JET BLACK

and the
NINJA WIND

Jet Black and the Ninja Wind
Area Map

忍者之風

HOKKAIDO

Sacred Mt. Osore

Kanabe
(Kuroi Family Village)

Mt. Hakkoda
(Aterui's Cave)

Sakata

SADO

JAPAN SEA

HONSHU

Kyoto

Tokyo

Mt. Fuji

Nara
(Ancient Capital)

SHIKOKU

KYUSHU

PACIFIC OCEAN

OKINAWA

JET
BLACK
and the
NINJA WIND

LEZA LOWITZ + SHOGO OKETANI

TUTTLE Publishing
Tokyo | Rutland, Vermont | Singapore

The Tuttle Story: "Books to Span the East and West"

Many people are surprised to learn that the world's largest publisher of books on Asia had its humble beginnings in the tiny American state of Vermont. The company's founder, Charles E. Tuttle, belonged to a New England family steeped in publishing.

Immediately after WW II, Tuttle served in Tokyo under General Douglas MacArthur and was tasked with reviving the Japanese publishing industry. He later founded the Charles E. Tuttle Publishing Company, which thrives today as one of the world's leading independent publishers.

Though a westerner, Tuttle was hugely instrumental in bringing a knowledge of Japan and Asia to a world hungry for information about the East. By the time of his death in 1993, Tuttle had published over 6,000 books on Asian culture, history and art—a legacy honored by the Japanese emperor with the "Order of the Sacred Treasure," the highest tribute Japan can bestow upon a non-Japanese.

With a backlist of 1,500 titles, Tuttle Publishing is more active today than at any time in its past—inspired by Charles Tuttle's core mission to publish fine books to span the East and West and provide a greater understanding of each.

Published by Tuttle Publishing, an imprint of Periplus Editions (HK) Ltd.

www.tuttlepublishing.com

Copyright © 2013 Leza Lowitz and Shogo Oketani

Area map created by Yuki Masuko

Owaranai Uta (Endless Song) chords and music: Masatoshi Mashima, Performed by The Blue Hearts. English Translation by Shogo Oketani and Leza Lowitz.

Tokyo is Burning—words: Anarchy (Japanese version), original music: Joe Strummer and Mick Jones. English translation by Shogo Oketani and Leza Lowitz.

Library of Congress Cataloging-in-Publication Data in Progress

ISBN 978-4-8053-1284-1

16 15 14 13   5 4 3 2 1   1307RP

Printed in China

Distributed by

North America, Latin America & Europe
Tuttle Publishing
364 Innovation Drive, North Clarendon
VT 05759-9436, USA
Tel: 1 (802) 773 8930; Fax: 1 (802) 773 6993
info@tuttlepublishing.com
www.tuttlepublishing.com

Japan
Tuttle Publishing
Yaekari Building 3rd Floor
5-4-12 Osaki Shinagawa-ku
Tokyo 1410032, Japan
Tel: (81) 3 5437 0171; Fax: (81) 3 5437 0755
sales@tuttle.co.jp; www.tuttle.co.jp

Asia Pacific
Berkeley Books Pte Ltd
61 Tai Seng Avenue #02-12, Singapore 534167
Tel: (65) 6280 1330; Fax: (65) 6280 6290
inquiries@periplus.com.sg; www.periplus.com

Indonesia
PT Java Books Indonesia
Jl. Rawa Gelam IV No. 9,
Kawasan Industri Pulogadung
Jakarta 13930, Indonesia
Tel: 62 (21) 4682 1088; Fax: 62 (21) 461 0206
crm@periplus.co.id; www.periplus.com

TUTTLE PUBLISHING® is a registered trademark of Tuttle Publishing, a division of Periplus Editions (HK) Ltd.

Contents

PART THREE
TOKYO 東京

PART FOUR
AMERICA 米国

PART FIVE
SENTO 戦闘 BATTLE

PART SIX
FURUSATO 故郷 HOMELAND

JAPAN 日本

winter solitude—
in a world of one color
the sound of the wind

–Bashō

Part One

BOUMEI

亡命

EXILE

CHAPTER 1

遊技 *Yugi*
The Game

The party had just started, and Jet stood in Amy Williams' kitchen, wearing the two-dollar black dress she'd bought at the thrift store.

"That's such a cool outfit," Amy told her, pushing a drink into her hand. The girls gathered, staring as if trying to remember whether they'd seen the dress in a catalog or a store window. Still, Jet knew it would've been cooler to have a date or to buy clothing that hadn't belonged to someone living in an old folks' home.

"Yeah," she said, "just put a hood on this thing, and I'd look like the grim reaper."

The girls in their sleek new outfits laughed. Jet could hardly believe it. She knew she'd changed, that people looked at her differently. Even her mother, staring at her one morning, had said, "The tomboy's gone. You've become a woman." Now Jet wanted nothing more than to spend the evening with the girls who'd always ignored her. But she couldn't. She had ten minutes before she had to leave. The game. Tonight was the night of the game. Saturday night had been ever since Jet could remember. She hated the game like she hated nothing else.

She took the drink anyway, not sure what it was—orange juice and something that smelled like rubbing alcohol. Amy Williams cranked the music. Boys were arriving. The girls began dancing in the living room just as the star quarterback threw open the door, a cooler on his shoulder. Jet tried to dance. How did they make it look so easy, swaying and turning gracefully? She'd have been more comfortable doing a spinning kick or a backflip. Now she had to make up her mind. Was it better to awkwardly explain she had to leave soon, or just slip out and invent a story later?

Her senses stilled. She took in the blaring music, the thudding baseline, the hollering boys, but behind all that, if she focused, there was the battering, off-rhythm engine of the truck turning onto Amy Williams' street. Kids were crowded around the door, so she went upstairs and into the bathroom. She took off her sandals, lifted the window screen and slipped out onto the roof's overhang, then jumped to the ground. She caught the top of the fence and swung herself over it. The truck was still moving, nearly to the house, when Jet reached the door and let herself in.

"Don't stop," she whispered to her mother, sliding down in her seat. A duffel with clothes for the game was on the floor, and as soon as they turned the corner, she began to change.

"Have fun?" her mother whispered, slumped at the wheel, more gaunt than ever.

"Best time of my life," Jet replied, "all ten minutes of it."

Satoko drove them out of the suburbs and into the mountains, over roads muddy and rutted from a week of heavy rains, though now the sky was clear, and the full moon hung in it as if Amy Williams herself had put it there.

The narrow road skirted the steep drop, hugging the edge of the mountain whose peaks glowed in the moonlight. As they went around a bend, the back wheels fishtailed. Jet gasped and clutched the seat. The truck almost turned sideways, skidding toward the cliff. Her mother jerked the wheel and hit the gas, and the truck slid back toward the mountain. She brought it under control and pulled it to a stop. She pressed her foot on the emergency brake, locking it in place. Her breathing sounded labored. She'd appeared unwell for months now.

"This is the last time," she told Jet.

"Really? You mean that?" Jet said.

"Have I ever said this before?" her mother asked. "Have I ever told you it was the last time?"

"No…"

"Well, it is. You'll never have to come up here again. The game will be over."

"Okay, Mom. I'm thrilled," Jet said, but the intensity of her mother's concentration distracted her.

Jet tried to keep her focus, staring out over the hood of the truck at the muddy road. Her mother seemed to have calmed. Jet could sense her exhaustion, the slowness of her breathing, even the tired beating of her heart. Satoko had said she had bronchitis, but her cough only got worse and worse, and Jet wondered for the hundredth time whether her mother's problem might be more serious. All week she would look exhausted and stay in bed, or meditate, and then, on the night of the game, she would pull herself together and become the woman Jet had always known her to be—strong, proud, still beautiful and fierce, like a raven. She would concentrate her energy, focusing herself, stilling her breath, her eyes becoming soft. Even now Jet could feel the slow expansion of calm around her, could see the precision in her movements. On the nights of the game, her mother would even cease to cough.

"You take the truck up to the parking spot," her mother told her.

"What?"

"Take it up. I'll get out here. You can find me."

"You mean like–"

"The same rules as always," her mother said.

She got out and stepped down into the mud. She slammed the door, and Jet slid over across the old vinyl seat whose split seams trailed bits of stuffing. When she looked out the window there was only the cliff alongside them, no sight of her mother. She released the parking brake and steered the truck up along the mountain. *What if it really is the last time?* she asked herself, trying not to be angry about the party. *If the game is over, what's next?*

The parking spot was no more than a widening in the road where the limbless trunk of a dead tree stood at the foot of a jumble of immense boulders. Hundreds of times, Jet had climbed the mountain, crouched, pausing to watch for movement. Now, she wrapped her body in black cloth and hid her face, leaving only a slit for her eyes. She got out of the truck, stopped, and stared up at the moon.

Like a sign written across the sky, it seemed to mock her, saying, "Loser. You're missing the coolest party ever, and you're going to graduate from high school without ever having been kissed."

She tried to think of a witty comeback. She stared at its face, at the craters like acne, and thought of the unpopular kids, the ones who didn't get invited to parties either. She'd never even had acne. That was her curse: forced to be *different*, to keep secrets.

There was a faint buzzing sound, and something, like a bird or a bat, flew close to her face. It brushed alongside her cheek, the sound clearer, a thin hiss of displaced air. A long knife struck the dead wood of the tree and embedded itself, quivering.

Jet dropped to a crouch, looking up and around her, then scuttled alongside the truck. Her mother couldn't have thrown it, could she? This wasn't part of the game. They didn't use real weapons, only sticks, rocks sometimes.

She was kneeling in the mud, her heart beating fast, moisture seeping through her pants, making them heavy. She shifted onto the balls of her feet.

Stay light, she told herself. Nothing moved on the mountainside. She didn't sense anything, not a single living creature, nothing.

"Mom?" she tried to call but the word stuck in her throat. How stupid could she be? Whoever had thrown the knife wouldn't miss again. Had her mother changed the game because it was the last time? She'd said "same rules as always," but maybe someone else was out there.

Staying in one place is dangerous! Jet told herself.

She sprinted and jumped, catching the handle of the knife and pulling it from the wood. She landed among the boulders and moved quickly, with small, darting steps against the stone, until she was on a perch in the middle of the jumble, hidden from sight.

She turned the blade over. It was an army knife of some sort, long, its handle heavy. It would be easy for her to use, but then she almost dropped it, realizing that someone had meant to kill her. Why? What had she done?

No, it had to be her mother who was trying to scare her. But how could Jet play this game if they were using real weapons? Maybe her mother wanted to teach her to take her training more seriously. Jet had once heard a story about a crazy war vet living up in these mountains, a man who'd gone AWOL on a visit home, and who hunted anyone who came onto his land. Maybe that's what was happening. Her mother might be in danger, too.

"Mom?" she shouted this time and moved quickly, changing her hiding spot. "Be careful!"

She placed her steps to leave the fewest traces. She ran along the side of a long flat boulder as big as a house, then crouched in a new hiding spot. There was no sound. Nothing. Who was out here with her?

"Mom," she shouted again, "if it's you, I don't want to play. Stop trying to scare me."

She changed places again and listened. Not a sound anywhere.

She knew every way up the mountain. The wind was picking up. Small clouds shuttled quickly across the sky, beneath the moon, their shadows gliding over the earth.

She concentrated her mind, listening, moving her senses out, watching the shape and hues of the landscape for traces of another person, the faintest pattern of footprints. But she sensed no one. Her mother had taught her to sit and feel everything for almost a mile around—birds, rabbits, people walking. The desert seemed empty, as if someone had cut Jet off from the world—or as if nothing was alive, or she wasn't.

She had two choices, to be slow and cautious, or to find her mother before someone else did. As a cloud passed beneath the moon, she sprinted, running into its shadow. No one could beat her in a race, and she would be a hard target, weaving and leaping.

Her ankle twisted and her foot was pulled from beneath her before she could even feel the pain. She struck the mud face-first and rolled. It had been a sharp tripwire. She could feel the swelling in her ankle, the blood filling the soft leather of her moccasin boot.

She wanted to cry, to scream her mother's name, but stopping now could get her killed. She leapt behind another long rock and lay, trying to become invisible. The mountainside was irregular, an obstacle course of stone and fallen trees, of mud and sheer cliffs. Her mother had chosen it for this, to teach Jet all of the skills that her mother claimed she would someday need. Up until now, Jet never had.

Maybe that was why she didn't cry now. The training. The lessons. The constant expectation that things would be more dangerous than they really were. She tried to sense what was around her, but her thoughts collapsed into fear. There was only her heart hammering in her chest, her body, her muddied arms and legs, her throbbing ankle, and her cold fingers still gripping the handle of the knife.

The wind was getting stronger. Jet took a few deep, slow breaths, as if pulling it into her body. It would help her. She had always been good in the wind. Her mother had taught her to move with it. She'd said it was Jet's gift.

Ignoring the pain in her ankle, she ran again, this time moving with the wind, fitting her body to its contours so that she brushed past stones, through trees, not traveling directly toward the peak where she normally found her mother during the game, but letting the wind carry her along an indirect route no one could know unless they too were running in the wind.

Her feet danced from rock to rock. She avoided the moonlight, threading her body along shadows. The texture of the wind pleased her, and she almost forgot her pain. But she didn't stop looking for the person who had thrown the knife and set the tripwire. She still couldn't sense them or see any trace.

The low, flat peak of the mountain came into sight past trees and boulders, and moments later, something brushed against her thigh, catching in the cloth of her pants. Even as her fingers touched it, she knew what it was. A dart, its metal tip barbed, maybe poisonous. In her mother's stories, they always were. She felt a sob building in her chest and tried to calm herself. Another one shot past and pinged off a rock. Where was her enemy? Above her, on the peak—that's where he had to be.

Move with the wind. Feel the elements. As she ran, the deep hum of the earth reached up through the mud. The fluctuations of the wind propelled her stride. The heat in her chest, the air in her lungs, the solidity of her body—all this she could blend. But whoever was up there had incredible vision and aim. Another dart flickered past her face. *Focus!*

And then her mind calmed and opened outward, and she could sense the world again, the life out there, across the desert's martian landscape that descended behind her. She knew each thing in its place. Lizards and snakes sleeping beneath rocks. Animals in burrows. A distant coyote sniffing the night air, sensing her. She had never felt this alive. Someone was on the peak, the presence faint, cloaked as if by an incredible act of focus, but still discernible. She directed her attention, searching into whoever it was.

Her enemy's energy hummed with anger, with hostility. In the body standing on the peak, she sensed an intention to hunt and kill her. Just feeling it, she was terrified.

What choice do I have? she asked herself. *I can't just run away. Mom is out here somewhere. I have to do this. Stay calm!*

Jet began to move again. Keeping close to shelter, she sprinted, twisting and leaping with the wind. She dimmed her presence, slowing her heart and breath even as she ran, to let her entire existence blur into the wind. It gusted hard, and she commanded her own life force to become faint, like a drop of water wiped along the surface of a dark window.

She didn't head directly for the peak, but around the mountain, to a cleft she knew, just at the back, at the base of a stand of gnarled trees, their branches misshapen from the wind. It was the only way she could think of to invade the higher ground. She timed it perfectly with a strong gust, with the brief passing of a small cloud over the moon, with the distant cry of the coyote that she sensed ready to howl, and then she was twisting through the air, taking shape, her foot reaching for the earth as she swung the knife. The figure stood on the flat surface of the peak and spun toward her.

Sparks flashed as her enemy lifted a blade and deflected the knife. Her opponent was wrapped in black, just as Jet was. This was no crazy war veteran, but someone far more dangerous. Someone who wanted to stay hidden.

The moon appeared from behind the cloud, and her enemy kept its back to it, silhouetted, the bright pallor shining into Jet's eyes as wind poured against the mountain with incredible force. Jet tried to use it, circling, feeling the pulse of the stone beneath her feet. But even as she twisted and leapt, the figure hardly seemed to move and yet avoided every strike, simply shifting slightly or again deflecting Jet's knife.

Jet never stopped, attacking repeatedly as she swirled close to the silhouetted figure. She timed her kicks and circled, trying to get the moonlight out of her eyes. She focused her strength and energy, but her fists and feet and knife passed as if through the wind.

All the while Jet was trying to sense the fighter's energy, at once masked and hostile, burning with a deep core of anger. But her enemy didn't act on this rage, didn't give in to impatience. It easily avoided every strike. All of the tricks Jet's mother had taught her, to dodge and fall back and attack, to follow the wind, letting herself retreat or stumble even as she struck—nothing worked.

Another small cloud passed between the moon and the mountain, and even as Jet began to formulate a strategy, she realized her mistake. She should have planned already, for the split second when the moonlight would vanish. Her enemy had done this.

As Jet was leaping to the side, trying to stay with the wind, a foot struck her stomach, suspending her in the air as if she'd been pinned there. And then she was falling, trying to find the earth with her feet, even as she couldn't breathe.

A hand caught the back of her head, gripping her hair through the black cloth. Her enemy jerked her head back and put the knife to her throat.

The wind suddenly died. The cloud passed from before the moon. The desolate landscape of the desert mountains stretched out like a vision of another world. Was this the last thing Jet would see?

"You've been lazy," the enemy hissed. "You've never wanted to learn."

Jet tried to pull away, but the blade stayed at her throat. The fist held her hair.

"What good are you to me? Tell me that!"

This time she heard the voice clearly: it was her mother's.

"Mom?!" Jet cried out in shock. "What are you doing? Are you crazy?"

Then her mother's lips were close to Jet's ear. There was a long silence. "I've trained you since you were old enough to walk, and all you think about is parties and clothes. Millions of kids go to parties and wear nice clothes. Only one or two people in the world get to learn what I've taught you. You still don't understand, do you?" She sheathed the knife and unwrapped her face.

Jet had begun to cry, shaking not just with fear and hurt, but with anger.

"You almost killed me! You could have–" she seethed.

"Jet," her mother took a step closer, but her knees buckled. Jet caught her mother's arm and held her up.

"This," her mother whispered, "really was the last time. I had to make you see. I didn't have the energy left, but I had to. I had to try to make you see."

"See what? What's wrong, Mom? Tell me. Tell me!"

"If you meet the dark leader, you must not be swayed. You mustn't be weak, like I was," Satoko said. "You must be strong."

"What dark leader?" Fear rose in the pit of Jet's stomach. "What do you mean, Mom?"

"Help me to the truck," her mother's voice came out, barely a whisper now.

Jet held her mother's arm as they walked toward the edge of the slope. Her mother leaned against her, gasping now, heavier than anything Jet had ever felt.

"What happened to you …?" Jet began to ask, recalling the warrior she had just fought, the figure shifting almost imperceptibly in the wind.

Her mother couldn't answer.

The walk down the mountain took an hour, Satoko leaning heavily against Jet with labored breath, her body exhausted in the night from which the wind had fled.

There were so many questions Jet longed to ask, so many her mother would never answer.

CHAPTER 2

物語り *Monogatari*
The Story

Back at the trailer, Jet helped her mother to bed, then bound her own ankle. Returning to her mother's side, Jet was surprised to see Satoko sitting up in bed, patching a hole in her jeans with a pink flower.

She looked so gentle, sewing quietly in the dark. Not like the woman on the mountain. Not like a threat.

Satoko guided the thread through her mouth to knot it, finishing her work. She folded the jeans and laid them next to her. Then she slid down in the bed, pale and spent.

"Get some rest," Jet said softly, pulling the blankets up to her mother's chin. Satoko sank beneath them, reaching out trembling fingers to take her daughter's hand.

"Wait. Tell me the story," she pleaded, gripping Jet tightly. Her ice cold skin sent a shiver up Jet's spine. Jet took a breath and stilled her thoughts, letting the stories her mother had told her come back from distant memory.

"Long ago, there was a country called 'Hinomoto.' It means 'land of the rising sun.' It was once governed by the Emishi, a native tribe. Their mountains and forests gave plenty of nuts, greens, and animals to live by, and their oceans and rivers gave them fish. Nature gave them so much wealth, they didn't have to fight."

Satoko's eyes narrowed. She nodded, urging Jet to continue.

"One day, a tribe called the Wa arrived from the mainland. They had many soldiers, and even more powerful weapons. Their king, who called himself the Mikado, said to the Emishi leader: 'You should give your country to me. I will change the forest into rice fields and build beautiful shrines. I promise you a much richer life than now.'"

At this, Satoko's jaw stiffened. In the dark, Jet couldn't see her mother's expression clearly, but she sensed her sadness. Her mother's inconsolable sadness was the only thing that helped Jet endure. She wanted to lift it, to make it disappear.

Jet sighed and continued. "The Emishi king replied: 'We don't need more wealth, and for us there is no greater shrine than nature. If you want to live on this land, we'll welcome you. But you must keep our laws. If you don't, then leave.'

"Well! No one had ever talked to the Mikado like that before!" Jet exclaimed, relieved to see the pleasure lightening her mother's tired face. "Everyone had surrendered to him for the promise of power and wealth. Enraged, the Mikado attacked the Emishi, who were quickly outnumbered."

"Go on," Satoko instructed.

Jet, too, was exhausted and shaken. In childhood, when she couldn't sleep, her mother had sat on the edge of her bed, spinning her tales. When her mother had spoken the words, each one had meant another night in their home, another moment of peace— not moving, not running, not scared. Jet wondered if the story was keeping Satoko alive now. Now it was her turn to be the strong one.

She took a breath and continued. "The Emishi abandoned their capital and fled north, where they built a new home surrounded by beautiful mountains and forests. But the Wa were not satisfied, and invaded there, too. This time, the Emishi decided to fight back. It was a long, long battle. Many Emishi died—women and children too."

Jet glanced over at Satoko, feeling grief wrap itself around her mother like a thick wool cape. She inhaled and carried on. "Finally, the Emishi surrendered. And here is the saddest part. They were sold as slaves to the Wa. Their only hope was of returning to their homeland someday. That dream kept them alive."

At this, her mother had always cried, and tonight was no different. Seeing the tears stream down her mother's face, Jet began to cry, too.

"What happened then?" Satoko urged her daughter.

"The age of the Mikado ended, and the samurai lords attained power. There were various classes of samurai, the lowest being mountain bandits...."

"No. They were ninja," Satoko murmured. "Those who hide quietly in the darkness, those who can put the heart over the blade."

"What?" Jet asked. She stopped, unsure as to whether to continue.

"Go on," Satoko urged.

"I don't know that part," Jet admitted, filled with concern.

"Well, I'll tell you," Satoko said in a raspy voice. "One day, a girl was born to the *genin*, the slaves, the ninja. She grew up to be beautiful, strong, and smart. The head of her *ryu* ordered her to infiltrate a samurai castle disguised as a servant so she could determine the lord's military strength and find out when he'd attack his rival."

"*Genin? Ryu?*" Jet puzzled over the words. Satoko had told her of the girl before, but never this. Satoko lifted her eyes to Jet and sat up taller, her spine straighter than before. She spoke more forcefully now, as if the words were giving her strength, feeding her energy.

"The girl was headstrong and willful. She saw only an opportunity for her people to be released from slavery, and nothing more. She became close to the lord, confided in him: 'My master has joined forces with your rival. He and other families are preparing to attack you. Now's a good chance to attack them first.'"

By now, a hint of color had returned to Satoko's gaunt face. "Furious, the lord attacked his rival and the tribes in the mountains and wiped them out. But the girl had already relayed her plan to the *genin*, who escaped before the attack."

Jet listened intently, almost holding her breath.

"That's how the slave tribes returned to their homeland as a free people," Satoko said. "They rebuilt their villages and lived peacefully in nature."

With a satisfied look, Satoko finished and lay back against the pillow, breathing deeply. She pulled Jet closer, guided her daughter's head onto her chest.

"Mom, hang on!" Jet called out, feeling her mother's life force grow faint.

Satoko's voice fell to a whisper. "Each new generation learns about this brave girl who helped their ancestors survive. But the generations are getting smaller and smaller, moving away, forgetting. If we aren't careful, they'll disappear altogether..."

"What can I do, Mother? What can I do?" Jet pleaded.

"You have to go back," Satoko spoke painstakingly, as if each word contained another diminishing ounce of strength.

"Back where?" Jet asked squeezing her mother's hand.

"To Hinomoto. To Japan."

"How can I go *back*, Mom? I've never been there before!" Jet caught herself as the familiar sarcasm edged into her voice. *No. Not now. Not now. Stop it!*

Satoko gripped Jet's hand with a strength she'd never feel again. "Well, that's all the more reason to go now, isn't it?" she answered.

Jet held back her frustration. "Why, Mom? Why?"

"Sometimes we have to risk everything in the present to gain the future," Satoko whispered and pressed something into Jet's palm. A rolled up paper.

"What's this?" Jet asked, surprised.

"Open it. It's from your grandfather Masakichi," she whispered. "Go see him in Aomori. For me."

"My grandfather?" Jet cried. She'd had only the vaguest notion of such a person. "Is he even still alive?"

Satoko smiled. "Very much so. Don't be afraid of him. Whatever he asks you, you must do. There's no time to lose."

"Why didn't you say anything about this?" Jet's words came out whispery with fear.

"There's so much more to learn, but you have the gift," Satoko said assuringly, a sense of urgency permeating her words.

Jet unrolled the paper. It was a hand-drawn map with a route to a mountain village.

She was about to ask her mother to explain more when the trailer door opened. A ray of light came in from the lamp outside. Satoko looked up. Jet turned to see a tall, quiet man standing above them. It was J-Bird, Satoko's boyfriend. She'd been waiting for his arrival. Waiting for him to come so she could go.

J-Bird's long, gray hair was tied back as always. He took his shoes off and sat quietly on the bed by her side. He dusted off his hands on his faded jeans and took Satoko's hands in his.

"Open the curtains," Satoko said.

Jet slid them aside. The torn yellowed curtains had never entirely covered the windows anyway, she realized. They'd been left over from their last house and didn't match the trailer's size. *Everything in my life is mismatched*, she thought.

Light from the full moon streamed in.

A smile spread across Satoko's lips. She told them about the *tsuki-mi-mado*—the moon-viewing window in her father's home, the way moonlight streamed in clear and shining like a crystal river. The thought seemed to touch something within her, calming her to the core.

Delirious now, Satoko asked if the moon one saw in America was the same one Jet would see in Japan.

"Of course, Mother!" Jet said. *But was it really the same?*

J-Bird moved aside. Jet lay her head on her mother's chest again, wanting to melt into it. "Don't go, Mom. I'll find Grandpa, I promise. And I'll tell you all about it when I come back," she said.

"Good," Satoko murmured. "I look forward to that." Satoko's breath was labored now.

Feeling her mother slipping away, Jet took her hand.

"Mom!" she cried. "Wait!"

But Satoko's eyes were closed.

Taking a deep breath, Jet looked into her mother's mind. She saw the ancient village, its crumbling walls, the thatched-roof farmhouse, a mountain path. Then a beautiful green forest appeared behind Satoko's eyelids, a small clean river flowing through it.

Jet saw Satoko as a little girl, walking along the river. As she walked, she could feel many animals alive and thriving under the brush. A white mist fell onto the forest.

"The forest is going to sleep…" Jet whispered as Satoko, too, fell into slumber.

Jet held onto Satoko's vision, filled with rich green and cool white air. She could almost smell the sap in the crack of a tree before the branch snapped off, the earth under her feet before the rain.

"Tell me the end of the story," Satoko murmured.

But Jet didn't know the end.

When I grow up, can I be like the brave girl who freed her people? Jet had always asked her mother as the story ended.

Of course you can, her mother had always replied. *Because you already are.*

But Jet had never heard her, just as Satoko, deep in the dream of the beautiful green forest she'd soon be walking upon, didn't hear her daughter end the story this very last time.

CHAPTER 3

約束 *Yakusoku*
The Promise

They dressed Satoko in a white paper kimono, left side folded under the right so she would travel in the correct direction in the afterworld. J-Bird set fire to the paper, which burned from its edges with a rushing sound.

The paper turned in upon itself as the flames spread, taking her mother with them. Jet watched the map of her past burn with her mother's life. She held her tears close to her body, as if they were a prayer book only she could read. She couldn't believe her mother was really gone. Only yesterday, on the mountain, she'd been so fierce, so strong. Determined to live.

J-Bird leaned toward Jet. "There's more your mother wanted to share with you. You should never use your real name, Rika. Kuroi—your family name—means 'black' in Japanese, so you must use that instead. Use your nickname in Japan. Just in case."

"Why?" Jet was alarmed. "Was Mom in that much trouble?"

He sighed, looking worried. "I promised Satoko I'd help you, but I don't know much more. We have to act quickly."

Jet swallowed, gazing at him in the half-light. Her mother had nicknamed her Jet when she was a little girl, because she ran like a rocket. J-Bird was the only one who knew.

They stood in silence as the fire consumed her mother's body.

Rika Kuroi is dying in these flames. Jet Black is being born. She felt her mother's presence guiding her thoughts. Why had she gone so quickly? Why wasn't there more time?

When the fire died down, Jet picked Satoko's bones out with long chopsticks and placed the white shards in a small urn. She poured the ashes into it, watching them stream before her, unable to believe that this dust had been her mother, a woman who had seemed capable of anything—surviving anything.

Later that evening, J-Bird and one of the elders, Neil Bluewolf, sang Navajo prayers in deep melodic voices, sending Satoko's spirit safely into the Big Sky. Jet watched their shadows sway on the wall, getting bigger or smaller in the candle's flame.

All those times I made you go up to the mountains, Satoko had said, frail and struggling to draw enough breath to speak–*all that hard training, you will soon understand why I made you do it. I hope you'll forgive me.*

Of course, Mom, Jet had told her, though she didn't really understand. Almost every night since she could remember she'd had to train in the forest behind their trailer. Or in dusty fields along the highway. She'd often shown up at school with her clothes mud-caked and torn, and had told her teachers it was from soccer practice. Then there were the bruises, scratches, and scars. Other kids called her crazy, but she couldn't explain. When the school bully started picking on her, she couldn't even use her training to fight back.

Though Jet was exhausted, she rarely found relief in sleep. When she turned over in bed, her bruises ached. Her heart ached, too, for even when she fell down and begged her mother to stop, she kept pushing her.

"Keep moving! When you give up, it's time to die," Satoko had said.

Spurred on by her mother's voice, she tried to avoid the barrage.

"Why do I always have to do this?" she pleaded, though she knew the answer.

"You have to protect yourself. I won't always be here to do it for you," Satoko had cautioned every time.

Even when her mother came back from work at dark, she took Jet to the desert, making her jump from tree to rock or run until her breath gave out, rolling on the ground until her clothes tore to shreds. On cold winter evenings, she forced Jet to hide behind boulders without moving.

And whenever Jet had asked her mom to explain why she'd fled Japan, Satoko's answer was always, "Later. We'll talk about it later."

But "later" never came.

Would she finally learn more, now that her mother was gone?

"You see," J-Bird confided, "The Kuroi family has a treasure. People all over Japan want it."

"Treasure? What kind of treasure?" Jet asked, picturing pearls, jade, and gold.

J-Bird shook his head. "I don't know. But I do know that your grandfather and your mother have been protecting it. Now that's up to you. Without you, it'll be lost forever. That's why you have to go back to Japan."

Jet frowned. "Why didn't she tell me this sooner?"

J-Bird closed his eyes and nodded. "Satoko knew that many people would try to find you to get it. Some of them even want to hurt you. The less you knew, the safer you were. I made a vow not to tell you, either. Until I had to. Until now."

Jet shook her head, disbelieving. "Why would anyone want to hurt me? I didn't do anything!"

"It's not what you've done, it's what you haven't done. Yet…" J-Bird said.

"I don't understand!" Jet said, voice quavering.

He put a hand on her shoulder. "I don't really either, but I do know that that's why you must protect yourself. You must use the skills your mother taught you. You'll have to dig deep down. Can you do that for Satoko?"

"What choice do I have?" She hated fighting and hated harming things. She always picked up ants, snails, and worms off the sidewalk and put them on trees to make sure they didn't get stepped on.

"I'm sorry, Jet. I really am. I wish I had been able to tell you more." J-Bird cast his eyes down.

Jet looked away, tears welling. His words troubled her deeply. All those years of training, and her mother had never mentioned any of this. How was that possible?

And what had Satoko meant about risking everything for the future?

Jet gripped the rolled-up map, hoping it might have the answers. A turquoise and silver ring J-Bird had given her years ago caught the light as she curled her fingers around the paper. It had been her power stone, and J-Bird had never led her astray. Would he now?

"I'll go to Japan," Jet said through clenched teeth. "I'll be strong for Mom like she was for me."

"That's my girl," J-Bird said, patting her back.

But Jet couldn't help but notice the anguish that lined his brow. *Still*, she thought, *what do I have to lose now that Mom is gone?*

CHAPTER 4

着物

The Kimono

Satoko had left her daughter her only kimono, a silk beauty with the pattern of blue irises for eternal spring, their stalks standing tall on the kimono's folds.

Jet put the kimono on. She hadn't worn it since trying it on so many years ago when Satoko had taught her how to tie the *obi*, how to stand tall and float her graces out to the world through the carriage of her spine as the silk fabric fanned out around her like waves.

She wondered when the last time Satoko had worn the Kimono was. On her wedding day to Jet's father, eighteen years ago? Where was he now? Another phantom man—dead, disappeared, gone. *Whatever.*

Jet tied the obi tight around her waist. It was her mother she wanted to honor. She merely hoped she'd have a happier occasion to wear it at in the future.

Then she wondered what Amy Williams and the girls would think of it. They knew she liked vintage clothes, liked to go to the flea market, where she discovered flowing skirts and old Navajo blankets, finding solace in the patterns as if they could give her the comforting childhood that had escaped her. She loved sifting through piles of clothes stacked on blankets, looking for things that had once been loved. She wanted to give these orphaned things a home. She sometimes wondered if the spirits of the owners still lived in their old clothes.

Jet realized with shock that she, too, was an orphan. But she quickly pushed the thought away. It wasn't exactly true, anyway, because she now knew that she had family in Japan. Like her eighty-year-old grandfather, Masakichi, whom she'd thought was dead.

Surprise! she'd say upon meeting him. *I'm your American grand-daughter!* Would he keel over in shock? Did he think she was dead, too?

Jet looked at herself in the mirror—tall, skin like lightly roasted barley tea, silky black hair. The kimono made her look entirely Japanese. And if she held herself a bit differently, a bit more softly, tenderly, she could transform herself from tough res girl to geisha. Her mother had taught her that, too.

Finally, Jet slipped off the kimono and put on the jeans her mother had patched. Then she gathered the kimono, obi, and a few of her things in an old black *furoshiki* and tied the ends together. She packed the *furoshiki* into an old leather suitcase and closed the latches.

J-Bird loaded the suitcase into the truck. Together they drove down the driveway, out of the Reservation, toward the strip malls, and to the airport—away from the only life Jet had ever known.

At the airport, J-Bird walked her to the gate. As the boarding call began, he stopped and reached into his satchel. Then he turned to her.

"Give this to your grandfather," he said, holding out a small wooden box tied with a red silk cord. "Your mother wanted you to bring it to Osore-zan. Your grandfather will know."

"Osore-zan?" Jet repeated the name. It was a sacred mountain. Her mother had told her about it in their bed-time tales.

"Yes. Be safe," he said gravely, locking his eyes on hers.

"I will. I hope," she stammered.

She knew what the box was, and clutched it to her chest.

"Satoko prepared this, too. She thought of everything." He held out a ceremonial envelope. Jet took it in her hands.

"Go on, open it," he urged, his soft eyes watering.

With trembling fingers, she slid the elaborate red and gold ribbon from the casing and eased the envelope out. Undoing its folds, she could see that it contained two stacks of crisp hundred dollar bills. She counted quickly. Two thousand dollars! She'd never seen so much money in her life.

"Your mother saved it up for you over the years. She didn't want you to be left with nothing," J-Bird explained.

"You mean all that time we were broke, all those times we ate just rice and beans, we could have had... steak?" Jet asked, stunned.

He laughed. "What? You love rice and beans! All that trouble you caused me being a vegetarian...!"

She laughed, too. "I know I'm a pain. I'm sorry. One day I'll make it up to you, I swear."

"I'm not going to hold my breath on that one." He chuckled, pushing her along.

Jet stood, frozen in place.

"Go on! You're going to miss your plane!" J-Bird put his hands on her shoulders and marched her toward the gate. She gave him a final hug.

"Go on," he said, waving her off.

The attendant tore off her ticket, and she took the stub. She turned to wave good-bye to the man who had been like her father for as long as she could remember.

"I love you," she called out.

"Me too," he mouthed, raising his hand in a salute.

When the plane took off, Jet's stomach lurched. She stared out the window, looking over the vast Southwestern desert as the plane lifted into the sky and the mesas and mountains disappeared. As her past trailed behind her and the huge mountains became mere specks in the clouds, Jet made a vow: she'd tell no one of her mother's secret training, the American father she hadn't seen for years, and the life she'd left behind. She'd go to fulfill her mission, whatever it might be.

Part Two

AOMORI

青森

THE OLD COUNTRY

CHAPTER 5

故郷 *Kokyo*
Homeland

In her dreams, Jet could vanish through a wall of smoke and climb the highest castle moat, but she still had to fly to Japan on an airplane like everyone else. Excitement tingled in her veins.

When she landed in Narita, no one was there to meet her. She slid into the crowds of dark-haired, dark-eyed people, happy for once to be invisible. She'd always stood out. Now she'd blend right in.

Surprisingly, she relaxed in Tokyo's crowds, its streets as large as dragons' tails, its silver trains carrying men in dark suits swiftly into glass buildings, women in fancy clothing shimmering like fireflies of many colors. Everyone and everything moved quickly. To where? To what? Why?

After a restless night's sleep at a business hotel and a dinner at the rotary sushi, she headed north to Morioka, an old castle town at the confluence of three rivers a hundred miles north from Tokyo. From there, she still had to catch a train to Aomori, the northernmost city of Honshu in the center of Mutsu Bay, nestled between the Tsugaru and Shimokita peninsulas.

Emboldened by a sense of purpose, Jet kept her senses alert and her eyes open, eager for her mission to begin. She managed to catch the Tohoku local, grabbing a quick lunch of *wanko-soba*—a local delicacy of thin flat buckwheat noodles—at a stand on the platform.

Satoko had spoken of the mountains as majestic as temples, the rivers where ancient trees bowed across old bridges, the rustic wooden houses where women moved freely in the front rooms instead of hiding on bended knee behind. But from the train window, Jet was disappointed to see the farmhouses covered with brown aluminum siding. Where was the old Japan?

She felt a little closer to it as she began to climb Mt. Hakkoda, following Satoko's directions. It had been almost eighteen years since her mother had ventured there. Why hadn't she returned? The question gnawed at Jet. She hoped she'd soon learn the answer.

The smell of the forest grew stronger as she climbed the mountain path. Jet looked at the map her mother had given her:

日本青森県十和田市金部村
Kanabe Village, Towada City, Aomori Prefecture, JAPAN

A twig snapped. Jet stared ahead, afraid to turn around. Was she being followed? The village lay at the bottom of the valley, north of Mt. Hakkoda, a mile away. It was getting dark and cold. She started to shiver.

She sensed a presence, but she forced herself to keep walking, listening. From the faint distant rhythm of breathing, she could tell that one of her followers was human and the other animal. Both were timing their movements with the sound of the wind. When the wind blew, they walked. When the wind stopped, they stopped and held their breath so the bamboo leaves wouldn't rustle around them. It was an excellent technique—*fu no kata*—moving like the wind. She was surprised to remember the name.

Suddenly, fear knifed through her. She didn't want her followers to know she'd caught on to their presence.

She bit back her fear and kept climbing through the beech, their thin gray trunks covered with bamboo grass. She made out the sound of falling water ahead. Her pursuers had stopped. They were probably listening to her footsteps to see which way she was heading.

Well, I'll throw them a bone, she thought.

A twenty-foot high waterfall appeared through the trees. On both sides were cliffs covered with deep green moss. She stopped and considered what to do.

She picked up a handful of stones and threw them into the bushes next to her. A flurry of mountain birds shot from the foliage.

At that exact moment, she made herself disappear.

The sudden flapping of wings broke the boy's concentration.

"Aska, let's go!" he called to his dog. "She'll get away!"

Hiro was twelve, with black bangs that covered his forehead like a curtain. His sharp features made him look intelligent and alert. Wearing well-worn country clothes, he moved confidently and swiftly, even though he was small for his age.

Aska, his large, light-brown Akita dog, rushed after the scent. Hiro ran, too, stepping into every footprint the girl had left to soften the sound of his movements. Just before the waterfall, he ducked into the ferns. He smelled the air and listened. A well-trained warrior could sense where his enemy was hiding, even when there was a breeze.

He worried that a single breath, his own, would break the silence. If that happened, he could be caught. He made up his mind: he had to corner her first.

The sound of cascading water grew louder. He concentrated. Across the river, a branch of red nandin nuts swayed. Was a breeze blowing there?

Then he noticed something blue in the leaves—the girl's backpack. Focusing even more deeply, he sensed a living presence behind it. He felt it and heard it: fluttering, a faint heartbeat. With a smile of victory, he picked up a small stone and threw it to the other side of the waterfall. It hit the nandin branch, but the backpack didn't move.

He picked up a thick branch and ran toward the river. Just before reaching it, he threw the branch ahead of him, onto the water. He jumped and before touching the surface, kicked his foot against the floating wood, using it to propel himself to the opposite bank. There was just one spot of water on the tip of his right shoe. His dog followed, leaping as if flying.

He climbed into the tree, toward the backpack, but as soon as he got onto the branch, it broke. He barely managed to land on his feet.

Laughter rang out behind him. He spun. A long-legged half-Japanese girl with black hair almost down to her waist was watching him. She had soft roasted-tea skin and deep, black eyes. Though she was pretty enough to be a movie star, she wasn't delicate. More like a tomboy. She seemed tough, and driven.

"At least you could try not to laugh," he shouted in his thick Tohoku accent.

"Sorry. I couldn't help it." Jet wasn't laughing at him, but because her ruse had worked and because she was relieved that she was only being followed by a boy and his dog. Then her tone softened. "Does your dog bite?"

"Only if I tell her to."

She sighed, relieved. *So he understood my Japanese.*

"Or if she senses danger," the boy added threateningly.

"Good, just like me," Jet said, smiling. She opened her backpack and a brown bird flew out.

"Thank you! *Sayonara!*" she called out after the bird.

"That was a lure? You tricked me!?" The boy seemed amazed.

Jet tried to conceal a smile. "Yeah, I guess I did. Sorry about that!"

"Sure you are. But this is still our mountain," he said angrily.

"I never said it wasn't," she shot back.

"Right, you're just like the others. Your people came from the dump last week and tried to get Ojiisan to let them use the mountain for landfill. They offered him lots of money. It's a good thing he didn't kick their butts!"

"Whoa, slow down a minute. I didn't say anything..." Jet stammered.

"Good, because if you did, you'd be lying. They said it would be good for the mountain because it would just be ashes and fertilizer. But the ashes contain poisons, like dioxin. I know all about it."

She held up her palm. "I can understand why you're mad. But I don't work at the dump. My mother was born in these mountains. I came here to meet my grandfather."

"Your grandfather?" His eyes brightened, then narrowed to slits.

Jet nodded. "Uh huh."

"Okay, if that's true, what's his name?"

She opened the suitcase and took out the wrinkled map. "Masakichi Kuroi." she said, sounding out each word.

The color drained from the boy's face.

"No way! Could you be…. Are you…Rika? I can't believe it. You came!"

Jet allowed herself a smile. "My friends call me Jet. And you would be…?

"Hiro. Wow! I mean," the boy switched to perfect English and paused, as if collecting his thoughts. "I thought you would look different… I mean, I thought you'd have dark skin, or blue eyes, like Ojiisan. I can't believe it. You came!"

"Wait a minute," Jet said. "Ojiisan has blue eyes?" She switched to English, too, wondering why her mom hadn't told her about that.

"Yeah. Many people have blue eyes here. We're different from the Wa." Hiro glanced around. "Hey, did anyone know you were coming?"

Jet turned around, too. "No. Why?"

"Good. We should hurry then," he said excitedly.

The dog at his side barked, looking up at Jet expectantly.

"Oh, I almost forgot. This is Aska." He ran his hand over the dog's fur. At his command, Aska slowly approached Jet, who reached out to pet her.

"Wait! Please don't move," Hiro said. Aska sniffed her feet and went back to Hiro's left side.

"Now it's safe." His face registered relief. "She has to smell you and record the scent for later. That's her enemy check routine."

"Oh," Jet said, wondering how often the boy and his dog had to check for enemies.

"It's getting dark," Hiro told her. "We'd better get going! You can't imagine how long I've been waiting for you. I've been hearing stories about you and your mother since I was little."

Before she could ask what kind of stories, or even express surprise that he'd known she existed, the boy and his dog took off along the mountain path.

She had to follow them, or she'd be lost.

"Hurry!" he called out. "We should tell Ojiisan right away."

Jet jogged behind him. As they emerged from the bamboo grove, the Ou Mountain range came into sight, peaked and majestic.

"There's our village," Hiro told her. "Come on! *Hayaku!* Faster!"

In the distance, flanked by the mountain and a river, was a cluster of old thatch-roof houses leaning into each other like people huddled in a circle. On either side stood sheer cliffs like hands lifted in prayer. A white mist hung over the valley like an ancient scroll painting. There was something otherworldly about the scene and Jet was unnerved. It was too quiet, too calm. Where were all the people?

But then Jet remembered her promise to Satoko, and the box from J-Bird. She stopped and knelt on the ground, taking the small box from her pack and clasping it to her heart.

"Mom," she whispered to her mother's ashes, "we made it to Kanabe. You're finally home."

CHAPTER 6

お祖父さん *Ojiisan*
Grandfather

An old man with white hair stood at a stone wall. Though eighty, he looked powerful and strong. His skin was smooth and brown, his eyes were—*how strange*—blue! Just like Hiro had said.

"It's Rika!" Hiro said. "She's finally here. Now we can–"

Ojiisan silenced him with a quick gesture, turning back to Jet.

"Granddaughter," he said gently, "thank you for coming all this way." Jet was happy to see a smile on his lips. She wasn't sure he'd welcome her, but his blue eyes twinkled warmly, and she felt herself relax.

"You look so much like your mother," he said in halting English.

He waved his hand, beckoning her closer. "I'm Masakichi. Hiro calls me *Ojiisan*, Grandpa, and you can, too."

He bowed deeply. She held out her hand. He laughed, held out his hand and took Jet's, shaking it vigorously. His fingers were calloused and rough.

Jet held on tightly as they made their way down the hill. The sun was descending in the distance, casting a golden hue on the valley. Hiro followed close, his nervous energy worrying Jet, making her think of her mother's warning.

But Ojiisan didn't seem worried. Jet felt that he'd known she was coming, even though she'd had no way to tell him, and had been warned by J-Bird she must arrive in secrecy.

Jet took a deep breath. The forest was preparing for winter, its smell different from the Southwestern desert's juniper, piñon, sage. That smell had been brisk and bracing. This forest was smoky, like freshly cut wood.

Ojiisan motioned to a two-story wooden farmhouse with a tri-angular thatched roof. Just like Satoko had described it.

"We're home. It's cold, so let's go inside."

He placed a hand on Jet's back, guiding her into the stone foyer. He took off his muddy boots, shook them, and gestured to Jet to do the same. She removed her own, the wooden floor smooth under her tired feet. The house smelled of moss and rain, as if she were still outdoors.

"Ojiisan," Jet said and handed her grandfather the box. "This is…"

Masakichi closed his eyes briefly and bowed low, understanding. He took the box gently into his hands, nodding at Jet to follow him as he carried it into a room with tatami mat floors and placed it on the Buddhist altar. He knelt to light a stick of incense and handed one to Jet so she could do the same. Fragrant cedar smoke swirled in the room, much sweeter than the piñon she was used to.

He closed his eyes and clasped his hands at his heart. "*Namu amida butsu*," he intoned. I pray to Lord Buddha. Jet repeated the words, calling forth the benevolent one. She felt Satoko with them almost as strongly as if she were really there. A chill ran up her spine.

After a while, Masakichi stood and went into the kitchen, mo-tioning for Jet to follow.

The kitchen had a dirt floor and stone oven in the corner, black-ened with soot. An iron pot with a thick, wooden lid gave off steam. There was a rusty water pump and a propane burner, too.

Masakichi stood a moment, as if remembering where he was, or trying to let go of his sadness.

"This house is over two hundred years old," he said. "I used to cook with Satoko here, just like my own parents cooked here with me."

"Two hundred years? Wow," Jet nodded, trying to imagine her mother at eighteen, in the same kitchen she was now standing in. "We never stayed in one place long enough to gather dust, let alone memories!"

Ojiisan's lip quivered and he looked away.

Jet wished she hadn't said anything. Awkwardly, she ran her fingers along the bowls, the stove, even crouched to slide them along the smooth wooden floor—touching the things her mother might have touched. Why couldn't they have come back together?

Jet didn't want to barrage her grandfather with questions though; they'd only just met. She tried to relax and see into his feelings, but her stomach growled loudly, breaking her concentration.

Ojiisan laughed and went to the fire. As he began grilling fish, Hiro set the table, dishing out rice.

"There's nothing like the taste of rice cooked over firewood," he said. He poured *miso* soup into bowls and placed red lacquered wooden tray tables on the tatami mat floor.

When the fish was cooked, Ojiisan set a fourth tray in front of the altar.

"For Satoko's spirit," he said, glancing over at Jet with warmth in his expression.

They sat down to eat. Jet sipped the warm *miso* soup. The *nameko* mushrooms smelled like wood, spreading a smoky taste through her mouth.

"Your mom loved this kind of miso," Ojiisan said. "As soon as fall came, she'd go hunting for nameko in the forest. She was a good hunter."

"Really?" Jet looked up, surprised. She'd only seen her mom hunt for food in the grocery store.

Then he leaned forward, lowering his voice. "Around here, people like me are called *matagi*. We're just hunters. If anyone asks you, that's what you should say. Okay?"

Jet nodded, though she was alarmed. *Weren't they?*

"The name of our town means 'bear' in the Ainu language," Hiro said, his chest radiating pride.

"That's right," Ojiisan replied. "Many families once hunted bear to survive. To the Ainu, the bear was a gift from God. They respected this powerful creature. He gave them his meat, his fur, his medicine. They gave him their gratitude and respect."

"And he kept the *Wa* away from the mountains. The *Wa* are afraid of bears. They're afraid of Kanabe." Hiro's eyes sparkled. "And us!"

"Are the *Wa* a gang?" Jet asked, remembering what Hiro had said.

"Not exactly," Masakichi said. "They're the Emperor's ancestors."

"They captured our ancestors and made them slaves," Hiro practically growled, making Aska's ears suddenly stick up. He stroked her fur and she moaned, ears softening.

"They haven't been around for a while, and we're happy to have them stay away from our mountain as long as they want," Ojiisan replied.

"Forever isn't long enough!" Hiro said fiercely.

"What do they want?" Jet asked, looking over at her grandfather.

Ojiisan hesitated. "The Kuroi family were nomads whose ancestors, the ancient Izumo people, traveled around Japan selling bamboo crafts to survive. As they traveled, they built a kind of network, picking up information and carrying it from town to town."

"And?" Jet asked. The hair on the back of her neck stood up.

Ojiisan sighed "In those days, that information was very rare and valuable. But in this day and age, there's email and iphones and satellites and even clones of animals—things your old grandpa couldn't have dreamed of fifty years ago. People can hear what we're talking about right now, even though they're thousands of miles away."

"That's true. But what does that have to do with us?" Jet asked nervously.

Ojiisan continued. "You see, our ancestors might have made some enemies. People didn't like their secret ways, didn't think there was a need for them anymore."

"But *you* don't think so, do you?" she replied. Her grandfather obviously liked the old ways. He still lived in a wooden house and cooked over a kindling fire. In fact, he seemed almost untouched by the twenty-first century.

Masakichi cleared his throat. His deep blue eyes sparkled as he looked into Jet's eyes. She stayed perfectly still.

"As long as there's a mountain, there will be a forest. As long as there is a forest, there will be bears and mushrooms and *yakuso*—medicinal herbs—and the village will survive. So we don't have to worry…"

Hiro frowned. "Yeah, but only if we protect it."

"How will you… we… protect it?" Jet asked quickly. There was so much she wanted to know.

Hiro looked over at Ojiisan, who laid down his chopsticks.

"You must be tired," he said softly but firmly, closing the subject.

"You could say that." She was almost too tired to keep her head up and eyes open. The train ride had been long. But still. Tension coursed through her body. She could see that Ojiisan didn't want the old ways to die. And neither had her mother. After all, Satoko had made Jet come all the way to Japan. And they were clearly being threatened. But by whom? And why now?

Jet didn't want to argue, to show Ojiisan her bad qualities. She would no longer be what her homeroom teacher had written in her progress report: "witty, sarcastic, at times cynical, and maybe a little antisocial." She'd determined not to be that way in Japan.

Ojiisan looked softly at Jet, as if understanding all she could not say.

"We should all get some rest. It's been a long day."

"I'll show Jet her room," Hiro said, picking up Jet's backpack and suitcase. Ojiisan quickly led them down a wooden hallway to a tatami mat room that opened onto a small stone garden. They brushed their teeth in a big metal sink. The toilet was a hole in the ground.

"The spare room is not very fancy, but we'll put out a futon, and you'll rest well. If you hear any strange noises, whistle like this."

Ojiisan made an owl's call from deep in his throat. Jet was star-tled—it was the same sound her mother and J-Bird had taught her in the desert.

"There are a lot of wild animals, you know. But don't worry, they're friendly. Most of them, that is. The bears are used to us."

Jet might have looked afraid, but she couldn't help but yawn.

"You've had a long journey," Ojiisan told her. "Come."

Jet said goodnight to Hiro after he put her bags down on the tat-ami. He opened his mouth, as if he wanted to say something, but Ojiisan ushered him and Aska back down the hall.

"Sleep well. Good night!" he said, eyes shining as he kissed her on the forehead tenderly like a child.

After he'd left, she changed out of her clothes and into her nightgown, which still smelled like Southwestern desert earth. How strange to think that just 48 hours ago, she'd been in America. Now she was here, a world away. Jet let herself sink into the folds of the many blankets. She heard him shut the front door, then bolt it. He closed the window shutters, locking them, too. She couldn't stop thinking about what Satoko had told her–that people would want to hurt her. She should have warned Ojiisan. Or did he already know? Hiro certainly knew something, Jet could feel it in her bones.

The thought of danger slowly faded. Jet had never felt safer. For so long it had been just Satoko, J-Bird, and herself. Now she had a grandfather and a cousin. Even a dog. She had the treasure she'd wanted for as long as she could remember—a family.

Was it too much to hope that she could keep it?

CHAPTER 7

壁抜けの術
Kabe Nuke No Jutsu
Passing Through Walls

Jet awoke to birdsong at daybreak. Masakichi was in the kitchen, whistling softly as he prepared the morning's meal.

"*Ohaiyo gozaimasu*," she called out cheerfully, practicing her Japanese.

"Good morning, Jet. Sleep well?"

"Like a log," she replied.

He looked at her, puzzled, then laughed.

"A big tree! Gotcha!" he said, eyes twinkling.

Jet laughed, too.

He handed her a cup of steaming hot green tea and said, "I've been thinking, and there's something I really need to ask you. Hiro told me that you used the art of *sozu* at the Fujin waterfall yesterday."

"*Sozu?*" she asked, bewildered.

He pursed his lips.

"Well, you hid your presence. You disguised your energy by muting your aura. Hiro was surprised. Even Aska couldn't detect you."

"Oh, that." She shrugged. "Mom taught me how to do that when I was little. She made me do lots of crazy things."

"Really? What else?"

Jet sipped the hot tea. It was slightly bitter but somehow comforting. "She would take me into the desert and tell me to walk on wet tissue paper. I was supposed to walk on it without tearing it, but no matter how hard I tried, I couldn't," she said.

"I would even imagine that my feet were like feathers, but the paper still tore. Then Mom told me that I hadn't understood. She said that it wasn't about walking carefully but that I should breathe as if my body was as light as a feather."

"Sounds like my daughter." He shook his head, laughing, and Jet felt that this peaceful old man couldn't possibly know about the danger her mother had mentioned.

Jet closed her eyes, trying to stay focused on her story.

"It was really hard. And I couldn't tell anyone about it. She swore me to secrecy." She sighed, recalling all the times she was taunted by the school bully. Because she'd promised her mother she'd never reveal her skills to anyone, she couldn't fight back.

"I know the feeling," Ojiisan told her. "My own grandfather, Jinzaemon, made me learn similar tricks. It was difficult. Impossible, really."

"Really?" Jet asked. "Like what?" She wanted to hear all about her family.

Ojiisan deflected her inquiry. "You'll have lots of time to learn about Jinzaemon later. Now I want to hear all about *you*."

"Okay," she replied, hoping he'd change his mind. "I was really awkward at first. But after three years. I managed to walk on wet tissue paper without tearing it." She remembered how proud she'd felt. Satoko had said, *Wonderful! You're as stealthy as a cat.* Jet hoped that Ojiisan didn't notice her eyes watering as she recalled the rare words of praise.

"So why don't you tell me what you did yesterday?" he asked softly.

"Well, when the birds flew out of the bush, I took advantage of the distraction. I caught one in my hand and put it in the backpack. Then I threw the backpack over to a branch across the waterfall.

The bird moved inside, and Hiro followed the movement. I was already hiding by then, holding my breath."

"That's a lot to do in a few seconds!" he exclaimed.

"I didn't say it was easy… I had to focus all of my energy. On top of that, I was scared. Anyway, was that *sozu*?"

"Indeed. *Sozu* is the old Japanese word for scarecrow. When a warrior wants to conceal his presence, he subdues his *ki*, or life force. He becomes one with nature."

"Mom taught me how to do that, to hide myself in any situation. I mastered it in high school, she said wistfully. "But it was hard. No one had any idea what my life was really like, or how much I had to train. I never really knew why. Maybe you can tell me…"

He laughed and shook his head, but didn't answer her question. His clear blue eyes made him look like an elf.

"You seem to have many talents," he said. "And since you've mastered the art of *sozu*, you should be able to learn the art of passing through walls quite easily!"

"Passing through walls?"

"Let's see… Where's a good place to try?" He looked around the kitchen.

"Right now?" she asked, dismayed.

He crossed the room and took off his *zori* sandals outside the pantry.

"Watch closely." He opened the pantry door and stepped inside. "I'm going to escape by passing through the wall. Watch from the kitchen, and you'll see that I won't open the door to get out. Pay close attention. It's a skill that could serve you well in the days to come."

Though she wanted to ask what he meant, she knew that it must involve the dangers her mother had warned her about. She understood that nothing in her life would ever be simple, so she fixed her gaze on the door.

"Come into the pantry," he told her. "I want to show you that this isn't a trick. Check it for trap doors."

She went inside and knocked on the walls, floor, and ceiling. Then she went back into the kitchen. He closed himself inside the panty, and she kept her eyes on the door, listening intently. There was no sound of moving floorboards or of a section of wall sliding. She concentrated. She still felt his presence inside. Thirty seconds went by. Suddenly, she lost the sense of his presence.

She opened the pantry door.

"Ojiisan!" she called. He wasn't there.

"Oi! Here I am!" he shouted from behind her.

She turned around. He was standing there, wearing the zori he'd removed.

"How did you do that?"

"Just now, when you went into the pantry, I walked right past you."

"How?" There was no way he could have done this unless he was invisible. "I didn't see you. And I was watching, believe me."

"Well, let's say you forgot that I walked past you," he said.

"You mean I lost my memory? You hypnotized me!"

"The minute you sensed that my presence had disappeared, your breathing became slightly irregular. I actually opened the pantry door and gave you a little hypnotic suggestion, then walked right past you. It's called *saiminjutsu*."

"But there wasn't even enough time to blink!"

"Well, it wasn't much time," he conceded, "but it was enough. You see, this isn't ordinary hypnotism," he remarked.

"What is it, then?"

"Everyone thinks he remembers what happened yesterday, but most people won't be able to remember what they did every minute. They just have a vague sense of what they've done, right?"

She mulled it over. You could forget something instantly. She certainly had, many times. Especially when it came to math. "I guess you're right," she said.

"The brain's memory center has two functions: remembering and forgetting. By tapping into the forgetfulness area, I can erase your memory. It just takes practice."

"But it seems so... so specific. How can you tap into that part?"

"I learned this trick from my grandfather, Jinzaemon. It helps a warrior subdue guards to break through to enemy territory."

This was the second time he'd used that word—warrior. Her mother had said he was a soba farmer, living off the land in the mountains. He himself had said he was a hunter. Jet definitely had her doubts.

"Did you say warrior? Are *you* a warrior?" she asked.

He looked down. "No, but there are always battles to fight."

"You mean the people from the dump?" she asked.

A sharp wind blew against the walls of the house. "Yes, that's right. You see, they used to come here a lot, trying to dump waste from Tokyo on our mountain, but we refused. So they hired some *yakuza*—mafia gangs—to harass us. Sorry for them, we fought back. Those people are very persistent. But so are we!" He laughed heartily.

Jet didn't see the humor. The thought of the mountain being used as a dump made her angry. "This mountain is too beautiful to ruin like that."

"It most certainly is," he agreed as he set food on the table. "But the truth is, there are always threats to mountain people like us. That's precisely why I taught Hiro *taijutsu*, and why your mother taught it to you—to protect yourself."

Jet nodded, but her head was spinning. Did the *yakuza* have something to do with her mother's warning? Was the mountain really in peril? The problems that had plagued her in high school no longer seemed so serious. She had to know more.

"Did the *yakuza* come to Kanabe too? Did they come to your house?" Jet leaned toward her grandfather.

"No," he said and his eyes shone with a fierceness that she hadn't seen before. "The *yakuza* are not the problem. The problem is the Wa."

Jet frowned. "Mom used to talk about the Wa, but I thought they lived a long time ago. Are they still around?"

"The Wa haven't been around for a while, but now that you're here, I'm afraid they'll be back again," he conceded.

"Really? Are they the people after me?" she asked, fear prickling her skin again.

"It's complicated," Ojiisan said gravely. "We were hoping you'd know. That's why I taught Hiro English. And why I learned a bit, too."

Jet sighed. "But I don't know a thing." She was about to ask if the Wa had anything to do with the treasure when Hiro burst into the room, Aska at his side.

"Hey, Rika. What's the plan for today?" he asked.

Ojiisan turned to Jet. "There's something we need to do, isn't there?"

"There is one thing…" Jet said softly. "Mom wanted me to go to Osore-zan."

Hiro's excitement grew. "We're in luck! It's a special time on the mountain, with the fall spirit festival going on."

"What's the fall spirit festival?" Jet asked.

"After death, everyone goes to the mountain. In old times, the Ainu communed with the spirits of the dead there. We carry on the tradition," Hiro replied.

"In summer and fall, the *itako*—blind female shamans—gather there. We talk to our ancestors through these *kuchiyose*… spirit mediums," Ojiisan explained.

"Can I talk to my mother?" Jet asked.

"Her spirit needs forty-nine days to cross over to the other side. I'm afraid it's too early," Ojiisan said.

Jet just nodded, trying to hide her disappointment.

Wait!" Hiro said brightly, "we can tell my mom and the others that Aunt Satoko is coming."

"Your mom? How… I mean, when?" Jet swallowed, ashamed. She'd been so focused on herself that she hadn't asked Hiro anything. How long had he lived with Ojiisan? How had his mother passed away? And where was his father?

"If we leave now, we can get there by noon. My mom's waiting!" Hiro exclaimed.

"It's settled then," Ojiisan told them. "Today we'll go to the mountain!"

Jet's mouth hung open. She couldn't believe how quickly they'd decided to go—too quickly. Suspicion rose in her gut. She wondered if they'd already planned it.

Hiro was smiling, but Ojiisan's expression was serious.

"It will be cold," he said, "So we'd better wear layers. And we'll have to take a few trains and buses. We might even have to sleep outdoors for a night or two. Let's prepare for any eventuality."

"Right," Hiro said, springing into action.

An ominous feeling fell over the home as they prepared for the trip. Jet wondered what Ojiisan knew. Then she wondered how much longer she'd have to wait before she knew it, too.

She hoped she'd learn more on the mountain.

She had the feeling there wasn't much time left.

CHAPTER 8

運命 *Un-Mei*
Destiny

The train sped alongside the ocean, passing old fishing villages, their harbors scattered with abandoned boats turned red with rust. Jet looked out the window. Batches of seaweed hung to dry from nets, withering in the sun. Aside from a few ramshackle dive shops sprinkled along the coast, it was desolate all the way to Tanabu, where Jet, Hiro, and Ojiisan got off with a crowd of pilgrims to catch a bus to Osore-zan, packs slung over their shoulders.

The rickety bus creaked as it wound its way up the steep slope into the forest. A cool breeze wafted through the open window. The fragrance of the forest was much stronger than on the mountain path to Kanabe. Jet sniffed the air from the bus window.

"The smell is Hiba." Ojiisan pointed to big trees shooting up to the sky.

"The wood our dinner trays were made from," Hiro added. "Remember?"

Jet nodded, struggling to focus on the trees and not on the unease in her stomach.

"Hiba's termite-proof and lasts a thousand years," Ojiisan said. "But now, unfortunately, almost all the Hiba forests are gone."

"At least we still have this one," Hiro sighed. "You can visit it every year in winter to see the flowers bloom. Their yellow pollen covers the snow."

"It must be beautiful." Jet said. She'd never paid that much attention to trees, but now that her grandfather had mentioned it, she realized trees had unique characteristics, too, like people.

"It's like the sun against heaven," Ojiisan replied. "We can come back together in the winter to see it. Hopefully, I'll still be alive," he chuckled.

"Of course you'll be alive!" Jet said, alarmed.

"It's just a joke," he replied.

Soon an aquamarine lake appeared, as if suspended in the white-gray landscape. Jet had never seen water so transparent and brilliant, like crystal.

"This is Lake Usori. It's Ainu for 'bay,'" Hiro explained.

When the bus doors opened, the scent of sulfur swept in on the cold air from the rugged hills that loomed beyond the temple walls, almost knocking Jet over.

"The lake used to be volcanic crater," Ojiisan pointed out as they walked around the grounds. Black burn marks scarred the hills' flanks. There was no trace of greenery or plant life. "In the ninth century, an oracle told the Chinese priest Ennin to travel east to a sacred mountain. It was supposed to take him thirty days. Ten years later, he found Osore-zan, a huge volcano surrounded by eight mountains," Ojiisan said.

"But our ancestors discovered Osore-zan long before Ennin did," Hiro said defiantly.

Ojiisan shot Hiro a look, but Hiro shrugged it off.

"I just want her to know the truth," he said.

"She'll find out soon enough," Ojiisan replied. "Let's show her the lake. Then we can go to the temple."

He took Jet's arm and led her up the hill. She felt urgency in his grip, and they walked quickly, their feet crunching against small ash-stones left from the scorching lava.

"It looks like a lotus. That's why it's a perfect place for sacred Buddhist land," Ojiisan said.

"A lotus!" Jet exclaimed. Whenever she'd complained about life, her mother spoke of the lotus, explaining to her how something so sacred, so beautiful, grew out of mud.

Remember, it's not what you come from, she'd said. *It's what you grow into.*

Soon, the aquamarine expanse of Lake Usori spread before them. The shimmering blue surface, uninterrupted by waves, accepted the soft rays from the autumn sky. Huge domes of lava were draped with braided ropes. The Emishi had put them there, Ojiisan explained. They'd believed the domes were deities themselves and that beyond the volcanic shores of Lake Usori was the home of the spirits.

The sulfur stung Jet's lungs. Steam rose from holes in the ground. A pure white beach glistened ahead.

"Why are mountains sacred places?" she asked, remembering the Navajo mountains back home.

"The spirits of the dead fly up to heaven. We want their journey to be as quick and easy as possible," Ojiisan said.

He dropped his gaze to the silk cloth containing the box of Satoko's ashes that Jet held close to her chest. He took off his shoes and socks, walking along the sandy beach for a while. Then he crouched beside the lake and motioned her forward.

"I think this is a good place. Don't you?"

Jet joined him and moved her hand along the surface of the water.

"Yes," she said solemnly. "I think this is what Mother wanted."

She handed the box to him.

"Satoko," he called out softly, "why didn't you come back sooner?"

He took out the urn and cradled it. Unbidden, tears fell from his blue eyes. He didn't try to wipe them away.

Jet hated to see her grandfather so sad. It was making her sad, too, and she couldn't afford to open that door—to think about her mother, her father, even Amy Williams and her high school friends who now seemed worlds away. She couldn't afford to think about all the people who were no longer there.

"Ojiisan," Jet cried, "why didn't Mom come back to Japan?"

"It's a long story... But, well, the village was attacked before you were born. Your mother had something those people wanted."

"What was it?" Jet pleaded. "Please tell me. I need to know."

"She understood a lot of things that most of us never will, and she had the courage to keep up the fight for years and not give them what it was that they wanted. When you arrived, I thought you'd have the answers. I'm still in shock that you don't."

Now it was Jet's turn to apologize.

"I'm so sorry, Ojiisan. I wish I did."

He nodded. "I only know that your mother was on the run all of those years."

"Is that why we lived in New Mexico?"

"Yes. But I didn't know that. For the longest time, I didn't know where she was. She believed we were being watched and feared that if she returned—or you did—the problems would start up all over again."

"I see," Jet said, mulling over his words. She had grown up in her mother's constant aura of fear and determination, thinking Satoko was crazy.

Ojiisan lit a bundle of incense and started to chant. The sun was slowly going down, the air cooling against Jet's skin.

"Your mother died too young," he said solemnly. "But it was her *en*, her karma. Only the dead can cut the ties of *en*."

Jet nodded. She didn't really believe in karma or fate. "Are you afraid of death, Ojiisan?" she asked.

He sighed. "If I were afraid of death, I'd be long gone by now. I simply want to *be*, like a rock that accepts the sunshine, rain, and wind peacefully. Death will come when it comes."

Jet watched as her grandfather released the stark gray ashes and white bones into the water. Instead of sinking, one small bone floated, moving gently like a butterfly over the surface. Satoko's *nodo-botoke*, the small bone of the Adam's apple.

"Every creature in the world is precious," he said softly, watching the water carry the ashes away. "Our survival depends on the animals and plants we eat. Our lives contain those lives and those deaths. The same is true with human beings—some take advantage of others. That's just life."

He looked at her meaningfully. "No one can escape the laws of this world. That's why our people know how to fight. We've been treated unfairly, and that's our *en*, our karma."

"Can't we change it?" Jet asked.

"Maybe. Maybe *you* can change it," Ojiisan said emphatically, holding her gaze.

"How?" she asked, her heart skipping a beat.

Ojiisan sighed. "That's what you came here to find out. We're here to help you however we can."

Reflexively, Jet made a fist and punched the earth. She'd wanted to stay calm, but she was rattled. It was like she was special in a way she couldn't possibly understand. Or believe. And yet, she'd made a promise to come here. To figure it out. So far, she'd gotten nowhere.

Ojiisan sighed. He stroked his chin as if gathering his words, then spoke clearly. "I know you've come back to help. And for that, I thank you with all of my heart. I know you are frustrated. But we must be patient. Your mother knew what she was doing, even if the rest of us don't," he laughed.

"Ojiisan," Jet whispered. "Grandpa...."

He wrapped her in his strong arms and pulled her close as her sobs released themselves. Letting herself surrender, she realized how good it felt to be held like this. She'd never had a father or a grandfather. She'd had men in her life, like J-Bird, but never that blood bond that would make her walk through fire and over water. She yearned for that closeness, that comfort, somewhere to belong. More than anything, that's what she wanted. Would Kanabe be it? Would she finally find a place to be herself, whoever that was?

CHAPTER 9

予言 *Yogen*
The Prophecy

Ojiisan led them down the path to the huge wooden gate before the temple, where people sat in small circles outside the prayer hall. In the middle of each circle, a blind female *itako* in a white kimono chanted as she fingered her prayer beads, clicking them together rhythmically.

"Hey! There she is!" Hiro shouted. He grabbed their hands and pulled them toward a stout old woman who appeared to be almost ninety.

"Hello there," he said. "Remember me?" He crouched next to where she sat. The woman squinted, tilting her head in his direction.

"Ah! I've heard that voice before. Yes, I remember! You're the boy who always comes with your Ojiisan from Mt. Hakkoda. Am I right?"

"Yes, that's me," Hiro answered.

"And you came with your Ojiisan today, too. But wait…" She turned toward Jet. "You're also with a young lady."

Hiro laughed. "I knew it! You're just pretending to be blind. You really *can* see!"

The old lady snorted. "Even if I can't see, I have a nose and ears. Even if my nose and ears don't work, I can feel someone's presence through my skin. Seeing is not the only way of receiving and perceiving. Understand?"

The sound of prayers rang out through the temple hall.

"I understand!" Hiro said confidently, then shifted his gaze to Jet. "Hey… My cousin came all the way from America to talk to the spirits. Here…" He pushed Jet in front of the *itako*.

She motioned Jet closer. She took a few breaths and placed her right hand on Jet's heart. It raced under the *itako's* touch, the woman's power charging her like electricity. Then words echoed from the *itako's* mouth, though they seemed to come from somewhere behind her body.

"The spirits are protecting you," she said, "but as you gain power in the present, you are being asked to go back to the past."

Jet opened her mouth to speak, but the woman's hand pressed her chest, as if stopping her words.

"You must find the treasure and save the magic mountain. It's what your mother trained you to do."

"How did you…." Jet stammered.

"You will save the mountain and its gods from destruction. You will be the one…."

Jet trembled in the cold air. "Me? How?" She also wanted to ask: *And how could a mountain be magic? Carpets, sure, and markers, too. But a mountain?* But she held her tongue.

The *itako* lifted her palm. "People from all over the world will come to the mountain for its blessings. It will become a symbol of peace. But only if you help."

"How! Tell me! How can I help?" Jet asked, her interest more piqued now than ever.

"Find your power. Then trust your power," the old woman said, nodding rhythmically as the words came out. "The women will guide you."

"What women? Where?" Jet said, struggling to understand.

The *itako* nodded. "Ahhh. Look within. We're always looking outside ourselves, but we're the ones with the power. Nature gives it to us, if we serve her."

"Nature?" Jet murmured, puzzling over the *itako's* words. "Serve her? How?"

"We've lost our connection," the *itako* said, head bobbing as the words spilled out in a rush. "It's there if we look."

"But I don't understand. I'm afraid," Jet said.

Light suffused the *itako's* ancient lined face, making her look young and radiant.

She pressed her palm into Jet's heart softly. "That's good. It's only through fear that we can discover our courage. If you're fearless, you don't need to be brave. Bravery comes from overcoming your fears."

"Hmmm. I never thought of it that way," Jet said, reassured.

"Use the feminine power to guide yourself and others. It's the only way."

"Teach me how," Jet stammered.

"I can't teach you. You are the teacher. Just trust, and let her emerge."

The *itako* shuddered, and the words stopped coming. Jet tried to let them sink in, but the message only confused her.

Suddenly, Ojiisan came to the *itako's* side and whispered something into her ear.

"Yes! You must go. Now!" the *itako* said.

"Wait!" Jet pleaded, "Tell me what to do."

"Not now, child. There is danger. Come back again."

Bowing to the old woman, Ojiisan wrapped his arm around Jet, guiding her to the gate.

"Thank you, thank you," Jet called out behind her as they boarded the bus.

"Quiet. Don't speak," Ojiisan whispered, glancing at the other passengers.

Jet nodded, frightened. Hiro looked down.

They rode in silence. Jet had no idea where they were going, and in the silence could only hear the *itako's* words ring out loudly in her head: *As you gain power in the present, you are being asked to go back to the past.*

What could that mean?

Soon the bus had descended the mountain and stopped at the train station. In a flash, they were back on the train.

Then the train stopped. Ojiisan stood up suddenly, taking Jet and Hiro by their arms. Hiro looked around quizically. It wasn't the right station!

"Quick!" Ojiisan whispered, pushing them both out to the platform.

They got off just as the doors slammed shut. Inside the train, two tall men in dark suits stood up and looked out the window. One shook his fist furiously. With a start, Jet recognized them. They'd been on the bus to Osore-zan!

Ojiisan led Hiro and Jet toward the train bound for Morioka Station—the opposite direction from Kanabe. Night was falling. He bought three sushi *bentos* at the platform kiosk.

"Where are we going?" Jet whispered. Again, Ojiisan motioned for them to be quiet. The next train arrived, and they boarded quickly. When they took a seat, Ojiisan handed them each a *bento*. It was just after six, and Jet wasn't hungry.

"Eat," he told her. "You'll need strength."

She did as he suggested. They broke apart their chopsticks and dug into the cold food, forcing themselves to eat. Ojiisan left half of his untouched and wrapped the box, then leaned back in his seat, eyes closed.

Jet held her chopsticks midair, recalling her mother's words from years ago.

"If you're completely hungry, you can't fight. If you're completely full, you can't fight."

Where did that memory come from? She looked carefully at the way Ojiisan was resting. She felt him gathering his energy, concentrating his power, storing it and restoring himself. She'd seen her mother sitting that way many times.

Outside, dusk was settling on the edges of the distant mountain. The bright autumn colors were gone. The outlines of trees stood darkly against the evening sky.

Ojiisan opened his eyes, looking intently at her. He lowered his voice.

"We're being followed. These men could be dangerous. They might be the people your mother feared. If so, we'll have to defend ourselves."

"What am I supposed to do?" Jet asked, desperation rising.

"Fall back on your training," he replied.

Jet's legs bounced up and down.

"Jet!" Hiro said, pushing her thighs down. "You're making me nervous!"

"I didn't even know I was doing that!" Jet said, embarrassed.

"Take a moment. Both of you," Ojiisan told them. "Remember—a warrior has to be in control of the body *and* mind—even to the extent of hiding who he is."

"*Oshaka-sama*," Hiro coughed. *Lord Buddha!* Then he closed his eyes and took deep, slow breaths. Jet watched his body relax. She wanted to be able to do the same. She tried, drinking in her breath like sips of hot chocolate. But then her concentration lapsed, and fear brimmed her chest.

"I can't!" she said, voice quavering.

Ojiisan looked at her kindly, his voice now light.

"Go ahead, try. It won't be so difficult for you, Jet, because you've already mastered the art of *sozu*. Right?"

"Right." She smiled, twisting the turquoise ring on her finger. Like she always did when she was nervous.

Ojiisan closed his eyes, turning inward, and Jet did the same, trying to calm her mind, breathing deeply. As vivid as if it were happening now, a memory washed up in her mind.

Once when she was twelve, walking home from school on a rainy day, she'd felt someone following her. She wasn't sure how she knew, but she sensed it clearly. She kept on walking, not turning back to look. As she rounded a corner, sure enough four girls came up quickly from behind and fenced her in. Instinctively, she put her right hand in her pocket. J-Bird had given her a beautiful turquoise ring for her birthday. She'd wanted to hide it so they wouldn't take this precious gift.

"Give us your money," one girl, the biggest, demanded.

Jet turned to run away. They came closer, encircling her.

"Take your hand out of your pocket, Chink," another one spat out the words.

They can't even get it right. I'm half-Japanese, not Chinese, she thought.

The rain started to fall harder. The rest was a blur of shouts, kicks, and pain.

The ring was gone and Jet came home with many scrapes and bruises on her body. She had been thoroughly defeated, shamed, and shocked. She hadn't really known what hit her. She told her mother what happened.

The next week, walking down the same street, Jet was surrounded again.

The big girl lunged toward her, reaching her right hand to attack. But this time, Jet stepped back to avoid the girl's hand. When the girl came at her with her left hand, Jet grabbed it and shifted back and to the right, locking the girl's joints and holding her in place, then jabbing her umbrella into her ribs. As the girl fell, the others stepped back in shock. Jet swung her umbrella in a low circle, hitting their ankles hard. She didn't know how badly she'd hurt them, but had plenty of time to run away.

When she came home, panting and out of breath, Satoko knew something had happened again. And yet her daughter's expression was completely different this time.

"Tell me about it," she said, making Jet a cup of hot chocolate.

Jet caught her breath. "I don't know what happened. I reached for the umbrella, and some *force* just took over. It was weird…"

Satoko smiled. "*Soujutsu*. In the old days, people had to use spears and lances. But nowadays, you can use an umbrella, a cane, a stick, or even a rolled-up newspaper. You did well!"

"Where'd I learn that?" Jet asked.

Satoko smiled. "I don't remember exactly, but I guess we covered it."

Jet had a vague memory of her mom teaching her this technique using sticks on a mountain, but her school teachers told her she had an "overactive imagination," and she was always daydreaming in class, so she couldn't be sure.

The following week Jet took the same route home. The girls were waiting for her again. But this time when she approached, they threw something on the sidewalk in front of her and ran away, scattering in different directions.

It was the ring from J-Bird, wrapped in a Taco Bell napkin. Jet had to laugh. She kept the napkin as a souvenir. Their white flag of surrender. She turned the ring on her finger now. If she could call upon those skills back then, maybe she could do it now. She felt a bit more reassured, remembering.

Jet snapped back into the present when the train stopped at a small station near Misawa Army base. Ojiisan quickly shuttled them out of the car.

The night's frozen air hit them on the platform, but Ojiisan didn't let them move until he was sure no other passengers had gotten off. Then, they headed up the street, stopping at a liquor store. Music streamed into the store from a back room. It sounded like it was coming from a TV game show.

"Anyone there?" Ojiisan called out casually over a blue curtain. Jet's eye travelled the many-shaped bottles lining the shelves.

"Oh, hello! Do you need something?" A plump rosy-faced woman peered from behind the curtain in a white apron.

"I'm sorry to bother you. Can we get a taxi? We got off at the wrong station. We wanted to go to Yaiyama, to see my nephew..." Ojiisan's voice trailed off.

The woman wiped her hands as she came into the store. Ojiisan rambled on. Jet watched the woman's cautious expression fade, the wrinkles on her brow ease. He was a harmless country bumpkin.

"Normally, you call a cab from the next town. It takes thirty minutes just to get here. But my husband got home early today, so he can drive you," she said pleasantly.

"No, no." Ojiisan shook his head. "I wouldn't want to put your husband out on a Sunday night. Besides, we're strangers. I'd feel bad for the inconvenience."

"Don't worry. When people have trouble, they should help each other. What goes around comes around." She parted the blue curtain and yelled for her husband.

"*Anta*, will you drive this old man and his grandkids to Yaiyama?"

A heavyset man with sleepy eyes emerged from the back room. When he saw them, his round face softened into a smile, just as hers had. They probably didn't get many visitors.

"No problem at all," he said jovially.

"Thank you. We know it's your precious day off." Ojiisan bowed.

Jet watched as Ojiisan's expression, attitude, gestures, and tone of voice completely changed. Was this *henge*, the art of disguise her mother had told her about? He was clearly a master, but Jet was too frightened to feel proud.

Ojiisan bowed and shuffled out, leading them out of the store. In the car, he chatted with the shopkeeper about baseball. Thirty minutes later, he abruptly asked the man to stop.

"We're not at the village yet, sir. It's just a few miles more." The man glanced outside at the dark dirt road nervously.

"It's all right. My nephew is kind of a hermit. He lives in the mountains. We can take a trail from here. I know this area like it's my own backyard."

"But it's pitch-black outside, sir. You can't see a thing," the man insisted.

"Not to worry. I could do it with my eyes closed!" Ojiisan laughed. He put a five-thousand yen bill on the dashboard and reached for the door. "Thank you so much. Here's some money for gas. Please take it."

"That's not necessary—" the man stammered.

"Please. It's the least we can do." Ojiisan opened the door and bowed to the man as Jet and Hiro got out.

After the car drove away, Ojiisan stood up straight, his voice clear and sharp again.

"We'll have to walk very quickly. Come on!" he commanded.

The lights of the village shone to the west, but where they stood was lit only by the glow of the crescent moon. Cold wind whistled against the mountainside. Jet shivered.

"Ojiisan… I'm tired!" Hiro said softly and yawned.

"I know. I am, too. But we have no choice. It will take us two hours to get home on the animal trails. Watch your step. And if you have to talk," he glanced at Hiro, "speak only in *shinobi kotoba*. Okay?"

Hiro nodded.

Jet looked at her cousin, eyebrows raised.

She sensed Hiro gathering energy from his core as he sent out breaths like smoke signals. She listened, remembering long ago when her mother spoke in this special way when they played "hide and seek" in the mountains. In daylight, her mother had taught her to use hand signals, but in the darkness—where their range of vision was limited—they used this same language. Now it had a name—*shinobi kotoba*.

"Do you understand me?" Hiro asked.

Jet nodded, remembering how words were made from the amount of air released when the mouth opened and closed. Ordinary people couldn't hear anything recognizable as language.

With a start, Jet realized she wasn't ordinary.

"Can you say something?" Hiro asked.

Jet opened her mouth, trying to let the air come through. She couldn't. This wasn't a game, it wasn't hide and seek in the mountains, and she'd never used *shinobi kotoba* when there was danger. *Focus. Think. Remember!* she willed herself, but only strange muffled gasps escaped her lips. Hiro couldn't understand her. There was no use.

"It's okay. Come on!" Hiro urged.

With heightened awareness, Jet stepped lightly behind her cousin and grandfather, moving swiftly in the darkness. The moon occasionally passed behind the black clouds carried on the strong north wind.

Then Ojiisan lifted his arm and stopped. It was as if his body had frozen. His mouth moved soundlessly in the secret language. Jet struggled to make sense of the word, and then, instinctively, it came to her. "Danger," he'd said. Hearing it gave her goosebumps.

Ojiisan crouched behind a tree and cocked his head, listening. Jet listened, too. The wind blew straight toward her, sending branches crashing into each other and casting leaves onto the ground. She couldn't feel any presence, not even a rabbit or a fox.

Jet tried to speak again, carefully shaping her lips around the air.

"Is someone there?" she asked, haltingly using her breath to push out sounds.

She waited for a response. Had she made sense?

"Yes, they're waiting for us. But we're still a bit away from them," Hiro replied.

Jet's heart pounded. "Why can't I feel them?" she asked in the secret tongue, the words coming more swiftly now.

"They aren't expecting us to come from this direction," Ojiisan said, "so they're focusing on the opposite direction. Once we go another mile toward them, you'll be able to feel them. And they'll be able to feel you, too. I'm sure they've raided the house."

"Ojiisan, what if they hurt Aska?" Hiro asked.

"Aska's tough. Don't worry." Ojiisan looked at the moon through the branches.

"It's five and a half miles to the southern mountain ridge. I'll go there to check on the house and make sure the village is secure. You two go east to Aterui's cave and wait for me. Okay?"

"We'll go with you," she insisted. "We should stay together. It's so dark, and—"

"Jet's right," Hiro added. "Let's go together. That way...."

"Hiro!" Ojiisan's body tensed. "The village is surrounded. If I bring you there, that will play right into their hands."

"No!" Hiro hissed.

"We must separate. You mustn't be afraid!" Ojiisan said sternly. "Wait ninety minutes at the cave. If I haven't come by then, get on a train and go find your uncle Soji in Tokyo. I'll come later."

Jet's mouth opened in astonishment. "Uncle? I have an uncle?"

"Yes. You do." Ojiisan smiled, but sadness shadowed his eyes. "Our family was being hunted. We had to go our own ways for safety."

"How horrible," Jet said, heart sinking. She couldn't help but feel that this was all somehow her fault. If only she could put an end to it, and soon!

"I put Soji's address in Hiro's wallet. Even though Hiro is very capable, he's still a boy, so please take care of him. Can you do that?"

"Yes, I promise. I will… But Ojiisan, please don't go!" Jet begged, more afraid than she'd ever been. This wasn't like the games against her mother. It wasn't even like the moment she feared she was fighting a stranger on the mountain. This danger was more serious than anything she had ever faced. It might be deadly.

Ojiisan looked at the sky. "You'll be strong. I know it. And don't worry about me. I've been here since I was younger than Hiro. I know where the gentian blossoms, where the salmon swim, and which tree has the best chestnuts. Even this wind is my friend. I'll survive."

"Please, grandpa. Be careful," Jet pleaded.

"I will, I promise," he answered as a harsh wind blew and the forest shuddered.

And then, quick as a sword slashing through the air, he was gone. He'd wrapped his body in the wind and been carried deep into the forest on its mighty wings.

CHAPTER 10

雨 の 匂 い *Ame no Nioi*
The Smell of the Rain

The wind blew stronger. Masakichi had to walk into its resistance, but his pace did not slow. The further he went, the faster he moved, soundlessly and forcefully. The earth smelled like rain. He had to find a way out. Alive.

His grandfather Jinzaemon had taught him how to find a straight path, even in the wind. Jinzaemon was born in 1848, twenty years before Japan first opened its doors to the West. He had taught Masakichi all about *ninjutsu*. "If you want to go straight against the wind, find a path in its folds and pass through it," he had said, although he'd never actually taught his grandson how to find it. Still, Masakichi had begged him.

"Even if I teach you where the path is, you won't be able to see it because the wind is always changing. If I show you the path in the wind one minute, the wind will shift and the path will disappear the next."

"Then how do I find it?" Masakichi had asked, worried he'd never be able to do it.

"You must find it anew each time," his grandfather smiled. "The only way to see the path in the wind is to become the wind itself. You have to be able to move like wind. Once you can pass through a narrow space or flow smoothly over a rough road just like the wind, then you will be able to see the path within it."

It wasn't until Jinzaemon died, not long after, that Masakichi had been able to see the path in the wind. He was ten years old. Jinzaemon was eighty and had lived a very long life.

Seventy years had gone by since then. As he swallowed, Masakichi's parched throat ached, and he realized he was now the same age that Jinzaemon had been when he died.

Ojiisan Jin would have told me to be tougher, Masakichi thought, although he knew he couldn't have ignored Hiro's feelings the way his own grandfather might have ignored his. He had to go rescue the dog. He had to check on the village. He knew he was taking a risk by entering enemy territory, but Aska was family, and Hiro would not be able to carry on if anything happened to her.

Compared to Jinzaemon, Masakichi was sentimental. That was his nature. And a fundamental ninja rule was not to go against nature—especially your own.

"Be impassive," Jinzaemon had taught his grandson. "If you are swayed by passion, your judgment falters. Then you get involved in situations you would normally avoid. If you do that, one day you'll end up in the enemy's trap."

"Yes, Grandpa," Masakichi had said earnestly.

"The ninja is not heroic. It's completely different from what you read about in comics and novels. It's unpolished and dirty. We have to let the samurai or *Wa* worry about honor and beautiful deaths. Understand?"

"Yes, grandpa," Masakichi said, his lip trembling.

"Good. Let them say what they will about us, but we have no laws to protect us, no lords to serve, no one to give us weapons or food or shelter. Ninja have to use whatever they can to survive. And that means we need to be decisive enough to use our master, parents, family, friends—even our children if necessary. *Wakaru-ka*? Do you understand?" His blue eyes cut into Masakichi's like ice.

"Does that mean you will kill me someday?" Masakichi asked anxiously, staring straight at his grandfather's face, which transformed into the face of an *oni*, the huge black devils that ate little children in his picture books.

"Yes! If necessary, I will use anybody—even you—to survive," Jinzaemon said. Masakichi's eyes watered. Jinzaemon softened his tone. "But it will never come to that. I would never allow such a dangerous situation to occur. So you don't have to worry. You are the most important thing in the world. You're the jewel of the Kuroi family. It's my job to protect you. And that I will do with my own life, if need be."

When Jinzaemon had finally smiled, Masakichi had felt relieved.

The smell of the rain came back to him now. Jinzaemon had taught him so many important things. Yet Masakichi knew he couldn't live in the past, in those words. To do so would take him out of the present, and that could be fatal.

The words of Zen priest Rinzai echoed in Masakichi's mind. *"When you meet the Buddha, kill the Buddha! When you meet your ancestors, kill your ancestors! When you meet a disciple of the Buddha, kill the disciple! When you meet your parents, kill your parents! When you meet your kin, kill your kin! Only thus will you attain enlightenment."*

He knew he lacked the severity that Jinzaemon had possessed. His grandfather had been as disciplined as a Zen priest. Masakichi understood why he couldn't be that severe. He didn't have absolute faith in *ninjutsu*. Masakichi knew that even if he had followed a strict discipline, even if he could move like the wind, he stood no chance against modern weaponry. His grandfather had been innocent, relying only on the power of his will, strength, and skills. But this was the twenty-first century. The invention of electricity had been the beginning of the end for the ninja. He meant what he told Jet, even though she had doubted him.

There was no use for the ninja anymore.

The smell of rain swept up from the earth like a tidal wave. Masakichi rubbed his nose as if trying to get rid of the smell. Now that Jet was here, however, maybe things would be different.

A new day had come.

The rains, too, would eventually clear.

CHAPTER 11

キリギリス *Kirigirisu*
Cricket

Masakichi crouched in the bushes, staring into the darkness. He could make out two shadows in the flat space at the bottom of the valley a few hundred yards away. He couldn't see the men clearly, but he didn't need to. He could tell where they were from the faint smell of cologne floating in the wind. He breathed a sigh of relief. The first to discover the opponent controlled the outcome.

They can't be professionals. A pro would never wear aftershave. And it's so dark, how can they see anything? They must be using a nightscope.

Fortunately, the moon was still covered by clouds. With a nightscope, you could see a target eight hundred yards away under the moonlight. Without moonlight, you could see less than five hundred yards. Masakichi wondered whether he should ignore whoever was following him completely, take an alternate route, and go straight to the village.

Suddenly a strong wind shook the forest. Jumping up into the wind, Masakichi rushed down the cliff, hiding in bamboo bushes that were taller than he was.

Masakichi smiled wryly to himself. Jinzaemon's lesson, "Use anything you can to survive," had stayed with him all those years. He stopped behind a tree, hugging its trunk.

He was still two hundred and fifty yards from the men. If he took one wrong step, they would find him. He had no weapons. He was sure that they did. His heart beat wildly.

He took a deep breath, listening to the crickets' song. There seemed to be hundreds of males in the grass, rubbing their wings to entice the females. He picked out the voice of a cricket whose song sounded like a high-pitched bell. Then he exhaled between clenched teeth, mimicking the cricket as he moved in the bamboo bush, carried along with the breeze.

> *How miserable*
> *the cricket singing*
> *under the helmet*

Masakichi recalled Bashō's haiku. The poet had written it when looking at the great warrior Saito Betto Sanemori's helmet. Saito was a medieval samurai who'd fought his last battle at seventy-three. Most people thought the poem expressed the pathos of being killed by a young samurai he'd once taught and served. His death was made even more tragic by the song of the cricket under his heavy iron helmet.

Masakichi disagreed. To him, the cricket was old Sanemori himself, facing certain death in battle with unwavering resolve. Like the cricket, he continued to sing right up to his death, even while the heavy helmet weighed down on him. He met his death with a song.

How painful to live in this world! Even at my age, when I should accept death quietly, why am I clinging to life? Masakichi asked himself.

Because there's so much left to do! Rika's just arrived. I must survive to give the secrets of our tribe to her so she can pass them on. Now that Satoko's gone, Rika and Hiro are the only link to the past.

Masakichi imagined that he was the cricket, singing as his life drew to an end. Staring at the faint shadows of the two men in the darkness, he laughed at himself. How ridiculous he was, mimicking the sound of a cricket! The two men, whoever they were, were staring intently in his direction.

What now? It's a waste of time to sit here chirping. Why do they want to kill me? He knew his life was in danger, the way he knew the very direction of the wind. *I must have done something really bad in my former life to end up like this in my dottage.*

Once again, the wind descended from the north, sweeping down from the top of the mountain. Masakichi picked up a fist-sized stone and threw it behind the two men. Just as the stone landed, the wind swept through the whole valley. Masakichi took off through the bamboo.

The misty rain covered the valley with a serene silence, lulling every creature to sleep. Masakichi stuck his palm out and let the rain fall into it. He tasted the fresh water, salty from his own skin. He wiped his face with the mist, as if purifying himself in it.

The last time I met death, I survived by accident. But this time....

Another strong northerly wind blew down from the mountain-top. When it reached the bottom of the valley and stirred the mist like smoke, Masakichi disappeared into it gracefully, just as he had done so many years before.

CHAPTER 12

アテルイの祠
Aterui no Hokora
Aterui's Cave

Jet and Hiro made their way down an animal trail into a bamboo grove where thick green stalks stood over seven feet tall.

As they walked, pushing aside the huge wet leaves, the sound of water became louder. They came to a pile of rocks on the mountainside.

"Here's the cave," Hiro said.

Jet hesitated. She didn't want to leave the bamboo grove. Satoko had taught her that a bamboo grove was the safest place in an earthquake, since the roots grew deep and strong, weaving to create a natural grid that locked the earth in place.

Jet surveyed the grove. If only the bamboo could offer safety now.

"Come on, follow me in," Hiro whispered.

"I can't," Jet stammered.

"Why not?"

"I'm scared," she replied.

In all the training her mother had made her endure, the one thing Jet hadn't conquered was this—a fear of small, dark spaces. Dark mountaintops, okay. Dark highways, okay. But caves? Jet shivered. She'd sooner sleep in a pit of vipers.

As the images flashed through her mind, Hiro stood beside her, waiting. *Was he seeing them, too?*

"I used to be afraid, too. But Ojiisan taught me how to conquer my fear."

"How?" Jet ventured.

"Well, first of all, don't deny it. Accept that it's there."

"Right," Jet said. "That's what the *itako* said, too."

"Yeah. Just try to call it something else. Not fear, but…." he bit his lip. "Extreme dislike, for example."

Jet laughed. "I can do that," she said.

"Good, that's a start…." he glanced around. "Anyway we better go in. It's not safe outside."

Hiro crouched and entered the cave. There was a candle near the wall. He cupped it in his hand, lighting the wick with matches. He then brought it to the entrance, showing Jet the cave's depths. In the flickering light, Jet saw how young he was. She sensed how afraid he must be. Yet, he carried on.

"Come on," he waved his hand, gesturing her towards the cave's opening.

She took a step inside. The air smelled of wet earth, and the wind echoed from outside like a howling animal.

"Look," he said, shining the candle toward a small wooden shrine deep in the cave. Hiro carried the candle there, pressed his palms together and bowed in front of the shrine. Jet stayed at the entrance, knees shaking, repeating his gesture.

Then Hiro sat on the damp earth as she stayed at the entrance, breathing deeply into her collar to warm herself.

"This is as far as I'm going." She sat down. "What is this place?"

"A shrine to our ancestor, Aterui."

Jet started. "*When the Emperor's troops invaded the north, Aterui led the resistance.*" She recalled the words from her mother's story, and repeated them to Hiro.

"Right! So you know about us!" he exclaimed.

"Not so much. I want to know more. Can you tell me? No one else seems to be able to," Jet sighed, frustrated.

Hiro smiled. "You *should* know more," he replied. "I'll teach you about the tribe. First of all, do you know why Japan is called Nippon?"

"No." She shook her head, wondering what—if anything—this had to do with the Kuroi family.

Hiro looked at her askance, as if—again—reading her mind. "Ojiisan says if you want to understand a people, look at their language. The words write the history, not the other way around."

She nodded, trying to quell her impatience, this shortcoming her mother had said came from her "American side."

"Nippon was translated into English as 'Jippon,' which became Jipang. When foreigners came, they had an easier time saying Japan than Jipang. So the name stuck. Here, hold out your hand," he said and traced two ideograms on her palm.

日本

"That's ni-hon," Jet said, proud that she'd remembered.

"Right. But you can also read them as *hinomoto*, the original name of Japan. 日 (Nichi) means sun and 本 (Hon) means origin."

"I get it!" Jet said. "The place where the sun rises! Is that why Japan's called 'The Land of the Rising Sun?'"

"Yes. Because that's what the Emishi called their ancient kingdom in Nara. The first king, queen, and residents of Hinomoto were the Emishi—our tribe!"

"I don't understand," Jet said, frowning. "What does this have to do with the Emishi?"

"Hinomoto is an Emishi word. Not a word of the *Wa*. Why? Because this was our kingdom first!"

"Weren't the imperial family the rulers of Nara?" Jet asked, confused.

Hiro sighed. "That's what they want you to believe, but it's only their version. Our ancestors were here first. The Emperor's army took the land from them. They wanted to 'civilize' the barbarians," he snorted.

Jet was dubious. "How do you know for sure?"

"Don't take my word for it. The *Kojiki* says, 'Emperor Jinmu advanced toward the East, defeating the 'barbarians' and 'relieving' Nara from the Emishi.'"

"So?"

"So, if Japan's oldest book says the Emperor had to 'relieve' it, clearly the Emishi were already there. Get it?"

"You must be right." Jet nodded, impressed. "Why doesn't everyone know this?"

"They should. Old Chinese records show the same thing. Some of the Emperor's family is buried in Nara, but those tombs date from the fifth century. Before that, the Emishi ruled the land. Peacefully. Until the *Wa* invaded… and re-wrote the history books."

"Oh, so that's why you hate them so much," Jet said, finally understanding.

"Yeah. You could say that. The Imperial Army drove survivors out of the West, and the Emishi kept moving north until they ended up here. They lived peacefully for a while. But then… gold was discovered nearby in the eighth century, so the Army came back again."

"Gold? I've never heard of that!" Jet said, astonished.

"Not many people have." Hiro shrugged. "Anyway, the Emishi fought hard, with Aterui leading. The battle lasted eleven long years. This shrine honors that battle."

"What happened to Aterui?" Jet asked.

"Finally, he had to surrender. He was sent to Kyoto and betrayed. He was executed. It was the saddest time in our history," Hiro said, turning toward the shrine and bowing again.

"And what happened to the tribe?" Jet asked, trying to recall her mother's stories.

"Many Emishi were captured and sent west as slaves. The ones who stayed were starving to death. The only way to survive was to sell their children. It sounds cruel, but that was all they had, and it was the only way for the kids to survive, too."

"That's horrible," Jet said, eyes wide.

"The Kuroi family were sold as *genin*. We did what we had to do to survive. Our ancestors suffered, but it was worth it, because our tribe is still alive. We wouldn't be here today…."

"*Genin!*" Jet recognized the word her mother had said on their last night together.

Hiro's eyebrow suddenly shot up. He cocked his head to the side.

"Wait. Listen!" he said. "Ojiisan's coming back… And he's with Aska!"

Sure enough, Ojiisan appeared in the mouth of the cave, Aska close behind.

"Ojiisan!" Hiro jumped up to hug him, making his grandfather stumble backward.

Aska jumped up and licked Hiro's face.

"Are you two all right?" Ojiisan rubbed Hiro's head.

"We're fine," Jet said, still reeling from the shock of Hiro's words. "Are you okay?" Her grandfather seemed exhausted.

"I'm still alive." He tried to smile. "Listen, here are some important documents—bank books, passports, and the title to the house. There's also money, credit cards, and a cell phone."

He handed a small backpack to Jet.

"Did you make it all the way back to the house?" Hiro asked.

"You bet! Just like I said I would. I found Aska in the backyard. They'd used a tranquilizer on her."

"A tranquilizer? Why?" Hiro asked, alarmed.

"No idea. No one was at the house…" He shook his head. "I thought they'd be waiting."

"Good thing Aska's a fighting dog, like her mother," Hiro said, petting the dog's wet fur.

"She'll be fine in no time," Ojiisan reassured him.

He stepped away from the cave, motioning for them to follow him.

In the distance, a red light flickered through the trees.

"Ojiisan! There's a fire!" Hiro exclaimed. "It's coming from Kanabe!"

"Don't worry about it." Ojiisan waved his hand. "We need to go right away."

"What? How can you not care?" Hiro fumed.

"Because I lit it!" Ojiisan replied, spinning on his heels and disappearing into the catherdral-like bamboo grove up ahead.

CHAPTER 13

死闘 *Shito*
Desperate Struggle

Aska suddenly crouched, snarling at the thick overgrowth in front of them.

Hiro and Jet jumped behind trees seconds before shots were fired.

Ojiisan leapt forward, spinning. He caught the man's cheek with his heel. As soon as the man fell, Aska was instantly on him, his throat in her jaws.

Another man, also dressed in black, his nose and mouth hidden by a scarf, ran at Ojiisan. Jet knew she should do something—anything—to help her grandfather, but she couldn't make herself move. It was as if she had suddenly become frozen, rooted to the earth like bamboo.

She tried to summon her power, but there was nothing there. Only fear and immobility. Why was this happening? She'd been able to fight her mother on the mountain, hadn't she?

Without hesitation, Hiro threw a ten-yen coin with such force that it gashed the man's forehead. Ojiisan turned and aimed his elbow at the man's throat, but the man caught his arm and threw him down. Ojiisan's shoulder struck the earth, and he grunted loudly.

Jet watched it all in a panic, as if in slow motion. Her mother had taught her how to run, jump, kick, fight in every imaginable circumstance. That was just it. Every *imaginable* circumstance. That was what she'd been trying to teach Jet that night on the mountain—what it felt like to *really* be threatened. This was different. This was real.

Jet took a breath, steeled herself. While his attacker held his arm, Ojiisan struck the back of his hand, the sound of breaking bones was unmistakable. He flipped to his feet and kicked the man's knee with the side of his foot. As his enemy fell, Ojiisan kicked his neck. Jet closed her eyes.

"*Oshaka-sama,*" he said in *shinobi kotoba.* "Lord Buddha! I knew there would be an attack, but this is worse than I expected. They're better fighters than we've ever faced."

Hiro was pale. He shivered as Aska came to his side. The dog had killed the other man, but the one Ojiisan had fought was still alive, lying face down.

"Let's go," he urged.

"Ojiisan!" Jet turned back toward the man. "We can't just leave him here."

"We have no choice. He's already chosen his destiny." Ojiisan crouched beside the man and took his rifle. He moved as if in pain, and she knew that if she'd fought alongside them, he might not have gotten hurt.

She sank to the ground in tears, her whole body trembling. Ojiisan took her arm and lifted her up.

He turned her to face him squarely. "You've got to snap out of it," he said.

"I can't fight. I don't want to fight," Jet murmured.

"Of course you don't. No one wants to fight. But you learn to shut out your emotions and defend yourself. You have to. You'll be hurt if you don't. Do you understand?" He gazed into her eyes.

She tried to look at him but couldn't see anything through her tears. She'd never seen anyone killed before. She couldn't have imagined how horrible it would be. She felt sick to her stomach.

"What if he had a wife and family?" she asked. "A daughter like me?"

Ojiisan sighed. "It's true, he might. And that is terribly sad. But he knew that when he took this line of work. And when you're under attack, you have no choice. It's either you or him. It is you who decides your own fate. Is his life worth more than yours?"

Jet sobbed. "No. Yes. I don't know."

He shook her gently, forcing her to meet his gaze.

"Well, I do. You can't have sympathy for a vicious attacker. This is battle. No one *likes* battle. If you want to live, you do what you can to survive. That's all. Blade over heart. That's what in battle means."

Jet's lip trembled. "I'm sorry, Ojiisan. I can't. I never wanted…."

"*No one* wants this. But it's who we are. We *must* go. Now!" he implored.

Jet sank to the earth again, thoughts whirling. When Satoko had taken her out to the desert to kick trees, she'd never liked doing it, convinced she was hurting them. She'd never imagined fighting with real people, their pain, their agony, their fear. She didn't want to hurt anyone ever. She had to get out of here, now.

"I can't. Even if they *are* Wa. Or *yakuza*. Or whatever. I'm sorry. I'm so so sorry," she said, collapsing further.

"Come on!" Hiro whispered insistently. This time he pulled her up and shook her like a rag doll. "I've waited years to meet you. I was so excited that you were coming, and I was amazed by what you did at the river… You can do this!"

Jet tried to move her feet but she couldn't. They were heavy, like stones.

"No, I can't. I can't. I'm sorry."

"Yes, you can," Ojiisan told her.

Jet took a breath in. She had to make herself clear.

"Ojiisan, even if I *can*, I don't want to. I won't."

"Your mother believed in you. She was trying to make you even stronger. She might have pushed you too hard sometimes, that's for sure. But she had to. Now you understand why."

"I don't understand. I don't," Jet shook her head, tears streaming down.

"If you give up now, everything your mom did for this family will have been in vain. Her entire life will have been wasted," Ojiisan said.

"I'm sorry I let you down." Jet sobbed, falling back down the ground. "All of you."

"If that's who you want to be, then fine. You have to decide on your own. Ojiisan, let's go," Hiro turned and began to walk away. Then her grandfather walked off, too, increasing their pace as they grew smaller in the distance.

Jet sank down, dejected.

She heard a low moan and looked from the fallen man to the one who lay wounded. His cry sounded so painful, so agonizing. She had to get away from it. Now.

She pulled herself up, spinning around frantically. Then she heard a twig snap, and fear kicked in. Were more people out there, waiting to attack?

She hadn't asked for this. Maybe the girl in her mother's story, the one who freed her people, hadn't asked to be a warrior, or to have so much responsibility, but that girl had had no choice back then. Times were different. Jet had a choice.

She didn't want to be here.

She breathed in deeply, tried to calm her thoughts.

True, she'd given her mother her word that she'd do whatever Ojiisan asked. She'd kept her word, and it had lead to this. Nothing good could come of it. A shot rang out in the distance.

Jet started, her body crouching into action.

She listened for another sound in the forest, but heard nothing. Nothing. Just the ricochet of her heart against her ribcage, battering away. Then she heard another shot.

Suddenly, anger raced through her body. What if Hiro and Ojiisan had been captured and hurt? What if they needed her, and she was just sitting here? *Get up!* a voice from somewhere deep inside said. *Don't be a victim! Conquer your fear!*

Suddenly some primal instinct took over, lifting her body from the ground.

Just this one more time. For them. Then I'm walking away. Who cares about ancient history anyway? It has nothing to do with me.

Soon she was walking stealthily through the forest, then running. Willing her limbs to move faster and faster until finally she made out Hiro, Aska, and Ojiisan, mere silhouettes along the animal trail, almost hidden by the tall swaying bamboo.

As soon as we get to safety, Jet thought, *I'll get on the first plane back to America. I don't belong here. I'm out of my element, way out of my league.*

She followed them in silence, knowing they felt her presence. Hadn't J-Bird once said: *A pack stays together. You never abandon your tribe.*

Eventually she caught up to them, chest heaving with exertion. Ojiisan led them into a thick bamboo grove. When he finally looked at her, there was sympathy in his gaze.

"Thank you for finding us. You understand that I had no choice but to push you."

"I know," she replied. Her expression must have shown how much she regretted coming here, making that promise to her mother.

Ojiisan looked from Jet to Hiro. "Our enemies are close. They know how to hide their energy and blend into the earth. I thought when we got through the forest and reached the highway, daybreak would come, and we'd be able to escape. But they've blocked the forest. It won't be easy to escape. If we stay here until daybreak, they'll encircle us. We'll be trapped."

"What can we do?" Hiro asked, desperation edging his voice.

"Go east. If you two run, you'll get to the ravine in thirty minutes. There used to be a wooden bridge there. It fell apart years ago. Do you remember where it was?"

Hiro nodded vigorously.

"I've been planning to rebuild it for years. I packed the materials up there little by little and put them in a storage shed. There's rope in it. While I'm dealing with our pursuers, I want you to use the rope to cross the ravine. Can you do that? I promise I'll come after you."

"Ojiisan, please, let's stay together. It's way too dangerous," Jet said, fighting back tears.

"It's the only way. I'll come for you, I promise." Then Ojiisan turned his gaze to his grandson. "I'll come back, just like I did with Aska. Keep your faith, son. Okay?"

"Okay," Hiro said. His lips were trembling.

"Jet," Ojiisan tilted his head toward hers and said in a near-whisper. "Even though your Ojiisan might look like a harmless old grandfather, he could be something totally different. So could anyone, for that matter…. *Wakaru*? Understand?"

Jet started. "Anyone?" She looked closely at Ojiisan. Though he was eighty, his skin was taut, his muscles lean and powerful. He moved with grace and stealth. He was strong and proud.

He nodded slowly, as if reading her mind.

Jet's gaze shot over to her cousin. He was just twelve, but he moved like an athlete. And though she'd just met him, it was clear he had a library in his mind. Why? Were they superhuman, or just super motivated?

Her eyes flickered between her cousin and grandfather as understanding washed over her, making her skin tingle.

"*Shinado* were born in an age without electricity, when people had to live in the darkness. Now, there's no such thing as darkness. And there are guns and atomic bombs and all sorts of sophisticated weapons…" Ojiisan trailed off, sadness tinging his words.

"*Shinado?*" Jet repeated. "You mean ninja?" She almost covered her mouth instinctively as the word floated out.

Ojiisan's deep blue eyes stilled as he looked into Jet's face. "The ninja has many codes to live by," he said. "Rule number one is: Keep secret things secret."

Jet gulped. That wouldn't be hard, she thought, because it was all a mystery to her.

"And number two is…?" she asked, bracing herself for the answer.

"Put the blade over the heart. Even if it means using those you love," he said, levelling his gaze, though she still felt warmth in his eyes.

"Ojiisan!" Jet gasped.

Ojiisan shook his head. "A ninja is not a hero. We had no laws to protect us, no one to give us food or shelter, let alone weapons or training. If the ninja had to, he used even the things dearest to him to survive. And we survived, despite the odds. We survived! If we don't fight for our tribe now, who will? We must do this to secure a future. A peaceful future."

Jet's brow furled.

Again, her grandfather seemed to read her mind.

"I know that sounds ironic, but it's the truth."

Jet let his words sink in. She didn't know what to say, for once. Ninja!

Hiro shot up, standing tall. "If you don't help us, we'll all die. And that's what those men want!"

Ojiisan's voice was fervent. "And that's what your mother didn't want, and why she spent every day of her life teaching you our wisdom, to insure it didn't happen. Do you understand?"

"I don't know," Jet stammered. "I don't know anything anymore."

"Our ancestors were *genin*—slaves even within ninja society." Ojiisan gazed down as he said the words Satoko couldn't say. "But we fought for freedom. We can't give it up now."

Aska cocked her ears. Jet caught the faint sound of a helicopter and sirens to the north.

People must be coming to put out the fire, Jet realized.

"Listen!" she whispered, heart sinking.

When she envisioned the beautiful thatch-roof house in flames, and the ancient village nothing but a pile of cinders, her heart was filled with pain. She imagined the fire licking the black beams, the white walls and shoji screens, everything burnt to ash and ruin. Burnt like Satoko.

If the ninja had to, he would use even the things dearest to him to survive.

So my mother... she too...

As Jet put the pieces together, she understood why her grandfather had set the fire. Because of the fire, the authorities would come and protect the village, keeping their attackers away. If the police and fire department came, this would give them time to escape.

Ojiisan never would have set the fire unless he had to.

"One more thing," Ojiisan told Jet and Hiro. "If you encounter into anyone, don't fight them head-on. Just run. But if you can't get away, then fight any way you can. Got that?"

"Got it," Hiro said bravely, looking to Jet.

Jet shook her head. She couldn't reply.

"Don't get hurt!" Ojiisan said as he straightened his back, rifle on his shoulder. "If something happens, go see Soji in Tokyo. Right away. He'll take care of you."

"Ojiisan, please!" Jet tried to turn away, but she couldn't.

He met her gaze with an expression that contained both fierceness and kindness, like the sky and earth joined.

"Jet! Your mother taught you well. Don't be afraid. She'll be with you. Always. Call upon her and the others. They're in your blood. They'll guide you, like the *itako* said."

"Ojiisan. Grandpa!" She reached out, and he held her in his strong arms. She didn't want to let him go. Ever. "Wait!" she pleaded.

"Now go! Run!" he said and released her.

Jet watched his figure fade into the mist, keeping her eyes on him as long as she could.

She had the terrible feeling that if she looked away, she might never see him again.

CHAPTER 14

夜明け *Yoake*

Daybreak

The sky brightened, shifting its canvas from black to deep blue. In that pale light before daybreak, Hiro and Jet found the shed and the thick nylon rope.

The ravine was more than two hundred feet high and almost sixty feet across. Jet and Hiro peered into its depths, dark cavernous places where even daybreak hadn't reached. Hiro's eyes were tired and his body looked weak. Jet took his hand.

"Let's go," she said. "We promised Ojiisan we'd cross."

Hiro pursed his lip, considering. "You're right. As soon as we set up the rope, he'll come. I'm sure of it."

The misty rain was still falling. Hiro tied a piece of wood to the rope and threw it to the other side of the ravine. It looped around the trunk of an old cedar. Together, they tied it tightly to a tree on their side.

Shots rang out in the distance. Jet looked back into the forest. She knew they were both thinking the same thing—about Ojiisan—but there was nothing they could do. They had to keep going and trust that he would make it to them safely.

Hiro wrapped his arms and legs around the taut rope, and hoisted himself across the ravine, knees bending and straightening like a frog's.

With an extra piece of rope, Jet made a harness and attached Aska to the line. Then she followed hand over hand, using her feet to push the dog. The autumn leaves below were orange, yellow, and gold. Halfway across, she stopped in exhaustion. This was harder than she'd expected.

Amegakurejutsu. The art of hiding in the rain. Making your body wet, slippery, part of nature, and drawing your strength from the elements. She needed to remind herself that she could use these skills. As she reached one hand over the other, she concentrated on bringing the rain into her body, seeing herself as water—no longer a girl hanging above a ravine, or a target.

But it was hard, so hard… She fought the desire to stop with fear, to drown in her confusion. She grit her teeth. Satako had believed in her. Ojiisan had believed in her. Hiro had believed in her. Now she had to believe in herself. Every time she felt herself being pulled down, she tried instead to imagine herself fluid, flowing like the great waves of the Pacific Ocean over which she had flown to arrive here. Slowly but surely, she felt her body melt into a vast blueness— like liquid, soft. Then it was easy—she gusted with the rain along the rope, pushing Aska forward with ease now. Briefly, she was no longer a girl but a part of nature. And then, before she knew it, she had reached the other side, gliding like water, then pouring like a wave onto the earth.

She'd made it! For a split second, she recalled that last time in the mountains, when her mother was so sick and weak, yet she still had fought so fiercely. Jet hadn't been able to transform herself so completely into the elements then. Now, it had happened with much more ease, and she hoped that if she had to, she could use this skill powerfully again. If only her mother could see her!

As Hiro untied Aska, she looked across the ravine. There was no sign of Ojiisan.

Jet glanced at her cousin worriedly. Where was their grandfather?

Suddenly, a tall man in black staggered from the forest, heading directly toward them.

"He's coming over here!" Hiro cried.

The man seized the rope and began crossing the ravine, advancing furiously, his hands moving with inhuman speed.

"Let's cut it!" Jet said.

"No! Ojiisan won't be able to cross!" Hiro shouted. "Look! He's wounded, and there are two of us. Three, including Aska. We can fight him!"

Jet looked back over at the man. He was halfway across. Blood covered his clothes. Then she saw it. A flash of silver. A blade flew out of the forest, striking his back. His hands slipped from the rope, and he fell, disappearing into the ravine.

Ojiisan staggered from the forest. His clothes were dark with blood—his or another's?

"Ojiisan!" Hiro shouted. "Hold on! I'm coming!" He began to cross the ravine.

Ojiisan held up his palm. "Stay where you are. There are no guarantees you can make it back over."

"I don't care!"

"Hiro, no! Remember what I taught you!" he shouted, but Hiro's gaze was elsewhere.

"Watch out!" Hiro shouted.

Ojiisan had already sensed the presence behind him. He turned, but there was no way to avoid the knife.

"Ojiisan!" Hiro cried as Ojiisan pulled the attacker against his own body, struggling to stand. By now, they were at the ravine's edge.

Jet couldn't tell what was happening or make out the man clearly. All she could see was that he was dressed in black, face smeared with dirt.

"Ojiisan!" Hiro wailed. Ojiisan threw his attacker over the cliff forcefully, even as he himself fell. Jet and Hiro watched helplessly as he separated from the other man midair, drifting down the ravine slowly like a piece of silk.

"Ojiisan! Ojiisan!" Jet cried. Aska came beside her, whining desperately.

Jet closed her eyes and held herself, rocking from side to side. As if guided by some unknown spirit, she began to chant *Namu*

Amidha Butsu over and over, hugging her body as she uttered the words Ojiisan might have said to himself as he fell.

This can't be real. It can't be happening, Jet thought.

"Ojiisan! Ojiisan!" Hiro echoed plaintively.

Hiro stomped on the ground, screaming, "I hate them! I hate them! I hate them!"

Jet pulled him against her to comfort him, but he struggled to break free.

"I could have saved him!" he shouted. "I should have saved him!"

"There was nothing you could have done!" Jet said, touching his shoulder, sensing how, every muscle every bone, every cell contracted.

"You could have saved him!" he cursed through his tears. "This is all your fault. If you hadn't come back, none of this would have happened!"

"I know. I never should have come here," she murmured.

"You didn't fight! You didn't even move!" he hissed.

"Hiro, I'm sorry. Sorrier than sorry. You have no idea," Jet moaned.

Sirens wailed louder in the distance. The smell of the fire crept up the mountain. Jet took a deep breath, trying to gather her strength.

"Hiro, please. Please come with me. We've got to get out of here now!"

"No!" he shouted. "We can't leave. I'll never leave Ojiisan! I'd rather die on this mountain with him than run away."

"Ojiisan wanted us to escape," Jet said gently.

"Ojiisan wanted us to *fight,*" Hiro said accusingly.

A thunderbolt cracked the sky.

Jet jolted, staring up.

"It's Ojiisan's spirit!" she exclaimed, "telling you to listen to me like you promised!"

"No. I won't listen! You don't know anything!"

"Well, I know this. I won't leave you here," Jet declared. Ojiisan had trusted her with Hiro's life. She wouldn't let him down again.

Jet took a breath and gathered all of her strength. She picked up Hiro by the collar and dragged him along the ground.

He struggled against her furiously, but she used every ounce of her strength to meet his power with her own, pushing him with her knees as she hauled him away from the ravine.

Aska whimpered and followed gingerly, unsure of what to do.

"Ojiisan! Ojiisan!" Hiro cried, flailing against her body, against all that he had suffered.

Jet held onto his wrists with iron fingers until she felt his will give in to exhaustion, and she knew he would let himself be carried down the mountain.

Aska followed behind them, head tilted to the ground as if she might hear Ojiisan's footsteps on the mountain's floor if she tried hard enough.

Jet summoned all her will to drag Hiro through the wall of trees, leaves, and branches. It was slippery underfoot, and she had to focus intently to keep her footing.

Suddenly, she stopped, sensing the presence of another being nearby.

A thick fog was settling into the woods, blanketing everything in a cottony white mist, and she couldn't be sure if it was her imagination or reality. Her instinct told her otherwise. She knew enough to listen.

Jet pulled Hiro to a stand of pine trees and pressed his head down, making them squat under the pine grove's thick cover. She steadied her breath and held onto Hiro tightly, stroking his head to keep him calm.

A dense black blur emerged from the cathedral of trees opposite where they were squatting. There was no mistaking this either. It was a bear.

The bear's thick round face looked intent as its eyes darted around the brush. Jet had never seen a real bear in its natural habitat, and didn't know if it was young, old, male, female, or a figment of her imagination. But when the bear lifted its long, curved, charcoal-covered claws to its face as if swatting away a fly, Jet knew it was real. Did Hiro see it, too? Jet held her breath.

Aska, too, seemed to hold her breath, looking up at Jet with

expectant eyes. The message in the dog's eyes was unmistake-
able: *You're the Alpha now.*

Jet sank closer to the earth. She could feel the bear's gaze boring
into her. She dared not look up, but she had to act fast. The gigan-
tic hump of black moved toward her.

Was this the bear's home? Had Jet intruded? She meant no harm.
Could she communicate this to the bear?

She stepped toward the bear softly, the way her mother had
taught her how to walk on paper. If the bear would let them leave
now, they'd go peacefully and never hunt again. She would hold
that promise in her heart. She'd tell the bear this. And it would let
them go, unharmed, down the mountain.

That's what would happen, Jet assured herself. If she thought
so, her thoughts could make it real. Isn't that what Satoko had always said? *Thought determines action, which determines reality.*

Ojiisan and Hiro might have been *matagi*, hunting the bear for
its many moons of meat, cooking grease that would fill two vats,
precious powerful medicines, and heavy covering to use as warmth
in the snow-covered thick of winter, but Jet was not a hunter. Now
she was the hunted.

Closer now, the bear loomed huge above her. She could almost
see its breath, steaming in the frigid air.

Jet steadied her gaze and sent the message through her mind and
out through her eyes, shooting her intention into the bear's eyes like
an arrow.

Her heart hammered in her chest. Hiro sat perfectly still, depleted.

The bear stood perfectly still, too, as if a statue of a bear in a wax
museum. Then it let its massive front legs relax by its sides. It appeared to be frozen.

Her *saiminjutsu* had worked! She had succeeded in hypnotizing
it! Now it was in receiving mode, waiting.

The bear's eyes met hers, the light of the two round black
moons boring into hers until their gazes melded into one. She felt
herself disappear into the bear's eyes, into its mind. Its belly was
empty, and it was hungry, seeking nandin nuts, hickory, and

chestnuts to gorge on. It had to feed its family, who were starving, too. That had been the only thing on its mind. But an intruder had come into its path, and it was scared. When Jet tapped into that thought, she sent her a message, loud and clear—she was *not* a hunter. She, too, was seeking sustenance and safety. Jet would not harm her if she would not harm Jet.

The bear blinked and lurched forward. Jet's heart shot into her throat and she crouched, covering Hiro. Aska leaned forward on her haunches.

But the bear ran right past them, lumbering off into the woods, leaving Jet and Hiro and Aska alone.

Aska whimpered. Jet finally exhaled. She wished someone could describe to her what she had just done so that she could know it had really happened. Until now, she'd doubted her powers, those of her body and of her mind. But if she could go into the bear's mind and soothe its fear, then why couldn't she do the same with her own? Her mother must have taught her well, and maybe all she had to do was turn inward to find the lessons she would need to keep her and Hiro alive.

She took his hand and led him away from the bear's lair, down the mountain. With a vacant gaze, he kept repeating their grandfather's name as they fled the fires of Kanabe that burned ferociously in the distance.

CHAPTER 15

終わらない歌 *Owaranai Uta*
Endless Song

The rain continued to fall quietly on the golden rice fields along the highway, washing everything in the silent drops.

Jet, Hiro, and Aska stood at the side of the Tohoku Expressway. She held out her thumb. Cars sped by, and Jet was drenched and feeling hopeless when a tattooed truck driver finally pulled to a stop and picked them up.

The driver kept his gaze on the road, occasionally offering them dried squid, rice crackers, and peanuts.

She didn't think she could eat. Her stomach still turned from the scene on the mountain. Why? Why? Why? As she forced a cracker down, swallowing the salty dry wafer, she realized that she was famished—and grateful to be in a warm, dry place, moving away from their pursuers.

The truck's window was slightly open. A charred wood smell permeated the air. Kanabe was still burning. Would anything be left when they returned? Jet's heart sank. *We can't let that happen. We have to stop them*, she thought. *But how? And was it already too late*?

Aska slept at Hiro's feet, breathing heavily. A Japanese rock song played on the radio, the angry cries of rebellion drifting futilely from the speakers.

"Can I turn up the volume?" Hiro asked, perking up.

"Sure. You like this song?" the driver said, flashing a chipped-toothed grin.

"Uhhn," Hiro nodded.

"You seem too young to know it."

"My mom liked it," Hiro told him. With his eyes closed, he hummed along.

> *Let's sing an endless song,*
> *for all the trash in the world.*
> *Let's sing an endless song,*
> *for this lousy world.*
> *Let's sing an endless song,*
> *for you, me and them.*
> *Let's sing an endless song*
> *so we can smile tomorrow.*

Jet kept her eyes on the road as they sped away from the mountains, down the highway toward Morioka. She replayed all that had happened in the past few days. Was this really what her mother had wanted for her? Hadn't Satoko herself escaped this very country, her very history? Why would she wish it on her daughter?

If only Jet had a better grip on what was happening. She felt she knew, yet did not know, like the way she knew an abacus was used for calculation, but did not know the method and couldn't find the solution. Her normal way of problem-solving simply didn't fit. She knew there was a secret, important and valuable, and that people were desperate to get it. Where it was hidden and how she would find it, only her mother and Japan knew.

Jet was exhausted and afraid. Here she was, wrapped up in a deadly battle she seemed to be at the center of. She'd had to fight to survive, but even her training wasn't enough. Grandpa was dead, and how many others on the other side were also gone?

She looked over at Hiro. His head bobbed gently against her shoulder as he surrendered, finally, to sleep. She wondered how Hiro had felt, growing up without a mother for so many years. Did he ever talk to her in his dreams? Did she come to him like the wind, stirring up memories and longing in her wake?

Whatever confidence Jet had felt facing the bear slipped away. She'd only succeeding in doing that because she was protecting Hiro. She was sure Ojiisan wouldn't have made her promise to bring him to Tokyo if he'd known how useless she was.

Wait a minute, Jet realized. *I only promised to **bring** him to Tokyo. I never promised to **stay** with him there.*

A wave of relief flooded Jet's body as she made up her mind. She'd take Hiro to Soji's as she promised, and then she'd disappear.

Hiro was a survivor. He was strong, a true warrior. Unlike her. He'd be fine.

It was for Hiro's own good. It was the best thing, really, for her to leave without a trace.

That she was good at.

Part Three

TOKYO

東京

CHAPTER 16

孤児 *Koji*

Orphans

Jet gripped Hiro's hand as he held Aska's leash. The rhythms of Tokyo pulsed in her veins—crows cawing in the eaves, trains rattling overhead on their tracks, cars honking, bicycle brakes screeching, waves of people coming and going, coming and going endlessly.

"What huge buildings!" Hiro looked up at the skyscrapers, his mouth open.

"Yes, it's so different from Kanabe, isn't it? Not at all like New Mexico either."

"There's not a tree anywhere," Hiro said, dejected and out of place.

All around, neon lights blinked their strange morse code. Jet, Hiro, and Aska made their way to Harajuku, where groups of kids with dyed hair, vintage clothes, tattoos, and piercings hung out on the streets. Hiro and Jet's mountain clothing was filthy and torn, so they used some of the money Ojiisan had given them to buy cheap vintage clothes at Hanjiro, a second-hand shop.

It was three stories tall and filled to the brim with used clothes of every stripe. Jet bought a miniskirt, velvet shirt, boots, and leggings. Hiro bought some black jeans, a turtleneck, hoodie, and some Converse hightops. Together it cost them less than 10,000 yen, about 100 dollars, Jet figured.

Hiro asked the platinum-coifed male cashier directions to a *sento* bathhouse, trying not to gape at his green eyeshadow and mascara.

Once at the baths, they tied Aska up outside and went in to clean off.

Jet peeled off her dirty clothes and stuffed them in a locker. She grabbed a bucket and found an empty stool in front of a faucet, pouring buckets of hot water over her body as she scrubbed her skin raw. Steam swirled in the air. Jet inhaled it, cleansing her lungs. She must have dumped ten buckets over herself, but still didn't feel purified of what she'd seen and done. She wondered if she ever would. Ojiisan said you never get rid of a battle. You lived with its scars, searing into your skin.

Exhausted, Jet dropped deep into the baths, letting the hot water ease the weight from her shoulders and cleanse her mind. Her body ached and her legs and arms were covered with scrapes and bruises, which she tried to hide with the small thin towel. The steaming hot water opened her pores and melted her tense muscles. The icy cold plunge bath reinvigorated her.

She looked around at the other women—bathing, chatting, and laughing as they scrubbed each other's backs, soap suds flying. How wonderful that they could do this for each other. She missed her mother, missed the warmth of her body, the beauty of her tired smile.

Finally, Jet toweled off and donned her new clothes, wadding up the old ones in the garbage. When she was dressed and done, Jet looked in the mirror, satisfied; she was finally like all the other teenagers on the street. No one would be able to see the pain she carried inside.

In the lobby, she was happy to see Hiro transformed as well. She wanted to avoid standing out at all costs. He appeared calmer, more composed, even though there were dark circles under his eyes.

They went back into the shopping district and bought a map, then began searching the narrow streets for their uncle's address. From time to time, they stopped and watched people pass on the sidewalk, making sure that they weren't being followed, that they didn't see the same people more than once.

Finally, they came to a tiny dead-end street lined with square houses that looked like oversized building blocks. At the end was an old-fashioned wooden temple with a garden.

Hiro was bewildered. "Why would Soji-san live at a temple?"

"Looks like we'll find out," she said, double-checking the address. It was right.

Hiro rolled open the temple gate. The grounds were perfectly manicured, with Japanese maples standing above moss-covered paths and carefully raked rock gardens. The great sweep of the temple's roof opened to the sky like the wings of a crane. They made their way toward the main building, walking softly.

An old lady in a white apron approached, carrying a thatch broom.

"Excuse me. Is Kuroi-Sensei here?" Jet asked politely.

"Oh? Sensei, did you say?" She eyed them suspiciously.

"Yes," Jet replied. "He's our uncle, and we came to visit him."

"The master went on a trip," the old lady told them in lilting Japanese.

Aska made her way to the old woman's side, sniffing her leg. She jumped back.

"I'm sorry! Don't worry. She's friendly," Hiro said, pulling Aska's leash.

"Where did the master go?" Jet asked, disappointed.

"Sensei goes on a lot of archaeological digs. This time, he went to Kyushu. He'll be here tomorrow afternoon."

"Thank you very much," she said. "We'll come back then."

The woman turned her back to them as she swept the broom over the ground.

"Excuse me, ma'am," Hiro called. "I have one more question. Does Soji-Sensei have blue eyes?"

The old lady turned, bemused. "Why as a matter of fact, yes. Like a European."

Hiro and Jet exchanged glances. "Thank you very much!" they said and left.

"Ojiisan never mentioned that Soji lived in a Dogenji, a Soto Zen temple," Hiro said. "Maybe because he knew I hate to meditate."

"Me too." She smiled. Her mother had often made her sit facing a blank wall. If Jet didn't focus on her breath and stay there, she wouldn't get dinner.

Not long afterward, as they wandered through the city again, Hiro pointed to a building.

"That sign says youth hostel. Let's get a room. And then let's eat. I'm starving!"

As Jet paid at the front desk, Hiro went around to the service entrance, sneaking Aska through the back.

In the tiny room, they turned on the small TV, but the news didn't mention anything unusual at Mount Hakkoda or about the fire in Kanabe.

They locked up and went downstairs to the cafeteria, where Jet ate *onigiri* rice balls with *umeboshi* pickled plum filling. Hiro's had tuna and mayonnaise inside. He ordered two salmon rice balls for Aska and put them in his pockets.

She ate her *onigiri* quietly, looking out the picture window at the crowded sidewalk. How did so many people avoid crashing into each other on such narrow paths? Her thoughts went back to what had happened on the mountain.

"Why didn't Ojiisan tell me how dangerous everything *really* was? We could have prepared."

Hiro stopped eating. "He hoped to have more time. He never thought we'd be attacked so soon."

"So he really did know we would be attacked?" Jet asked, incredulous.

"He always told me that I would have to be ready, because when you came back, you would need our help," Hiro considered.

"But why me? Why do they care about me?"

"I don't know." He looked out the window, then down. "You were supposed to be special."

Jet swallowed, ashamed. "My mom trained me, but it wasn't like this. This was life or… or…" She couldn't bring herself to say it. Ojiisan was dead.

"Ojiisan used to tell me how harshly his grandfather Jinzaemon trained him. Now I understand why. Battle isn't a game," Hiro replied.

"I'm sorry, Hiro. I can never apologize enough. I've ruined everything. I was supposed to learn more about the elements from Ojiisan. Now it's too late" Jet said. Regret coursed through her.

Hiro frowned. "Great-great grandpa Jinzaemon taught Ojiisan about the wind, taught him never to go straight against the wind, but to find a path in its folds. Ojiisan used to say, 'Even if I teach you where the path is, you won't be able to see it because the wind is always changing. If I show you the path one second, the wind will shift and the path will disappear.' Jinzaemon told him that every second he had to find a new path, and that the only way to do that was to become the wind itself. I finally understand what he meant."

Jet nodded, sensing it was better just to let Hiro talk than to try to say something pointless. But she resolved stronger than ever now to slip out as soon as night fell, make herself one with the darkness, disappear from his life and into the maze of the city.

"Battle is like wind," he told her. "I understand that now. You can't just use what you've practiced. It's always different. You have to find a new path every second. You have to *become* the battle."

Jet bit her lip. Satoko had said things like this before. They'd made sense in her mind, but now she knew that her body couldn't master the techniques. She wasn't who her mother had thought she was.

"I'm worried that Ojiisan didn't prepare me enough," Hiro said pointedly. "Great-great grandpa Jinzaemon was harsh, but Ojiisan was sentimental. That was his nature, and he used to tell me that the main ninja rule is not to go against nature—especially your own."

Jet stared at her cousin. Again, his words seemed to have been meant especially for her. She thought of how kind her grandfather had been, though he barely knew her. His nature must have made him a gentle teacher. What was her nature, and what had it made her? Her mother had thought she was some kind of ninja, but what kind of ninja is afraid of dark places? Her mother had been wrong. Obviously, tragically wrong.

"There was one lesson that he always repeated from his years of training with Jinzaemon," Hiro said. "'Be impassive. Swayed by passion, your judgment falters. When that happens, you'll end up in the enemy's trap.'"

Jet listened guiltily. Had Ojiisan been swayed by passion? Had he been so moved by his granddaughter's return and the desire to place his daughter's ashes in the lake that he'd imperiled them all? Or had he sacrificed the village and given his own life so that they might live and discover the treasure? Had he led them to this point on purpose?

Jet understood that he had done as his own grandfather would have. He had sacrificed everything.

"Ojiisan always said that the Kuroi family women were the true masters," Hiro said. He sat and stared out the window, his expression determined, eyes focused. Jet sensed he was seeing his duty, becoming more and more determined to be the ninja that his grandfather had taught him to be.

She, on the other hand, was shrinking farther and farther away from it.

So I have special powers, she reflected. *Don't we all? Doesn't everyone have a hidden reserve of power waiting to be tapped into when needed?* She thought about the stories she'd heard, mothers lifting cars off children, soldiers jumping impossible distances to catch wounded comrades, incredible feats of strength and endurance beyond what we thought humanly possible.

What's so special about my *special power?* Jet thought, *and why I am the last one to know about it?*

CHAPTER 17

風来坊 *Furaibo*
Roaming Like the Wind

Hiro fell asleep on the floor. He insisted he'd be more comfortable there, lying next to Aska. But he didn't seem comforatble at all. Though exhausted, he tossed and turned, cried out in his sleep. *He must be dreaming about Ojiisan and the fight on the mountain*, Jet thought with a wave of regret.

She knew she'd failed Ojiisan and Hiro. She wanted nothing more than to slip away forever. But Hiro too was restless, surely he or Aska would hear her leave.

Lying in bed, she began to send out her awareness, moving it through the hostel, sensing who was in the rooms nearby, who was asleep and who, like herself, was awake. As she expanded her awareness, she began to sense something unusual. She couldn't name it, but it was a presence, an energy that seemed stronger than the others, like a beacon out in the vast city.

There was no way she would fall asleep now. Maybe the presence was their enemy. If so, she needed to protect them and ready herself, so she concentrated her breath and energy. The presence grew stronger. Jet's heart pounded. She knew she had to stalk it, to find it before it found them.

She sent her focus to Hiro and Aska, covering them in a net of calm and safety. She kept her awareness on them, laser-like, until they sank into the net, let it embrace them in its comfort. Only when Hiro was snoring and Aska's body was twitching, did Jet ease out of bed, put her pack over her shoulder, and say a silent good-bye. Her heart was heavy, but she couldn't linger.

Walking as if on tissue paper the way her mother had taught her, she slipped out of the room and closed the door silently behind her.

She moved through the hostel, pausing in shadows, searching into the awareness of others so that she could sense them before they noticed her. Then she practiced what Ojiisan had taught her by making people forget they'd even seen her. It was easier than she realized. She made it past the front desk without the receptionist noticing her. She slipped past a group of youths coming in through the sliding doors.

She'd made it. She was free!

Now what?

She roamed the streets, zigzagging through alleys and boulevards, making herself invisible, even in the bright neon glare. And all the while she was sensing the energy somewhere in the city, not too far away, it seemed, a keen awareness, a searching presence.

What could it be? Each time she thought she'd drawn close to it, there was nothing—it vanished. She stood and felt out around her, as far as she was able, but couldn't sense it anywhere.

Was it the people from the mountain, trailing her?

No longer tired, she decided to move her body like she'd always done to calm herself. Out in the alleys she jumped and rolled, scaling a brick wall only to let herself drop soundlessly to the earth and roll past a group of laughing office girls in high heels. No one noticed her. In a small park, she practiced her kicks and strikes. In dark lanes, she did backflips and spins, cutting the air with her foot.

When she'd finished, she was calmer, and she was hungry. She crossed a large intersection, spotting a brightly-lit Ramen shop, a bowl of steaming neon noodles flashing in the window.

She slid open the door. A row of black-suited salarymen sat at the counter, hunched over their bowls of noodles, slurping loudly. Seeing them, she had a memory of high school, of going into the cafeteria and trying to find a place to sit alone, of not belonging to any group. The suited men looked so comfortable, all dressed alike, all eating the same thing, almost in unison. They were drunk and hopelessly exhausted, but there was strength in numbers. They belonged.

In high school, she had mastered hiding herself, but how she'd envied the popular girls who sat in the cafeteria, heads held high. Pressed up against each other, they all wore the same expensive designer clothes, the same make-up and hairstyles. Jet remembered how they laughed as they pointed at her clothes, made jokes.

She turned away, stung by the memory. No matter how hard she tried, it seemed, she was always going to be on the outside, skirting the margins of the world.

There would be no family, no home, no comfort. Now there would be only wandering, endless wandering. Could she ever find peace in that?

She sat at a table, but there was no menu. A young man came in and sat down nearby. He put his backpack on the chair opposite him and took a book of dogeared *manga* from the pile of comic books spilling from the ramen-shop shelf.

"May I borrow this?" Jet asked, pointing to the menu on his table.

He looked up. His light brown eyes were the color of roasted barley tea, with a streak of green. Jet's breath fell away.

He nodded politely, then went back to his manga.

She studied the menu, trying to take him in without his noticing. His long black hair was tied back. His skin was brown and luminous. His arms were sinewy and muscled beneath the sleeves of his t-shirt.

After she had placed her order in Japanese, he turned to her.

"You're American, right?" he said.

"Half and half."

"You grew up there?"

"Yeah," she kept her answers short.

"Are you traveling here alone?"

She shrugged and nodded, not wanting to say too much.

"Are you also traveling?" she asked.

"Yeah. In the old days, drifters were called *furaibo*. It means 'roaming like the wind.' They were carried on the gusts that blew in the world. That's what I'm doing. Just exploring."

"*Furaibo*. I like that word a lot," she said, smiling. "I like the wind."

He raised an eyebrow.

"Is that a strange thing to say?" she asked, suddenly full of doubt.

"It's honest," he replied. "Would you like to join me?"

Her heart almost skipped a beat. She hadn't had any contact with people her age in weeks, but she didn't want to seem too eager.

"Are you sure?" she asked.

"Please," he said, moving his pack so she could take the seat opposite him.

Jet sat down and looked at the boy more closely. She couldn't judge his age. Was he still a boy, or was he a man? He looked down shyly.

The clearly defined lines of his jaw and neck made him look strong, fierce even, and yet there was a softness to him, a vulnerability. He seemed to her like a hawk that had been wounded.

She could feel him looking at her too, taking her in intently.

Thankfully, their noodles came, and she dug into the steaming bowl so quickly that the broth burned her tongue.

Then she realized he wasn't eating. Had she been rude to just dig in?

The young man smiled, looking at her with a playful expression, as if he might laugh at her, almost as if he knew something that she didn't.

"I'm Takumi," he said. "Tell me your name."

"Jet."

"Jet? That's an interesting name. Is it your real name?"

"Real as anything," she said.

Again, he smiled. Then he took some chopsticks from his pack, and two apples.

He wiped the chopsticks on a cloth, and offered thanks for his food before lifting some noodles to his mouth.

She looked at the apples.

"Oh! Right!" he said. "I have to eat these today or they'll go bad. Would you like one?"

"Sure," she said. He handed her the apple, and as the tips of their fingers touched, she felt a wave of energy radiate through her, like nothing she had ever felt. It moved up her arm to her heart, and she almost gasped. She could feel power and something else she couldn't name... just from the tips of his fingers.

His light brown eyes were studying her, his playful expression clearer than before as she tried to hide her response.

"Are you okay?" he asked, amused.

"Yeah. I'm fine." She set the apple on the table. "The last few weeks have been hard, that's all."

"Oh? Why?" He genuinely seemed to want to know.

"It's nothing," she said.

"What's so hard about nothing?" he replied, grinning.

Despite herself, Jet smiled.

"Go on," he urged.

What would happen if she told him? She'd felt reigned in for weeks now. But by what? Her mother wasn't here anymore to guide her, or to disapprove. And as far as a father, well, she'd never really had one. Of course, there was J-Bird. His dark, lined face came into view. What would he do?

Advise me to be careful, to listen to my heart.

Jet took a breath.

What if those were mutually exclusive? Reluctantly at first, she told him about her mother's death and her childhood in the Southwest. He nodded intently. Before she knew it, she'd told him more than she'd meant to.

The way he looked at her, she had the sense that, if she wanted to, she could tell him even more, about her training and maybe the attack the night before. But she didn't. She couldn't read him clearly. He wasn't much older than her, maybe twenty, but he seemed calm and confident.

When she stopped talking, the playful light in his eyes had turned serious.

"Your childhood actually reminds me of how I grew up," he said.

"Really?" she stammered.

"Yeah. But it was in Brazil. My father was Japanese, but I'm like you. I don't come from here. I often felt the way you did." As he told her about his cold demanding father and the difficulty of fitting in, his expression became younger, like that of a boy.

"Your life sounds so familiar," she said, relieved. "That's how I felt in New Mexico."

"I've been there," he said. "It's beautiful."

"Well, I guess. It was pretty rough where I was growing up."

"In Albuquerque?"

"No. All over the place." She named a few towns but didn't mention the reservation. She wondered if she had already said too much. But she couldn't help herself. It was so rare to find someone to talk to like this, honestly, without masks.

They spoke some more about living as outsiders, going to school where there were no other Asians. She found herself laughing and smiling, feeling so light that she almost forgot all of the troubles she'd been through.

"So you're just traveling now—visiting Japan?" she asked.

A look of confusion flashed across his face.

"Yeah, for a while, I don't know," he said.

"You don't? You just travel? That's all."

"Actually, no—I mean, I have a job. It involves traveling, but I don't want to bore you…"

"No, please tell me. I'm interested."

With the same look of vexation, he told her that for his work he'd visited the United States, Russia, Korea, China, and many other countries. He said he spoke six languages and wanted to learn more.

She was impressed. "Six languages! I can barely speak two!"

Takumi laughed.

The clock on the wall read three in the morning. She felt that they had been talking for only ten minutes!

"We should probably go," he told her.

She didn't want to leave. And besides which, she'd already decided to leave Hiro and Aska. She couldn't go back. She had nowhere to go.

The feeling made her heavy, like a lead weight pulling her down.

"Yes," she said, but before she could stand, he touched her hand accidentally, then pulled his back, as if burned.

She almost gasped at the sensation of being drawn toward him, into him. Her body thrummed with energy. The feeling startled her, and she tried to compose herself. She had always been very sensitive to smells, sights, sounds. But touch? This was a first. Or maybe it was him—did he have some special power of touch that magnified sensations?

"It was nice talking to you," he said, holding her gaze. She could hardly feel her own body anymore.

He moved away, and she stood up.

"Good night," she told him, taking one last look at his strong set jaw, the sharp lines of his cheeks, the deep brown of his eyes. Light shone on his face from the neon outside, as if he were gilded in moonlight.

She tried to clear her mind. Her head felt cloudy. She wanted to stay here forever.

"I hope we can…." she stuttered, intending to ask him how she could find him again, but she lost her nerve and turned toward the door.

She was a few steps away from him when she heard—or sensed— the quick motion behind her, the shift in the air. Without looking back, she swung her arm over her shoulder. Her hand caught the apple in midair as she spun into a fighting stance.

Instantly, she slouched out of the stance, catching herself.

His playful expression was back, but faint now, as if startled.

"You forgot your apple," he told her sheepishly, and she blushed.

"Oh, thanks," she managed to say, flustered.

In that one motion, she felt that she'd told him everything about herself. More than she'd told anyone, ever. Including herself.

More rattled than before, she wondered if even though she'd frozen on the mountain, she *was* a warrior. Was it in her body and in her blood, deeper than she'd thought? Deeper than she'd let herself believe? How had this man managed to unearth her skill where the battle on the mountain hadn't?

Maybe Hiro and Ojiisan had been right. Maybe she was a ninja after all. Hadn't this power surfaced now, just when she was determined to walk away from her promise, and her mission, leaving Hiro to fend for himself?

Wasn't that also a power, to know when you've stepped too close to the brink and to reel yourself back in? A sense of responsibility flooded her heart, overriding her guilt and the desire to run away.

I've left Hiro alone for too long. I'd better go check on him. What if he's not there!?

Panic coursed through her as she rushed back through Tokyo's darkened streets to the hostel, heart pounding.

What if it was already too late?

She slid open the gate, opened the front door, and slipped back into her room, relieved to find Hiro still there, relieved to see he hadn't awakened. Or had he?

She thought she sensed his awareness brightening when she unlocked the door without making a noise. Did his eye register the half-light streaming through from the hallway?

He was skilled enough to hide it, and to hide his breathing, too.

She put her pack down and slid soundlessly back into bed.

I'll stay and fulfill my promise to my mother, to J-Bird, and Ojiisan. What good is my word if I can't keep it? It's the only thing I really have.

Only when Jet was safely back in bed did she think to ask herself why Takumi had thrown the apple at her back. She wondered at the look in his eyes, sometimes knowing, sometimes confused, but strangely familiar.

She hoped he hadn't noticed how eagerly she'd leaned into him, waiting for him to come closer, just an inch, to feel him near.

Had her *henge* been good enough to hide her feelings? Or for the first time ever, had she not wanted to hide at all?

CHAPTER 18

曖昧 *Aimai*
Ambiguity

The next morning, Jet, Hiro, and Aska left the hostel. Jet kept watch as they wove their way through Tokyo's small alleys back to Soji's temple, stopping frequently to check behind them, to survey their surroundings.

Hiro was jumpy, convinced that someone was following them. Jet was, too, but she kept wondering if that someone was Takumi. Like an animal sensing an earthquake, she could feel his presence not far off. She wondered if that had been what she had felt the previous night, too.

When they got to the temple, the gate was locked. Leaves had piled on the pavement. The old lady with the broom was nowhere in sight.

"Do temples usually lock their gates?" Jet asked.

"I have no idea." Hiro took off his boot and used it to pound on the gate.

Finally, a man in black monk's robes with a shaved head appeared at the wooden slats. He peered out.

"May I help you?" his voice boomed.

Hiro struggled to balance on one foot as he put his boot back on.

"Are you Soji-san?" he asked nervously.

"I am indeed." The man nodded.

"I'm your nephew, Hiro Kuroi. Remember me?"

"What's that you say? Hiro?" he said, peering around to size up the boy, then chuckled. "Of course! You're so big now! You've grown up there in the mountains. Must be all that healthy food!"

Hiro pushed Jet forward. "And this is Rika. I mean Jet, my cousin."

"You came all the way from America?" Soji bowed to her.

She nodded, surprised that he knew of her. "Yes. Nice to meet you."

"Well, please, come in." Soji unlocked the heavy gate and slid it open. She was relieved to see that his eyes were blue, just like Oji-isan's. He was tall and stood straight and proud, looking formidable, even noble. She tried to decide if he resembled her mother.

"Just a minute," Hiro said as Aska came forward and sniffed Soji's feet. She returned to Hiro's side, where she sat down and looked up at him with expectant eyes.

"Good girl," he said.

Soji closed the gate behind them.

"Ojiisan sent us here from Aomori," Jet told him. "We got to Tokyo yesterday. We came here, but we couldn't find you." She hesitated, unsure of how to tell him about their grandfather.

"I'm sorry I wasn't here," Soji said. "I went to take a look at some newly discovered ruins."

He beckoned Jet and Hiro into the temple grounds, but then hesitated. "Where's Masakichi?" he asked.

Hiro swallowed as if to hold back tears, and Jet made herself speak. "There was an accident on the mountain. We were ambushed, and Ojiisan…" She couldn't get the words out.

But she didn't have to. Soji seemed to understand.

"How horrible. Horrible for all of us," he said, clasping his hands to his heart.

Jet was relieved that she didn't have to finish telling him what had happened on the mountain.

"The people who attacked us might still be after us," she said. "Ojiisan made us promise to come here and find you."

"I'm so glad you did. We'll go under lockdown," he said gravely. "We'll have the place fully protected. If anyone comes, we'll be ready."

"Thank you," Jet said, relieved.

"I'll look into the attack on the mountain and see what I can find out. We'll need to be active," Soji said.

"Right!" Hiro said, nodding vigorously.

"Hiro, you can stay with me. Jet, you should go out and do *takuhatsu*—begging for alms, like a monk. That way you can keep an eye on the streets nearby. It's just a disguise."

"Got it!" she agreed.

"What about Aska?" Hiro asked softly.

"Well, she can be a guard dog. She'll let us know if any intruders come in, won't she? She's probably quite capable of defense, right?"

"Oh, yes," Hiro said.

"And there are tons of *noraneko*—stray cats—around to keep her busy."

"Aska's favorite toys!" Hiro smiled through his sadness, and he let Aska play off the leash on the temple grounds.

"Can I run with her?"

"Absolutely," Soji replied.

While Hiro and Aska were running, Soji asked Jet to walk with him on a stone path toward the library.

"I've been expecting you for a long time," he told her. "We all have. So I'm going to speak to you as if I have known you for years, because that's how it feels."

She nodded, finding it hard to swallow.

"Yesterday," he told her, "I went to Kyushu, and I think that a few of the people I saw there had something to do with the attack in Kanabe."

"What do you mean?"

"Some ancient petroglyphs were discovered there, and I went to inspect them. Do you know what a petroglyph is?"

"Like a Native American cave drawing?" Jet ventured.

"That's right. The ones I saw in Kyushu might help uncover our ancestors' lost history." He turned and looked at her with a shy smile that reminded her of Ojiisan. "Unfortunately, I met some suspicious people there. They were from a computer company. This isn't the first time I've run across them. In fact, I expected them."

"Why would a computer company be interested in petroglyphs?" she asked.

He ran his hand along his shaved head, over the shadow of black stubble there.

"The company is called New Language Systems. They gather symbols from all over the world. The CEO, a man named Davison Harter, collects artifacts. He's obsessed with dead languages. Apparently, NLS develops and breaks codes for the American government. They are putting together a huge secret code library."

Jet stopped, looking at her uncle quizically.

"What is it?" he asked.

"Does this have to do with the Kuroi family treasure?" She inquired. Though she didn't know much more about it than she had before, Jet now knew this much: she had a duty to find the treasure, whatever it was. And it certainly must be valuable if Ojiisan had given his life to protect it.

Soji pursed his lips. "Well, according to legend, the family passed a treasure from generation to generation. I don't know what it is, but there are a lot of myths, and you can't take any of them too seriously. Some say it was a sacred bone." He hesitated, watching her reaction. "The most far-fetched theory is that it was Jesus' *nodobotoke*—his Buddha bone."

She frowned, skeptical. "Jesus' Adam's apple? How could that be?"

"Some historians believe the person who died at Golgotha was Jesus' brother, not Jesus himself."

"Jesus had a brother?" Jet asked, incredulous.

"According to the Bible, yes. These historians think the real Jesus traveled across Asia and died in Japan. It's probably a myth, but there's evidence that many Jewish people and groups from the Middle East came here a long time ago. Jesus was Jewish, after all."

"Hmm…" She thought it over. "What kind of evidence?"

"Well, for instance, the imperial family crest is a chrysanthemum, and the ancient symbol on the Wailing Wall in Jerusalem is almost exactly like it. But in the fifth century, Japan had trade with Persia through the Silk Road, and the Imperial family might have adopted the symbol used by royal families in the Middle East."

Jet mulled this over.

Soji took a large, leatherbound book from a high shelf, opened it, and passed it to her. "See this? It's the Star of David. It's carved on an old stone lantern at Ise shrine in Nara, which is directly connected to the Imperial family. Some of the oldest families of the Omi merchant classes used the Star of David as their family crest in Western Japan."

"This doesn't necessarily mean it came from Judaism," Jet said.

"True. In Japan, the star was called *Roku Bou Sei*—a Taoist protective talisman brought from China. In Hindu religions and in Tantra, it's the symbol of a unified man and woman. It represents heaven and earth, light and dark, male and female, the yin/yang circle. The Jews began using this symbol only in the seventeenth century."

"So that doesn't prove anything about the bone belonging to Jesus. Why would people attack the village and kill Ojiisan over a myth?" Jet asked. "I mean, they were *vicious!*"

Soji sighed. "I am sorry you had to go through that. It must have been horrible."

Jet's lip trembled.

"Anyway, to be honest, it's mainly occultists who believe in the Jesus theory, or think that the lost Jewish tribe came to Japan," Soji admitted, "but there are all sorts of theories linking ancient Japanese and Jewish cultures which are not yet disproven."

"For example?" She was curious to learn more.

"Well, one myth is that the treasure of King Solomon was buried in the mountains of Shikoku, though archeologists haven't found evidence yet. And in Shingu village in Aomori, there's an old grave where people say Jesus is buried. The village's ancient name was Herai, which sounds like the Japanese word for Hebrew, Hebrai."

"It sounds too far fetched," Jet said, recalling what little she knew about King Solomon from a Hollywood movie she'd seen about treasure hunters in the African jungles. And who could believe Hollywood?

"It has to be a myth," she confirmed.

"Well, there's still an odd custom in Aomori," Soji said. "After a baby is born, the parents draw a cross on its forehead to protect it from evil before they take it outside. That's what the Jews did in ancient Egypt—they painted an X on their doors to prevent their first-born sons from getting killed."

"Okay," she acquiesed. "Let's say it's true. What does any of that have to do with the Kuroi family?"

Soji took a deep breath. "That's just the problem. None of us knows...."

She crossed her arms, frustrated. "So what do we know?"

"We know this," he reassured her, "in the north, many people have blue eyes like Ojiisan's, or light brown eyes. Usually, the gene for colored eyes is weaker than for black. If either parent has black eyes, a kid's eyes will be black. But in the north, people have blue or gray-blue, or green eyes no matter what color their parents' eyes are."

"What does that mean?" Jet prompted.

"Northern Japanese pass down the dominant gene for blue eyes. Some believe it came from the Middle East. If that's true, so did our ancient ancestors." He paused, letting this information sink in.

"You mean," she asked, "we might be connected to Jesus? I mean, our ancestors?"

"Yes! That's right. Or, conversely, this might have nothing to do with Jesus. And the truth is I don't know what the treasure is."

"Great," she said, dejected.

"I'm sorry, Jet. I'm frustrated too. The secret wasn't entrusted to me. It was passed from woman to woman in the Kuroi family. The men never knew."

Her eyes widened. "Woman to woman? Is that why everyone thinks I know?"

"Yes. That's exactly right."

"But I don't! My mother never told me, and she and every other woman in the Kuroi family is... is...." Again she couldn't bring herself to say the word.

"I know. And I'm sorrier than sorry," he said.

"Hiro's mother, too," she added.

"Someone tried to kidnap her. They must have thought she knew. The police said she was fighting off thieves, but we know the truth."

"It's so awful," Jet said.

"She wasn't even related to us by blood. Her husband—Hiro's father—was my brother. He died at a construction site." Soji sighed.

"Hiro's lost everyone," she said softly, glancing over to where Hiro was playing with Aska. "It's terrible."

"It is. But he's strong," Soji told her. "And so are you."

She shook her head, knowing she'd have to face men like those who'd hunted them in the forest. "What are we going to do now? We can't just wait to be attacked again!" Jet shuddered at the thought.

"We need to be patient," he told her. "Our enemies are obviously sophisticated and very dangerous. We'll have to get our information straight. I'll find out if NLS is involved."

As they came to the library door, she hesitated. "Uncle Soji," she said, taking a deep breath to calm herself, "I'm sorry about Ojiisan."

He put a hand on her shoulder. "It wasn't your fault."

She nodded but didn't believe him. A lump rose in her throat.

"No one expected this to be easy," he said, "and even if we knew that you would return, we also realized there would be great dangers."

She looked down. Neither spoke for a moment.

"I never imagined…" Jet trailed off.

"I know… Well you should get some rest," he said.

"Yes, uncle."

"Let me show you where to put your things. Rest a bit, then we'll have a meal before going out."

"Thank you." She bowed.

He led her to her room—a small wooden cabin at the edge of the temple compound—and closed the door behind him, leaving her.

Wind rattled the closed windows, the air heavy as if warning of a coming storm. The old house seemed designed to let the weather in. With its sagging, waterlogged roof and broken tiles, it had a simple *wabi-sabi* beauty. Imperfect and temporal. Fragile and real.

Jet shivered. Though cold, she realized she didn't really mind. The cold was energizing, bracing. She had the feeling she'd have to stay alert. The cold helped keep her on edge.

She stretched out on the futon and looked at the ornate calligraphy that hung in the room's *tokonoma* altar, determined to decipher its curves. It read *mu*, the Zen symbol of nothingness. In it, to her surprise, she saw the line of Takumi's eyebrows, the shape of his face. Why had he affected her so deeply? How could she be thinking of him now when their lives were in danger? Was he in danger, too?

CHAPTER 19

微睡み *Madoromi*
Takumi's Dream

The luminous hands of Takumi's watch stood out in the dark. Ten minutes to five. He was trained to be fully alert on four hours of sleep. The most he usually napped was five minutes, so a one-hour catnap was enough to take him into the evening, or even well into the next day. But since he'd met Jet, his sleep had been restless and filled with dreams. Rather than get up, he tried to remember the one he'd just had.

In it, he was a child, and he'd gone into the jungle at night, not for his usual training with his father, but to catch a bird with golden wings that he'd seen in a marsh. During the dry season, when the moon was full, the birds came to drink, and children tried to catch them. An old white man came from the city to buy the birds. He smelled of tobacco and sweat, but Takumi liked him because he didn't discriminate between the kids. He bought the best birds, and he paid white kids and Indio kids the same prices.

The birds were as small as a child's palm and had brilliant feathers, and they sang beautifully. When they drank, they moved quickly and furtively, so that they could barely be seen, and they were not easy to catch. The children tied small limes to the ends of bamboo rods and swung them toward the birds at the exact instant they stopped to drink. They knocked the limes into the birds, throwing them off balance so they could catch them.

Takumi went deep into the jungle, walking toward a marsh he had discovered. Even in the dry season, the air smelled of dead, damp leaves. He parted the bushes, and the blue of the water appeared. He crouched. He could wait for hours. He loved the silence of the jungle. His father had taught him how to conceal himself and subdue his breath, and he dropped instantly into that state of being and non-being. There was no sign of the golden bird, but the moon would be full tonight, and he knew the bird would come.

The sun went down in the west, and moonlight from the east illuminated the marsh. He waited, motionless, and suddenly, a soft tone echoed in the jungle. The white bird with golden wings appeared. It was the most beautiful bird he had ever seen. Each plume was a clear golden color, and its beak and legs were the same bright hue.

I can sell this bird for more money than I ever dreamed, he thought. *And then I can be free of this place.*

But the longer he watched the bird, the more its beauty entranced him. It circled for a long time until finally it began to descend toward the water.

He gripped his bamboo pole, and just as the bird dipped its beak into the water, he swung. The lime hit it, and the bird lost its balance. With panic in its big brown eyes, it seemed to understand its fate and began to flap its wings. He caught it in the string and pulled it back to him, but as he reached to untie it, the bird cried out.

"I'm not going to hurt you," he told it, trying to unwind the tangled string, but the bird flapped its wings more desperately, becoming entangled.

"Be still! Be quiet!" he said, almost crying himself. So many golden feathers came off in his hands that the bird's pale skin was visible. And the song, which had been soft and ethereal like a flute, was now a grating, high-pitched squawk. The bird soon lost all of its golden feathers and, exhausted from the effort of fighting, stopped moving.

He held it in his palm and stroked its small body as tears ran down his cheeks.

What have I done? he woke up asking, but there were no golden birds in the jungle near that poor village. It was odd to dream of it like this when almost every night of his childhood, after he'd finished school and his father had left the coffee fields, they'd gone into its secrecy to train. The jungle had always represented poverty and fighting.

He lay in the dark, thinking about how he'd come to this point.

"*Ninjutsu,*" his father had told him, "are only skills to trick people and steal their secrets. I'm just teaching you how to survive on your own."

Life was hard, his father insisted. The proof was everywhere, and he wanted options for his son. Though the training was demanding, Takumi knew it was his only hope of a better life. He mastered one technique after another while his father constantly reminded him never to show off. He thought his father had been afraid that the secret fighting techniques would be revealed to the villagers. But now he understood that his father had wanted to show him by example that even if he became a master, there was no way for a ninja to live except as a tool for others. Still, he'd devoted himself to *ninjutsu,* imagining his return to Japan where he would prove his mastery and gain his freedom.

Until now, Takumi had been pleased with his success. He had money, ate in five-star restaurants, traveled the world, slept in the best hotels. Yet, meeting Jet had uncovered a lingering disastisfaction with it all. He felt like a dragonfly skimming the surface of the world. Everything seemed fleeting and shallow.

What am I trying to attain? I was poor all my life, lived on beans and potatoes. My Indio mother couldn't read or write, my father survived by clinging to the pride of his ancient tribe. That's how I managed to find the strength to leave. I made my way in the world only to find a life as a modern-day slave with a knife and a gun.

What was it about Jet that rattled him so? Yes, she was beautiful, her glowing skin, dark hair, and piercing eyes. Two worlds— the East and the West—shone from her expressions: openness and discipline, the desire to reveal who she was and the mask behind which she hid. He sensed her contradictions in the way she spoke and hesitated, in the way she studied him cautiously.

She'd appeared so authentic, so hungry for connection. She'd touched something in him, something buried: all that he hid in his own solitude. She, too, had been cast off, living outside, on the margins. He hadn't intended to get along with her, let alone find it impossible to shake her from his thoughts.

He frowned, wondering if she had orchestrated their meeting as much as he had. She was certainly capable of that—and more. And had she sensed his ninja energy at the ramen shop, even though he'd done everything possible to mute it? He was shaking. He took a deep breath. She made him weak. He couldn't afford to be weak. He had to get the job done.

He closed his eyes with resolve. He didn't believe in victory anymore. Only survival.

Weak meant only one thing: dead.

CHAPTER 20

餓鬼 *Gaki*

Hungry Ghosts

Storm clouds gathered above the city as Jet played her role of begging monk. She wore robes and white *tabi* toe socks. She prayed that Uncle Soji wouldn't make her shave her head as he'd joked, and her prayers were answered because, as he claimed, he needed a new flat razor to get through all of her hair. Hiro wasn't so lucky.

For now, Jet kept her hair tucked into a black cap.

As night illuminated the city with neon, she walked the streets beyond the temple, chanting the sutras she'd memorized. Plastic bags swirled in the bone-chilling wind.

She had been standing in the sea of people for more than an hour, her robes flapping, her breath deep and slow to warm her body. Few people had noticed her, fewer still had stopped to put money in her begging bowl. She was about to turn in for the night when a five-hundred yen coin dropped in, then another. She looked up to meet the eyes of the benefactor. The lights of the plaza danced on the sculpted planes of his face. There was no mistaking him.

"Takumi!" Her heart raced faster now. "How did you…?"

"I wanted to see you again," he said softly. His eyes flickered down to her clothes, but he didn't ask why she was begging or dressed like a nun.

"Can we talk?"

"Yes. Of course…" she said, but there was something different about his expression. What had happened?

"Come with me," he said, pulling her away from the plaza.

His brown eyes flashed in fear as he led her into the darkness of a back alley, looking over his shoulder. She turned as well. No one was behind them.

She knew she was putting herself in danger by not staying in public where her enemies couldn't attack her openly, but she couldn't help it. She couldn't risk losing him again.

"Takumi…How did you find me?"

"Please." He put his finger to her lips. "Don't ask me questions. Just follow me."

The alley bled into another, and another, a labyrinth in the city's underbelly. He led her through a dark underpass near the station. A row of cardboard houses stood against the wall, old shoes lined up neatly outside them. Jet was surprised that the homeless adhered to ritual, taking their shoes off before entering their paper-box homes.

Takumi led her to a quiet part of the underpass, where they could stand in the shadows. Jet began to speak, but he turned and stared at her, and in his expression she saw anguish. He stepped forward and leaned into her, bringing his body close to hers.

"Wait," she said, "we don't really know each other." But she knew that wasn't quite the truth. She felt that she did—through her senses, her intuition.

He reached for her hand. For all his power and recklessness, his fingers were soft in hers, seeking out warmth. She wanted to protest, but her body awoke like fire under his touch.

"Jet," he said, wrapping his arm around her. "You can't imagine what it feels like to see you again."

"I think I can," she said, aching to be closer.

They stared at each other, hearts racing.

As if of its own volition, her body was being pulled inexorably toward him.

"Takumi, what do you want from me?" she asked.

He stared at her, hesitating.

Then, impetuously, daringly, she kissed him, their lips drawing together, warm and hungry. Her lips melted into his, his into hers. She was lost. She was on fire. Did he feel the same?

"I just wanted to see you… one last time," he said, sadness shadowing his face.

"What do you mean, one last time?" she gazed into his eyes, seeing the well of loneliness there.

"I can't be with you. That's all." He tried to back away, but her grip was firm.

"But you are! Here we are. What do you mean?" She felt his heart beating next to hers, almost leaping out of his body, though his breath was soft and quiet. Wind gusted into the underpass, wrapping around them.

"It's not safe," he whispered. "That's all."

"Safe for who?" A chill ran through her, even as she felt the heat wavering between them.

He sighed and closed his eyes. "If you knew who I was, you wouldn't want me…"

"How can you say that?" she asked, fighting back fear.

"What if I told you that I came here… to… to capture you?" he said, not meeting her gaze.

She couldn't breathe as her mind struggled to comprehend.

"You're joking, right?" She tried to laugh.

His face flushed. "I'm serious. I wanted to warn you, but then I saw you, and I couldn't stop…."

"Then why don't you take me?" she said. "Here I am." She held her arms open wide.

"Listen!" He said, intensity in his words. "I mean it!"

She tried to straighten her clothes, her hair, the jumble of thoughts that crowded her brain.

"Why would you want to capture me?"

"It's not what I want. It's what *they* want me to do," he said, looking quickly over his shoulder.

She looked behind Takumi at what he was looking at, but there was nothing there.

Then she stepped away. "Is this your idea of a game?"

He shook his head.

"Then what is going on? Tell me! This isn't making sense!" she said, frustration lacing her words.

"When we talked at the restaurant, I didn't expect to feel this way. It's that… you made sense to me. I felt something…"

"…I did, too," she said softly, her face hot. Her heart hammered in her ribs as if it would burst.

"But I have a duty," he stammered. "I have my life and my oaths."

"To who? What oath is that important?"

"I work for the Matsumura family. I cannot break my oath to them. This is the best life I've had. If I don't have this, I'll have nothing."

"Kidnapping innocent people? Is that the best life you could have? Somehow I doubt it." Her eyes locked on his.

"I doubt it too," he said, then spun and walked toward the street.

Her mother had trained her well, it was true, but the one part of her that couldn't be trained was her heart. She wanted to be loved—wildly, fearlessly, dangerously. She *wanted* to be unsafe, to let down her guard.

"Wait!" she called out.

Takumi turned.

His hair shone in the faint light, and in his frustration, a force radiated from him more powerfully than anything she'd ever felt. But a force was also growing inside of her, too, determined and wild. A sudden understanding fell upon her, like a dark curtain.

"There's something I need to ask you!" she grabbed his shoulder, spun him around. "Were you at the mountain?" She asked the question slowly, deliberately. *If he had anything to do with Ojiisan's death, I'll…*

He didn't answer.

"Takumi," she hissed. "Were you? I need to know."

"…Come with me." He shook his head.

"No! You must tell me!" she insisted.

"Jet," he said with a desperate look in his eyes. "You just have to tell my boss where the treasure is, and then we'll be free. Let's go. It will be quick. Easy. You'll see."

"Your boss?" she spat. "Is he behind all of this? Is it that computer company?"

The conversation with Soji swirled in the far reaches of her brain as Takumi watched her, saying nothing.

"I would if I could," she told him. "The problem is, I don't know where it is...I really don't!"

"Do you think I believe that?" He shot her a seething glare.

"You have to," she said. "It's the truth."

Takumi scowled. "Look... if it's some jewelry or an artifact, who cares? You'll be free of it. You can have your life back." He reached for her wrist.

"Honestly," she said, trying to curb the panic in her voice, "I don't *know* where the treasure is—or what it is. You have to believe me!" Her heart wavered, and she thought about making up some lie just to see what he'd do.

At the moment of her indecision, he caught her in his arms.

"I wish I could." He stiffened.

She felt as if she'd always belonged with him, next to him. Her body leaned toward his, and she longed to touch the thick muscles of his chest, the hollow of his smooth, strong stomach. She let herself melt into this desire, despite her training.

Then, more quickly than she could have imagined, he bent at the knees and threw his arms around her, threw her over his shoulder like a hunted deer, and started to run carrying her. She was stunned by his speed. Automatically, the fight kicked in. She tried to knee his face, then flexed the ball of her foot to kick him.

He threw her down, but she jumped back up immediately and assumed a fighting stance. He paused, taking her posture in. Indecision flickered in his eyes, and for a moment, she thought he would fight her.

But he swung around, his back resolutely to hers, and moved away.

"I have to go," he said.

"No. Not yet," she begged.

"Don't say I didn't warn you."

"Takumi!" she called out after him, but it was too late. He had already slipped away, back into the endless Tokyo night and out of her life once again.

CHAPTER 21

く ノ 一 *Kunoichi*
Female Ninja

Jet lay in bed back at the temple, wondering if she should tell Soji what had happened. How could she begin to explain? She turned Takumi's warnings around in her mind, more determined than ever to get at the heart of the mystery.

She hadn't been able to save Satoko. She hadn't been able to save Ojiisan, either. Could she still save Kanabe? She knew she couldn't let Ojiisan's fall from the ravine be for nothing.

Ojiisan had known the end could come anytime, but something told Jet this was only the beginning. Jet tossed and turned all night, the questions spinning in her mind. What kind of destiny could this be? Always being hunted, or hunting. Is this how Satoko had felt, all those years?

Was this the present she'd have to give up to allow the future to emerge?

All she could see were Takumi's eyes, brown, fierce, beautiful. And the feel of his soft lips against hers…. There was no way to speak of it, any of it.

Sometime before dawn, Jet finally slept. She woke to the sun streaming through the windows and a chill in the air. She resolved to quell her desires in meditation. It was her seventeenth birthday, and she would celebrate it in the prayer room.

Bundling herself in a blanket, she left her small bungalow and made her way to the prayer hall, where she took her place on a round cushion warmed by a patch of sun through the shoji screen window. She sat and waited for the others to arrive.

The sound of the meditation bell traveled up her spine, making her shiver. She tried to remember the teachings. *The body was impermanent. You got sick, grew old, and died. No one could escape the cycles of karma. Birth. Death. Rebirth. Transcend your desires, as they only cause suffering.*

How true that was! She tried to anchor her thoughts in the breath. Her mind reeled. Her body hummed with equal parts passion and pain.

When she was young, Satoko had made her sit and meditate. She'd passed the time by making up stories in her mind. Eventually, she'd gotten bored of the stories, so she'd watched her breath. Watching her breath made it slow down. Then, inexplicably, her thoughts slowed down too, and she noticed space between thoughts. It was quiet and peaceful in that gap, and soon, she began to like going there. It helped her forget about things like tests, homework, not being invited to the popular kids' parties, and most of all, her mother for making her stare at a wall.

Now, the stories she was telling herself were real, and the conflicts dangerous. She breathed deeply, trying to find the gaps, hoping to steady her heart. Maybe too deeply, for she heard Soji's swift footsteps approaching from her across the hall. Then there was the sound of a sword cutting through the air, and Jet's heart skipped a beat. But he was only swatting her back with the *keisaku* stick, used to keep monks from falling asleep during meditation. Not hard, but just enough to let her know she was walking a thin line and he knew it.

Ojiisan was dead, she and Hiro were hiding from vicious attackers, and the first guy she'd kissed said he'd been sent to capture her. Even if it wasn't true, she was nothing but trouble, as her mother had always joked. Satoko's words came back to her. *Many people will try to find you... Some of them may even want to hurt you.…. But you can protect yourself, though you may not remember how. You'll have to dig deep down. Can you do that? For me?*

Once more, Soji's stick thwacked her back, rattling her thoughts. And yet, she felt all the tension held there being released at the contact, allowing her to drop more deeply into the rhythm of her breath, as if coming home to something more elemental than the mind and its endless thoughts. She felt like an animal, following its instincts as it searched for peace. It wasn't a bad feeling.

Jet didn't know how much time had passed when the bell sounded again and Soji clapped the wooden sticks together. Meditation was over.

"Jet," he said, "come speak with me."

As they crossed the long main hall, the floorboards squeaked beneath their feet.

"In the old days," he told her, "builders of palaces and temples put hinges between the cracks of floorboards. They're called nightingales. That way, when the enemy tried to ambush, the nightingales sang."

"Ambushed in a temple?" she asked, dubious.

"Nowhere's safe," he said. "As for the priests and monks, they were the best warriors. It was the perfect disguise."

She thought she detected a note of admiration in his voice. Was Soji a warrior too?

"Now," he said, "more importantly, it's good that you are meditating. If you can control your mind, you can control your emotions. Then you can be strong."

She looked away, afraid that he was disappointed in her.

"Whatever you do," he said, "do it with awareness. That's why we meditate. To stop the inner noise of thinking and notice the silence. In the silence, you can hear your inner voice. You can train yourself to trust your instincts."

"What good are my instincts if Ojiisan died because of me?" Jet asked, anguish washing over her.

He sighed and looked at her pointedly. "Your grandfather was not killed because of you."

"That's not true. If I had been stronger on the mountain, if I had been quicker to respond, he'd still be here now."

"Not so. But you will have to forgive yourself for that," he said solemnly. Then he motioned for her to follow him out of the meditation hall into his study, closing the door behind them.

Floor-to-ceiling bookshelves lined the darkened room. Rows of leatherbound books, scrolls in wooden boxes, and manuscripts cluttered the shelves. Stacks of books rose from the floor like columns in an ancient fortress. He walked over to a trunk near some bookshelves and pulled an envelope from the papers there, then blew off the dust.

"I promised Masakichi I would give this to you when the time was right."

He handed it to her.

"Can I open it?" she asked.

"Go ahead."

Trembling, she peeled back the flap and shook the contents toward her. A gold locket with an ideogram engraved in the front fell into her palm.

女

"Is this....?" She held the object in her hand, feeling a faint vibration. The locket sent a subtle energy coursing through her body, as if she'd been switched on by an invisible current. Her face flushed as she realized it was the same feeling she'd had when Takumi's fingers had touched hers.

"It's the character for 'woman,'" Soji said. "The radicals that make up the ideogram are: く ノ 一."

"く *ku* means 9. ノ *no* is a possessive, and 一 *ichi* means one. Some people say it means ten..." He looked down, then said in a voice so soft that only a spider traversing the floorboards could have heard it, "...holes."

Jet blushed, understanding. "Like a woman's body?"

"Yes." He cleared his throat. "Whether it means that or not, however, is immaterial, as those three characters mean *kunoichi*."

She took a breath. "And *kunoichi* means...?"

"Female ninja," Soji whispered.

She looked at him apprehensively.

"And…?"

"The lineage is symbolized by this locket. Those who wear it are few, and hidden. The power of that tradition is embodied in this amulet."

She deepened her breath to harness the energy that was coursing through her as she held the talisman.

"But," she stammered, "it's just a locket."

"Yes, and no. It contains your history, which is the seat of your power. Open it."

She did. Inside were pictures of her mother and another woman, both in beautiful kimonos, their black hair pulled back in buns.

"That's your grandmother, *Momoko*." He smiled.

"*Momoko*. That means peach child…" she murmured, recalling her mother mentioning the name.

"Right. She was the most powerful woman warrior in the Kuroi clan…" He lowered his voice and gazed directly into her eyes, making her tremble, "…as your mother was after her."

"What?" she asked, startled. Her fingers clutched the locket involuntarily, as fear gripped her insides.

"As soon as your mother knew she was pregnant with a girl, she and your father left Japan to make a new life in America. She wanted to protect you from the struggles she had in Kanabe."

Jet drew her clenched fist close to her heart. Her mind stuck on one word.

"My… father?"

"Yes, he was still with her then. After that, I don't know…"

Soji smiled softly and crooked his fingers, signalling for Jet to return the locket.

She gave it back, but the thrumming didn't stop.

"You'll keep it here, then?" she asked, relieved to be free of its power and message.

"No." He shook his head, smiling. "It belongs to you." He twirled his fingers in the air, signalling for her to turn around. She did.

Gently, he put the locket's chain around her neck and clasped it.

"There now. Turn around and let me see."

She did as he asked, and he stepped back to study her.

"Very good," he said, the lines of his face softening. "You are a ninja, and you must protect this symbol of that secret life. Happy birthday, Kunoichi."

Though she was afraid, her chest sang more vibrantly now, as if the locket itself were humming. She touched the silver pendant, fighting back tears, tears at not knowing all the things her mother had promised to tell her someday.

"You should understand," Soji said, "that all those years your mother was isolated from her family, she was trying to protect you. That's why she did it. Please forgive her."

"I know," Jet murmured. Hearing her uncle's words, she felt all her resentment from her mother's harsh training and survival games melt into appreciation and gratitude. *Mom, you were just protecting me! I hope you'll forgive me, wherever you are.*

"She wanted to protect the tribe," he said, studying her. "The ninja blood is in you, and your mother believed it was strong—that we would need you."

"Maybe she got sick and died because it was too hard to hold it all inside, to keep so many secrets," Jet said, feeling her stomach tighten.

"No. That's not it." Soji put a strong hand on her shoulder. "It was her time to go. You can't blame anyone—especially not yourself."

"At least she had J-Bird," Jet cried, realizing that although her mother was thousands of miles and an ocean away from her homeland, she had managed to make a home.

"Yes. And she loved you both very much." Soji nodded in agreement.

Jet's heart skipped a beat. "Wait a minute! J-Bird! J-Bird must have known about this. Why didn't he tell me?"

Soji bowed his head. "Well, it seems that J-Bird did know some things, but it wasn't his place to tell you. You had to discover your connection to the past yourself."

"Why?" She shook her head. It seemed so complicated, so strange. When they'd put Satoko in the white kimono and sent her off to heaven, J-Bird had said nothing. Had he betrayed her, too?

"Some people can be trained to have great strength, awareness and even power, but some are born with it in their blood. Like you. The locket is a symbol of that inheritance. It was passed down from the young woman who freed the Kuroi family from slavery."

"The one in the stories?" Jet asked, startled to realize that her mother's story about the girl might have been more than a myth.

"Yes," he said. "She was a true master of the elements, and the women in her bloodline drew their power from the land, from the elements of the world in which they grew up, especially the wind."

"But I didn't grow up here."

"The Kuroi clan women are deeply connected to the earth. Japan is in your blood, but so is America. You can draw your power from two tribal lands. You can be doubly powerful."

Soji's eyes shone in the darkness.

Jet glanced at the ground, uncertain. After Takumi's betrayal, after her failure to help Ojiisan, now she learned it was her role to protect her family, to use whatever powers she had inherited from her ancestors and from both lands to do it. But could she? It seemed impossible, superhuman.

"I don't know," she stammered.

"Take some time to think it over. The choice has already been made," he said. A gentle smile curved his lips. "It's just a matter of accepting it."

Jet bit her lip. She tried to remember what had given her the determination to battle her mother on the mountain when she'd thought she was facing a stranger.

It was fear for her mother's life, she realized—the desire to protect her. Yes, that was it. This she could fight for—to protect Hiro, Soji, Aska—to defend what was left of her family. That she could do. But how far would she go to do it?

"There's one thing I've wanted to ask." Her voice faltered. "My mother said something about a dark leader. What did she mean?"

"Ah, that." Soji took a deep breath. "Ninja almost always ended up fighting each other. Because they were bought, they often found themselves on opposing sides. The dark leader is the ninja who sells his soul for money, the one willing to betray the others."

"Is there more than one?" she asked nervously.

Soji shook his head. "I don't know. Maybe she foresaw something, or maybe she was just referring to history. Let's hope it's not a real threat…"

A jolt ran through her body as she saw Takumi, saw his face as he admitted his true purpose. Takumi!

She closed her eyes. Was she ready to accept what she was, even if it meant coming up against someone like Takumi? Is that what her mother had warned her about?

She settled into her breath, then directed the movement of her breath into her belly.

A memory surfaced. On the reservation, J-Bird had given her costumes to put on as a child. No matter how clumsy she was, when she put on a ballerina's pink tutu, she felt graceful and beautiful. When she'd worn the leather moccasins, dress, and feathers of J-Bird's people, she'd felt strong and protected by the tribe and its animal spirits. *What's to stop me from becoming a ninja when I put on this locket?* she wondered. Had J-Bird been preparing me, too?

She took a breath, felt the locket rise and fall on her chest. *Isn't this* henge, *too? Using what you have to fit in?* The thought made her smile. *Isn't that ironic. I've never fit in anywhere before. A ninja's strongest skill is the ability to blend in.*

"Uncle Soji? Is it all right if I call J-Bird?" She needed to ask him for the truth. All of it. And soon!

"Of course," he told her. "I have to go out to do an errand, but I'll lock the place down."

"Thank you," she said, quickly collecting her things and rushing out of the room.

She ran back to her bungalow and picked up the phone Ojiisan had given them. As she dialed J-Bird in New Mexico, she ran her fingers over the locket as if it might give her the answers she desperately sought. It felt alive against her skin, and she tried to breathe in its power, its history, its magic.

The phone rang and rang.

Guide me, Mom! she pleaded, holding the locket. *Teach me, Obaachan!* she begged of her grandmother, Momoko, whose spirit too was embodied in the sacred feminine symbol.

Help me become the kunoichi *you were. And quickly!*

She knew that there was no time to lose.

Let this locket be my armor. Let it be strong and true.

CHAPTER 22

ねむらない 街

Nemuranai Machi

The Town That Never Sleeps

Hiro had skipped out of the temple and was snaking through the throngs of people in West Shinjuku, Aska by his side. He had six thousand yen in his pocket. Soji had given him the money early that morning while Jet slept.

"Here's some money. You might need it," Soji had said, lifting his hand from the sutra he was copying in *sumi* ink to give Hiro an envelope with money inside. "Cleaning a temple and studying all day must be boring. You haven't seen much of Tokyo at all. Isn't there someplace you want to go?"

"Actually, yes. Shinjuku," Hiro answered immediately. He thought Soji's request was strange. It was dangerous, even, to go. Yet, Hiro knew enough to realize that Soji must have had a plan and had wanted him to make himself scarce for a while. His uncle didn't do anything randomly, so Hiro agreed to leave.

"You can't take Aska on the train," Soji said. "You'll have to walk." He dipped his brush in the ink and drew out a route to Shinjuku on the *washi* paper used for copying the sutras.

It took Hiro and Aska an hour to get to Shinjuku from Shibuya. Now they were walking on Shinjuku Dori, passing department stores where models wore expensive autumn clothes and drifting by fancy cake shops from which warm, sweet smells wafted up onto the sidewalk. Aska's nose twitched repeatedly. Hiro had to laugh.

For long time, he'd imagined what it would be like to leave Kanabe and come to a huge city like Tokyo. He and Ojiisan had often talked about the city and its twenty-four-hour-life.

Hiro thought he'd already gotten used to the people walking quickly on the street, staring ahead as if programmed for their offices, and the fact that you couldn't see the tops of the enormous buildings without craning your neck to the sky. He even felt desensitized to the incessant noise of cars and trains, the heavy pollution choking the air. He understood that this was city life, that living here meant accepting these things. Your body adapted to them just as it adapted to nature. But it seemed counterintuitive.

In the mountains, he felt healthy and alive because there were places of stillness, places where even the rivers and wind were silent. Though it had only been days, it seemed like months since he'd walked in the forest with Aska, chasing rabbits or skipping stones. Here, he felt disoriented, out of touch with his body and the rhythms of the earth. He concentrated on his breath—in and out—centering his awareness in the earth, somewhere far beneath the concrete under his feet. Could he still feel the earth energy there and bring it back up into his body?

Even though he was no longer in the mountains, the mountains were in him, in his blood. Perhaps that's what Ojiisan had meant when he said that the spirit of nature was alive in the trees, rocks, dirt. Had that spirit transmitted itself to Hiro? Even if you cut the forest down, the seed could be replanted. The mountain, the river, the earth were in his skin. The spirit of nature was under his skin, in his cells, alive and breathing there.

Hiro walked more slowly, feeling the stillness of the earth spirit as he let it re-enter his body. He puzzled over the events of the last few days. He knew that Jet had tried to abandon him and Aska in the hotel room. He couldn't say he blamed her. It was tempting to just walk away from one's duty and start all over again.

He could do that now, with Aska, slip into the shadows of the city and never be found again. But that would be a waste. He'd given his word, and Ojiisan had died for them. They had to complete this mission. What kind of ninja was he if he just walked away from his word?

Besides which, he wondered where Jet had gone that night, and if she'd put them in jeopardy. He had a sinking feeling that she had. He shook his head in consternation. Aska hung hers low.

They walked toward Shinjuku station but didn't go in. Instead, Hiro bought a small bunch of orange Chinese bellflowers from a kiosk on the corner. It cost eight hundred yen but he could have picked as many as he wanted in the mountains of Kanabe for nothing.

Aska walked alongside, her nose bumping into Hiro's calf every so often as if to confirm that he were still there. She seemed to understand his feelings. They went into a dark narrow tunnel under the railroad that led to the West side.

A foul smell came up from the wet pavement inside, and when a train passed overhead, the narrow space filled with a deafening rattle. A blind man sat on a half-broken chair in the middle of the tunnel playing blues on a harmonica, but the melody was drowned out by the noise of the passing train. Hiro didn't know the music, but the low tune hung sadly in the wet, dark air and made time stand still for just a moment. He stopped in front of the man and put a few coins in his empty red can and kept on walking.

Once out of the tunnel, they wound their way through the office buildings and luxury hotels of West Shinjuku until they hit Yamate Dori, a big street with down-on-their-luck lunchrooms, cramped electronic stores, and car showrooms. Hiro looked at the map that Soji had drawn for him and found "Yamate Dori" and "Honan Dori" with a circle drawn on the intersection. Hiro was surprised. Soji had understood exactly where in the vast area of Shinjuku Hiro had wanted to go. But then again, his uncle had powers. Of that, he was sure.

Hiro stopped at the intersection and put the flowers on the ground. Then he crouched and placed his palms on the concrete, feeling the warmth of the autumn sunshine on the pavement.

He knew that the trains and the subways ran deep beneath this ground, just as the water from high up on the mountaintop ran down to the village, coursing beneath Kanabe. Underneath the stillness was motion. In the motion was stillness, if you could find it. That much Masakichi had told him. Could he find the stillness in the city that never slept?

The warmth Hiro felt on his palms was his father's warmth. He closed his eyes and tried to conjure his father's face. Hiro's father had gone to Tokyo as a seasonal worker, helping to construct the new subway line.

From November to March, Northern Japan was completely snowed in. If people were animals, they would have gone into hibernation, awaiting the arrival of spring from their caves. But humans don't hibernate, and there were mouths to feed. So the men in northern Japan left for Tokyo or Osaka to get work. There, they did the dirty, dangerous jobs others wouldn't do.

His father had never come home again. When Hiro was three years old, his father had been hurt on the job, just underneath where he now stood.

Perhaps he was humiliated that he could no longer support his family, perhaps his spirit had been crushed. Hiro's mother had hated Tokyo for having stolen her husband. By the time she herself died, she wondered if he was even still alive.

Hiro understood his mother's feelings and for a long time, he'd agreed with her. Tokyo represented all that had oppressed his tribe, his people, his history. Yet, nature was also to blame. Nature was beautiful, but it was also harsh and unrelenting. It created life, but it had incredible destructive power to take life away. That was the law of nature. Ojiisan had taught him that everything grows, flourishes, and dies. Kanabe had not been able to sustain the men and their families, so they had no choice but to come to the cities, where progress would give them money to sustain their old village lives. You couldn't have one without the other. The old villages kept history and culture alive. The new cities sustained them.

Even though Tokyo had claimed his father, Hiro understood that it was filled with an energy he'd never imagined. He wanted to find a way to harness it. He felt the city rebuffed him, and yet, there was something there, something indefinable, something sparkling and alluring.

Kneeling on the ground, he asked his father's spirit:

Where is the place earth and sky meet? City and country? Where does one root and the other branch?

He folded his hands over the deep orange bellflowers he'd lain on the street in the hopes that his father, who'd disappeared into the wet, dark underground of Tokyo, might return to the tranquility of Mt. Osore and spend a peaceful life there with his mother as spirits in the netherworld.

Then he got up and took the leash firmly in his hand, leading Aska back toward the temple, heart heavy.

I'll never forget, he promised.

CHAPTER 23

火の玉族 *Hi no Tama Zoku*
The Fire Tribe

The warm autumn sun poured onto the concrete. The smell of *yakitori* and roasting sweet potatoes floated down the street.

Hiro and Aska had walked for an hour and stopped to rest on the steps of the fountain at Shinjuku Koma Theater in the center of Kabuki-cho, the biggest red-light-district in Japan. On either side of them were honkytonk bars, strip joints, massage parlors, hostess halls, and gay bars. Hiro let down his guard. No one would go to look for a kid here.

They'd just finished lunch. Hiro had eaten five sticks of *yakitori* from a cart on the street. He'd splurged and bought his favorite, *tsukune*—the tender round chicken meatballs, and *negima*—thin chunks of breast meat skewered with green onions. He'd bought Aska a double bacon cheeseburger at McDonald's. He could see Jet turning up her nose, saying, "That's so disgusting and greasy!" but it was the first meat either had eaten since they'd come to Soji's temple. There, they couldn't eat meat, fish, eggs, or any strong-smelling vegetables like onion, leek, and garlic, which were considered too stimulating for monks.

I'm no monk, Hiro laughed to himself.

For the past week, he'd eaten rice, *miso* soup, Japanese eggplant, green pepper, *shiso*, lotus, tofu, and soybeans every day. The taste of meat was comforting to this *matagi*. Aska had made extremely short work of her bacon cheeseburger and was lying comfortably on her side, her full belly heaving gently.

The streets of Kabuki-cho were dark from exhaust fumes. The whole area was littered with paper, tin cans, and cigarette butts. Hiro glanced at the people walking between the plaza and the theater. Women in glittery clothes, heavy make-up, and thick perfume laughed loudly as they clicked along the street in high-heeled shoes. Many were from Russia and Southeast Asia. Hiro wondered if any of them had been brought here against their will. A pack of short-haired *yakuza* in black jackets and red shirts swaggered to the center of the street like wolves.

If Grandpa saw me here, he'd definitely disapprove. Hiro smiled to himself. He was comfortable in the anarchy of this place. The people of Kabuki-cho showed their real faces. He wanted to show his.

Hiro stretched his arms and looked at the clock in the center of the square. It was two o'clock. If they left Shinjuku at three, he would be back at the temple before five and could still help make dinner. Jet might have missed him, but Soji would explain.

Soji asked me to take a holiday today, he thought, *so I shouldn't go back too soon. I've still got a few more hours, though. What should I do?*

A group of teenagers walked in front of him, talking loudly in slang and laughing. Their hair was dyed blonde, blue, pink, and red, their pants were ripped and shredded. They were carrying a lot of heavy black bags. They stopped at the side of a fountain and rested.

Hiro directed his attention toward them, keeping his hand on the coins in his pocket. He observed their body language, the way they laughed and jostled each other. They all had pierced ears, noses, lips, cheeks, and eyebrows. One even had a pierced chin. They were tough, but Hiro didn't feel any danger from them.

"They're punks," Hiro whispered to Aska. "*Oshaka-sama!* It must hurt to have so many piercings, don't you think?"

Aska turned to the kids and let out a slight sound as she yawned.

"Wow, that's a big Akita!" One boy whose blue hair stuck up like a hedgehog had heard her. He approached Aska and crouched beside her. He had a pierced nose and a large safety pin stuck through his cheek.

"Can I pet your dog?" he asked. He seemed to be little bit older than Hiro.

"Sure. Just a second," Hiro answered. Then he turned to Aska and gave her the go-ahead signal.

Aska immediately stood up slowly and walked around the boy, sniffing him. Then she returned to Hiro's side and looked up at him patiently.

"Okay. Now you can pet her."

The boy sat on the ground. "So, you're a girl, are you?" Aska lay on her back and exposed her belly. The boy petted Aska gently.

"What's your name?"

"Mine or my dog's?"

"Both." The boy laughed and waved his hand in the air. There were big silver rings on each of his fingers.

"My name is Hiro, and her name is Aska."

"Hello, Aska. I'm Akira." The boy seemed to love Aska. He lay down on the ground just like her, and continued to pet her.

"Are you from Northern Japan?" he asked.

"Well, yes." Hiro blushed. Akira had picked up on his accent.

Akira turned to Hiro and noticed his flushed cheeks. "My dad's from Akita-ken. He still has an accent—just like yours. That's how I knew. I didn't mean to make you feel bad about it. Sorry."

"I didn't feel bad." Hiro shook his head, smiling. Even though Akira looked menacing, the way he considered Hiro's feelings made him feel comfortable.

A girl with dyed red hair, a frilly white shirt, and red and white striped pants came up to Akira. Hiro thought she looked like a Raggedy Ann doll.

"Let's go. Are you ready?" she said, motioning for him to get up.

"Yep." Akira stood up and turned to Hiro. "If you have time, come with us. We're going to put on a concert in the plaza." Then he dashed into the circle of punks who looked like brightly dressed gypsies.

"Really?" Hiro and Aska started to walk toward the plaza, where a loud sound roared into the sky like a sonic boom.

"Sure!" Akira called back.

People walking along the plaza stopped in their tracks. With the aggressive rhythm of an electric guitar, bass, and drums, the music was a huge ball of sound hitting the asphalt and rebounding against the sides of the buildings, filling the plaza.

The punk rockers started to dance, jumping and shaking their heads wildly. More punks scurried out of the alleys and joined the group. Hiro rushed into the circle with Aska. In the center was Akira, holding the microphone in his hands and shouting into it ferociously. Hiro listened for the words, but what came out of Akira's mouth were less like words and more like some kind of powerwail squeezed from his body. He sunk down to the ground and shouted at the concrete in an unbelievably loud voice.

> *Tokyo is burning, Tokyo is burning!*
> *I'm so frigging mad!*
> *They feed you for nothing,*
> *it bugs the hell out of me—*
> *your slow, easy life!*
> *You don't even have to work!*
> *You grew up without a care in the world!*
> *Friggin' symbol of Japan.*
> *Don't criticize me, because you don't even lift a finger!*

Then he lifted his third finger and jutted it into the air. The people gathered in the square cheered. They were dancing along the rim and pushing in toward the center. Akira sank way down to the ground, and when his head almost touched the pavement, he leapt back up and shouted into the sky. High or low, he never stopped shouting out the words, as if they had climbed up inside him and clawed their way back out again.

> *Silly prince, without a care in the world,*
> *brought up by your servants with a silver spoon,*
> *in your beautiful clothes, talking about nothing—*

Friggin' symbol of Japan!
Just because you were born into that family!
Tokyo is burning,
Tokyo is burning.

Akira ran back and forth, jumping up and down, coursing with energy. Hiro's body buzzed to Akira's voice. He let himself get carried away into the sounds and into the crowd, which was swelling with the music.

Soon, Hiro was dancing and jumping in the center of the circle. Sweat poured down his back. He felt his body grow light as if he were running through the mountains back home. Aska was dancing, too, putting her paws up on Hiro's thighs. Before long, other boys and girls were taking turns dancing with Aska. Her tongue was hanging out happily as she roamed from punk to punk. Even though he was moving wildly, Hiro felt that his entire body had been transported to a pure place. A place of stillness within this frantic motion.

Hiro sensed that the whole city was charged with a kind of energy just beneath the surface. Did cities have spirits too? And then there was no Hiro. There was no city. Only energy. Only oneness. Hiro basked in that feeling, let himself be embraced by it.

Suddenly, police sirens rang out.

"The cops are here!" Akira shouted.

In a split second, a few policemen clomped forward in their heavy boots, night-sticks clacking at their sides as they tried to break into the circle.

The band stopped playing and the punks started running, carrying their instruments, speakers, and amplifiers away from the plaza.

"Hiro, come on!" Akira waved his hand, still holding the microphone.

Hiro ran after Akira. Aska followed. "Stop right there!" the policemen shouted into a bullhorn from behind them.

Of course, no one was stupid enough to stop at a policeman's words.

Hiro turned back to see the gypsies laughing.

They ran through the narrow alleys fast, faster than light, almost as fast as Hiro ran through the mountains. They ran so fast that the dirty gray walls disappeared one after another. A stray cat rummaging through a garbage can at the back door of a bar was surprised by Akira, Hiro, and Aska's swift approach. It bounded up to the roof, spilling garbage out onto the alley. Hiro and Akira laughed gleefully.

To Hiro, the gray walls looked like the mountain's walls of trees, and the cat looked like a squirrel jumping to a high branch. He felt as if he had found the mountain of his homeland in the dirty, foul-smelling streets of Kabuki-cho.

Hiro didn't know where they were running to and he didn't care. He felt himself transcending time and place. Just being in the wind. Carried on the wind. Weightless. Free.

After a while, they came to a small park. Akira stopped at a bench and sat down, motioning for Hiro to do the same. Their breath heaved in unison.

The sun was going down to the west, drawing three long shadows on the street—Akira, Hiro, and Aska. Akira's shadow had a microphone in its hand.

"Hope everyone else got away safely." Hiro sat on the ground, leaning against the chain-link fence. Aska lay down beside him. The silver and green-striped trains of the Yamanote line passed just outside the fence.

"I'm sure they did! We do this all the time." Akira smiled. "It's our entertainment."

"You mean the music?" Hiro asked.

"No. Running away from the cops. We're always going to be faster than them. They're old and fat and they don't like our sound." Akira laughed.

Hiro laughed easily, and Aska leaned into his leg.

"I like the first song you played," he said.

"That one? I like it too." Akira nodded. "The original was by the Clash, about twenty years ago. Anarchy put the lyrics into Japanese. They rewrote the song about the Emperor instead of the Royal Family."

"Anarchy?" Hiro asked.

"Yeah. You probably never heard of Anarchy. They were a great punk band."

"What happened to them?"

"They criticized the Emperor too directly. The record company had to bleep out the words. When the CD came out later on, that song was cut."

"That sucks," Hiro said.

"Yeah. It's their best song, but it couldn't find a place."

"But you give it one, out in the streets," Hiro exclaimed.

"You're right. And I guess that's where it belongs," Akira said, hope shining from his eyes.

To Hiro, Akira's punk band sent their music up to the sky like smoke signals, a tribal call to find a way to belong, even though the world had not carved out a place for them.

The waning sun cast a dark orange glow on everything. Akira's body became drenched in saffron. Tokyo was burning in the autumn light, and Hiro thought that it was beautiful.

They sat on the concrete, watching the trains go by as the sun went down between the buildings. Hiro breathed in deeply. The chilly autumn breeze coursed through his whole body like brand new energy. Maybe *that* was the energy of the city. He felt rejuvenated.

It was almost five o'clock.

"Well….We've really got to get going." Hiro stood up. Aska got up, too. *I hope Soji and Jet are safe at the temple. We've been gone for hours*, he realized, fear once again rising.

It's what Soji wanted, he reminded himself. And it had felt good to hang out, be a regular boy. *When's the last time I've done that?* he wondered.

Have I ever?

"If you stay in the city, come check us out. We play in Shibuya, Harajuku, Ikebukuro, everywhere." Akira smiled.

"Yeah. I'd like that," Hiro said, grinning.

"Next time, I'll sing you a song I wrote myself." Akira put his nose to Aska's nose and said good-bye.

"Cool. I hope we meet again." Hiro held out his hand.

"Thanks. Me too." Akira shook Hiro's hand with a strong grip.

Aska and Hiro started walking toward the station. Hiro looked back to see Akira waving to them with the microphone, and Hiro waved back. Then he walked toward the glowing red sun. It was the same sun he'd seen in the mountains near Kanabe.

Ojiisan had been right, Hiro realized. The mountains could live in the city. The city could live in the mountains, too. Both could live inside you wherever you were, as long as there was light and energy.

As long as there was a fire within.

CHAPTER 24

必然 *Hitsuzen*

Necessity

Takumi went to the window. Tokyo looked flat and lifeless from the top floor of this fifty-storey building. Neon banners and billboards shouted into the sky below. Then there was that glowing red sun, the same one he'd seen in the jungle. No place could be further from the lush green jungles of Brazil. Would those rainforests someday look like this—concrete and steel?

He turned to face his boss. Matsumura Fuhio looked Takumi over and clucked his tongue. "Takumi-san," he said sternly, "I was worried that you were too young to be in charge of the operation in Aomori. Now I'm even more concerned."

He leaned back in his chair, arms behind his head as if trying to give his best warrior the benefit of the doubt. "Please tell me I'm wrong." He folded his hands on his lap and leaned back into his chair.

"There won't be any problem this time," Takumi said, quelling his emotions. He was a trained assassin. He could take down anyone—a head of state, a warlord, or a guerilla fighter. So why did this man have to keep asserting himself? Takumi could kill him in an instant, too, and leave no shred of evidence.

Matsumura tapped his fingers on the table. "I have already invested over five million dollars in this project. Nothing can prevent it from happening. Is that clear?"

Takumi looked at Matsumura's thin, cunning eyes.

"Yes, sir. It's clear." He forced himself to sound respectful. After all, Matsumura was the direct descendent of a seventh-century Japanese aristocrat whose family had been in power for centuries. One had been president around seventy-five years ago. They acted as if they were still in control of the country.

"Harter and I have been lenient with you," Matsumura said. "We've wined you and dined you, put you up in my seaside villa, pampered you so you would be ready to do the job. Now it's time to stop playing. Get busy and bring the girl in. There will be dire consequences if we continue in this manner."

Takumi knew there was no room for regret. He was doing as his father had done, using his skills to survive. *But if my father knew what I've done with what he taught me...*

At their last meeting, Matsumura had shown Takumi Jet's photograph and sent him to stake her out. He'd followed her to the hotel. She'd lead him to the ramen shop. Takumi understood that he'd been tested.

"Did you hear me?" Matsumura asked.

"*Hai.*" Takumi nodded. He understood all too well. He remembered the promises Harter had made: *Come with us. We'll give you everything you need.*

Takumi smiled ruefully. Harter had no idea what he needed, because he himself hadn't known at all. He'd been seduced by the promise of food, shelter, even possibly school. But none of that was going to happen. And now he was backed into a corner. The only way out was to kill or be killed.

Lines from the *Rinzai Roku*, the sayings of the great Zen master, came to him: *Your deep doubt will become solid like the ground to throw you off balance. Your deep attachment will transform into water to drown you. Your deep anger will transform into fire to burn you. Your deep pleasure will transform into the wind to carry you away.*

That's what it is, Takumi thought. *Pleasure is a wind.* He wanted to be carried away on that wind. Instead, he had to hunt the source of it—Jet. He had to capture her, maybe even harm her. But first, he needed her to tell him what she knew. She had the information that would make them all rich. That's why he was here, after all. To secure his future. A better future. And only money could do that. That's what he'd always been taught. Was it wrong to believe what his father had told him since he was old enough to listen?

Damn the fate that had made a woman so beautiful into the one he had to fight. What twisted karma would lead him to this? He ached to touch her again, and he cursed himself for his weakness. He took a deep breath and centered his energy in his *hara*.

Even if you succeed in getting rid of your attachments, the only thing that comes of it in the end is a way to save your own life, he thought, shaking his head. It was better to look at things practically. He was a mercenary. He had to survive. If he failed or refused, they would try to kill him. He knew too much to back out.

"A human life is almost the same as the life of a car. It runs as long as it can. And when it breaks down, you have to abandon it," Matsumura told him.

"Yes, sir," Takumi agreed, bile rising in his gut as he realized that his boss was talking about *him*, how dispensable *he* was.

"Get to it," Matsumura snarled as he left, closing the door behind him.

Takumi stared out the window. The sun had gone down, and the city spread out flat and dark beneath him, its neon lights switched on, snaking around buildings like the tails of digital dragons.

How would it would feel to fall from this height? he wondered.

Cars shone like chips of colored glass in each lane. This busy little world was nothing, its inhabitants insignificant specks. His men, the people he had to capture, Jet, even himself, all of them were pointless. His warriors were ready to assault the Buddhist temple. But though he needed to gather everyone in the Kuroi family and interrogate them, he wasn't convinced that they knew the secret to the treasure, or that there even *was* a treasure. People with great wealth didn't behave like this. They didn't run. They used their power. Still, he would do his job. He would learn what they knew and get rid of them if he had to. Matsumura and Harter wanted no loose ends. They'd been working toward this goal for years. Failure was not an option.

Takumi felt dizzy. He steadied himself. He had men to manage, a mission to fulfill. He'd lied and told Matsumura that he was twenty-four, but he was only nineteen, in charge of a contingent of well-trained men, and this was his first big mission. At the outset, no one had questioned his age. His skills had quelled any doubts they might have had. If he failed, his future would be certain failure as well.

Nothing goes well living as a ninja, his father had said.

Takumi hadn't believed him. He'd thought he could make it go well. After all, there were many kinds of wars and warriors. He'd force himself to be the best.

He hadn't counted on something in her awakening something in him. He hadn't factored that in at all. He'd thought he could steel himself against anything. But he'd been wrong. He'd never met a *kunoichi*.

He shook off thoughts of the girl and went out to meet his men. He had a job to do, and a plan to put it into motion. He was a professional, and as such, had no room for emotion. He would do his job, and do it well. No wind, no woman, nothing would stop him.

CHAPTER 25

アスカの魔法 *Aska no Maho*
Aska's Magic

Jet moved through the temple with the cell phone pressed up to her ear, cocking her head and trying to get good reception. J-Bird hadn't answered yet. *Where could he be?*

She was dialing again when she heard the nightingale floor sing in the distance. The temple had become eerily quiet. She'd been so intent on getting through to J-Bird that she hadn't noticed.

Gomen kudasai… she called out as she walked into the dining room, but there was no response. Then she went more quickly, through the monks' quarters, Shoji's room, the library, and the shelter near the shrine. All were empty.

"Hiro!" she shouted, suddenly panicked. "Hiro! Come here now!" Where had that boy gone?

But there was no reply. Instead, she heard a woman's voice calling from outside the gate.

"Hello? Is anyone there?"

Jet peered through the gate.

It was the old woman who usually swept.

"Is everything okay?" Jet asked.

"Not really." The woman's voice was urgent. "I came to tell you something important. Soji Sensei's been in a car accident on Aoyama Street. You should go to the hospital."

"What?" Jet's heart raced. "Is he okay?"

"I think it's serious. I'll take you there. There's a car waiting."

"Thank you for letting me know! I'll go get my things." Jet ran across the temple grounds. She got the coat and backpack from her room and sprinted back to the gate.

When she returned, Hiro and Aska were coming up the hill toward the temple.

"Hiro!" Jet was astonished that he'd broken the rules and gone out with Aska.

"Jet! Where are you going?" he cried out.

"I'll explain later. We've got to go now!" she exclaimed, grabbing Hiro's arm and pulling him toward the old woman.

Aska blocked her way. She stopped in front of the woman and sniffed her leg.

Then she went to Hiro's right side and sat down.

"Come on!" Jet urged. "Uncle Soji's been hurt! We've got to get to the hospital!"

Hiro caught her sleeve, holding her back with surprising strength.

"I mean it, let's get going!" She pulled her arm free. But instead of following, Hiro touched Aska's back and commanded, "Go!"

Aska lunged at the old woman, knocking her down.

"Hiro! Aska! Stop it! Stop it!" Jet shouted, but it was too late. Aska had pinned the woman, her fangs at her throat.

"Jet, no!" Hiro shouted. "Look!" He ran to the woman and pulled at her hair, jerking her head back. Jet's mouth opened to scream in protest, but she stopped mid-scream as the woman's hair came free along with the face.

"What a lame disguise!" Hiro said to the thin little thug sweating underneath. Hiro rolled him over with his foot, crouched down to search him, and removed a silver pistol from his waist.

"How did Aska know?" Jet asked, astonished.

"When she smells someone for the first time," he told her, "she goes to my right side. But if it's someone she's met before, she goes to the left. She never forgets someone's smell."

"Good job," Jet told Hiro.

Then she crouched above the thug. "Where's Soji?" she demanded.

The man grunted. "Get your dog off me."

"Tell us where he is!" Jet lifted her fist above his face.

He sneered. "Halfway across the world by now if I had to guess."

Jet felt someone approaching from the side. Two men ran from the temple garden, moving quickly and seamlessly. One sailed toward her, a flash of blond. A Westerner! He swept a knife from his waist, then dove, curling into a ball as he rolled. He bounded up to assume a *kosei no kamae* fighting stance.

This time, Jet didn't stop to think as she ran toward him. Surprised at her speed, he thrust his knife toward her wildly. She swung her right leg in a clipped spin and hit his wrist with her foot, sending the knife clattering to the ground. Using the velocity of her kick, she turned and sent a backspin kick to his face, but he ducked.

She landed as he launched himself against her, his thick hand grasping her wrist from behind. Unable to break free, she bent down and reached toward the ground for his fallen knife. He grabbed her elbow with his thumb and index finger, locking his fingertips like iron into two pressure points. Suddenly, she couldn't move. Pain wracked her body. Her heart pounded in her chest.

To her side, Aska was still on the thug, and Hiro had the pistol trained on the other man who'd approached them. They were all watching the struggle between Jet and the blond. She reached out, trying to claw his face. He shifted just out of her range of motion.

"Stop trying to scratch me, girl," he said.

She swung again. He laughed, only increasing her fury. Where were her powers? Why couldn't she handle this thug?

"Your fighting needs some fine-tuning," he told her. "When I've got you in these two pressure points, you're immobile. Not even a gorilla could move."

"Do I look like a gorilla?" she grunted. Her comment gave her enough time to shoot her left leg up, aiming her foot at his face. But he anticipated her move and jerked her into place, pinching her right elbow.

"If I put a little more pressure with my fingers, your arm will be disabled forever," he said. His calm tone told her that he wasn't exaggerating. She was furious and desperate. These were grown men, trained as mercenaries. She stood no chance against them.

"Where's the family treasure?" he asked. "Is it hidden in the temple?"

"I don't know," she snarled.

He applied more pressure, gritting his teeth, it seemed to Jet, in pleasure.

"I swear. I don't even know what it is!" she cried out, trying to buy time, to focus her mind. She had to—for her mother, for Oji-isan...

Hiro edged closer to her while the other man circled. Jet slowed her breath, slowed her heart and let her senses expand, drawing energy up from the earth, letting her awareness move into the wind and rain.

"Come on. You've got to do better than that, sister," the blond man sneered.

And then her rage faded to the silence of meditation, and the falling raindrops seemed to slow, as if each were suspended in the air. Her senses opened outward so that she could feel everything around her—Hiro, Aska, the three men. It was as if she were in the mountains again, with her mother during a rainstorm, blocking her attacks as they moved between boulders in the dark. *Amegakurejutsu*. The art of hiding in the rain.

She sensed how her mother used the rain to mask her presence and then projected her energy toward her before attacking from a different direction so that Jet felt as if she were fighting two, sometimes three people. She moved into that deep, silent space of instinct. Her left hand was all that was free. *Ninja use what they have.*

She would have to be fast enough to save both herself and Hiro once she'd started.

"Hiro!" she cried out, as if to warn him, and he spun toward her, lifting his gun. She projected her energy to his side without moving a muscle and simultaneously merged her physical body with the rain, imperceptibly staying put. The blond man lurched forward as if to keep her in place, though she hadn't budged. The other man—the one Hiro had covered with the gun—sprinted at him.

She crooked the index and middle fingers of her free hand—the *shako ken* claw strike—and with a cry, she jammed them into the blond man's face.

"This is how this girl scratches, jerk!" she said.

A chilling sound came from his mouth, and he released her, clutching his eye. She dodged forward, beneath the line of Hiro's gun, to intercept his attacker. She skipped to the right, swinging her left leg at the pit of his stomach. It hit like a whip, and he dropped to his knees.

Hiro had the gun trained, but the blond man was wearing a bulletproof vest, she realized.

A flak jacket can stop a bullet, but it can't stop the force of a kick that holds every ounce of a body's ki. *My* ki. Jet became like the rain, moving with a gust, then shifting so that she seemed to come at him from two directions and struck. He staggered, his wounded eye partially blinding him as she bunched her fist and shot it at his temple. He fell, and she caught her breath. It seemed to her that her body was moving by instinct alone. She shook her head and tried to come back to the moment.

She looked around to make sure that there were no other attackers, and then she thought she saw someone else standing in the temple garden watching, his eyes narrowed, a faint twist to his lips as if he were smiling.

"Let's go!" Hiro shouted, and Aska followed him. Jet glanced back one more time, but there was no one there. Had he been there or not? Or had she wanted to see him so badly that she'd conjured him from thin air?

Jet shook her head, clearing the thought from her mind. Then she sprinted after Hiro, her feet barely touching the ground.

The three ninjas ran into the crowded streets of Tokyo as the rain poured down, soaking them to the core.

CHAPTER 26

変化 *Henge*
Transformation

They moved through Tokyo for the next hour, weaving between back streets and crossing through crowded intersections before taking to the main roads again. Finally, when they could no longer sense anyone following them, Hiro paused and caught Jet's arm.

"Aska's bleeding," he said. He knelt and held his dog.

"She is? I didn't see her get hurt," Jet replied.

"I didn't either. It looks like an infection. Maybe something happened on the mountain and we didn't notice. We need to get her treated immediately."

"There must be vets in Roppongi!" Jet said, recalling that many foreigners lived in this popular mini-America. Foreigners had pets, she reasoned, and pets would need treatment.

They made their way down Killer Boulevard, which swarmed with soldiers on leave, dark-suited businessmen on expense accounts, and body-conscious girls in lamé miniskirts swinging gold-chained Chanel purses, angling to meet their *gaijin* prince charming.

"So this is city life, eh?" Hiro said, his mouth hanging open.

Jet, too, was overwhelmed by all the activity, the sheer masses of people crammed into such small spaces.

Hiro tightened Aska's leash as a blond woman with a small white papillon walked down the Avenue. They fell in behind her, following her down one of the "eel alleys," behind the big boulevard where expatriate companies had homes for their foreign workers. As the woman fumbled with her keys, Hiro asked her if she knew of a vet. Her dog strained on its leash, trying to stay away from Aska as she directed them to a veterinarian's office down an alley lined with purple potted plants that looked like mutant cabbages.

There, the vet examined Aska, agreeing to treat her immediately. He then took an X-ray. When he came back into the waiting room, he wore a confused expression.

"It looks as if your dog had a microchip implanted in her neck. That's what caused the infection."

"A what?" Hiro asked.

"A computer chip that stores information about the owner in case the dog gets lost. We have them in America," Jet said, enjoying the look on her cousin's face. It was the rare time that she knew something he didn't.

"That's right," the vet said. "But this one is more sophisticated. It's actually a kind of sensor."

Hiro looked at Jet with wide eyes. Someone was tracking Aska's movements! He had to think fast so that the vet wouldn't be worried.

"I just remembered!" he said. "Ojiisan used to take her hunting for mushrooms in the mountains, and she'd sometimes wander off to chase rabbits. He must have wanted to track her when she took off."

"That's right," Jet jumped in. "But now that we live in the city, we no longer need it. Can you take it out?"

The vet looked at them quizzically. "Okay," he told them. "I'll just use a local anesthetic so we won't have to keep her overnight. Give me a few minutes, okay?"

As soon as he left the room, Hiro lowered her voice. "That's how those men found us! They used a tranquilizer on her. That means they've probably followed us here, too."

Hiro got up and went to the receptionist desk. He asked if he could change yen bills for coins. Jet knew instantly what he was doing.

They didn't have regular *tsubute*—ninja throwing stones—so he would use coins. They were less effective, but if he put his *ki* into each attack, they could become deadly.

"Shouldn't we call the police?" she asked,

Hiro shook his head vehemently. "No way. I'll never ask *Wa* policemen for help. I'd rather die."

She sighed. "Hiro, is everyone *Wa* to you?"

He bit his lip, considering. "On the mainland, probably. Anyone in power."

"Whatever," she said. She took out the cell phone again. "I'm calling J-Bird."

Hiro shifted on his feet, a look of concern etched on his face.

"Is he safe?" he asked.

"Hiro, of course he's safe. He was my mother's boyfriend. He's like a father to me."

He frowned. He wasn't buying it.

"I know, my dad doesn't have the best track record," she said, understanding. "But J-Bird is different."

"I hope you're right," he said.

"Me too." She sighed. Everyone was suspect now, it seemed.

Hiro left to see how Aska was doing, and Jet went into the bathroom and dialed J-Bird. Was Hiro right? Could he be trusted? A tingling fear went up her spine. Would he, too, betray her? She had to be on guard.

It was 6 AM in New Mexico. The phone rang seven times before he finally picked up.

"J-Bird! It's me, Rika. I mean, Jet," she whispered.

"Jet? Where are you? Are you okay? It's so good to hear your voice." Relief flooded his voice.

"I'm… I'm fine. I'm in Tokyo with my cousin, Hiro. Some people attacked us in Kanabe, and grandpa was murdered."

"What?" J-Bird's words hung heavy in the distance between them. "How terrible for everyone."

"I know." Jet tried to sound collected, but the words came spilling out like pachinko balls. "We went to stay with Uncle Soji in Tokyo, but now he's been kidnapped! What should we do?"

J-Bird's voice was steady, measured. "Wait a minute. Slow down. Explain everything from the start."

Jet did just that, speaking in a hushed voice. Finally, she told him that she and Hiro had probably been tracked, and that the men would certainly be waiting for them outside the vet's office when they left.

She could hear him swallowing, as if digesting all of this information.

"Good," he finally said.

"Good? What could possibly be *good* about anything I just said?" Jet's face flushed with fury. Had Hiro been right?

"I'm sorry, Jet. We should have explained all of this to you sooner, but we couldn't take the risk."

"What are you saying?" she asked, more terrified and angry than she'd ever been.

"Plans changed when your mother passed," he told her gently. "We knew people were after the treasure, but we didn't know who. We were working on that—Satoko, Masakichi, Soji, and me, that is."

"What?" Jet asked, shocked. "You were all in contact?" Outrage coursed through her veins, and it was all she could do not to slam the phone shut.

J-Bird sensed her anger. "Wait! Just barely. While your mother was in New Mexico, her enemies were desperately trying to find her. They seemed to have stepped up their tactics. So we had to change strategies. We were trying to figure out how to draw them out so we could see who we were fighting. But then," his voice quavered, "then your mother got sick…"

"Why didn't you tell me any of this?" she demanded, digging the fingernails of her free hand into her palm as she made a fist.

"I can't explain yet, but I will. I promise. You have to trust me."

Jet grit her teeth. She couldn't afford to make another mistake, and yet, J-Bird was family. If she didn't trust him, who could she trust? "Please don't lie to me, J-Bird," she said, strongly.

"Never," he assured her. "Listen," J-Bird said, "here's what you have to do. You have to get away, but that shouldn't be too hard. They don't want to hurt you now. They just want to chase you until you lead them to the treasure."

Jet gasped. "What do you mean *now*?"

J-Bird sighed. "Steady... I mean you have to let them know that you're coming back to America—to New Mexico."

"And then what?" Jet asked, seething. She definitely didn't trust him anymore. How could she?

"Go to the airport and fly back here. I'll book two seats for you and Hiro for tomorrow night. If you need anything, use the credit card Masakichi gave you."

"Actually," Jet said, hesitating. "They already know where I'm from, so they're probably expecting us to go back..."

"What? How do they know?" J-Bird stammered.

"Because I told them," she said, remembering how she and Takumi had talked about where they'd lived at the ramen shop. Trying to keep her emotions under control, she explained this to J-Bird.

She heard him taking a deep breath. "I'm glad you let me know that. They won't be able to find me right away, but they'll be asking around. It's not as if there are a lot of Japanese people around here."

"That's for sure," Jet said. Still, she didn't regret talking to Takumi. It had been natural, and wonderful. She was happy just thinking back on it. Especially in light of everything else that had happened recently.

"Even so, it should take them a few days to trace Satoko to me. By then you and Hiro will be here, and we'll be ready," J-Bird broke her train of thought.

"Ready for what?"

"Without knowing it, they'll lead us to their headquarters."

Jet swallowed. "Then what?"

"I'm afraid we'll have to take them on there," he said. "And get rid of them, once and for all."

"Get rid of them?" Jet gulped. She didn't like the sound of that. ""J-Bird," she ventured, "who do you think they are?"

"I'm pretty sure it's NLS. Soji sent me a message–"

"Soji!? Is he okay? I mean, do you know where he is?"

"I think they've kidnapped him," J-Bird said solemnly. "He must have sent the message just before they got him."

Jet felt her body deflate. "What are we going to do?"

"Jet!" J-Bird urged, as if he could sense her collapsing through the phone. "Soji thought NLS was behind this. It's what we always suspected. They've been building databases of ancient languages to break codes so they can find hidden treasures all over the world. They've been amassing enormous wealth and power for years. They're nearly unstoppable."

Jet tried to steady herself. "You mean you knew about this all along?" She felt she was falling, crumbling into dust.

"A lot of it, yes," J-Bird admitted.

"Tell me what you know. Now," Jet said in her strongest voice.

Jet could hear J-Bird inhale on the other end of the line. "Years ago, a very greedy, heartless man found out only the Kuroi family women were entrusted with the secret," he began. "All of them were lost fighting to defend the family's treasure. Only Satoko escaped."

Jet sank to her knees. "Oh, god…"

"They were waiting for you to return to Japan. We couldn't let you know too much. If you got captured and knew anything, we'd all be at risk—especially you. If you ever had to face them, your mother wanted you to face them as if you knew nothing–"

"That wouldn't be hard to do," she wailed. "I *don't* know anything!"

"Well, it's not that simple," J-Bird said. "But we can talk about that later. We didn't think they'd come out so strong. Still, it could have been worse."

"How much worse could it be? Ojiisan died. Soji's gone, and…" Jet's voice trailed off.

"I know. It's terrible. But we can still win," he said forcefully. "On our own turf. That's why you must com back."

"How am I going to explain this to Hiro?" Jet bemoaned.

"My father used to say that a coyote who's wandered from its territory loses its power. It's strongest in the place it knows best. So that's our plan. Tell Hiro we're going to let them know you're coming back, have them follow you, and fight them on our own turf. In the meantime, I'll keep researching New Language Systems and try to find out everything I can."

"J-Bird. How do I know I can tr…?" Jet said, shame rising in her throat.

"Jet…" he coughed, avoiding the unformed question. "Soji mentioned Aska. If you fly with her, she'll be quarantined in customs for weeks. She can only skip quarantine if Hiro pretends he's blind, though. She'll have to be his guide dog. So from the moment he gets to the airport until when he gets off, he'll need to wear dark glasses and carry a white stick."

Jet frowned. "Where are we going to get that kind of stuff?"

"Soji gave me an address for a place you can buy just about anything for disguises."

He read it out to her, and she wrote it down.

"Okay. I'll do it," she said.

"Be careful," he told her. "And yes, you can trust me. I would give my life for you, Jet. As I would have for Satoko. I loved her more than anyone in the world."

Jet felt a lump in her throat.

She was about to say goodbye, but remembered one more thing.

"J-Bird. I have to ask you honestly," she paused. "Did you know I'm *kunoichi*?"

"Kuno-what?" he said unconvincingly. His bad acting made Jet laugh despite herself.

"It's okay," she said softly. "I just wish I'd found out I was a princess or something. That would have been so much easier."

"A princess? What a bore!" he said. "Why on earth would you want to sit up in a castle all day, letting the knights have all the fun?"

"You're right, J-Bird." She laughed, relieved to hear he still had a sense of humor.

"That's my girl," he said.

"I love you," she said. She hadn't meant to say this; it just slipped out.

"I love you, too," he said. "And by the way, happy birthday."

"You remembered!"

"Wouldn't forget your birthday for the world," he replied.

"Thank you," she said, and softly closed her phone.

She held onto those three words and all he'd said. She and Hiro were going back to America. America! Her heart pounded. What would happen if their enemies took the bait and followed them back? She shuddered to think of it, but she knew J-Bird was right. They had to rescue Soji. She couldn't let what happened to Ojiisan happen to Soji, too. She had to find the strength to be the *kunoichi* everyone thought she was.

CHAPTER 27

黒い風 *Kuroi Kaze*
Black Wind

Jet went back out into the waiting room. Hiro was taking out two soft dog biscuits from an old-fashioned round glass jar at the reception desk.

"You're going to spoil that dog rotten," she said.

"No," he told her, "I'm going to spoil *someone else's* dog rotten." He flashed the tiny microchip at her before sliding it into the biscuit.

"Our enemies might be masters of *henge*, but we're going to do some *henge* on this signal," he said in *shinobi kotoba* as they made their way back to the waiting room.

Hiro went up to pet a big French bulldog owned by a rich-looking white man with a shaved head and red plastic glasses.

"Can I feed your pup?" Hiro asked.

"Sure. Why not? One more biscuit's not going to do too much damage," the man answered in a British accent and smiled. "She did so well with her shots, after all."

Hiro kept a straight face as he returned to Jet, but when she told him about her conversation, his expression changed.

"We should leave soon," she said, "or else they'll notice that the signal isn't with us. It would be great if they thought they were still tracking us."

Aska's operation was done, so Jet, Hiro, and Aska left the

animal hospital cautiously, following close behind the British man and his dog after he'd settled his bill.

"Let's get into a crowd as soon as possible," Hiro said. "It shouldn't be hard in this neighborhood."

They came to an upscale shopping mall and went through a side door to enter it, ditching the British man.

Jet, Hiro, and Aska hurried through the stylish women in designer clothes and men dressed in Brooks Brothers casual who milled around three floors of designer boutiques and restaurants, laden with shopping bags. They wove their way through families sitting on benches eating ice cream and bentos. Suddenly, Jet felt a surge of power. She turned almost imperceptibly to see a gray-haired Japanese businessman falling into step beside her. He caught her arm, and briefly, their eyes met. Her heart jumped. Had she seen him before?

Suddenly, a black wind swept in front of them, tunneling through the crowd. The man covered his neck with his right arm just as the black wind struck. People in the shopping center turned to watch, some screaming, others calling for the police.

It was Aska. Her fangs clamped down on the man's forearm, but the man didn't release Jet from his grip. She tried to throw him down, slamming her full weight into him in a *shizen ken* move, but he widened his stance. She took advantage of that moment to break from his grip. *His right hand is free*, she thought. *That's not good. Now he can hurt Aska.*

She was right. With a sharp *kiai* cry, he shoved his palm into Aska's ribs. The Akita lifted into the air, but she didn't release her grip. Rather, she growled from the bottom of her throat, sinking her teeth deeper.

Akitas were sometimes used to hunt bears in northern Japan, Jet knew. They could fend off an attack with their sharp claws, but their strong jaws could kill a bear in a single bite. Aska had shown her breeding, and yet, amazingly, the man's face revealed no pain. He must be directing his *ki* to his arm. He grabbed Aska's neck, but Jet executed a *soku gyaku* toe strike, hitting the pressure point hard beneath his shoulder, and he immediately let go of Aska.

In that split second, Jet looked over the crowd to see that Hiro had been fending off another man, throwing coins at his face to slow his approach.

What should I do? Jet's mind raced. She had to act fast.

The rubbernecking crowd was too thick for her and Hiro to run through, but Ojiisan had taught her that a ninja had to take advantage of everything to survive.

What do I have? she considered. In her bag was the silver Colt 38-caliber handgun she'd taken from the man earlier, but it was too dangerous to use in the mall, with all these people around. The thought triggered another idea.

"Everyone get down! That man has a gun!" she shouted, pointing at the gray-haired businessman.

The solid wall of humanity dispersed as people ran for cover or dropped to the ground. The gray-haired businessman finally threw Aska off and leapt toward Jet in a *kosei no kamae* fighting stance, one arm up in front of his body and one arm behind it. But just as quickly, Hiro flicked his coins at him. The man protected his face, but three coins cut into his arm and stuck. He shook his forearm sharply, making no sound, showing no feeling at all.

"Let's go!" Hiro shouted, commanding Aska to leave.

Jet, Aska, and Hiro sprinted through the rotunda and onto the street, but just outside, another man, a strongly-built Japanese fighter, was waiting. He lunged out, slinging Hiro over his shoulder, and ran. Hiro began to kick him with his heels, and Aska sank her teeth into his boot.

When Hiro's attacker saw Jet coming, he threw Hiro down like a sack of potatoes and assumed a fighting stance. She jumped in a *tobi keri*, sending a kick to his cheek, her toe slamming the bone. She leapt again, this time aiming her heel at his neck. Even as he fell back, he twisted to avoid her, striking her leg away. She lost her balance and fell.

Jet tried to get her bearings. Hiro and Aska were fighting one of the men from the mall, but the gray-haired businessman wasn't there yet. When he came back, Jet and Hiro would be outnumbered.

Before she could stand, her opponent caught her right arm between his legs and pulled her down, hooking his legs around her neck.

Get up! You were winning! she told herself.

But he overextended her arm, straining her shoulder, and she bit her lip to block the pain. She reached her free arm to try to break his grip, but couldn't. She gathered strength in her *hara*, working two spheres of energy against each other in swirling circles of *ki*, then swiftly pulled her right arm. But he anticipated her. He held tight and jerked her arm back to his side. Pain shot through her shoulder. Enraged, she bit his leg. He kicked her hard in the neck. Then he released her wrist. His thick hands crushed down on her throat.

This is it... she thought. *Namu Amida Butsu. Namu Amida Butsu. Namu...*

Just as she began to drift from sensation, Aska took a diving leap, sinking her teeth into the man's neck. He let go of Jet and crouched, desperately squeezing the Akita's snout, trying to force her mouth open.

Their other attacker was a wiry fighter with a shaved head and dark clothes. No longer having to fight Aska and Hiro at the same time, he was striking rapidly at her cousin, blows that the boy barely avoided. Jet leapt onto the man's back, her knees aimed at his kidneys. Hiro's *tsumasaki-geri* toe kick caught him in the forehead and sent him tumbling. But he got up, still strong and angry. She rushed and kicked him between the legs with the top of her foot, striking swiftly. He doubled over as she sent a spin kick to his temple. She heard a bone crack. He fell and didn't move, and she stood, stunned, realizing what she'd done.

Aska's bite had felled the other man, and she panted heavily, her whole body moving with her breath.

"Are you okay?" Hiro asked Jet. She was holding her arm. Her shoulder throbbed.

People had cleared from the mall but for a few daring spectators. The gray-haired businessman stepped through the doors. He stopped, looked at the man on the ground, then reached up and peeled his face off. It was Takumi!

A wave of terror, then longing washed over Jet, the two emotions struggling with each other.

Silver flashed toward him as Hiro threw a coin, but he ducked. "Wait, Hiro!" she yelled, then faced Takumi. "What do you want?"

"I've been watching you," he said. "It's true, you have the gift."

"You can't win. It won't happen." As she spoke, she tried to keep her emotions from her face, to hide her hurt and disappointment.

He gently reached forward and touched her shoulder. Her arm pulsed with pain, but the electric current in his body moved into hers again.

"You've dislocated your shoulder," he said. "You need to be careful. Don't let men who are stronger than you get so close to you. They're good, but you're still the better fighter."

"So you're giving me fighting tips now?" She shook her head in disbelief. The nerve!

Aska crouched beside them, growling.

"An impressive creature," he said. "But my boss has his own animal guardian named Inanna. If it came down to both of them…."

"Aska can take her, whoever she is," Hiro said. "We can beat you all!"

"Don't be so sure," Takumi said. "Inanna is a black panther."

"You sound proud of that," Jet spat.

"No. I'm just stating the facts."

"What do you care about the facts?" Jet asked, her voice devoid of emotion. "All you want to do is capture me, right? What are you waiting for? Go ahead."

Again she stretched out her arms in front of her, wrists turned up.

She saw something—regret or anger—flash in his light brown eyes.

"No, not now," he said, shaking his head. "I want to fight when you're at your best."

"You won't get another chance," she stated. "I'm going back to America. This is the last you'll see of me."

His eyes narrowed, as if searching hers for the truth, but Hiro distracted him. "You don't want to fight her because you know you can't win."

"Oh. I can win. And I will when I have to," Takumi said. Then he softened his voice. "But I'd rather you join me."

"And what would that look like?" she asked.

"You hand the treasure over. Your uncle has already joined us. He's in America. We're just waiting for your help, and then we'll all be rich."

"Forget it," she said. "I'd rather fight. Besides, you're lying about Uncle Soji." There was no way he—or she for that matter—would betray her grandfather and her mother.

"So be it," he told her and turned. They watched him walk back into the mall and soon disappear from sight.

Sirens began to blare in the distance, coming closer as Hiro faced her.

"How do you know him?" Hiro asked, distrust in his eyes. She saw the determination in his face, the will to fight and to survive at all costs. He was no longer the boy he used to be.

"I don't know him," she said, instinctively touching her turquoise ring as if it were a worry stone that would calm her mind. "I thought he was someone, but I was wrong."

The sirens grew louder. The two men lay on the ground.

Jet stood above their bodies. She felt sick and helpless.

"What now?" Hiro asked.

A million thoughts raced through Jet's mind. A month ago she'd been a mere girl, but so much had changed. She'd lost two people she loved. She'd trusted a man, even if only briefly, and had been betrayed. And now she'd taken a life. The sound of breaking bone was etched in her memory forever. She'd never be able to erase it.

This must be my karma. But what kind of person would have such karma?

She closed her eyes. Unconsciously, she brought her hands to her throat and felt the locket Soji had given her.

She had the locket. Now she just had to access its power.

She grit her teeth. She had no choice but to focus on the future and forget these men.

"We're going to America," she said, "but first I'm going to get the haircut Soji didn't have the chance to give me. Then we need to turn you into a blind man with a seeing-eye dog."

"*Henge.* I think that's a good idea," he agreed.

"Glad you think so," she said. But she was thinking about deeper change. She'd ended someone's life. Sure, it had been in self-defense but she could never undo this fact. She'd never be the same girl again. She'd never be a girl again. She was a woman. But more than that, she was *kunoichi*. Like her mother.

She said a silent prayer for her mother's spirit, floating somewhere between worlds. It took forty-nine days to reach Nirvana, if that was even where Satoko was going.

"Let's go! Now!" she said, shaking such thoughts from her mind.

Then she turned to Hiro. "I talked to J-Bird. He told me the plan. I was going to tell you, but all hell broke loose."

"I know," Hiro nodded. "I get it. We'll have to disguise ourselves if we want to stay alive."

Part Four

AMERICA

米国

CHAPTER 28

砂漠 *Sabaku*

Desert

J-Bird was waiting for them at the Albuquerque airport when they arrived in the hot thick air. The sky was deepened by shades of orange and red in the big picture windows of the airport as they deplaned. Even beneath the harsh florescent lights, J-Bird's clear coppery brown skin radiated the warmth of a desert sunset. His cheekbones and jaw were strong and firm. Only the long silver-gray hair he kept tied back in a band revealed him to be in his fifties. He wore jeans and a blue work-shirt. It was the same thing he'd worn the night they burned Satoko, the same thing he always wore.

Jet quickened her pace, forgetting Hiro and Aska as she jumped into his arms, crying out with relief.

J-Bird held her tightly. "Jet, hey! I feel like I haven't seen you in ten years!"

"More like a hundred!" she replied.

"I'm so glad you made it home safely. Wait a minute, you got a haircut!"

"Yeah. You like it?" The new cut framed her face, and she shook her head, twirling her short hair like a pinwheel, but her injured shoulder ached and she stopped. She'd also tweezed her eyebrows into a softer arc, applied thick fifties-style eyeliner, powdered her face until it glowed, and put on shiny red lipstick. She wore a sleek miniskirt and patent-leather white boots that reached up to her thighs. That had been her disguise leaving Tokyo, and she felt like a movie star.

All through high school she'd wished she'd had the money to buy clothes like this, and now she had, for a reason her mother might actually have approved of—*henge*. Jet wanted to allow herself this brief pleasure, knowing that she'd soon be dressed to fight in the shadows again.

Hiro approached with Aska on the guide leash, dark glasses hiding his eyes, white cane in hand, tapping the floor.

"Oh, I'm sorry," Jet said, gesturing to her cousin. "This is Hiro. And this is his best friend, Aska."

"Nice to meet you. I'm J-Bird." He held out his hand. "What does Hiro mean?"

"Big-heart man," Hiro answered shyly, shaking J-Bird's hand.

"Well, that's a good name. And she's an Akita, isn't she?"

"Yes, her name's Aska. It means 'flying bird.'"

"Cool name."

"It suits her," Jet said, recalling how Aska had fought on the mountain in Kanabe, jumping and landing so precisely. Her name was perfect. She must have once been an eagle. A fierce, righteous eagle.

"And you pulled off the *henge* well."

"Thank you. But wait," Hiro told J-Bird, pushing the sunglasses to the top of his head. "Please stop there for a moment."

Hiro dropped Aska's leash. As usual, Aska walked around J-Bird, sniffing his feet. Then she returned to sit at Hiro's right.

"Is her ritual over?" J-Bird scratched Aska behind her ears, and she sighed with satisfaction, closing her eyes.

"Yes. Once she smells you, she'll never forget the smell. She remembers everything."

"I see." J-Bird crouched to Aska's eye level and put his nose to her black, wet nose. Aska licked his face with her big tongue.

"She likes you a lot," Hiro said. "She usually doesn't take to people so quickly."

J-Bird nodded pleasantly. "Well then, I'm honored. Anyway, I arranged to get off early from work. Let's go."

He took their bags, led them to the parking lot, and they got into his old blue Ford Falcon. Soon they were on Highway 40, sunshine streaming from the clear desert sky. Jet took a deep breath. Sage and piñon filled her lungs. The smell rejuvenated her, took away the heavy feeling in her heart about what she'd done in Japan and the knowledge that things had not gone the way anyone had expected.

Hiro stuck his head out the window, breathing the hot, dry air, gazing into the huge expanse of sky and earth across the blacktop.

"Hey, Aska! Look at that! Can you believe it's a cactus? It's so big!" He stroked Aska, and she sensed his excitement, her tail thumping against the seat.

J-Bird glanced in the rearview mirror, and Hiro kept his eyes on the side. So far, the coast was clear. Jet wondered how long this lull would last.

The highway stretched on, light brown desert on either side. The cacti stood as tall as people, with thorns as long as chopsticks. There were also small trees that resembled cedar, and little bushes everywhere. Shades of red, brown, and orange striated the craggy mountains.

"I thought the desert would be totally empty," Hiro said, "no trees or grass, maybe only sand. But this is different. I've never seen colors like this in nature before."

"I felt the same way in Japan," Jet admitted. "The mountains were so dense, so mysterious. Almost otherworldly."

Hiro hummed as they made their way down the ribbon of highway. Along the road stood orange-brown adobe structures where people sat outside on blankets, selling their wares.

"Hey! Look at her!" Hiro pointed to a Native woman sitting at a roadside stand, selling jewelry and woven blankets. Three small kids were at her feet. "She looks like a lady in my village. She went to Aomori city everyday to sell vegetables, just like that, on the side of the road. They could be sisters!"

Jet laughed. Hiro stroked Aska's neck, her nose twitching in the air that blew in from the open window. Her whiskers moved as she sniffed the new smells.

Further on, the desert reached to the line of the horizon. It seemed as if the barrier between earth and sky had disappeared. Huge crevice-like valleys appeared like optical illusions. Tall, thousand-year-old trees were scattered amidst the sagebrush.

"This is the land of the Diné," J-Bird told Hiro. "That's what we Navajo call ourselves."

"We'll be home soon," Jet said, keeping her eyes on the long, empty New Mexico highway. How many times had she and Satoko packed up and headed down the road? She recalled the story of how her father had disappeared, apparently owing a lot of people money, and her mom hadn't been able to pay them back.

"If I go to jail, there'll be nobody to take care of you," Satoko had said. "So we have to stay on the road. *Sho ga nai*—it can't be helped."

"Okay," Jet had replied, trying to hide her disappointment.

Satoko had said, "Please try to understand."

Jet had tried, but she couldn't believe there was nothing they could do. She thought her mother was weak, defeated. They'd driven the highways in silence, the heat shimmering off the pavement like phantom smoke, their stomachs as empty as the road.

"Let's stop here," Satoko had said one autumn night, pulling into a dusty truck stop near the Navajo reservation. Jet was two, and they'd been gypsies for years. But they'd never ventured onto a reservation before. That was where they had met J-Bird, cooking over a metal grate, singing as he tended the fire.

"Come on in," he'd said slowly, stirring a thick soup. "Sit down. Have some food."

"Thank you so much!" her mother had said. "The gods must be smiling down on us."

"Indeed," J-Bird had agreed jokingly. Satoko had bowed, holding her hands together in a small steeple at her chest before they sat down to the meal of rice, beans, sautéed zucchini, and tortillas that this kind man had cooked for them.

He let them live on the reservation. Jet grew up there, and grew to understand that they were safe, that a reservation was invisible to all but those who lived on it.

After that, they didn't have to move. But Jet was shy meeting new people, slow to make friends. She stayed on the outside, quietly observing the other kids at school, responding only when she was asked a question.

Likewise, she stopped asking about her father and let J-Bird guide them. But still, something haunted her sleep, a worry, a gnawing sense of absence. All she knew about her father was that he'd been in the military and had left them. She waited for the time when her mother would teach her more about the family she'd left so abruptly when Jet was a baby.

But the time never came.

The sweet smell of juniper wafted through the window, and Jet gazed out at the desert. Though barren, the landscape was beautiful, transformed subtly as the sun shone on the deep earth reds and oranges. Even though the land had been taken from the Native Americans, its spirit, the nature spirit, remained in it. One of her mother's words came back to her: *natsukashii*. It meant a kind of nostalgia. Nostalgia only came from belonging somewhere. Satoko must have felt that she belonged here, in America, in the desert.

Jet felt she belonged here, too. But now there was Kanabe.

Was it possible to belong to more than one place? Or was the truth simpler—that you could inhabit yourself so fully that you belonged everywhere you went, making a home wherever you were?

The sun had begun to set, making Jet realize that time was passing quickly. She was no closer now to finding the treasure than when she'd left America a month ago. Two people she loved were now gone, and Soji was missing. Jet hoped that the coming days would bring her the answers their lives depended on.

CHAPTER 29

隠し砦 *Kakushi Toride*
Hidden Fortress

Cold air drifted from the transparent blue sky, making Hiro shiver.

"It was so hot just an hour ago. Now it's cold, like winter!"

"We're going into the mountains, that's why," Jet told him. "This is where I grew up."

"I didn't know you grew up in the mountains, too."

"Yeah, we have that in common," Jet said, settling into the cracked red leather seat. In the past few days, it seemed Hiro had forgiven her for what happened on the mountain. She was comforted by that, and relieved. They would have to be a strong team to face whatever was next. Jet was sure of it.

Speaking calmly, J-Bird said, "Look behind us carefully. Don't make it obvious. Two cars have been following us for a while."

She and Hiro glanced in the side mirrors. One car, in the right lane behind a big truck, was a shiny black Lincoln Continental. The other was a brown Buick Skylark.

J-Bird sped up. Both cars accelerated.

"Fasten your seat-belts! They're definitely after us," he said and continued to accelerate. Jet felt the gravity pulling at her body. They were going ninety-five miles an hour, but the two cars kept up.

Ahead of them, a big truck with a silver back door was in the middle lane, with more cars on either side. Even though J-Bird was fast approaching, no one changed lanes to let him pass. Clearly, they were together, waiting to surround the Falcon from the front and back. J-Bird was blocked in, unable to make a U-turn because of a concrete barrier in the center of the highway.

"Hold on tight!" he said as they approached the huge back door of the truck at a hundred and twenty miles an hour. The two cars behind them fell back.

"I didn't think this old Falcon had it in her!" he yelled, grinning. He shifted between lanes, going toward the rear of the truck. With a crunch, the left front headlight of the Falcon hit the right tail lamp of the truck, sending it crashing to the center barrier. The impact shook the car, and J-Bird held the wheel tightly to keep from spinning out to the right.

"Jet, hand Hiro the bag under your seat!" he said.

She pulled out the bag. It was heavier than she expected, and she had to drag it out with both hands.

"Throw everything in it out the window!"

When Hiro opened the window, the cold air rushed in. The bag held pyramid-shaped objects made from two nails bent into L-shapes and tied at the middle with wire.

"*Tetsubishi!*" Hiro shouted, dumping the bag's contents into the wind. The sharp metal pieces tumbled along the asphalt, and the cars chasing them spun out, braking hard on flat tires, skidding on their wheel rims, sparks flying from the pavement in the seconds before they crashed into each other.

"The shape is like a pyramid, so a sharpened end always points up no matter which way it lands, sticking into tires or even feet," Hiro explained.

"Satoko taught me how to make them," J-Bird said. "I've had them in the car for about ten years. They were getting rusty!" He wiped the sweat from his forehead, but kept his speed at ninety-five as they flew down the highway, alone now.

Finally, they came to a trailer park at the end of a forest that spread along the north side of Mt. Taylor. They quickly turned in, checking behind them.

"Coast is clear," J-Bird said, pulling in to a forested area where the trailer homes were almost completely hidden by the branches of fat cedar trees that covered the mountain.

"Come on, quick." He ushered them out of the car. From somewhere deep in the forest, the cries of an owl echoed like an ancient clock, keeping time in the darkness.

"It's an owl!" Hiro exclaimed, grabbing Aska's leash and taking his things from the trunk.

"We call her the Night Eagle. In our medicine wheel, she sits in the East, the place of illumination," J-Bird said.

"We have them in our village, too. Cool!" Hiro said, awed as much by J-Bird as by the owl.

"She represents magic and is drawn to others who practice it. She might feel a kinship with you," J-Bird told him. "Or she might be asking you to key into your powers of seeing. She might have a message."

"What kind of message?" Hiro asked.

"If it's for you," J-Bird said, "only you can understand it."

He led them down a small path, passing little trailers lined up next to each other.

"See the outline of the mountain?" He pointed ahead. "*Tsotsil* is our name for it. It's a sacred mountain to the Navajo."

"Why?" Hiro asked, squinting. Darkness had fallen.

"Over a hundred years ago, our tribes were overwhelmed by the army. We were banished from our homes and sent East. But there wasn't much water, and the soil was bad. We couldn't grow anything. All the crops failed. We didn't have enough food or clothes for the harsh winters. After two years, we were allowed to go back home. On the way, we passed Tsotsil, and we knew we were on our way home. Everyone cried with joy."

Hiro nodded. His lip quivered, as if he were fighting back tears.

"The same thing happened to your people, didn't it?" J-Bird added.

"People need a homeland," J-Bird said, looking behind him at Jet and Hiro with warm, soft eyes.

"Ojiisan always said the same thing," Hiro told him. "There's a sacred mountain in my homeland, too. Osore-zan. Everyone goes there when this life is over. Maybe I'll go there too."

"That's a long way away, my boy," J-Bird said.

"Yeah, I'm definitely not ready!" Hiro agreed vehemently.

"But when you are, we'll wave to each other across the ocean."

Hiro smiled. Jet was happy to see him at ease.

They approached J-Bird's trailer. He opened the door, glancing behind them.

"Welcome to the Hidden Fortress," he said. "I hope you don't mind that I live in a trailer."

"No way!" Hiro said enthusiastically. "It's like in the X-Files!"

"Well, I don't have a TV I'm afraid," J-Bird apologized.

"I used to go to the restaurant in town to watch it. We didn't have one either."

"Well then," J-Bird replied, "I hope you'll feel right at home."

CHAPTER 30

過去 *Kako*
The Past

Jet took her bags from her shoulder, wincing. It had been throbbing for days.

"Let me have a look," J-Bird said. She let him feel around the joint.

"You've dislocated it," he told her, "but I can put it back for you. It's going to hurt while I'm doing it, but you'll feel better after. Up for it?"

"I'd do anything to feel better," she said, taking a breath in.

J-Bird stood behind her and folded his right arm into her back, wrapping his left arm around her shoulder. On the count of three he used his full body weight to put the shoulder back into its socket. It snapped back in place.

"Aaaaaargh!" she cried out.

"Sorry about that," he winced.

Jet bent over in pain. Aska crept up to her face and began to lick her cheeks. Finally, Jet stood up and braced herself.

"You're right. It does feel a lot better. Thank you!"

"Let's get some ice on it." J-Bird gave her an icepack, turned on the heater next to the small table and made coffee in an old blue enamel pot. Then he cooked oatmeal. Jet put butter and brown sugar on hers. Hiro found some soy sauce, then cracked a raw egg onto his porridge and mixed it together.

"Yuck!" Jet said.

"Same to you," Hiro retorted. "Americans always make everything so sweet."

J-Bird laughed, studying Hiro's dark skin, eyes, and hair.

"If I didn't know it, I'd think you were one of us, son. You could be Navajo."

Hiro beamed. No one had called him "son" in a very long time.

"Well, the first Japanese and the Native Americans had the same ancestors," Hiro said, smiling.

"Really?" J-Bird said, looking at Hiro's big eyes, with their thick, almond-shaped eyelids.

"Yeah. The first Japanese were part of the ancient Mongolian tribes that lived in Indochina. Before the end of the glacial age, they started to move toward the east. At that time, the Bering Strait was a land bridge. Japan was connected."

"I see." J-Bird poured his coffee, eyebrows raised.

"They separated into two groups. One went south, the other continued east. The group that went south became the first indigenous Japanese. The other went to America and became the Native Americans. Ojiisan told me that Japanese and Native Americans still have the same type of immunities."

"Really?" J-Bird raised his eyebrows. "I'm impressed. You sure know a lot for a boy your age, don't you?"

"Not really," Hiro said, flashing a shy grin. "Ojiisan taught me everything I know. And I like to read. Especially history."

"That's special enough these days." J-Bird dropped his gaze to his hands, which were folded in his lap. He traced the lines of his left palm with his thumb.

Jet sat at the table. She knew what this gesture meant. It was a kind of signal that he was collecting his thoughts before he spoke. It was time to sit quietly and listen.

"I'm glad you both made it back safely," he said. "There are some things you need to know, and now's as good a time as any to tell you."

Jet put her spoon down. She had always counted on J-Bird to guide her, and she was relieved that he wouldn't let her and Hiro down.

"Hiro, you might not know it, but I served in Vietnam. Jet's father Jack was there, too."

Hiro nodded.

"I never knew him," J-Bird said. "When the war ended, I returned to the reservation, hoping for the best. But nothing had changed. It was the same miserable place I'd left. I was pretty beaten down. I lost hope. So I started drinking. I drank every day straight for years. Then one day, this incredible woman showed up. I thought God had sent me an angel. She was so kind, so gentle. And very, very hungry."

"My mom!" Jet laughed.

"You got that. And she was with this beautiful little girl." J-Bird smiled, remembering.

"Jet!" Hiro exclaimed.

"Right. Jet was about two. I told Satoko they could stay on the reservation until she found a job. Well, she found a job that day and the month turned into many years," he said, chuckling.

Jet laughed, and for a moment she forgot all that had happened in Japan.

"I stopped drinking and started to put my life back together," J-Bird looked at Jet, and she returned his gaze, staring at his watery eyes that seemed to absorb everything.

"Anyway, I never asked her much about your father," J-Bird said, "but just before Satoko died, she told me what she thought I should know."

Jet listened intently.

"In Vietnam, your father was known as the Rambler. He liked to wander, which is a good thing, as you have no choice but to keep moving on the battlefield. But sometime during his tour, he went AWOL. He was a very good soldier, but he just reached a point where he didn't want to fight anymore. He walked off into the jungle. Disappeared."

"Where did he go?" Hiro asked.

"No one knows. He could have fallen sick, or gotten killed, but he survived. He was very strong."

Jet frowned. She wasn't impressed. Her father might have had great survival skills, but he hadn't been very generous in sharing them with his family. He'd left when she was a baby, after all. Where was the virtue in that?

"He made it out of the jungle," J-Bird continued, "but had nowhere to go. And since he'd gone AWOL, he couldn't get an honorable discharge. He was wanted by the FBI, so he changed his name and went into hiding. The only work he could get was as a mercenary."

"A mercy-mary?" Hiro repeated the strange words.

Jet laughed despite herself. J-Bird shot her a sideways glance.

"Mercenary—a soldier for hire. Corporations, governments, the military, even the CIA hire them," he explained.

Hiro took out a piece of paper and wrote the word down.

"Anyway," J-Bird continued, "he did that work for a few years, and eventually wound up in the Japanese countryside, working on a mission with some other combat vets who could navigate jungles. They were looking for some kind of treasure."

Hiro almost jumped out of his seat. "Was he after our family treasure?"

J-Bird looked over at Jet soberly. "Yes, I think he was. He must have been following the Kuroi family to get information about the whereabouts. But then he met your mom on the mountain. She was out picking mushrooms."

Jet gasped. Ojiisan had said that Satoko was a good hunter of *nameko*.

"He almost attacked her. But then she looked up, and well," J-Bird told her, "they fell in love pretty much on the spot."

Jet's mouth fell open. Was that what her mother had meant when she'd said, *Don't let yourself fall—like me*?

"And then what happened?" Hiro leaned forward.

"Well, your Ojiisan would have been furious if he found out. And Jack's boss would have killed him, so he and Satoko met secretly in Sendai, where she worked at a restaurant."

"What happened next?" Jet prompted.

"Well your mom got pregnant, and your dad started to think about the baby. You." He looked at Jet with a gaze full of quiet insight, the kind of understanding that only someone who has accepted his fate could have.

Jet looked down. She'd never had much goodwill towards the man who had abandoned her, and it was hard to start now.

"Anyway," J-Bird cleared his throat, "Jack decided to quit the operation, move in with your mom, and work the land, growing buckwheat. The problem was he knew too much, and his boss didn't want that information to get out. And he didn't trust your dad to keep quiet."

"Why not?" Jet asked, biting her lip.

"In that line of work, you trust someone, you wind up six feet under. And like I said, your dad was a strong soldier."

"What happened then?" Hiro asked.

"Sure enough, Kanabe was attacked that winter."

"Who attacked it? The people working for my father's ex-boss?" Jet asked.

"Seems so, but they made a mistake. They thought it would be easy to steal a treasure from a mountain village, but they overlooked two things. One is that the Kuroi family are descendants of ninja."

"And the other?" Hiro asked, leaning forward in his swivel chair.

"Snow. They didn't know the power of snow in Northern Japan. Even though they were well armed, they didn't know how to fight in snow well."

"But the villagers did!" Hiro added proudly.

"Right." J-Bird closed his eyes. "Your grandmother Momoko died, and Masakichi was heartbroken. So was Satoko. She believed it was all her fault."

"How horrible," Jet said. The image of Ojiisan cooking dinner in Kanabe flashed in her mind. She couldn't believe how much he'd suffered, how many of his loved ones he'd lost. What treasure was worth that much?

"Most of the attackers died, too," Hiro said quickly, swinging his feet under the table nervously. "Ojiisan told me about that battle. The village fought hard."

"I wish none of this had ever happened," she said.

"Jet, listen to me," J-Bird said resolutely. "You can't help who you fall in love with. Satoko fell in love with your father, he fell in love with her. If he'd known what would happen to Kanabe, he wouldn't have stayed with her, no matter how much he loved her. I'm sure of that."

"I don't know," Jet said, trying to quell the bitterness in her heart, and the fear that she was more like her mother than she'd ever known.

"Why didn't you tell me all this before?"

"Could you imagine knowing all of this when you met Ojiisan? Would you have gone to Japan if you'd known?"

Jet took a spoonful of oatmeal, hoping the warmth and sweetness of the maple syrup would comfort her.

"You're right," she said. "I might not have."

After all, she'd gone back because she'd promised Satoko, and it had seemed important. But now she wondered... Had her mother kept so many secrets because she'd been afraid Jet would reveal them, endangering them all?

"Your dad was trying to protect Satoko. That's why they came to America," J-Bird said, finally.

"It was his idea?" Jet asked, astounded. "All this time, I thought Ojiisan was against my mom's marriage! But he wasn't, was he?"

"Well, he was... At first. But then he saw how hard Jack defended the village against his own people to protect Kanabe. Masakichi wanted to save what was left of the family. Jack did, too. That was *you*. You were born in July of that year.

"After that, your mom made three decisions. The first was to protect her daughter. The second was to avenge the attack."

"And the third?" Hiro asked.

"The third was to keep the Kuroi family treasure away from them at all costs. Jet's father agreed. So they went underground in America. They lived for a year under different names, but your father realized they were being followed."

J-Bird hesitated. "By then, they were tired of running."

Jet sighed. She understood the feeling of being on the run all too well.

"So what did they do then?" she asked.

"They decided to meet their fate head-on. Your mom and dad wanted to get to the source. You see, when Jack worked in the field, he'd been hired by a secret agent, so he never knew the identity of his real boss. But he made up his mind to find out. Jack began doing research, going undercover. He was sure he'd found out who was after them, but one day in February he disappeared. He was almost certainly... J-Bird stopped, unable to say the word.

"Killed?" Jet asked, swallowing hard.

J-Bird looked down, nodding.

Jet didn't know what to say. All her life she'd assumed that her father had left them because he didn't want to be with them. Now there was more to the story. He had left to protect them. She had a hard time accepting this.

"Jack might have made a lot of mistakes," J-Bird told her, "but he was only human. I believe he loved your mom, and she loved him. And I know he loved you, too."

Jet's eyes began to water. "Thanks for saying that," she said, swallowing hard. She finally understood the dark cloud that hung over her mother's life. And hers.

J-Bird looked down at his hands. "There's more," he said. "You see, your mother and I avenged the deaths of Jack and the Kanabe villagers."

Jet felt the hair on the back of her neck stand up.

"Avenged? How?" she asked, not sure if she really wanted to know.

"We used the information that Jack had gathered to track down a man named Harter, a treasure collector and smuggler who ran a ring of mercenaries. We did it because Satoko wanted a normal life for you. She thought if he were gone, it would finally be possible."

Jet swallowed, choosing her words. "So if Harter is dead, who's after us now?"

J-Bird glanced from Hiro to Jet. "His son. We never knew he had one. He runs a military technology company..."

"NLS! New Language Systems," Hiro exclaimed, jumping up from his chair.

"Right," J-Bird said, "and he vowed not only to get revenge but to find the treasure once and for all. He'll stop at nothing."

"Uncle Soji told us about them," Hiro said. "He's been researching them for years, trying to figure out what they're up to."

"Yes. And even though Satoko took Harter out, she never went back to Japan because there were reports of people spying on Kanabe. She knew they were still searching for the treasure, but she didn't want to bring any more trouble to the village."

"So what changed?" Jet asked, holding her breath.

"I think you know by now that only the Kuroi family women knew the location of the treasure, and she believed that the secret was safer here. But then she got sick, and she knew she didn't have much time left. So she made a plan. She decided to send you back to Japan to draw them out. She hoped to end things once and for all."

Jet closed her eyes, feeling the weight of all she was learning. Only *she* could avenge her entire family and set things right. She was their last chance. If they didn't succeed, the village of Kanabe and the history of her people would vanish.

Jet shook in anguish. It was too much to bear.

J-Bird steadied her with a hand on her shoulder.

"Jet, your mother made a promise you would never have to fear for your life the way she'd feared for hers. She loved you more than she loved herself. That's why she trained you so hard. She knew that only by learning where you came from could you go safely into your future."

Jet shook her head. "That's what the *itako*—female shaman— said on Osore-zan, too. But maybe I would have been more at peace if I had known the truth from the beginning."

"I know you think that now, but if she *had* told you, what would you have done?" J-Bird's eyes locked on hers.

Jet bit her lip. "I don't know. But that was my choice to make. I had a right to know!"

"Listen," he said slowly. "You're right. But just imagine if she'd told you about the treasure. Wouldn't you have run away to try to find it?"

"Who knows?" Jet shrugged.

J-Bird laid a hand on her shoulder. "Well, *I* know," he said. "I know you, and I can tell you that you were safer not knowing. If you were captured and knew more than you already do, it would have put everyone at risk. That's a chance we couldn't afford to take," J-Bird insisted.

"If there really is a treasure, why didn't Mom claim it? We were so poor. You know that, J-Bird!" Jet sighed.

"The Kuroi family treasure exists. It *is* real, and it is very well hidden," he said emphatically.

"So well hidden that no one can find it!" Jet exclaimed.

"Exactly. Only the Kuroi family women knew where it was and why it's important."

"Great. There's just one problem. They're all gone," Jet said, dejected.

"Not all of them," Hiro said, looking at her meaningfully.

Jet brushed him off. "I didn't even know the treasure existed until last month. How can I know where it's hidden?" She looked intently at J-Bird. "Well?"

J-Bird didn't answer. He just looked at her intently before speaking. "I know it sounds backwards, but you—you had to shine light on your shadow self to let it emerge. You had to uncover your warrior nature so that someday you—and the Kuroi clan—could live a peaceful life."

"I really wish people would stop saying things like that," Jet said. "It makes no sense at all."

"Not now. But it will later," J-Bird promised.

Jet closed her eyes and sighed. *Why is my life so strange?*

"You've done everything your mother had hoped you would. I know it's been treacherous, and dangerous. But here we are. And I know your mother—and father—would be very proud of you," he said. "I know I am."

Jet turned away. She didn't know how much more of this cat and mouse game she could take. She hoped it would end soon.

CHAPTER 31

箱舟 *Hakobune*
The Ark

Hiro pushed his oatmeal around in his bowl, puzzling over what he'd learned. "Why does NLS want the treasure so badly? It it that valuable?" he asked.

"I've been gathering information," J-Bird said. "New Language Systems is a lot more dangerous than their name suggests. They're interested in archaeology, but their main involvement is with the US military."

"How, exactly?" Hiro wondered.

"Well, I asked a few of my old army pals, who said the things NLS does are incredibly advanced. For example, the military used to need special computers to launch interceptor missiles at incoming enemy missiles. But then NLS created a high-tech laptop that could accurately calculate the route of a missile. Things like that. There's only one big problem."

"What's that?" Jet asked.

"Their products are so innovative that they've monopolized the field. They have no competition at all. Also, if they used military technology for private purposes, it could be very dangerous."

"I still don't understand why they would want Jesus's *nodobotoke*," she said.

"*Nodo* what?" J-Bird asked.

"Adam's apple," Hiro told him. "It's 'Buddha bone' in Japanese."

J-Bird shook his head, considering the oddity of it all. "A bone named after the apple that led to the fall from grace in the Garden of Eden. And it's called the Buddha bone, though it belonged to Jesus. How strange can you get…?"

Hiro and Jet smiled, but J-Bird grew serious.

"Anyway, NLS's CEO, Davison Harter, inherited many obsessions from his father, who made his fortune smuggling artifacts. Finding Jesus' bone was Harter's holy grail, so maybe he thinks the Kuroi family treasure is connected to that. There's a special division at NLS called Enki Systems dealing solely with artifacts. Everything at Enki is shrouded in secrecy. Except asking for money," J-Bird said, his brow wrinkling in distaste.

"So he's a good businessman," Jet said.

"He is, but he's also a wild card. He believes in the occult and makes decisions based on astrology, and will use any means possible to get what he's after. Five years ago, he led the excavation of an ark in Iran. The project was the subject of great controversy, and didn't make him any friends in the field."

"Did you say ark? Like Noah's ark?" Jet asked.

"Well, yeah. Apparently, this one predates that even. The story of an ark was inscribed on a stone tablet that predates *The Book of Genesis.*"

"How do you know all this?" Jet asked, impressed.

"Actually your mother researched it all," he replied.

"Mom? What else did she learn?"

J-Bird stroked his chin. "Well, apparently, in the *Gilgamesh Epic*, there's a story of a man who built an ark to escape the floods. The *Gilgamesh* tablets were found in the mid-nineteenth century and were a huge sensation in Europe. People became interested in Mesopotamian civilization again, so archeologists started to dig again."

"Did they find anything?" Hiro asked.

J-Bird nodded. "Yes. Evidence of a flood was found in the layers of ruins, and this sparked great interest worldwide. When Harter's researchers snuck into Iran, they looked for the ark. But the Iranian police discovered Harter's team, and believe it or not, these so-called 'researchers' were armed and dangerous! The Iranian government complained to American about the incident, but it was covered up."

"Why?" Hiro asked.

"No one wanted news of an archeological find to spread. If a rumor like that got out, can you imagine how many Christians would have tried to get into Iran? Can you imagine? The fundamentalists would not have been too happy."

Jet looked down, troubled. "Wait a minute. Even if the Kuroi family treasure *was* Jesus' bone, how could anyone prove it?"

J-Bird flashed a fleeting smile. "It would be very difficult, because, according to Christianity, Jesus ascended to heaven, so there's nothing left of him on earth."

"Yeah," Hiro concurred. "And if Jesus' bone is around somewhere, it would prove that the events in the Bible aren't accurate."

"And that would totally go against Christianity," Jet said vigorously as understanding dawned on her, too.

"But that might be why Harter would want the bone—to upset Christian society!" Hiro exclaimed.

"Right!" Jet added. "Someone who wants ultimate power wants to control the spread of religion, too."

"Like Japan tried to suppress Christianity in Nagasaki a few hundred years ago," Hiro said excitedly.

J-Bird pushed his hand down, as if tamping down the air. "Okay. Enough speculation for now. We can't worry too much about what their motives are. Your mother was the only person left who knew what the treasure was. She guarded the knowledge very carefully, though, and made a complicated plan. That's what we've all been trying to figure out."

Hiro agreed. "We all have parts in finding it, don't we?"

J-Bird put his hand on Hiro's shoulder. "Yes. And Satoko set it up so that no one of us individually could know the whole plan. We're just supposed to carry out our individual parts, and if we do—if we trust her and do what we're supposed to—we'll find the treasure and be able to protect it for future generations."

Jet's hand instinctively went to the locket at her neck. She closed her eyes and tried to connect to its power. Considering the debacle on the mountain and all that had happened since then, she couldn't help but concede that she had failed her mission.

"J-Bird, I let Mom down," she groaned.

"How is that?" J-Bird asked, putting a hand on her shoulder. "You promised her you'd return to Kanabe and meet your grandfather. You did."

"Yeah, but I came back to America without the treasure!" she said, dejected.

"No," J-Bird told her. "That was part of the plan. Your mother was smarter than we'll ever know."

"But how can I succeed at this when no one else has been able to?" she asked, aloud.

"It's your destiny," J-Bird said, softly. "It can only unfold."

Hiro chewed his lip. "Soji's being held captive at the NLS compound, and us coming back to help save him, was that all part of Aunt Satoko's plan, too?" he asked.

J-Bird nodded. "Uh huh. You've drawn out the enemy without even realizing it. That was also part of Satoko's plan."

Confusion shadowed Jet's face as she thought of one thing that hadn't gone according to plan. She'd faced the dark leader her mother had warned her about, and she'd let herself fall. Should she tell J-Bird about it?

Jet kept her fingers on the locket. With surprise, she realized that the turquoise ring was touching the sacred amulet from her ancestral homeland. Jet took a deep breath in, feeling a subtle melding of worlds. She decided not to say anything yet. There was too much at stake.

"Here's the next part of the plan," J-Bird said, breaking her train of thought. "Your mother left something for you. I guess we could call it another kind of ark."

"An ark?" Jet asked, curious.

J-Bird knelt and reached under a bench covered by an old Navajo blanket. He pulled out a dusty wooden chest. Jet took a step back.

"Is that the family treasure?" Hiro's eyes lit up.

J-Bird smiled. "In a way, yes. I guess you could say that!"

Jet knew instinctively what it was. She remembered seeing this mystery box years ago, as toddler. She blew a plume of dust from the lid and opened it. Inside was a black cloth for disguise and beneath that, her mother's weapons.

"Help me with these," she told Hiro. "Remind me of their names."

"Let's see," he said gleefully, reaching into the cache. "Two bamboo *fukiya* blowguns, five *shuriken* throwing stars, a *shinobi gatana*…"

"Ninja sword?" she asked, excitement flooding her veins.

"Small for better concealment," he replied.

One after another, he unloaded the stockpile, arms moving like a pinwheel as he fished into the trunk's depths and uncovered more surprises.

"*Shinobi-zue* staff, *tessen* iron fan, *kyoketsu shoge* chains and a set each of *shuko* and *ashiko* bands. Cool!" He carefully attached a set of iron bands around his feet, then another set around his hands. Sharp metal prongs jutted out from each band. The bands, whose spikes were used for climbing walls and for defense, looked truly fierce.

He curled his hand like a cat's paw and swiped the air in front of them. Aska jumped up and barked.

"Not so fast. I've got this," Jet said, flicking the *tessen* iron fan open in front of her, instantly deflecting his attack. The two metals clashed with a screeching sound.

Jet looked up at J-Bird. It was quite the stash.

"You forgot one thing," J-Bird said, taking a large white net from the bottom of the box.

"What's that?" Jet asked Hiro, shaking it out.

"It's a fish net," Hiro said without hesitation.

"A net?" Jet laughed. "What's that for?"

"For *toami no jutsu*. To reel in your catch," Hiro said.

"Great. Other girls get bridal trousseaus. I get a ninja toolbox!" She humphed.

"Sounds like Satoko." J-Bird laughed.

"All you need is the groom!" Hiro teased.

"Who needs that when I have all these great weapons?" she said, hitting her cousin playfully.

There was one more thing in the box. A diamond-studded *kanzashi*. Beautiful, and potentially lethal. Jet held it in her palm, marveling as it shimmered in the half-light of the trailer's dim camping lanterns. She twirled her long hair into a bun and stuck the *kanzashi* ornament in her hair.

"Thank you," Jet said, looking warmly at J-Bird.

"It suits you," he replied.

"You kids decide who gets what. I'll take what you can't carry. Meanwhile, you should sleep for an hour. That's all we can risk." He brought out blankets and spread them out on the banquettes on either side of the folding table. Then he lit a candle on the stove.

"Go on, now. Hit the sack! I'll keep watch outside."

He propped up a few pillows at their heads, then said goodnight. Hiro curled up in a sleeping bag with Aska at his feet.

Just before J-Bird went outside, he knelt down and touched Jet's shoulder. "Try to sleep, and not to think too much about everything I've said. You're going to have to be ready for anything."

"*Hai!*" she said as she lay down.

Aska talked in little half-barks as she dreamed. Jet couldn't sleep.

In the flickering candlelight, she pictured her mother driving in the desert, heading toward the horizon, sun streaming into her eyes. The orange glow of the sun in Jet's memory melted into the yellow flicker of the flame. Jet longed for a chance to speak to Satoko again, to thank her and tell her she loved her.

She protected me, gave me all her love and learning, and I didn't know the extent of her sacrifice.

She tried to conjure an image of her father. What did he look like? Speak like? Smell like? She wanted to thank him, too, and apologize for thinking he didn't love her.

An uneasy feeling came over her. After all they'd gone through, she wasn't sure she wanted to find the Kuroi family treasure. It had brought so much hardship to everyone. If she had the treasure, wouldn't her life be an endless struggle to protect it, like her mother's had been to hide it? And wouldn't the cycle continue then, as it had for centuries?

Jet forced down the doubts that roiled within her. She had to break through her doubts and fears. If she really was *kunoichi*, she'd use all her powers to find a way.

CHAPTER 32

迂直の計 *Uchoku no Kei*
The Strategy of Going Around to Go Straight

The night was not as cold as Takumi expected. He was lying on his stomach, hiding beneath ferns, gazing into the dense fog covering the forest.

His mission should have been over by now. He had given Jet chance after chance, and hadn't been able to hand her over to Matsumura and extricate himself from the whole thing. Now he was even more enmeshed in Matsumura's plan, overseeing operations at Harter's villa. And his feelings for Jet tore at his insides like a claw.

At Kanabe, the men he'd led hadn't followed his orders. They'd thought he was too young and that they knew better. As a result the old man had taken them out. In the city, Hiro, Jet, and the dog had brought down his best fighters, making it look easy. Still, he felt he could have prevented this. It was inevitable that he would catch her and hand her over, and each day he hesitated to do so further tarnished his reputation.

Just yesterday, he'd stood in front of Matsumura and the American named Harter—that overwrought man with his even more overwrought pet, a panther tethered to a golden chain—and admitted that he'd failed.

"I did suggest more training for the men," he said.

Harter was furious. "Regardless of the reasons, failure is failure. Even with more men and better equipment, you didn't capture the girl. There's no excuse."

At the show of his master's displeasure, the panther growled. Harter, enthralled with the animal's aggression, rewarded the panther's bloodlust by stroking it between the ears and promising it a steak.

Takumi could barely contain his disgust. He felt disdain for the panther. The sleekest of natural predators, one of the most graceful and powerful rulers of the animal kingdom, had let itself be tamed so thoroughly, and for what—the promise of a few cheap steaks delievered to its golden cage daily? And yet, somehow he recognized himself in the beast's servitude.

How different am I from that animal?

"Are you with me?" Harter asked, exasperated.

"Yes, sir," he said dryly.

"I've made my best effort to stop the Japanese police from investigating the trouble you made in the north," Matsumura said between clenched teeth. "And that wasn't easy. I need you to capture the girl immediately!"

"Yes sir. I'll take care of it." Takumi had bowed and left the room.

"You'd better, boy. It's your last chance," Harter had called out haughtily.

Takumi grimaced, touching the wound on his right forearm. The Tohoku boy must have had incredibly good training to throw coins like that. Takumi shook his head in admiration. He'd also been trained to throw coins. It was easy to fight with *shuriken*—throwing stars or spheres—but you had to concentrate the body's *ki* into the fingertips to turn a mere coin into a weapon. To learn that, you had to throw coins hundreds, thousands of times at tree trunks as practice. Yes, the boy's grandfather had taught him well. It was a shame that the old man had to die.

In fact, they could have spared his life, but Takumi's men didn't know how to fight in the heat of the moment. He had seen the whole thing from the ridge, watching with disgust. That old man had been worth a thousand of Harter's footsoldiers. As he'd fallen into the ravine, Takumi had thought he'd heard him chanting *Namu Amida Butsu*. Did he go to Nirvana? To Heaven? Did one have to leave this world in order to find peace? And was there really another world to go to?

It would be easy to walk away, Takumi had thought. Well, not easy, but not impossible. He could call the whole thing off and take Jet with him. But where would they go, and would she even forgive him? She must hate him with every drop of blood in her body.

He pushed up the sleeve of his black shirt to look at his watch. Twelve-fifteen.

He thought of the men injured in the car chase. He admired Jet and the boy for their ingenuity, throwing that bag of tricks at them. He couldn't have done better.

Although he'd commanded his warriors to catch them, his main purpose was to make them agitated, tire them out. He knew they would escape, but they would be confused and spent. He'd always been a believer in the principles laid out hundreds of years ago by Sun Tzu in the *Art of War*, and he'd employed the strategy of *uchoku no kei*.

U meant the roundabout way, *choku* meant directness, and *kei* meant strategy. You couldn't always win a battle by attack. You had to use a combination of action and inaction, throwing the enemy off-guard psychologically as well as physically.

A real ninja backed his target into a corner using various strategies before even considering drawing a weapon. The true skill was deciding which strategy and scheme to employ, thus avoiding having to do battle at all. Having a back-up plan was also necessary. And a back-up to the back-up.

Jet is an amazing warrior, he thought involuntarily. When Matsumura had approached him about this mission, Takumi hadn't known the particulars. It was the money that attracted him. Too much to turn down for what he thought would be an easy take.

Then he'd met Jet. She was the only girl he'd ever felt would understand him. They were like the same spirit in two different bodies. He swallowed hard. He knew how to cut off his emotions. That was second nature in his vocation. But he'd never really met anyone who came close to testing him like this. Cutting out his feelings for her was like ripping out his own heart.

He watched as the forest settled into even deeper darkness.

I'm so tired of this, he thought.

He tore off a fern leaf and put it in his mouth. The first time he'd gone to Japan, he'd visited his father's ancestral village in Aomori. But he hadn't found the rich land surrounded by nature that his father had told him about. Instead, he'd found a decrepit mountain ghost-village. If the land had been fertile, his father wouldn't have left for Brazil. Takumi had looked on the village from the top of the cliff: a cluster of wooden houses with the roofs caved in, overgrown with weeds and grass. So this was his promised land.

The bitter taste of the fern leaf spread in his mouth.

He'd often wondered what his life would look like if he'd stayed in the jungle and worked coffee, marrying an Indio woman and having a kid or two. Would he accept that life as his father had, working from sunrise to sunset just for the day's meal, reminiscing about some ancestral village and believing in a paradise after death that would purify his hardened heart?

More myth. More smoke and mirrors. Everything was ninja, indeed. Even that.

"What are you laughing at?" one of his comrades asked, a tall blond soldier-for-hire named Rossi.

Takumi hadn't realized he was laughing. "Nothing," he said.

"Well, stop it. When a guy like you laughs, something bad is going to happen."

Takumi laughed again, loud enough this time to hear it himself. He swallowed the bitter leaf. An owl cried three times in the forest. Takumi stood and blinked his flashlight rapidly, throwing its code into the forest. A few shadows stood from the darkness and set out with him. He ran so fast he almost flew through the thick white mist. There was no time to think about the past, or the future. He had to be in the moment.

The chase was back on.

CHAPTER 33

危機 *Kiki*
Facing Death

"We need to find their headquarters," J-Bird said, spreading a map of Harter's compound out on the fold-out table, pointing to a large building in the center. "One of us needs to get inside."

"How?" Jet asked, looking down at the map. She was still curled up in the blankets, though she hadn't slept at all.

Hiro was looking at J-Bird, eyes still, expression slightly concerned yet calm. "Oh... I get it," he whispered. "One of us needs to get caught. That's it, right?"

J-Bird nodded.

"And it can't be Jet," Hiro realized, "because she's too important."

Again J-Bird nodded.

"I'm in!" Hiro exclaimed.

"You don't have to do it," J-Bird said kindly.

"I know," Hiro said, chest lifted, "but I want to."

J-Bird smiled proudly. "Good. I've done some research. The easiest thing would be to put a tracking chip on you, but..."

"No!" Jet said. "What if they hurt him? There has to be another way."

"That's not going to happen. He's more useful to them as a hostage," J-Bird replied.

"I'll be fine, and we can't wait much longer. They're getting ready to attack."

"Hiro's right," J-Bird said. "They're looking for us, probably already know where we are. If they get one of us, they'll think they've got the advantage and that we're on the run. We can make a surprise attack as soon as we figure out where they are."

Jet shook her head, furious. "No way, J-Bird. He's just a kid!"

Hiro stomped the floor. "No, I'm not! I'm a ninja. And I'm not afraid."

"I know, but…" Jet looked over at Hiro with compassion. He *was* brave. *Much braver than me*, she thought.

Hiro was determined. "Ninjas have to take risks, and sometimes we win by looking as if we've lost," he said.

Jet flushed, recalling her own fear on the mountain. She knew how willful Hiro was, and that he'd rather die trying than give up after having come this far.

"Okay. Do your stuff, J-Bird." Jet said.

"Yessss!" Hiro pumped his fist into the air.

Jet was thinking what an amazing man Hiro was going to be some day. He'd grown up on the mountain, learned English, mastered *taijutsu*, and taken care of his grandfather and the akita. He never complained or demanded anything. And now he was sacrificing himself for them. Jet felt proud that she could call him family. She hoped he'd feel the same way about her some day.

J-Bird had a GPS microchip similar to the one used on Aska. The plan was this: Hiro would swallow it just before leaving. As long as it was in his stomach long enough for him to be taken to Harter's headquarters, he'd be easy to track down.

While J-Bird tested the chip transmitter and receiver, Hiro sat with Aska and read in the candlelight. Jet joined him.

"What's the book?" she asked.

"The *Epic of Gilgamesh*. J-Bird had it on his shelf. It was your mother's copy. J-Bird said Harter was obsessed with it. I figured I'd be better prepared if I read it."

Jet admired Hiro's discipline and clarity of mind.

"Come here," he said, patting the pillow next to him.

"Sorry, Aska. You can trade places with Jet," he said as the dog bounded off. Jet scooted over to him. He opened the book, a page spread on each of their laps.

> *Gilgamesh whither runnest thou?*
> *The life which thou seekest thou wilt not find;*
> *For when the gods created mankind,*
> *They allotted death to mankind.*

Gilgamesh had been half-god and half-human, but hadn't been able to save the life of his best friend Enkidu, who'd died after the angry goddess Ishtar cast a curse down upon the earth.

"Enkidu!" Jet exclaimed, recognition washing over her. "You mean like Harter's Enki division?"

"Exactly!" Hiro nodded, eyes wide with excitement.

They read on, learning that the powerful grass Gilgamesh found after an impossible quest—the grass that could have made Enkidu immortal—was eaten by a snake. Gilgamesh was overcome by grief. Even a hero who triumphed over the forest and its dragons, who killed the heavenly bull Ishtar sent to wreak havoc on earth—even one such as he couldn't triumph over his fate.

Jet understood his anguish, but she also understood the force of Ishtar, the feminine embodiment of power and grace.

"Why was Ishtar angry?" Hiro asked.

"Ishtar wanted Gilgamesh to be her partner, but he rejected her," Jet said, reading.

She continued to read aloud. Ishtar was the embodiment of the sacred feminine worshipped for centuries as the leader of the Venus Path. Thought to be the original Aphrodite, Ishtar was the name Assyrians and Babylonians gave her. In ancient Sumerian, it was Inanna.

"Inanna!" Hiro shouted. "Isn't that what that guy said about the panther?"

"Yeah. Wait. What?" Jet murmured, stunned. Did Hiro know about Takumi?

"That guy with brown eyes. I'm pretty sure he said the name of his boss's panther was Inanna!"

"Yes he did, didn't he?" She stammered.

"So the question is, why would Harter name his panther Inanna?" Hiro frowned.

Jet thought fast. "Gilgamesh is about power and the quest for immortality. The quest to overcome death. Maybe he wants that for himself. Doesn't everyone?"

"No," Hiro shook his head in disagreement, looking intently at Jet. "Our people wanted to secure the future for their society, not for individual gain. And they lived *with* nature, not against it. That's what the sacred feminine is—mother earth."

"Wait a minute," Jet remarked, suddenly recalling the *itako's* words on Osore-zan. It felt like years ago, but the *itako's* words rang loud and clear in her head. Could this be what the shaman meant about serving nature?

Hiro spoke louder, confidence rising in his voice. "Of course, there were conflicts, but the tribe worked together. They understood they didn't *inherit* the earth from their ancestors, but rather that they *borrowed* it from their grandchildren. The *Wa* never understood that. They just use and use until they use things up."

Jet nodded, thinking of the people in Japan who'd wanted to use the mountain for a trash dump. She thought of the people in America who'd taken the land from J-Bird's tribe, depleting the resources until there was nothing left.

It was time to change course. Maybe past time. Was it already too late?

J-Bird had told her that their brothers the Hopi had a name for this lack of harmony: *Koyanisquatsi*. Life out of balance. He'd said this about where they lived in the Southwest, too: *The white man wanted more and more. First, they wanted the land to harvest the crops for themselves. Then, they wanted more land for crops to sell to others. Then they wanted even more land to raise cows. In the end, they wanted all the land—even the desert—until there was none left.* Jet had always wondered how people could be so greedy.

She looked over at Hiro, concern etched on her face.

Jet felt that now, the earth was shouting in protest—floods, earthquakes, tsunamis, drought. Mother earth had had enough abuse.

Hiro closed the book, handed it to Jet, and ran his hand along Aska's fur. They sat in silence for a while. Finally, Aska stirred, nudging her nose into Hiro's chest.

"Anyway, I'm worried about leaving Aska," he said. "We're always together. Even when I go to school, she comes with me and waits so that we can go home together. She only obeys people she totally trusts."

"We'll leave her here. She'll be safe," Jet promised.

"Good thing she knows how to defend herself," Hiro conceded, scratching Aska behind the ears.

Jet gazed at the dog, their eyes locking. Aska pleaded with her not to leave her behind. Jet gave the dog a sympathetic look, and turned away. She knew that Hiro wouldn't be able to bear it if anything happened to his beloved companion. Jet couldn't let that happen.

"Work with me on this," she said wordlessly to the akita.

Aska let out a howl.

A shy smile spread on Hiro's lips. He'd broken into their conversation.

"Okay, kids," J-Bird said suddenly rising from the table. "Hiro," he said, "it's time. We're got to go. You need to act like you're scouting the land around here, keeping watch over the trailer. Pretend we're still inside."

Jet closed the book and put it under the cushion on the bench.

She understood Gilgamesh's desire to never die, but knew it was impossible. She understood Ishtar's desire for revenge, but that too was pointless. All one could do was live out one's destiny. Most people never got the chance. Now she would. It was too late to turn back. Jet brought her face close to Hiro's.

"Don't give up until you find the man with the light brown eyes," she whispered.

"Got it," Hiro's voice echoed confidently.

"The other men might hurt you, but he won't," she said.

"How do you know?" Hiro asked.

"Because he understands your value. He wants the treasure. That's more important to him, I'm sure. He has self-control. The others might not," Jet said knowingly.

Hiro nodded slowly.

"And don't worry," Jet told him. "We'll look after Aska. Then we'll come get you. And we'll fight together. We'll win!"

She wrapped her arms around Hiro and said good-bye.

"*Ganbarimashou*," he said, let's do our best.

"For Ojiisan," Jet said.

He gave her the raised fist salute Akira had given the crowd of punk rockers in Shinjuku. Ojiisan had trained him to face death, and he wasn't afraid.

CHAPTER 34

降伏 *Kofuku*
Surrender

J-Bird and Jet crept over the mountain to a hogan, a harvest cottage on the Reservation ten miles north of the trailer. Aska hadn't wanted to leave Hiro's side, but Hiro had spoken to her strongly. "Go with them, Aska. Your job is to protect them." Her ears had turned down sadly, but she'd obeyed.

Hiro had stayed at the trailer, guarding it as if Jet and J-Bird were still inside.

He'd collected quarters, even though he wasn't supposed to fight. He had to pretend to escape and then surrender, but he hated the idea of giving in so easily. Why not take on as many of the enemy as he could? He focused his senses into the dark forest, catching every sound, scent, and movement. He noticed faint breathing, the smell of skin, a slight rustling different than the stirring of the wind.

He counted three people hiding, located them in the void. But then he briefly sensed a faint shift that frightened him, the presence of a more skillful warrior who'd almost completely assimilated into the darkness, hiding his *ki*.

Hiro went inside the trailer, retrieved a sleeping bag from inside, then focused his energy again on his surroundings.

The men in the forest saw a small shadow jump from behind the trailer. Three of them ran toward it. As soon as they attacked it, they realized it was a stuffed sleeping bag—Hiro's *kawarimi* transforming skill.

Then he attacked them from an *ichimonji no kamae* stance, low and strong, moving like water rushing over river rocks. He struck their knees and chests, running faster than he ever had to the other side of the trailer.

He used *shoten no jutsu*—vertical surface running—to run up the tall tree trunk in front of him, throwing his pursuers into confusion. As they approached, he aimed his quarters decisively. The *tsubute* knocked them unconscious, one by one as they tried to shield themselves. All three were down.

Hiro returned to the ground, careful now. How could he surrender without risking danger to his own life? *This is harder than I expected.* In the darkness, he felt the faint human energy again.

Someone approached from behind. He turned and ducked and threw a coin. It ricocheted off a tree trunk. The person had disappeared. He couldn't sense where he'd gone. He held his breath. This must be the man with the light brown eyes. Hiro had to make his surrender look believable, but for the first time since the mountain, he was afraid.

"*Oi! Ore nara koko ni iruzo!*" A voice shouted in rough Japanese. *Here I am!*

Hiro's fear deepened. He climbed a tree, but his knees started to shake, so he breathed deeply into his belly to push away the panic. If he let it overtake him, he wouldn't be able to regain his composure. Whoever was there was only ten feet away. Normally, Hiro could have sensed his presence, even been able to ascertain his body temperature. But this man had completely hidden himself in the darkness. Hiro was overwhelmed. No one had ever been able to hide from him so fully.

Never lose your focus. Ever, Ojiisan had taught him. Hiro reminded himself that he was supposed to surrender. *Okay.* He took a deep breath. His fear would make his capture look genuine.

Gathering his strength, he jumped to the ground in *zenpo ukemi*, falling straight and landing on all fours. Then he crawled into the bushes and ran like a small animal chased by hunting dogs. The sharp tips of branches tore at his clothes, scraped his face and hands. He ran as if to escape his growing fear, to outdistance his own weakness.

A cliff appeared before him, and he stopped in front of it, his heart beating wildly. His breath caught in his throat as he remembered the ravine Ojiisan had fallen into. He felt the same helplessness he had while watching his grandfather tumble into the darkness. Now he was even more determined not to go without a struggle: Why should he surrender when he could get revenge on the warrior who'd caused Ojiisan's death?

"The chase is over," the man said softly. His tone suggested that he took no pleasure in this capture. He didn't seem to be relishing this victory at all. He was giving Hiro a last bit of dignity, letting him accept defeat like a man.

Hiro turned. The fog had lifted. A tall powerful warrior stood in the moonlight.

Hiro estimated the distance between them. Almost forty feet. He still had a few coins.

I'm close enough to hit him. We can end this here. For Ojiisan!

"Don't waste your energy." The man said. He had read Hiro's thoughts.

He was now less than ten feet away. Hiro couldn't give up without a fight. It wouldn't be believable. No ninja would. And yet he had to survive. He still wanted to fight, but he felt the intensely silent gravity of the man's strength and skill.

Hiro stood, calming his mind.

A real warrior knows when he's overpowered. There's more dignity in surrender than in messy defeat.

Hiro breathed deeply, offering all that he was to the memory of his beloved grandfather and parents. He hoped they'd been watching from above, and that he'd made them proud.

The man's light brown eyes flickered as they met Hiro's. Hiro had caught him off guard by his strength and wisdom. The man perceived Hiro's fighting will disappear from his body.

He laughed softly. It wasn't wicked, nor was it with pleasure or amusement.

Strange, Hiro thought. In another world, they might have been comrades. The man might have given him a gentle punch on the arm and taken him under his wing.

But in this world, Hiro was bound and blindfolded, then brought to a concrete dungeon in the desert and thrown in a cell without windows deep beneath the earth.

CHAPTER 35

捕囚 *Hoshu*
Trapped

"Don't underestimate the kid!" the brown-eyed man cautioned Hiro's guards. "He has enough skill to kill you before you know it."

Hiro blinked. He hated that he'd had to give up, but knew that even if he'd fought, he would have been defeated. How could Jet and J-Bird possibly have saved him from such a strong warrior? It would have been a miracle.

He was led down a dark corridor that dead-ended in a thick metal door. The guard opened the plastic cover of a keypad beside the door and input a six-digit number before putting a key into the hole.

673944. 673944. 673944. Hiro memorized the number.

Then he was handcuffed to a steel chair, motionless, conserving his energy.

"So Takumi, now what should we do with him?" asked a tough-looking blond wearing a black eye patch.

"Nothing, Rossi. We just wait for the woman to come get him," the brown-eyed man replied.

"Why don't we play with him a little to get some information?" He grinned at Hiro, cracking his knuckles.

"It's not going to work," Takumi said harshly. "He doesn't know where the others are. And even if he did, he wouldn't tell you."

"Is that so?" the blond sneered.

Takumi stiffened. "He's been well trained. He's quite an impressive boy. Let's just use him for bait. It's the best we can do."

Hiro blinked. He remembered the blond man now. He'd attacked them in Tokyo, and Jet had clawed at his eye. He couldn't help but smile at the memory.

"*Usunoro!*" he said and spat on the ground. *Idiot!*

Even if Rossi didn't understand Japanese, Hiro's tone was crystal clear. The blond swung a fist into Hiro's face. Hiro fell down, still in the chair.

"Stop it," Takumi said wearily, putting his hand on the American's shoulder.

"What? You want to protect this kid because of some tribal allegiance, is that it?"

Takumi looked away. "The kid's right. You're an idiot. I shouldn't even grace you with a response."

"Fine. You think you're so high and mighty." Rossi seethed.

"Just to educate you, when you tried to hit him, he absorbed the energy of your punch by falling down. You didn't even hurt him."

Who is this guy? Hiro wondered. *Whose side is he on?*

"Keep a good eye on him. Don't forget," Takumi added, "he's been trained from birth to take advantage of the smallest opening."

Then he turned to Hiro. "As for you," he said, "don't forget your dignity."

"What's that supposed to mean?" Hiro growled.

"Stand up! You can stand up even with your hands tied behind your back! You can swim with your hands and legs tied! This man can't even walk and chew gum at the same time. Show him how to be a man."

Hiro suppressed a smile. *So brown-eyes understands!* Hiro's mind flashed to the fact that samurai used to train by swimming in armor, but ninja trained by swimming with their hands and legs tied. They had to prepare for every possible circumstance. Like the one he was in now.

Reluctantly, Hiro righted himself by engaging the muscles in his back. His fallen chair flipped back onto its feet as he came back up.

Takumi smiled faintly.

"Well done," he said. Then he turned and left, motioning for the blond to follow.

The door slid shut. Now Hiro was alone in the cell. He looked around. There was a toilet in the corner. A square vent hole in the ceiling covered by a metal grate was the only opening, but the ceiling was almost twenty feet high.

Hiro sat on the concrete floor and used his feet to slide his shoes off. Then he rubbed his feet together to circulate warmth through his body. He was exhausted. He tried to stay awake by remembering passages from books, stories Ojiisan had told him, songs his mother had sung. But he needed rest and strength, and his eyes became heavy.

When he closed his eyes, a vision of his mother appeared. She was sewing beside the hearth in the living room, and Ojiisan was there, too, reading the newspaper and drinking sake. Hiro didn't have any real memory of his father, who'd died at the construction site in Tokyo he'd worked at over winters. From his earliest recollection, the only image of his father had been of a man with big arms, and the stoic but soft face in the black and white memorial photo placed on the Buddhist altar.

He looked closely at his mother's image before him. She was young, her hair short in a stylish bob, her face shining with health and delight. She was plump, and liked to sing, and always encouraged him to be strong. Once, he came home from school after failing a test. He'd been humiliated in front of the class by his teacher, and he told his mom how the whole class had laughed at him, even his friends. She held his hand tightly and said, "Even when things get hard, you mustn't cry. You're a strong boy."

"*Kachan!*" he called out to her. How long it had been since he had seen her this way, so happy and healthy. He wanted to touch her, to feel her warm hand in his. She lifted her face and smiled.

"You'll never guess where I am! America!" he said proudly. "I came here with Jet. We drove through the desert. It was incredibly big and wide. It's nothing like Japan."

In his vision, Hiro put a pillow under his mother's knees, the way she liked to rest. A good smell, like the fragrance of small white *nanohana* flowers blossoming at the beginning of spring, came from her somewhere in the reaches of memory. He wanted to tell her what he'd seen, that there were wolves named coyotes that howled in the far mountains. *Wauu, Wauu.* And when they'd howled, Aska had awoken with a surprised expression, her ears sticking straight up. She seemed to be thinking, *Who are they? Are they my enemies? Are they my friends? I might have known them a long time ago.*

"I wish you could have seen Aska's face."

This memory made him realize that Aska wasn't there. It was strange to be without his best friend. He imagined it might be like losing a limb.

Suddenly alert, Hiro awoke. He stared again at the dark gray concrete wall in front of him, and behind him, and to the sides.

He was closed in, with no way to escape.

The smell of his mother hung like sweet incense in the air. If being here brought him closer to avenging her and Ojiisan, then he was happy to be in this place, even if it was a cell. Hiro leaned back against the wall and settled in to his breath.

He'd been taught the art of patience and would practice it well. For her.

CHAPTER 36

歴史 *Rekishi*

History

Thirty video monitors showed every angle of what was happening inside and outside the villa.

Takumi sat in a chair looking steadily at one of them, where Hiro's small figure was resting against the concrete wall. He didn't expect any new information from the image. He was watching the screen out of curiosity, to see how this boy—who had inflicted serious damage on Takumi's subordinates and caused Takumi himself no small amount of worry—would behave in a situation where it was next to impossible to escape.

After a while, the small figure seemed to fall asleep. He was now squatting with his back against the wall. Takumi guessed that this rest was not only from exhaustion, but that the boy had been taught how to behave as a captive, and one of the first lessons was to grab any amount of rest when the opportunity presented itself.

That's what my father taught me, too. Takumi smiled bitterly, remembering how his father had reprimanded him harshly when they were hiding in the bushes during training. Takumi, who'd been no more than eight, had moved slightly when a mosquito bit his neck. "You have no discipline!" his father had said.

Takumi had tried to tell him about the mosquito, but his father had cut him off.

"Don't you have any pride? What kind of warrior are you, making excuses like that? If you're captured, the enemy will have no mercy for your poor explanations."

After that Takumi had endured the mosquitoes biting his neck and the itchy red spots. His father's words were harder to endure. Takumi had always wanted to show his father that he was strong and good, but his father had never once said he loved him. That was not their way.

This boy must have had the same kind of training as I did, he thought.

"Watch these screens," he told the young man next to him and left the room, walking soundlessly down the narrow corridor. Jet was coming. He could feel it.

From outside, Harter's villa appeared to be a three-story pueblo, a style typical in the Southwest, but this place was different. The inside was made of concrete, triple-reinforced with iron. Three underground floors were fully equipped military facilities with weapons storage and a control center to monitor the sophisticated surveillance system. Harter was scheduled to arrive by private helicopter that afternoon, and the villa was under heavy security.

Takumi took the elevator three floors underground. The door opened to reveal a white, quiet corridor. A guard sitting in front of Soji's cell at the end of the corridor stood as Takumi approached.

"Open the door," Takumi commanded.

The guard punched in the code and put in the key. The iron door slid back.

"Are you enjoying yourself?" Takumi asked the monk sitting in lotus position on the bed.

Dark stubble covered Soji's drawn cheeks. Even though Takumi had entered the cell, walked around, and fixed his gaze on the man, Soji remained immobile, his face toward the wall in silence.

"You can speak to the wall all day, but it'll never answer you," Takumi said.

Soji turned and slowly opened his gray-blue eyes. He held his wordless gaze on Takumi.

"Soji," Takumi said, getting accustomed to the long silence

between them, "are you chaneling some medieval priest who thought meditation could turn him into the Buddha?"

Still Soji said nothing.

"Will a polished crock become a mirror?" Takumi spoke the words of the great Zen Buddhist monk, Dogen, throwing them at Soji like cold water. "When the polished crock becomes a mirror," he said, "a man will become the Buddha."

"You underestimate the importance of polishing the crock," Soji said finally, standing from the bed and turning to face Takumi. "That action itself contains the essence of the Buddha."

"Even if a crock is polished, it won't become the mirror," Takumi replied. "Zen is just a smokescreen to give priests a job."

"That may be so," Soji said crisply, "but you didn't go out of your way to come here and discuss Zen with me, did you?"

"You're right." Takumi stepped closer. "I came to tell you that last night we caught Hiro. He's in this building. Don't you want to see your family member?"

Soji's eyes flickered. "If he's my family, he must be related to you, too. Certainly you have the same blood as we do. It's obvious from your eyes. We're all brothers."

Takumi shrugged. He didn't care.

"Judging by your features," Soji continued, "I'd say you have a lot of Mongolian blood. But your light brown eyes come from the same blood that bore the original Japanese people. And your accent is like my grandfather's. He was born in Sasa."

"So what?" Takumi replied in a quiet, cold voice. Still, he was impressed with how much Soji had ascertained in such a short time.

"I just thought I'd mention it. No meaning." Soji shrugged.

Takumi looked steadily at him. "What do I care if we're from the same tribe? If I cared about that so much, I'd be just like the *Wa*, always going on about family lineage, bloodlines, duty, and honor. In the end, we all spill the same blood, die the same deaths. It's all meaningless."

Soji lowered his gaze. "Not so," he countered. "The village you raided, Kanabe, was your father's homeland, wasn't it? That means it was your own ancestral home. Doesn't that bother you?"

Takumi ground his heel into the concrete. He was tired of it all. "What's done is done. I've already cut the ties of race, history, and family. What does it matter?"

Soji took a step toward Takumi. "What I mean is—"

Takumi didn't budge as the older man approached him. "What? I'll hear you out this time. But make it quick."

Soji swallowed. "Let's use an allegory. Imagine you're seeking to define the essence of stone, not by describing the essence itself, but by saying what stone is *not*. For example, stone is not flower, stone is not soul, and stone is not air." Soji paused briefly.

"Go on," Takumi sighed. *Another tiresome lesson from some self-righteous scholar.*

"But soon you've negated all of the words and attributes that could be used to characterize stone itself."

"And so?"

"In the same way, you're denying your essence, destroying yourself, which is exactly what they want you to do. Only you do it for them, so it makes you even worse than them."

"Ok, Mr. Philosopher. I appreciate the profound analysis, but what's your point?"

"I've made my point," Soji replied.

"Good, then save the rest of your lecture for the classroom. And don't forget you're a prisoner here—my prisoner."

"Let me ask you something." Soji steadied his gaze on the young man. "Why did you take part in this mission?"

"The money," Takumi said matter-of-factly.

"Really?" Soji asked dubiously. "Is that all?"

Takumi laughed. "You know how miserable army pay is. How else can one survive?"

Soji neither agreed nor disagreed.

"After this," Takumi told him, "I'll retire. Anyway, do you think I really believe that the treasure of the Ancient Orient is hidden in Japan? King Solomon's treasure? Jesus's bone?"

"Perhaps. Perhaps not," Soji conceded.

"Who cares? I won't see any of the riches. But if I do my job, at least I'll get paid for it."

"That's it, then," Soji said, eyes narrowing.

"Right. That's it. It's just a job," Takumi replied.

Soji sighed. "I *do* know that wherever and whatever the Kuroi family treasure is, it's been passed down from generation to generation. We're not going to let it go lightly."

"That's more than obvious," Takumi said. So far, truth serum, lie detectors, voice-layering analysis and drugs had not been able to get any information out of Soji. His men had interrogated him about evidence that he'd traveled to America in March of 1996, possibly to meet Satoko. But it was as if his mind had been erased. Even under hypnosis, he could recall virtually nothing of that journey.

"So you don't believe that this treasure really exists?" Soji asked.

"Me? No." Takumi looked into Soji's eyes. "The reason legends like that exist is to prop up morale. Family treasures, national treasures and great historical artifacts are basically fantasy, ways for people and nations to feel important."

"And why is that?" Soji looked back into his eyes.

"You should know!" Takumi saw what Soji was trying to do. It reminded him of his father.

"Tell me anyway," Soji challenged.

Takumi frowned. "Countries want to prove their superiority. Every time a new artifact is found, leaders want to prove how advanced and intelligent the ancient people in that country were. Those people were most likely slaves or artisans working for nothing so that those in power could live in palaces and be surrounded by beautiful things..."

"Go on," Soji urged.

Takumi paused. His emotions were getting the better of him. He couldn't let that happen.

"Like the bone of Christ. So what if it turns out to be real? The people in power at the time killed Jesus."

Soji shrugged. "What if there's a message on that bone, a message that has as much power today as it had thousands of years ago? What if learning this message from an enlightened being would help people today? Wouldn't you want them to hear it?"

"Maybe it will help some, but maybe it will anger others. Who's to say?" Takumi replied.

"At least those defending it are trying to protect their own history. Otherwise it will be erased."

Takumi paused, considering. "It doesn't matter. Over time, the truth will be lost. History belongs to the victors. Everyone knows that."

"That's my point!" Soji exclaimed. "Our ancestral lands were stolen by the Emperor's army, and our tribes were enslaved. And they didn't stop at stealing the capital—they took the name of the country, too. What else are we going to let them take?"

"That proves *my* point. Why keep such a sad history? We've already lost it, and nothing's changed. We're still slaves," Takumi replied, voice rising in anger.

"Oh, but it has," Soji said, suddenly animated. "The Imperial family made up a history in which they were the rulers of Japan from the beginning. The Emishi were just one of the tribes that obstructed the Emperor's progress, so they wiped us out of the history books."

"Exactly. What does this have to do with the Kuroi family treasure?" Takumi asked.

"The very act of protecting the treasure symbolizes our will to recover our lost history. That's the real meaning and value of the Kuroi family treasure. It has nothing to do with material riches. But then again, you wouldn't understand that, would you?"

"I wasn't expecting such a sermon," Takumi told him. "Obviously, Harter is wasting his money and time searching for this so-called treasure. For all he knows, it could be a piece of an old grandmother's *furoshiki*."

"The truth will emerge," Soji said. "If the truth-tellers are brave enough to speak it. Our history is the treasure. You must know that. You must feel that, somewhere in your blood." He searched Takumi's face for an opening, a vulnerability, a recognition. Briefly, Takumi hesitated and Soji thought he saw a flicker of doubt, but then the young warrior went cold.

Darkness shaded Takumi's features. "You're deluding yourself," he said. "History shows us that those who've been invaded turn around and invade other territories. Maybe you think the Imperial family rewrote history to suit themselves, but the Kuroi family rewrote their history, too. Anyway, it's not my business. It's not worth losing my life over."

"You think it's not your business, but it is. You're already dead working for the *Wa*. You've sold yourself to the enemy," Soji said, disappointment saturating his voice. "You tell yourself it doesn't matter, but it does."

Takumi's face flushed. He grabbed Soji's shirt and pushed him. Soji lost his balance and fell.

"If you want to protect your history, you should learn to stand on your own two feet," Takumi said.

"Why don't you come back to the side you belong on?" Soji stepped back up and steadied himself.

"I belong to no one," Takumi replied, but Soji's words had cut into him, shaken him.

"You have a choice," Soji insisted.

"I can't see where your choice would lead me to somewhere better than I am now," Takumi replied.

"Just because you can't see it, doesn't mean it's not there. Have some faith."

"Faith?" Takumi scoffed, disbelieving. "Don't talk to me about faith, blood, and lineage. You're just like them, spouting the party line. It's just the other party. I don't care about any of that, don't you see? I want to be someone who thinks for himself."

"Is that who you are?" Soji's stare burned into Takumi's eyes. "Really?"

"At least I don't pretend to be someone I'm not." Takumi glared back at the priest, not backing down. Then he turned and left, walking back down the hall to the elevator, fuming.

He shook his head.

How dare that priest speak to me as if he knows me, as if he cares? He just wants another acolyte. Someone to spout his family mythology to the next generations to pump up their defeated pride.

At least with Harter, he knew where he was headed. If he went out on his own, there would be too many surprises. Once you stepped into the unknown, it expanded. It became the unknowable. Takumi wasn't sure he could handle that.

All he wanted was for the mission to be over. All he had to do was wait for Jet to try to rescue the boy. Harter believed that only the Kuroi women knew the secret to the treasure, and Takumi felt that in that, for once, his boss was right. He sensed that he was days away from finding it, and when that happened, Takumi would be done with this madness once and for all.

Part Five

SENTO

戦闘

BATTLE

CHAPTER 37

奇襲 *Kishu*
Sudden Attack

The wind on Blanca Peak carried the chill of winter. Jet hid in the bushes and breathed deeply to warm herself, but the bone-chilling cold penetrated the down jacket, turtleneck sweater, and thermal underwear J-Bird had bought her. He crouched beside her. She could see his silvery breath in the moonlit sky.

Harter's mansion was nestled in the southern foothills of the fourteen-thousand-foot mountain in the far south of the Rockies. According to Navajo legend, there were four sacred mountains surrounding the territory, branching out in the four directions. To the Navajo, Blanca Peak was Sis Najimi, the Sacred Mountain of the East. J-Bird and Jet had followed Hiro's signal to Colorado, where they'd easily found Harter's villa, northeast of Fort Garland.

It had been two days since Hiro's capture. Jet knew that Harter was waiting for her to rescue him, so she and J-Bird had spent a few hours navigating the area. The villa was situated on four acres surrounded by a tall, double-wire fence. The only way in was through a heavy iron gate on the east side, where four armed guards kept watch. Even if she could get through the gate, she'd still be almost a mile from the main building.

A dense cedar forest stretched from the north side of Blanca Peak to the west side. That would be the logical place to enter, but she and J-Bird agreed to do the least expected. They chose the grassy lawn of the south side, even though they'd be totally exposed. The land was so flat and open that no one in his right mind would come through that way, so the security there would probably be lax.

Jet and J-Bird crawled into the bushes outside the southern fence. It was almost half a mile from the fence to the main building. Earlier that day, they'd seen metal poles everywhere on the grounds, certainly holding motion sensors and infrared cameras.

Though Aska might have been useful, and she certainly wanted to come find her master, they'd decided to leave her back at the trailer. It was too dangerous to bring her along. She'd cried and howled at having to stay back, but she'd already gone through enough. It was just too big of a risk to bring her into the battleground.

Jet stroked Aska's ears the way she'd seen Hiro do, whispering assurances. She thanked Aska for her loyal service. When the dog woke up, hopefully Hiro would be by her side, and all would be forgiven. The alternative was too devastating to consider.

On the drive there, J-Bird had told Jet how he'd helped Satoko hunt down Michael Harter, Davison's father. They'd gone to his villa on Lake Michigan, plotted it all out: made a floor plan, checked for hidden cameras, located the guards. They'd taken advantage of the heavy snow, dressing in white and engaging in *inton*, the art of blending into the environment. Satoko had moved with some deer while J-Bird stood watch. She'd made quick work of Harter, in and out like a dagger.

With no evidence of break-in or a struggle, the police had no choice but to rule Michael Harter's death accidental.

The situation Jet and J-Bird now faced was completely different. They had no floor plan and no information on how many guards were on site. The technology was also much more sophisticated than it had been back then. The only possibility was to create a distraction, causing enough confusion to break in. They had one advantage. Earlier, they'd seen a helicopter arrive. It was clear that Harter or another VIP was there. Some of the guards would have been pulled to protect him, and there would be fewer at the gates. Regardless, even if they saved Soji and Hiro, they still had to get Harter. Until then, they'd never be safe. He'd never leave Kanabe alone while he was alive.

J-Bird looked up at the crescent moon and prayed. When he had finished, Jet signalled that it was almost time. To stop her cold lips from trembling, she tried to smile.

"You smile just like your mother," he said, his voice tinged with sadness. Jet wondered what losing Satoko must have been like for him. Then again, she thought she knew.

The wind blew, and he motioned farewell. She huddled, waiting. Her hands were trembling.

Jet looked down at her hands, seeing her mother's hands there, strong and determined. She remember the way Satoko's hands slapped the flour against the stone as she made tortillas, or flicked skillfully across the bamboo sheet as she rolled up *nori* to make sushi.

How had her mother done it, kept both worlds—east and west—hidden and revealed at the same time? Or had this very secret self burned its regret deep under her skin like a tattoo, like the locket Jet herself was not safe to reveal?

And was that why Satoko vowed that Jet wouldn't feel the same pain, why she'd made Jet promise to return to Japan to fulfill the mission?

Jet sighed and felt the locket rise and fall on her chest. She wasn't done yet. She hadn't accomplished the mission her mother had entrusted her with. She asked the locket for the strength to carry on, to see the quest through to the end.

As she summoned her mother's spirit, she swore the locket hummed its energy into her chest, singing the ancient secret song of Satoko, Momoko, and all the unknown Kuroi woman warriors before her, the ones whose strength hid in the darkness, vast as the night itself.

Ninja are trained to fight. And those who are born to fight will one day end up in battle.

She knew the time was near.

An explosion flared from the north side of the property, flames shooting into the sky. J-Bird had planted the pack of dynamite and would now go to cut the electrical cables. He'd also shoot at guards to create further distraction.

An alarm screamed through the night as flames illuminated the sky, embers raining on the grounds. Guards ran across the property to the north side, where they thought the intrusion was taking place.

Jet wrapped a black *zukin* cloth over her face and took off her jacket. Underneath, she had on the traditional ninja *kuro shozoku* night outfit to blend into the darkness. She took a deep breath and steeled herself. She was ready.

She ran toward the fence, holding a twelve-foot long *shinobi-zue*, a fiberglass pole used for vaulting. She picked up speed. All along the fence, guards jumped into sight, and she stuck the pole into the ground a foot in front of the fence. She soared into the air, over the fence, savoring the sensation of floating until the ground rushed close and she felt its touch on her right shoulder. She curled into a ball and rolled down the hill, letting gravity speed her descent. It was second nature now. In the distance, she saw flames spreading around the front gate. When she reached the bottom of the slope, she ran toward the main building.

If there had been just two or three lights on posts, Jet would have shot them out, but there were more than ten poles every hundred feet. Shooting them would tell the enemy where she was. She had to make it into the inner sanctum and take advantage of the confusion to create more confusion. Besides, they wouldn't shoot her. They needed her if they wanted to find the treasure, even if she didn't know why.

From the rooftop, a spotlight began to follow her. A guard with a submachine gun came her way, and she hid in a row of hedges. The light stayed on her, but the guard wasn't shooting. He must have orders not to kill her. She'd counted on this.

"The game is up!" he shouted. He approached the bushes, his gun trained on what he thought was her. When he got close, he saw that what he'd mistaken for a crouched person was just pieces of ripped black cloth strung up in a bush.

Then the spotlight turned off, and all of the compound lights went dead. J-Bird had succeeded in cutting the cables!

Jet slipped behind the guard, put her dagger to his throat.

"Don't say a word!" she whispered, pulling him into the bushes.

The fire at the eastern gate was still burning under the inky black sky.

"Where are the boy and his uncle?" Jet demanded.

"I don't know." His knees were shaking.

"I don't like liars." She pressed the dagger harder against his throat.

"I'm not...ly...lying," he stammered, his adam's apple thrumming under the blade. "All I know is that there are two Japanese in underground cells. Is that...that...who you mean?"

"Take off your jacket and give me a short tour, will you?" She grabbed his shirt and dragged him out of the bushes.

He protested, but she kicked him back. "If you do what I say, you'll survive."

It was pitch dark around the compound. J-Bird had done a good job, but a generator could kick in any minute.

Sure enough, seconds later, light flooded the grounds. But Jet and her captive had already disappeared.

CHAPTER 38

捕獲 *Hokaku*
Capture

Light streamed from the chandeliers, spilling over the marble floor of the grand entrance hall to the villa. The outside of the mansion was pueblo, but the interior was ornate and European, with black and white marble floors, eighteenth-century Turner and Barbizon landscapes lining the walls, and Greek and Roman statues dotting the high-ceilinged corridors.

Armed guards were everywhere, their voices shouting in confusion. A thin pale man cursed and shouted, his voice louder than the others. Davison Harter.

"You're useless, completely useless! How many people have made it onto the grounds? I want you to tear this place apart until you find them. Move! Now!"

"Mr. Harter, it's dangerous for you to be out here. Please go to your room," a bodyguard said calmly, taking Harter by the elbow and leading him away.

"Where is Takumi? That idiot!" He swung his arms like an angry child, trying to throw the bodyguard off.

"I'm right here," Takumi said, concealing his rage. How dare Harter call him an idiot!

"Do you know how many security cameras we have here? Fifty! Fifty cameras. They're not for decoration. And do you know how many guards I pay to protect this property? Twenty. And not one of you has a single brain cell!"

The red blood vessels in Harter's forehead looked as if they would burst.

Takumi glanced down. He'd known Jet would make it to the villa, but he hadn't expected her to find it so quickly, or to attack so well. The guards had been totally incompetent, and when the explosion occurred, he'd been taking a wolf-nap in his room, a five-minute refresher that could hold him over for hours. He woke with a start and commanded the guards to go into the forest to the north. But she'd gone against expectation by entering from the south, where she'd been totally exposed. He couldn't help but admire her daring.

"Yes, sir!" he said, hating the pleading tone in his voice.

Still, he had her now. Even the *tedare*—highly skilled warriors—could hide themselves in the confusion for no more than ten seconds.

Harter stormed around the control room flanked by wide-shouldered bodyguards.

"Are they in the building already?" he asked.

"No, it's impossible. Whenever there's a breach in the security system, all the doors and windows immediately lock, except the main entrance. The intruders would have to enter from there. You know that," Takumi said, but he didn't put it past Jet. If she'd timed the blackout just right, the security system would have been rebooting. He felt rattled.

"I want this dealt with immediately," Harter commanded.

"Yes, Mr. Harter. Please go back to your suite. We'll take care of it," Takumi said.

"You'd better!" Harter shouted, walking briskly to the door. The fire at the north fence had been put out, and men whose faces were black with soot were walking toward the main hall, laughing with relief, unaware of Harter's presence. The smell of fire permeated the air. Their voices were loud and distracting.

The hair on the back of Takumi's neck stood up. Something was about to happen. Something very bad. Listening to his intuition, he rushed toward Harter, grabbing the back of his jacket and throwing him forward.

"No one move!" Takumi's voice silenced the room. Guns were readied, aiming in his direction.

"*You* don't move!" a woman's voice rang out in the hall. Takumi froze. Soft light from the chandelier exposed the woman's almond eyes. She was dressed in black from head to toe and held a gun to a guard's neck.

Takumi took a deep breath. "You won't be able to escape," he said. "And don't think that killing that guy will mean a thing to me. I don't care if you do."

"It's not him you should be worried about," she said slowly, her eyes on his face.

He willed himself to be cold. Did she understand what kind of man he really was? He had to stay strong. He was a warrior.

"I meant what I said," he told her as he neared. "Go ahead and kill him if you want!"

At that she moved the gun from the man's neck and shot the chandelier's chain. It fell, its many crystals shattering, their shards scattering across the floor.

In the dark, guards shone their flashlights about, and shadows moved. A few gunshots rang out. Takumi knew exactly where she would be in less than a second, and he propelled his body through the space. He could sense her presence rushing toward Harter. It felt as if catching a gust of wind, but he reached out and grabbed hold of her from behind, spinning her around and putting the blade to her throat.

Flashlights illuminated them. Harter lay on the floor at their feet, looking up, eyes wide with confusion.

"You think it's that easy," Takumi whispered in her ear, pulling her head back. "I was closer to him than you were. Don't assume everyone is weaker than you are."

He could feel her heart beating wildly, but he kept the knife fixed at her pale throat. She turned her face to his, and seeing her like this, so close, so very close, he had to steady himself. He tried to shake off the lingering warmth of her breath as it landed on his body like gossamer. He tried to shake the way his own fingers longed to stay on her skin just a little bit longer. It was more than attraction. Perhaps even more than love. It was as if destiny itself had taken form before him—her form—and called him out. But his destiny was to live in the shadows, wasn't it? Isn't that what ninja did?

An unsettled feeling rose in the pit of his stomach. Takumi drew his breath in and waited for his heart to settle back down to where he'd buried it for as long as he'd remembered.

But the shock, the sense of betrayal flickering in her eyes, made him feel something he'd never known. Regret.

His heart battered against his chest.

He'd have to steel himself against it, or die trying.

CHAPTER 39

抵抗 *Teiko*
Resistance

Jet looked up at the gray ceiling and shivered. It felt as though the cold space was closing in on her. She wanted to shut her eyes, to wipe out what was happening, to dissolve into nothingness. Mercifully, Takumi did it for her. He ordered his men to bind her. They put steel rings on her legs and wrists, and then threaded four metal wires through smaller rings. Then they clamped them to hooks in the wall. She shrank into her shackles.

"Pay attention, gentlemen. Don't think because she's a woman she's any less dangerous," Takumi said, touching the wires as if strumming a guitar to check for slack. They were taut and strong. She'd be able to move only her fingers. Jet looked at him, awaiting his next move. She felt a strange sense of detachment, amazed at his cruel precision.

"You almost got away with it," he said softly, as if consoling her. "If I hadn't noticed your shape, you'd have defeated us."

She tried to turn her head toward him. Everything had happened at the speed of light. What shape? she wondered.

"The shape of your body," he said, as if reading her mind. "I saw your shadow. There's no way I could have missed you out there. Even before you spoke." His lips hung on the words, and Jet tried to press her way into them, back into him, but he had gone cold.

"How long will you keep me here?" she asked.

"Until we find the treasure," he told her. "If you cooperate, we'll let all of you go with your lives."

"Why are you doing this?" She tried to hold his gaze, but he looked away. In his downcast eyes, she thought she still saw a glimmer of the man she'd met in the ramen shop, the one who'd talked about his upbringing, which was so much like hers.

"It's too late for questions and answers," he replied coldly.

"It's never too late," she said, daring him to turn around.

But he didn't. The air hung compressed around them, like a cyclone frozen in the sky.

Then he abruptly turned and left the cell. The door slid shut behind him heavily, as if in a vault.

She twisted in her binds, finding no give. Shaking with frustration, she closed her eyes. *If I hadn't noticed your shape, you would have defeated us.* What he meant was: If you hadn't been a woman. All her training, all her mother's suffering, all her ancestors' battles, nothing could change that. *Yes, I'm a woman,* she thought, heart thudding in her chest.

She breathed deeply, directing her energy to her heart center, where the locket hung undetected. She focussed her breath on its mysterious kanji. Woman.

Send me your power, she intoned. *Show me the way.* For now she knew there was *always* a way. She had to use everything around her to win, like Ojiisan had said. All she had to do was be subtler and more determined than Takumi. She grit her teeth, filled with determination. She had to be the warrior her mother and Ojiisan believed she was destined to become.

The girl had died, the woman had been born. Now the woman warrior, the *kunoichi* who'd been locked in Jet's heart for years, must finally emerge.

Their lives depended on it. They always had.

In the silence, Jet became aware of another sound: the faint blowing of air from the square vent on the ceiling. She surveyed the rough gray surface of the windowless wall, the heavy metal door. *There must be a hidden camera somewhere. I have to find it!*

Suddenly, the door opened. A tall blond man wearing an eye patch entered. He looked smug, like a child who'd gotten away with something naughty.

He stroked her cheek. She tried to kick him away.

He laughed, enjoying her reaction.

"I was going to punish your cousin for what you did to my eye," he said, "but now that you're here, it only seems fair that I deal with you directly."

"Your eye?" she said, uncomprehending.

He pointed to the eyepatch. "What's the matter? Lost your short-term memory?"

Then she remembered. The man she'd clawed in Tokyo!

He looked up at a black spot on the wall and spoke. "Rossi here. Deactivate the cameras and mikes in this room for a while." Then he turned back to Jet.

"No one will bother us now," he chuckled, taking a long knife from his belt and touching the blade with his finger. He trailed it along Jet's throat, watching her flinch. Was he going to torture her like this for a while? Or were his intentions far worse?

Jet had a feeling they were. Revulsion rose in her belly. She had to get out of there.

I can't sit back and let this happen. I have to think of something quickly. Anything. What would get me out of here?

Breath rose high into her chest. The locket heaved as she breathed.

That's it! I could encourage him, pretend to be interested…

The thought disgusted her, but she knew it was her only way out. She took a breath in, made her voice sweet and inviting. *Henge,* she told herself. Transformation.

"Why don't you release my legs from the vise?" she said sweetly. "That way I can move better."

For a second, he hesitated, as if considering it.

Then understanding shadowed his face, and he became angry.

"You think I'm that stupid?" He kept the knife at her throat as he fumbled with his clothes. "Is that what you think?"

"No," Jet shook her head vehemently. "Of course not."

All she could do was close her eyes to escape what was happening.

Then she jolted upright. *Never close your eyes. At any time, in any situation, keep them open!* a voice inside her said. She shook her head. *Never close your eyes! Face your fears!*

She looked straight at him, as if her gaze could burn through his skin. At first she didn't realize what she was doing. Desperation had set her into motion, and now she knew that her mother had trained her in ways she could barely recall, as if she'd hypnotized Jet to give her other, deeper lessons.

Ojiisan had told her about tapping into the mind of your enemy, and Jet tried to remember how he'd done it to her in the kitchen when they passed through the walls. She continued staring, calling on the wisdom in her blood, the power and knowledge of the generations of ninja that had gone before her, and the lessons that her mother had taught her since she was a child.

Rossi sneered as her gaze burned through his eyes into his brain.

"You won't get away with it!" she told him. "Your karma will catch up to you!"

"Karma, schmarma," he scoffed.

But his movements were slowing. His fingers couldn't find belt-holes or zippers. Jet continued to stare, gathering her energy and boring her gaze into him like a sword. The wider she opened her eyes to what was happening, the less afraid she was, the more she felt in control. She sensed the hesitation in him. Doubt. Desire. Anger. Fear. He was not a meditator—a decent fighter, maybe, but a brain like Swiss cheese. She understood. So this was why the best ninjas meditated. You could win with the body and still lose with the mind.

The light within the room filled Jet's eyes, and within it, she saw the darkness of her own mind. It was a place where she could act freely. And in that darkness, Jet saw the light that would lead her not only to survival, but to victory.

Summoning all of her strength, she made her move, and it was decisive.

CHAPTER 40

闇 *Yami*
Darkness

Right before Takumi's eyes, Jet had done what he'd failed to do—fight for her ideals, not for someone else's glory or profit. He admired her for it, but at the same time it hurt him to see how far he'd come from his own youthful dreams.

Soji's steady voice came back to him: *You're trying to deny who you are and what you came from.*

Who am I? he asked himself. A poor peasant with a false hope of freedom. He felt rage toward Soji, suddenly wanting to go to his cell and throttle him. With a shock, he realized that he'd never wanted to hurt someone so badly. He'd mastered the art of fighting the way others mastered ordinary skills like carpentry or farming. He did his job automatically, professionally, without putting his heart into it. But since he'd met Jet, his heart had gotten in the way of everything.

A thought struck him. If he really didn't care about what Soji had said, if he really did live without illusions, why was he so angry?

His right thigh pulsed in pain. A bullet from one of his men's guns had hit him in the pandemonium of the main hall. He didn't think the wound was that serious, and at any rate, he had to finish the job. He grit his teeth and endured the pain. The stupidity of his own men injured him more than the wound itself.

I'm nothing but a dog. Once my job is finished, my master will take me into the forest and leave me there to fend for myself. Just like I always do.

A few men in the control room were talking about the explosion and drinking coffee, relaxing. One of them facing the hall coughed to alert the others that Takumi had come in. The room fell silent. He was used to it. Even in the Foreign Legion, or in the desert with Green Berets, he'd had the same experience. As soon as he went into a room, not only his comrades but even his superiors stopped talking. He understood that his coolness made even the most ruthless mercenaries tense.

"Did you take a nap?" Takumi asked, looking around the quiet room.

"Yes, sir. I slept for two hours," a young man said, standing up to offer Takumi a seat in front of the monitors.

Takumi motioned for the man to sit. He stood with his arms crossed, looking at the screens. On one screen, Soji still sat on the bed facing the wall, but the screen for Jet's room was dark. The one where the boy was imprisoned looked like it was covered in dust.

"What happened to these monitors?" he asked harshly.

The guard appeared confused.

"Oh, man! Jeez! The Japanese kid must have spit on the camera," he said. "And the guard I replaced said he'd turned the girl's camera off by orders from Rossi."

"Orders from Rossi?" The blood rushed to Takumi's cheeks. His blond lieutenant was always pushing the envelope, the insubordinate!

"Well, turn it back on, damn it!"

The screen showed Jet's room. An unconscious guard lay on the floor. Jet was gone. Gone! Takumi's stomach churned. Not because she was gone, but because the sickening thought that Rossi might have harmed her crept into his awareness. He clenched his fists.

"We have an emergency!" Takumi shouted. "Did any one see anything before?" He turned around, eyes blazing at his men.

"A tall man who looked like Rossi was on the third floor underground monitor. But I couldn't tell for sure," a young guard answered nervously.

"Was he alone?" Takumi asked.

"No, sir. He was with a shorter guard."

"Sound the alarm immediately!" Takumi called into a tiny microphone he took from his waist. Just as he commanded his men
to Harter's suite, the emergency siren sounded, obscuring his
voice. Then the lights went out, throwing the mansion into total
darkness. He looked at his watch. 5:20 in the morning. Nearly dawn.
The sun was still moving slowly at the eastern edge of the horizon.
Sunlight wouldn't reach the compound for another hour.

He frowned. It was the perfect environment for people accustomed to the dark. People like Jet and her kind. *His* kind.

Shinobi.

Ninja.

CHAPTER 41

継承 *Keisho*
Inheritance

Ojiisan had told her it was ordinary hypnotism, but it was not. Now she knew that to find the unguarded part of your opponent's mind and make it bend to your will required something more than ordinary hypnotism.

Instinctively—or because of her training—she'd done that. She'd taken the strength in her *hara* and projected it with a short sharp yell, like the *kiai* she used when kicking or punching. She didn't know why she was doing it, but she sensed it was her only way out. Her arms and legs were shackled, and the yell expressed her inner fire and power. Her body shook from the force of the energy moving up with the sound. Nothing could counter it.

Rossi froze where he stood before her. His cruel expression replaced by the quivering grimace of a frightened child.

"Get away from me!" she said harshly. To her immense surprise, he did as he was told. If she'd been in doubt before, she now knew she was in full possession of his mind. He was under her control.

She kept her own mind in sharp focus on his, as if practicing *kyuudo* archery. She had to keep her focus on the bulls' eye and couldn't waver from the target. She commanded him to open her shackles, holding his thoughts steady. Then she had him call a guard inside. She knocked the man out with a quick strike and changed into his uniform.

Then she had Rossi take her to the master circuit breaker. She shut it off and smashed the main switch. The wail of the alarm stopped as soon as darkness descended. She had him return the weapons that had been stripped from her: her *shuriken* throwing stars and *shinobi gatana* ninja sword, as well as the spiked *shuko* and *ashiko* arm and leg bands.

Now Rossi led her to Soji's cell. She incapacitated the guard with one strike under his nose, all her energy coiled into the palm of her hand, flicking it up.

Inside the cell, Soji sat as still as a statue, slowly exhaling from his nose.

"Soji…Soji…." she said in *shinobi kotoba*.

Her uncle turned his head without interrupting the rhythm of his breathing.

"Jet!" He stood, and in the dark she saw the vague outline of his exhausted face.

"We have to find Hiro," she said. He nodded almost imperceptibly, then resumed his breathing, walking out of his cell stealthily.

"What about him?" he shot a glance at Rossi, inert beside her.

"His brain is tofu." She laughed. "Don't worry."

They moved down the hall, Jet going first, gliding along the wall as if shadows, wearing the black air like a cape. She struck out one guard after another along the corridor until they found Hiro's cell, a small glass cut-out enabling them to see inside.

Sensing their presence, Hiro stood inside and mouthed the password in *shinobi kotoba*.

Jet keyed in the number: 673944. The door slid open with a hydraulic *woosh*.

Hiro was shocked to see Rossi, but Jet waved her hand in front of his eyes, and Hiro soon understood.

"*Saiminjutsu!*" he said. "You've been busy!"

Jet nodded, then turned to Rossi. "How do we get out of here?"

"The elevator, or the fire stairs," he answered in a sleepy voice.

"Impossible," she told Hiro. "The power is out, so the elevator won't be running. And I'm sure they've staked out the stairs."

"We could climb the elevator cables," Hiro said, "but brown-eyes probably thought of that already. He'll have put men there."

Jet nodded. She knew he was right. Takumi would have anticipated their next movements. He wouldn't make the same mistakes twice. No doubt, he was already one step ahead of them. They had to think fast.

"Plan B?" Jet whispered.

Hiro gave her the thumbs-up and swung into gear.

CHAPTER 42

目つぶし *Metsubushi*
Smoke and Mirrors

Only a minute had passed since the power went out. Takumi figured Jet was still underground as she needed time to rescue Soji and Hiro. He put himself in her mindset. She would have to get to the ground floor to escape. The elevators were out. If they climbed the cables, they would encounter guards on every floor. Jet, her cousin, and uncle were sealed in.

His men wanted to use nightscopes, but Takumi was against it. The images weren't good in a closed space, and they could mistake each other for the enemy. He had them use flashlights and laser targets instead.

How in the world did she get out of her cell? he wondered, leading his men down the stairs. *Saiminjutsu?* He realized he was enjoying this in spite of himself. As long as she was free, he could see her as the enemy. And he knew what to do with the enemy. He could be the trained assassin he'd always been. On the other hand, when she was captive, he felt a crushing sense of responsibility and a fear of the emptiness that awaited him when she would be gone.

Yes. Let her be free for now. At least I'll have a worthy opponent.

"Separate into two groups," he commanded the six guards with him at the door. He worried that he was running out of men. "Half of you come with me to search this floor. The rest stay here. Whatever you do, don't shoot without my command."

"Yes, sir!" they replied in unison.

He felt a fleeting sense of satisfaction and the hope that things might go his way after all.

He braced himself and kicked the door open. Flashlights and laser beams crossed in the dark space. The door to one of the cells was open. Someone was there. But who? Jet and the boy knew how to mute their auras, so it must be the priest.

Takumi flashed a hand signal to his men to release smoke into the room—*metsubushi*, smoke and mirrors, or as the ninja called it, eye blinders. A canister released heavy mist. The men waited, breathing through gas masks.

One, two, three, Takumi counted in his head.

Then, illuminated by flashlights, a shadow emerged, covering its face with both arms. The red lights of dozens of lasers targeted the man as he staggered toward them.

"Stop. Don't move!" Takumi called out as two guards grabbed the man's arms and pulled them down. Takumi rushed to the man, astonished to discover that it was Rossi.

His blond footsoldier was coughing and swearing. His unexpected appearance shocked the men, who immediately lowered their flashlights and lasers.

"Give him a mask!" Takumi shouted. "We've been tricked!"

CHAPTER 43

忍びの風 *Shinobi no Kaze*
The Ninja Wind

Jet smelled the smoke creeping into the cell.

"Come on! Quick!" she said from the ceiling vent, helping Soji and Hiro up. The ceiling was over twenty feet high, so they'd stood on each other's shoulders. They had no idea where the vent would lead, but decided to take the risk. Besides which, they had no other options.

Soon it angled straight up through the building, and Jet climbed to the main floor using counter-pressure and the *shuko* and *ashiko* bands. Then she dropped them down, and Hiro and Soji followed. Jet steeled her focus, knowing she'd face Takumi again. She'd have to draw on all her skills. She knew her own weakness. Now all she had to do was guard against it.

If only it were that simple.

The vent opened on a grate in the ceiling of the hall on the main floor.

Speaking in *shinobi kotoba*, Jet told the others to stay in the vent.

"Where are *you* going?" Hiro asked.

"I've got go straight to the top—to get Harter."

"You can't! It's too dangerous," Hiro pleaded, "Please!"

"We've come this far. Now's the time," she said, steadying her voice.

"Are you ready?" Hiro asked.

Jet swallowed. "Yes. I'm ready."

"No. It's too dangerous. I'll go with you," Hiro said.

"You must stay here with Soji," Jet insisted. "He's weak. We can't leave him alone."

Jet couldn't see Hiro's face in the dark vent, but she felt his strong sense of duty, and his even stronger desire to avenge his mother and Ojiisan.

Jet took a deep breath in. "Hiro. I know you want to come with me, but if something should happen, it's better that one of us is…" She stopped mid-sentence. "Do you understand?" she asked.

Hiro came closer. "You're right. I know you're right. But I…."

"Nothing's going to change unless I defeat him," she said calmly. "It's why I went to Japan. It's why you came to America. We have to finish what our mothers started. For them."

Hiro nodded. He understood. "Be careful," he whispered.

"*Hai!*" she cried, knocking open the grate and dropping down between two guards in an instant. She moved like lightening, knocked them out by jabbing them behind the ears with her fingers in a *shishin ken* strike. More guards on either side of them turned toward her and drew their weapons.

Takumi came into the hall just as they took aim.

"Don't shoot!" he called out, but it was too late.

A hail of bullets rained across the room, guards hitting each other on either side of where Jet had stood.

Standing before them, she'd timed her presence for what seemed a second too long, just enough to confuse them and make them wonder why she wasn't running. And in that brief confusion, she passed through the wall—*kabe nuke no jutsu*. Instantly, she found a small breeze through the building and followed it out.

In the stillness within her motion, she heard the sound of the wind outside the walls. A chill ran through her body. Ojiisan had told her that about the ninja wind. It lived in all of her tribe. It propelled them forward. This was it. It lived within her, too.

The sound shook her soul and pushed her into action. The sound was the desire to live, the force of her will, her *ki*, coming from within her heart. It was her inheritance.

Moving like a gathering storm, she felt her power and strength.

To survive this night, she'd have to master the ninja wind. She'd have to become it, and let it become her.

Her hand instinctively went to the locket, but nothing was there. Her fingers fluttered across her chest, searching but not finding the sacred locus of her power.

Panic rose within her. *When had she lost it, and where? In the cell with Rossi? Sliding through the air vent? I have to find it!*

Jet's heart pounded, her pulse raced like never before.

She was doomed.

In the moment she needed her power the most, it was gone.

CHAPTER 44

夜明け *Yoake*

Daybreak

A huge mahogany door took up the entire wall in front of her.

There must be another door of steel behind it, Jet thought.

She groped the wall, feeling for a keypad.

When she had it, she lifted its plastic cover. It lit up. She took a breath, entered the word.

Inanna.

She'd asked Rossi how to get into Harter's suite, and he'd told her while under hypnosis. The name of Harter's panther, named after Ishtar.

Jet swallowed her distaste at this perversion. *No one could own the sacred feminine. No one could tame it. How arrogant and misguided. How much we've all paid.*

There was a slight whirring as the door slid open. She heard a helicopter outside, its rotors still turning. It had probably brought Harter here and was planning to take him away.

Tall candles were lit all over the enormous ornate room, their flames wavering when the door opened, sending shadows dancing over the ceiling.

Jet stopped, awed wherever she turned: marble sculptures, valiant bronze horses rearing up in battle, a gorgeous baroque armoire carved with a magnificent design of a weeping willow, two rococo couches in red velvet with elegant curves. Jet tried to avert her eyes from the beauty, turning her gaze to the far corner of the room.

"So, you managed to outsmart them, did you?" a voice said in liquid Japanese.

She turned. A man she took to be Harter sat on a plush crimson couch embroidered with white roses. He was thin, pale, and impeccably dressed. A Japanese man sat beside him, straight as a sword in an expensive dark blue suit. He had the bearing of an aristocrat.

And then she saw it. At Harter's feet, its fur black and glistening, was the panther. Inanna.

Just outside an immense window was a landing pad, the helicopter's rotors turning, throwing leaves and dust up against the glass.

"*Most* of them," she corrected in polite Japanese. Then she fired Rossi's pistol toward a seraglio curtain against the wall. A man collapsed behind it, pulling the curtain down with him.

"There's someone else hiding. Come out now or I'll kill you," she said, aiming at another curtain on the other side of the window.

A terrified man emerged, holding up both hands.

"Are you the bodyguard?"

With the gun, she motioned for him to stand near Harter.

"No Ma'am. I'm just the helicopter pilot." His legs were shaking, he could barely stand from fear.

"Then behave like one and fly out of here." She pointed the gun at him. It felt strange, dirty in her hand, and she hesitated. In that moment, her intuition told her to jump to the right, behind the bronze statue of a horse. She did.

A *shuriken* throwing star shot past where her leg had been and struck the wall. It would have incapacitated her.

"It's useless to hide in such a place," a deep voice echoed from across the room.

"Takumi? Is that you? Good job, boy!" Harter stood up with a huge smile on his face, clapping his hands. "Finally. You did something right!"

Takumi grimaced. His right thigh was bleeding more now, from when he'd been shot by his own men. Was the wound deeper than he'd realized? He cursed his men's incompetence.

He aimed his gun toward Jet, but looked to the couch.

"Don't you ever call me *boy*." He threw the words at Harter, then flicked his gun toward a Chinese ebony screen next to the couch and pulled the trigger, shattering the image of a mountaintop pagoda. Harter dropped onto the couch as if he'd been shot. Matsumura scrambled onto the couch next to him. The pilot dove between them, shaking in fear.

"Don't move. Stay there until I say otherwise!" Takumi commanded, brandishing the gun in their direction.

Jet's heart pounded. She glanced past the sculpture at Takumi, staring into his light brown eyes. His gaze caught hers for a split second, and she felt him falter. Maybe his connection to her hadn't been faked. Maybe he felt torn. She was sure of it.

Boldly, she stepped from behind the pillar, but he then aimed the gun at her.

The night cracked open. The pale glow of dawn streamed into the room, mixing softly with the faint light of the candles. She looked at his face, softly illuminated against the shadows. It was still the most beautiful face she'd ever seen.

Takumi kept the gun trained on her as he moved toward her slowly, dragging his injured leg. "Why don't you just surrender and turn over the treasure? That will satisfy Harter, and you can go free."

"I don't have the treasure. I don't even know where it is," she said, keeping her eyes on his, trying to still her heart with her breath.

"How can I possibly believe that?" He tried to keep his voice steady to mask the confusion he felt within.

"I've believed things that seemed impossible, too," she said pointedly.

Takumi's eyes darted toward Harter and Matsumura, then back to her. "There's one thing I want to know," he said, his gaze now burning into hers. "Why are you fighting so hard?"

"I'm fighting to defend what's important to my tribe. The land we cherish. My mother's home. It's where our history has roots."

"No," he said frowning. "It's *your* history. Not mine."

"We're connected, Takumi. We're both ninja."

"I have no connection to anything," he insisted.

"What about me? We're connected," she said, searching his face.

"Us?" He laughed ruefully. "You're *kunoichi*. You used ninja magic to make me care! You didn't really feel anything for me, did you?"

"No, that's not true! I did care. I *do* care!" She rushed toward him, and in his eyes she saw surprise at the undeniable truth of her declaration.

He shook his head, as if shaking her out of his mind. "I'm sorry. I have no choice," he said.

"You *do* have a choice," Jet said emphatically.

Swallowing hard, he forced the words out. "I have a job to do."

Then he threw his gun down and leapt at her, unleashing a stream of powerful kicks. Instinctively, she raised her hands to block them, spun her body to avoid his rapid blows. She swayed under his immense power, trying to meet it with her own. She held her ground.

He turned to kick her in the chest, but she jumped over him, flipping and twisting. She landed behind him and launched a spin kick at his face. He leaned back while striking her ribs with the side of his hand in a stinging *kiten-ken*. It would have broken her ribcage if she hadn't jumped backward and rolled on the floor in a *zenpo kaiten*.

He didn't give her the chance to stand up, raining sharp kicks down on her. She rolled backward and forward to avoid his attacks. Then, using the strength of her core, she fell back on her elbows and kicked his ankle. As he regained his stance, she flipped to her feet and faced him. Pain throbbed at her side.

She couldn't imagine defeating him, even if he was wounded. But maybe she could make him see all he'd tried to deny.

Takumi seemed to read Jet's hesitation. He jumped at her, but she grabbed a damask cloth from a couch and threw it like a fishnet in *toami no jutsu*. It spread in the air, blocking her from sight, and she kicked him through it with all of her *ki*. He fell to the floor beneath it. Pulling the ninja sword from her belt, she yanked the cloth back.

But he was already gone.

The tinny taste of fear pervaded her mouth. *Where did he go? He's got to be somewhere in this room. There's no way he could have gotten away so quickly! I have to find him!*

She moved toward the shadows at the back of the room. Harter and Matsumura remained frozen on the couch, the frightened pilot huddled with them.

The helicopter whirred on the landing pad outside the window.

Jet sensed something behind her and jumped to the side as a saber passed through the space where she'd been.

"It's no use hiding," she said, repeating Takumi's own words.

She breathed deeply, stilling her mind.

Don't be impatient. Think! She focused her senses. Light from the window reached into the room. *He's trying to hide in the dark.* She tried to put herself into Takumi's shoes. How would she act now, if she were him?

Even if you can't see, you have a nose and ears. The *Itako's* voice echoed in her head. *Even if your nose and ears don't work, you can feel human presence through the skin. There's much more to perception than what you see.*

She realized how much she had been depending on daybreak to decide her fate. With the loss of darkness, she no longer had the advantage. How could she win?

She concentrated more deeply. The faint metallic smell of blood hit her nose. It was coming from behind a couch. Gripping the sword, she considered *unyo no tachi*, but was she skilled enough? And did she want to harm him? Her mother had taught her the art of *Jigen-Ryu*, sword fighting. The style was so simple, so deadly, that one stroke could end an opponent's life. But the skills needed to ensure the proper speed for charging and the incredible force required for the sword stroke were far beyond that of any other school of swordsmanship. The timing had to be exact. The masters of *Jigen-Ryu* had been able to fell an opponent thirty feet away in one stroke, in an *unyo*, a fraction of a heartbeat. That's what *unyo no tachi* meant.

Jet didn't know the answers to the questions that flooded her mind, but instinct took over and she leapt forward. Instantly Takumi emerged in an *unyo*, holding a dagger. Sparks flew as he deflected her sword. He grappled her fiercely, pinning her as he brought his blade toward her face. She leaned back, but he turned the knife and brought it to the side of her neck. She wanted to reason with him, to bring this extraordinary warrior to her side, but she knew that she had no choice but to fight truly with all her skill. His anger was too great. He would fight until the end. It was all he knew how to do.

Jet held her sword in both hands, using it as a shield. Takumi funneled all of his power into his blade and tried to push it down on her. She grit her teeth, trying to hold his blade back. If only she had the locket, she would be stronger, she told herself. If only she hadn't lost it.

Suddenly, the image of her mother returned to her, on the mountain that night, the last night of the game. In a flash, she understood. That had been her final lesson. Satoko hadn't had the locket. She hadn't needed it. She'd been born into her tradition, and her powers were her birthright. She'd been trying to teach Jet her true power—that they were women, and brute force wasn't their skill. It wasn't going to be possible for her to beat Takumi like this. Her mother had been sick and frail, yet had still won by being totally present. She'd endured using everything, the moonlight and the wind, her awareness of the earth, to harness her last remaining power. Now Jet understood that what her mother had taught her in that last game on the mountain was how to fight when you were weaker than your opponent.

Gratitude flooded Jet's heart, and she knew what she had to do. There was only one way she could defeat Takumi, and she would have to embrace it, no matter how difficult. It was the gift that her mother had bequeathed to her. Satoko had sacrificed her life to give it to her, and Jet could no longer refuse it.

She took a deep breath, deep as the ocean. Then she caught Takumi's wrist with one hand and threw her sword with the other, using all of her strength. His eyes lifted briefly as her blade spun and struck the large window. The glass shattered, jagged pieces falling to the floor as the wind from the helicopter's rotors rushed into the room.

Here it was again, this time undeniable—the wind her mother had told her to study, to feel, to follow, the wind Ojiisan had shown her. Locket or not, Jet's *hara* thrummed with power and resolve. *Kunoichi is not something outside myself,* she finally understood. *It's not something given to me or inherited. It's something claimed from within.*

This time, she knew she had to let her body join the ninja wind, to move with it, dance with it, embrace it, *be* it. She surrendered and it poured over her and into her. She twisted along its invisible lines, slipping from Takumi's grip and entering the wind.

Following its currents, she came to her feet and moved away from him as he propelled himself up. He charged fiercely, as if he could feel nothing, not his wound or his heart, and she again leapt away, dancing along the wind, letting her mind grow still in this final, silent meditation: empty, being nothing but the moment that arises, the very present instant, smaller than any fraction of a second, and yet also infinite, until each second seemed a hundred years, and each of her movements—a blur of speeding motion in the eyes of the others—felt to her like floating, drifting past those around her who were now so slow they appeared frozen. Even Takumi seemed to move in slow motion. She embodied the wind, and the world opened before her.

Then Jet spun away, grabbing the saber he'd thrown at her. She followed the wind around the room, her feet brushing over furniture and sculptures. She ceased to think and jumped toward him. He leaned back, striking out with a tight spin kick.

She slipped past his foot, moving into the gust, rolling over the floor, and attacking again before he could see where she was. Her saber clashed with his knife.

Go to the right, a voice spoke from within the stillness of her mind.

She did, hearing the wisdom in her blood, bending her body with the wind from the helicopter's rotors. She crouched and spun and kicked his wounded thigh with all of the *ki* she could summon. He dropped to his knees. Now his leg was bleeding heavily. His face was pale.

She lifted her sword to his throat.

No... No. I can't....

She held the sword there, taking in his beautiful, suffering face, the light brown eyes. She still wanted to save him, to make him see what was real in her, in him.

Then she felt it. The cold muzzle of a pistol against the back of her head.

"Drop the sword. Get on your knees."

It was Harter.

"I've been waiting for this all my life," he said. "I've been torn between killing you to get revenge for my father, or getting the treasure. I'll settle for the treasure."

"Let me do it," Takumi said harshly. He got up slowly. He took the gun from Harter. The muzzle brushed her head, and she closed her eyes. *I'm sorry mother. I tried. I did my best.* She imagined light all around her body, enveloping her. She steadied herself for the bullet.

Then she felt the gun move away.

Takumi was pointing it at Harter.

Jet was breathless, stunned. Was Takumi crazy? Or had he come around? Her heart held in her chest.

"Listen to me, Harter, and listen well," he said. "For a long time, I thought of myself as a stray dog, begging for scraps of food and shelter. I was willing to do anything if the pay was high enough. But there comes a day when even a dog would rather run into traffic than be kicked by an owner who's dumber than he is."

"No one betrays me!" Harter said, eyes bulging with rage. Matsumura was standing by the couch, his posture suggesting fury, but Takumi ignored him.

"Me?" he said. "Betray you? You're even dumber than I thought. Because you believed there was such a thing as trust between us. Our relationship doesn't go beyond money. I thought I could be your dog, but it turns out that some things are worth more than money."

"You ungrateful fool!" Harter shouted. "I was the only one who would hire you. Everyone else said you were too hard to predict. I should have listened to them."

"Takumi," Matsumura shouted. "Are you insane? You'll never work again!"

"Shut up, Matsumura!" Harter yelled, then glared at Takumi, assessing the situation.

"If it's money you're after, I can understand. Money is power," he said. "How much do you want?"

Takumi smiled. "Of course, you would think that. But there's one thing worth more than money."

"Yeah? And what's that? Love?" Harter sneered.

Jet held her breath, looking at Takumi.

He paused. "Respect. I respect anyone who fights like they do," he nodded in Jet's direction. "And I don't respect you at all."

Harter walked away from Takumi as if unafraid. He took Inanna's chain and motioned for the helicopter pilot to follow him. Wind rushed through the room, and Jet sensed it all happening at once: Takumi's exhaustion as he lowered the gun, the click of the trigger across the room. Matsumura fired, striking Takumi in the chest.

Jet screamed. Like a hurricane, she hurled herself into the few remaining shadows in the room. Guards rushed through the door as Harter and Matsumura ran to the helicopter. Jet wanted to go after them, but Takumi was lying on the floor, looking up at her. He was the only one who could see where she stood in the darkness.

A faint light shone on his face. Jet felt herself pulled into the vortex of his despair. His eyelids began to close. The helicopter took off.

She knew she needed to flee, to find Hiro and Soji and escape, but there weren't many guards left, and she could easily defeat them and then find help for Takumi.

The softness of his gaze called to her the world he had lost, his jungles and the quiet of its trees. His gaze softened. Was that a slight smile on his lips, like the mysterious smile of the Buddha, containing worlds?

She knew she should chant *Namu Amida Butsu*, but she refused to believe it was his time. Sunlight flashed over his face like the wings of a golden bird.

"No!" Jet pleaded with someone. God, Buddha, anyone. She couldn't let him go.

She had to find a way to save him, even if he couldn't save himself.

CHAPTER 45

涙 *Namida*
Tears

J-Bird drove Hiro, Soji, and Jet along the highway. Soon after they'd crossed the Colorado border into New Mexico, snow began to fall.

"*Yuki!* Snow!" Hiro leaned against the window. Though he hid them well, Jet could feel Hiro's emotions. *He's still just a kid*, she remembered. *Not even a teenager yet.*

Before long, the hills along the freeway were draped in soft white. Looking at the tableau, Jet felt its cool sparseness. This feeling of emptiness was a relief.

"What happened to the man with the light brown eyes?" Soji asked.

"I left him for dead," Jet said, staring at the snow.

"I see." Soji's jaw tightened. "What a waste." He, too, kept his eyes on the road in front of them, and the white mountains glittered in the cold silence.

"Completely," Jet said, stifling her own emotions. Unconsciously, though, she rubbed her hands as if the smell of blood remained there. Takumi had still been breathing when she'd left him. After incapacitating the guards who hadn't fled, she'd called an ambulance and bound his wound. Then she'd interrogated several of the injured men, finding out where Harter would have gone.

Had Takumi sacrificed himself so she could live? And yet she knew that if she'd killed him then, she would have died at Harter's hand. What another might have called weakness had been her strength. It had allowed her to survive.

Turmoil would always exist beneath the surface, but what lay hidden in the depths of the ocean, the crevices of a cave, the folds of the wind, the chambers of the heart? A longing for tranquility filled her. Yes, she could locate the point on the forehead where a flattened palm would knock a man unconscious, or knee someone hard and swift enough to make someone crumble, or twist herself deep into a man's unconscious mind, sticking there like a fly in a spiderweb to confuse and disorient. But none of that had helped her when Takumi lay wounded.

It was just as Ojiisan said: one could survive only at the expense of others.

She grit her teeth. The fight was still not over.

"Take me to the airport," she said, her voice thick with resolve.

"What?" J-Bird asked, stunned. "Why?"

"It's not over yet, J-Bird. You know that. We need to finish this."

He looked over at her, his eyes glinting.

"I know I need to let you go," he said. "But I want to go with you."

"I know. Trust me. I'll be back," she promised.

He reached out and gripped her hand.

"You will," he said, knowing that only she could finish what her mother had started.

"I'm sure of it. Satoko knew you could do this, too."

"Thank you for everything, J-Bird," Jet said, her mind made up.

As he gazed at her attentively, he hoped in his heart of hearts that she would. He'd lost one Kuroi woman. He couldn't bear to lose another.

CHAPTER 46

重荷 *Omoni*
Burden

Harter sat behind his desk, watching the lights of San Francisco flicker fifty floors below. It was eight o'clock in the evening, but it could have been midnight for all he knew. Things had not gone well, not at all.

The entire operation had gone terribly wrong. Takumi might have been gifted, but he had been too young and volatile to trust. Harter kicked himself. He should have known. He *did* know. He just hadn't trusted his instincts. Never again. Failure was not an option. They were so close, after so many years, so many losses, so many millions of dollars. He could taste victory, and that would all be worth it. The treasure would be his. He'd finally get recognition for all of his hard work, resourcefulness, and faith that such a magnificent historically significant treasure existed. No one would ever mock him again, and his father's martyrdom would be seen for the highest form of sacrifice that it was.

He stared out at the skyline, half expecting to see it explode.

"Mr. Harter, excuse my bluntness, but what are you going to do?" Matsumura's high-pitched voice broke the silence. "As your primary backer, I invested seven million dollars in your enterprise. I gave you the information you needed to launch operations in Japan. You promised me a significant return on my investment, but so far, nothing has gone as planned. I'm sure you know that half of the money came from Japanese investors whom I personally assured would see a substantial return. How am I going to satisfy them?"

Harter kept looking at the lights. Inanna put her head on his foot and rubbed her nose with her paw.

"I'm someone who always succeeds, Mr. Harter." Matsumura cleared his throat. "Every time the investors call me asking for a status report, I manage to come up with enough news of progress to hold them over. But if the situation doesn't change soon, I'll never be able to go back to Japan. Do you understand?"

"That's your problem, isn't it?" Harter said, not looking at him.

"I realize that you don't have a lot of sympathy for me," Matsumura went on, "but try to put yourself in my shoes."

Harter tried. The Matsumura clan was notorious for walking on the backs of others to make their fortunes. Yet, this was par for the course. What successful clan or business didn't do the same?

"Fine," Harter said. "Now put yourself in mine. There are only a few companies that deserve to be called enterprises. How many do you know that had steady sales increases during the recession? Just a handful, I can assure you. I'm one of the select few who leads those companies. Companies that prop up the world economy, mind you! Do you understand that the global economy depends on people like me?"

Harter closed his eyes. The losses on his estate would be in the millions. There would be payments to the families of the men who'd been killed, hush money to the injured men and the local police station, fire department, and media. New Language Systems couldn't write off the losses. They'd be too great for the books. Stockholders would be outraged. He'd have to cover the costs personally. It enraged him to think that his carefully conceived plan had almost been crushed by a young woman. He clenched his fists. He would do everything to stop her.

"Mr. Harter, please say something," Matsumura said. "You must take responsibility! That's the only thing my Japanese investors will understand!"

"Mr. Matsumura, if you're so worried about your investors, why don't you commit *hara-kiri*. Then they'll forgive you. Isn't that the way of the virtuous samurai?" Harter's eyes narrowed as he turned to look at his colleague's reddening face. Matsumura's expensively tailored light gray suit seemed to exaggerate the lines of his diminishing body. It hung as if on a skeleton.

"Risk is a necessary part of any business, Mr. Matsumura," Harter continued. "If you wanted to avoid risk, you should have put your money under your futon."

"Don't mock me!" Matsumura's voice tore into Harter like ripping metal. "You were the one who came and asked me to put my trust in you. You bowed down and begged me to help you undertake this project, for the good of world history. World history! That's what you said. But now I see that it was your *own* history you were concerned about. Your own gain. That's why things have not gone well."

"That would make me just like you, wouldn't it?" Harter said smoothly, stroking Inanna with his foot, enjoying this little power play.

"First," Matsumura said, his voice shaking, "you wanted me to help you gain access to sites in Japan, assuring me you'd take total responsibility for the excavation costs. But as the project grew, you practically begged me to invest, so I managed to collect the funds from my circle of contacts, men I've known for years, men whose families have been tied to mine for generations. Now you dismiss my generosity by saying it was 'just business.' How selfish can you be? If my losses are so easily dismissed, what would lead me to believe that any of our gains would be shared?"

"*My* gains," Harter corrected him.

"No. *Our* gains," Matsumura countered. "Let me tell you something about history. The treasure you call King Solomon's treasure should have belonged to my ancestors."

"What?" Harter whirled around. "And how is that?" he scoffed.

"In the fourth century, when Emperor Jinmu conquered Western Japan, my ancestors fought hard under his name. They distinguished themselves," he said, his chest lifting. "As a reward, they received the power to govern Japan on the Emperor's behalf. The

Matsumura were his faithful retainers in Kyoto, members of the aristocracy until the country bumpkins you call 'virtuous samurai' raised their swords and took over."

Harter laughed.

"So you see, the fortune should be *ours*!" he exclaimed, the blood draining from his face with rage at Harter's mockery.

"Mr. Matsumura, no doubt you're proud of your roots, but you aren't the only one who has lost money. I don't know how long your family has held onto its fortunes, but if you're so proud of its long, rich history, you'd better just kiss away what you've lost. It's just a trickle in the ocean, isn't it? Kyoto aristocrats leeching off the emperor always exaggerated their status. You seem to be typical of the aristocracy."

"No one insults me!" Matsumura moved toward Harter. Inanna, who had been resting, suddenly growled. She opened her mouth, exposing two sharply curved fangs.

Matsumura backed away, trying to smile.

"Mr. Harter," he said in the friendliest voice he could muster, "I don't want to fight with you. I just want you to understand my situation. Please be reasonable."

Matsumura bowed humbly, smiling at both Harter and Inanna. But Inanna seemed to have understood that Matsumura's smile was disingenuous. She crouched, preparing to attack.

"Please say something to your pet. I never intended to harm you."

Harter smiled. "Okay. Inanna, back off!" He stroked her shining black fur, but she didn't stop growling. She moved toward Matsumura, tensing her shoulders.

"Mr. Harter, please. It's not a joke. Please call her off!" Matsumura cowered near the couch as the panther took another step and growled.

"Inanna, enough! Back off! Back off!" Harter grabbed her neck, but she shook free of his grip. She lifted her face and roared.

"Ahhh!" Matsumura cried, crouching against the couch. He fumbled in his pockets, forgetting that he'd disposed of the gun he'd used to shoot Takumi, anxious about it being used as evidence.

"Inanna, no! Stay!" Harter shouted. But the animal kept advancing. He opened his desk drawer and pulled out his pistol. He aimed it at her, prepared to shoot.

Matsumura's entire body was shaking.

"Stay!" Harter shouted. Inanna's growl resonated, but as if distracted by something, she moved away from Matsumura, padding sleekly toward a white door in the far corner of the room.

Suddenly, she stopped ten feet in front of it and raised her head.

"Who's there?" Harter shouted, pointing his gun at the door.

The door swung open violently. Jet rushed into the room, holding a gun. Harter pulled the trigger, but she anticipated his clumsy shot and ducked.

"I won't hesitate to shoot you," she said. "And my aim is better than yours."

"That remains to be seen," Harter told her and shot again, but Jet quickly and easily stepped aside.

She fired a single shot, knocking the gun from his hand. He cried out, clutching his fingers.

Inanna exposed her teeth with a growl, shifted her weight to her rear legs.

"Shush, Miss Kitty," Jet whispered, boring her gaze into the panther's. "You should be better trained."

The panther grew silent, watching her intently.

"How did you get in here?" Harter shouted.

"It wasn't very difficult," she said. She'd used *kabe nuke no jutsu* to enter, then hypnotized the guard, getting the code and access to the emergency stairs connected to the penthouse.

"Stand up!" Harter shouted at Matsumura.

Matsumura stood meekly, hands splayed out to cover a spot that had spread on his gray pants.

Harter smiled. "Tell your jittery band of Japanese investors that even though the first stage of the project might not have met expectations, the termination of the opposition was a success. And tell them it's Harter who'll get King Solomon's treasure in the end. So sit back and enjoy the show."

Then he turned to Inanna. "Kill her," he commanded.

Jet's eyes windened.

Inanna growled, but Jet put her finger to lips. The panther quieted again. Jet looked into Inanna's eyes and took a step toward her, moving slowly and lightly, the way her mother had taught her how to walk on wet tissue. Almost imperceptibly. Weightless.

Inanna growled, but Jet took another step, gazing into the panther's crystalline eyes. She flashed to the bear on the mountain in Aomori. If she could talk to a wild bear whose mountain lair she'd invaded, she could talk to a domesticated panther in an urban highrise. She steadied her breath, focussed her mind on the panther's.

"Inanna, get her! Kill!" Harter yelled, snapping his fingers in the air.

Jet neared the animal. Inanna backed away from her.

"Inanna, what are you doing? Kill her, kill her!" Harter shouted, panic straining his voice.

Inanna froze. Her eyes closed as if to avoid Jet's gaze.

Jet continued to approach the panther slowly and stealthily, as if she herself had transformed into a sleek black feline. Inanna rolled onto her back and exposed her belly. Jet felt sorry she'd been taken from her habitat in the jungle. What kind of life was this for a wild animal to be at the short end of some power-hungry fanatic's golden leash?

"Good girl!" she whispered, crouching and stroking the beast's black body. Inanna purred like a cat, paws up in the air, her body undulating in ripples of joy.

"Inanna! I'm your owner! Obey me! Kill her!" Harter shouted, clutching his injured hand. Blood seeped from his wound.

Inanna rolled to her feet and shook her body angrily. She turned to Harter and opened her mouth, roaring. Then she looked toward Jet, as if awaiting instruction. Gazing into Jet's eyes, she moved toward Harter with slow, deliberate steps. Smelling blood. His blood.

"I'm your master! Stop! Stop! Now!" Harter's face was distorted with fear. He dropped to the floor and scrambled for his fallen gun.

"I'm not the bad guy," he pleaded, fear choking his words. "My quest put your ragtag tribe onto the global stage. I could turn the world's attention to your village. I could make it culturally signifi-cant, make it thrive. Let's work together. I beg of you," he pleaded.

But it was too late. Jet watched Inanna's beautiful body leap twenty feet in an instant, landing on its prey. How graceful and ef-fortless it was.

Jet turned and walked toward the white door. She stepped into the dim narrow space of the stairwell. Her footsteps echoed heav-ily. They sounded like the footsteps of a *sarariman* tired of his job, tired of his life.

Behind her were the terrible screams, then silence.

Jet wasn't proud to have avenged Ojiisan. She felt only that she'd carried out her duty, lived out her destiny in the only way she could. The smell of blood hung in the air, sending waves of revul-sion through her. She wanted to wash it off, to purify herself in the cold mountain water she'd sipped from the bamboo ladle on Osore-zan not even a month ago.

My mother must have known this feeling. She tried to protect me from it, and in the end, she couldn't. So she trained me well so that I'd be able to accept my destiny with humility and respect.

Jet walked out of the building and through Chinatown, where she bought some incense and a lighter. Then she walked down Mar-ket Street to the Embarcadero, where she sat on the pier as the waves of the Pacific crashed against the rocks as sea lions barked raucously.

Looking out toward Japan, she thought of Ojiisan. He was right. You couldn't escape your *en*, your karma. The most you could do was try to live your life, hoping to do as little harm as pos-sible. She'd done enough for several lifetimes.

She breathed the cold air. She'd given herself over to her weak-ness and conquered it for her mother, grandmother, and Hiro's mother. For her father and Ojiisan. For generations of her family. *People who've been forced to die unecessary deaths should be hon-ored. The dead can't remember the dead*, she realized, *only the sur-vivors can.*

Jet was a survivor. The ocean breeze washed over her. She prayed it would cleanse her.

She lit the incense and prayed for the souls of those she had done battle with, those who had gone on to other shores. She prayed for forgiveness for all she had done.

As dusk settled on the city, she stood up again. It was time to return to her family.

But first she'd go get the panther. J-Bird knew an animal shelter that would place it in a wildlife refuge. She'd have to clean up the evidence, somehow.

Jet crept back into the building and found Inanna in the mayhem of the room, roaming disorientedly. She made a leash with Harter's belt, checked the hallway to make sure it was clear, then guided the panther down into a service elevator and out into the basement parking garage, where she tied Inanna to a post. Then she used a tranquilizer dart from her mother's ninja trousseau and knocked the panther out. Using a payphone on the street, she called the SPCA and reported a large cat in the parking garage.

Then she ran as far away as she could get.

Regret brimmed her chest. Ojiisan had said that being a ninja meant putting the blade over the heart, subduing one's personal desires over one's duty for the tribe, for history, for the future. She resolved to take care of Hiro and return to Kanabe, taking her rightful place in the tribe. Though she couldn't take back what had happened, she resolved to spill no more blood, to stop the cycle.

Rika Kuroi was just a distant memory. Now she was truly Jet Black, *kunoichi*, able to put the blade over the heart.

If only Amy Williams could see me now, she thought.

Part Six

FURUSATO

故郷

HOMELAND

CHAPTER 47

暗号 *Ango*
Cryptography

Soji, Hiro, and Jet gathered in J-Bird's trailer. Ever since they'd returned from Harter's compound, Aska had not let Hiro out of her sight. For his part, Hiro had practically been glued to her side.

Aska licked Hiro's face repeatedly as they sat with an old Native American man respected for his wisdom. His name was Neil Bluewolf, and he'd helped perform the rites for Satoko's funeral. Jet was curious as to why he was here now. His face was dark and weathered, his brow and the bridge of his nose prominent.

"Harter is gone. The mission is complete," J-Bird said, nodding at Neil.

"Everyone's here, finally. It's time to discover the treasure," Neil said softly.

Jet and Hiro's eyes lit up. J-Bird looked at them with a calm, serious expression.

J-Bird spoke. "As you know, Kanabe was attacked years ago by people who were after the treasure. The villagers fought bravely, but when it was over, some questioned whether the treasure existed at all. And if it did, was it worth all they'd given?"

Jet nodded. She wondered the same thing. Was it worth it? She envisioned the lonely village at the bottom of the valley. She could smell the forest and remembered the odd sense of timelessness she'd felt walking the old roads. The mountains encircling the village had been red, the color of autumn. In their light, Ojiisan had stood with a calm smile on his face.

After a short silence, J-Bird began to speak again.

"Satoko took the loss very hard. After the attack, she decided to hide her knowledge of the treasure in a place no one would ever think to look."

"We know!" Hiro said, excitement building.

J-Bird paused. "And that place was Jet's mind."

Hiro gasped. "You mean she buried a map in Jet's head?"

J-Bird looked around the room. "Yes. I mean, she hypnotized Jet and hid the information in the depths of Jet's consciousness."

"What? Why didn't you tell us before?" Jet asked, astonished.

"Soji was central to unlocking the mystery. He held information in his brain, too. It was the only way to make sure that Jet's information was protected."

"And that's why you needed us both together!" Jet exclaimed.

"Right! And here we are," J-Bird replied. "Finally! With the danger gone."

Something didn't sit right with Jet. "Why didn't we all just get together before? Why did so many people have to get hurt along the way?"

"It wasn't necessary before. The teaching was always that the secret should stay secret," J-Bird said. "But then NLS stepped up its attacks, Satoko got sick, and she feared it would be lost forever."

"If that happened, the tribe's future would be imperilled forever," Soji said.

Jet frowned. "Couldn't someone have just hypnotized us and drawn out the information anytime?"

J-Bird shook his head. "That's exactly what NLS thought. That's why they wanted to capture you, and that's why they caught and interrogated Soji."

"Oh, I get it!" Hiro exclaimed.

"If we'd used ordinary information, they'd have succeeded," J-Bird continued, "but Satoko met Neil, and Neil and I encoded the information in such a way that no one would be able to decipher it."

"Encoded?" Hiro's eyes widened.

"Yes. Neil was a Navajo Code Talker. My father Wayne and Neil served in counter-intelligence together at the end of World War II."

Hiro jumped up. "During the Pacific War, the American military used a code based on the Navajo language. It was the only code the Japanese military couldn't break!"

"Right!" J-Bird looked proudly at Hiro, then turned to Neil, who continued the story.

"We'd just turned twenty," he said in a deep voice. "We went into the Marines and to boot camp. Afterward, we were sent to Camp Elliot, where we found out we were supposed to use our language to translate official orders in the Iwo Jima combat zone. You see, when the Pacific War broke out, military intelligence needed to create a code that the Japanese army couldn't break. They found out about our language from a white man who knew it, and decided to use it for their code."

"How did it work?" Jet asked, eyes wide.

"Native American languages differ from tribe to tribe. Even if someone can understand Hopi, that linguistic knowledge won't transfer to another tribal language like Navajo. The wording of the Navajo language is so special that it's not even easy for Native Americans to master. Even if someone could understand Navajo, they couldn't break the code," Neil said.

"Brilliant!" Hiro enthused.

Neil shook his head. "You know the sad history of our people, don't you. Well, as hard as the war was for people in the outside world, the situation on the reservation was worse. We had no money. Few homes had water or electricity. The schools were terrible, and the men had no work. The only thing we had was alcohol. It was everywhere…" He sighed.

J-Bird interjected. "Anyway, we had every reason to reject the U.S. Army's proposal to use our code to help win the war. We wondered how the war was going to benefit us, especially if we were going to lose our lives and lend our language to it."

Neil nodded, speaking carefully. "But then we had a big tribal meeting and learned about the Japanese army's brutalities in

China. Hundreds of thousands of people were being killed. It reminded us of The Long Walk in our own history, when we had to leave our lands and go to the reservations. So many died."

J-Bird looked down. "We felt we couldn't sit and watch. We decided to help because no one had helped us."

"Right," Neil said. "The way we saw it, being Code Talkers meant saving as many people as possible from what we ourselves had suffered. That's the way to turn the tide of history."

"So you were a hero!" Hiro said.

Neil shook his head. "Not at all. We just did what we felt was right. We were stationed on the front lines. Wayne and I translated radio-transmitted orders issued from the Code Talkers at command posts. They had it much worse."

"So there were only two of you?" Jet asked.

"No. Twenty-nine of us created the code. We made up about five hundred words. The army used other languages for code, too, like Cherokee, Comanche, and Choctaw. In 1945, our poor Navajo comrades were captured and tortured by the Japanese, who couldn't break the code. Some of our own men didn't even know the code. Even if they admitted to understanding each word, they still couldn't figure out the code. What a lot of grief we caused them," Neil said, shuddering.

"Without the help of the Navajo Marines," J-Bird said, "we—America, that is—probably wouldn't have won the war."

"It helped capture Iwo Jima, and that was decisive," Neil said solemnly, as if recalling the horrible battle.

"Why haven't I ever heard anything about the Code Talkers?" Jet asked, surprised.

"After the war, we weren't supposed to tell anyone about it because the army used the Navajo code again in the Korean War. Then it was broken and the news of the Code Talkers came out. But it wasn't until recently that we got any recognition. You know, I even got a call from Washington the other day," he said proudly.

"From the president?" Hiro asked excitedly.

"Well, from his office. There's going to be a ceremony at the Capitol." He looked at Hiro's sparkling eyes. "Want to come?"

"I have to go back to Japan," Hiro said, looking disappointed.

"Let's see if they can work around your schedule," Neil said, smiling.

"So what does this have to do with the treasure?" Jet asked.

"My father was on the front lines with Neil," J-Bird told her. "So when Satoko needed help hiding the tribal treasure, I thought of Neil and the code. I thought it could be useful."

Neil nodded slowly. "When J-Bird introduced me to Satoko, she told me the story of her family. I saw my own history all over again—the theft of our land, how we'd been oppressed. That's why we agreed to help her."

"Wow! You did that for a stranger?" Jet marvelled.

"No. I did it for a *friend*. You know, the Navajo have a saying. 'We are all connected.' And it's true."

"Except to the *Wa!*" Hiro said, defiant. "They're our enemies. Descendents of the Emperor who stole our lands!"

"No," Neil disagreed. "To *everyone*. Our enemies make us rise to what we have to overcome in the world—and in ourselves. They're not always *out there*. They're often *within*."

Jet bit her lip, thinking of Takumi.

"How does it work? What is it that I know?" she asked, letting out a deep breath. She wanted to solve the mystery, and now.

Neil closed his eyes. "We needed two people to secure the information. One holds the key to open and close the door to the unconscious mind of the other. That's Soji."

"And the other?" Hiro asked, eyebrows raised.

"Jet holds the map. Anyone who wanted to find the treasure first needed to bring the two of you together. Then they needed to know that you held the map and the key."

J-Bird looked at Jet. "This is one of the reasons so little was explained to you. We knew that you wouldn't be safe if you knew the whole story."

"But I don't!" Jet said, feeling the old frustration rising again.

J-Bird put his hand on her shoulder, steadying her.

"Well, you *think* you don't. Since you were both hypnotized, you have no memory of knowing. But some part of your mind knows. That's what we have to open."

"Real *saiminjutsu!*" Hiro exclaimed. "Your tribe has it too!"

"Yes." Neil looked around the table, meeting the eyes of everyone sitting there. "Now that we're all here and the danger is gone, it's time to unlock the door."

Jet's body tingled in anticipation.

J-Bird put a candle in the middle of the table and lit it. Then he turned off the lights so the flame softly illuminated their faces. There was no sound except for a slight wind and the melting snow dripping from the roof to the ground.

"Wait!" Jet said. "There's one more thing I have to do."

She took her suitcase and went into the bathroom. When she came out a few minutes later, she was dressed in her mother's kimono, the one with the spring iris pattern emboldened on its silk brocade. The diamond-studded *kanzashi* sparkled from her hair. Neil beamed. Soji clapped his hands together in delight. Hiro smiled broadly.

"I just wanted to put this on for my mom," Jet said. She couldn't really explain why, but she knew it was something she had to do.

J-Bird looked up from the candle, eyes glistening.

"Satoko would have been honored," he said.

Then he nodded, motioning for Jet to sit down. She slid gracefully into the metal folding chair at the table in the tiny trailer.

"Jet, Soji, look at the flame. No one else say anything."

Jet and Soji looked at the flame until their eyes began to tear up.

"Please close your eyes. Let all the sounds around you come into your ears."

The wind outside blew harder. The silence seemed endless.

"What do you hear?" J-Bird asked.

"The wind. The sound of the wind," Jet answered.

"Yes, try to remember the last time you heard this sound," he said, pausing to let them drop deeper into concentration.

"All the winds in the world are contained in that sound. The echo of wind you hear bears the original echo of the wind that blew on earth in the beginning of time. It covers the four corners of the world. It's ageless and timeless. It will continue blowing forever, carrying the same ancient echoes."

Jet breathed deeply, following his words.

"Just like the wind," he intoned, "you've been alive forever, holding ancient memories in your consciousness. Deep inside your mind, you'll find the echo of your old memories. Listen to the echo. Find the echo of your memories in the echo of the wind."

Jet and Soji began to sway.

"It's December fifteenth, 1996," J-Bird said.

"December… fifteenth… 1996…" Jet repeated his words as if in a trance.

"Yes. December fifteenth, 1996. Soji, what do you hear?"

"The sound… of… water… running… down… from the mountains… still covered… with deep snow." His low voice vibrated within the room like a temple bell.

"Yes, the rush of a spring river," J-Bird said gently, as if talking to a child.

Soji's body moved in his chair rhythmically, like a pendulum.

"Soji, you have something to say to Jet, don't you?"

Soji nodded.

"Please tell her," J-Bird said.

The words came out slowly, as if Soji was talking under water. "*Haa la hoodzaa sit naaaas. Haaateedee la aniti.*"

Hiro looked at J-Bird with surprise. It was a language he had never heard before: Navajo.

"Jet," J-Bird prompted, "Soji just asked you, What happened? Where did you come from?"

Her body swayed to the flicker of the candlelight. Now she stopped and leaned back in her chair. With her eyes still closed, she opened her mouth. Words tumbled out in a slow stream.

"*Doolado hozhoo lagi nishwood, sixt naa'aasoo.*"

The words reverberated in the small room, their mysterious echo like the song of an ancient bird Hiro never imagined could exist.

As she spoke, Neil wrote down her words.

Then they stopped. Silence filled the room again.

"Is that it?" J-Bird asked Neil. He nodded. J-Bird looked at Jet and Soji.

"I will count to three. While I'm counting, you will begin to wake up. And when I say three, you will wake up completely."

"One, Two, Three!" His deep voice boomed.

Jet and Soji's bodies jolted, and their eyes sprung open.

"Are you awake?" J-Bird asked Jet.

She blinked. "Yes. Was I sleeping?"

"You and Soji were asleep for five minutes."

"Really?" Jet yawned and leaned back in her chair, looking at the flame on the table.

"Soji? Are you back?" J-Bird asked.

"*Hai!*" Soji said, rubbing his eyes.

J-Bird smiled. "Good work. Now it's up to Neil to decode. He's the specialist."

Neil signaled for J-Bird to turn on the light. Jet and Shoji looked at the mysterious words on the paper, waiting for their meaning to be revealed.

"What happened on December fifteenth?" Hiro asked, unable to hold back.

J-Bird explained. "When we decided to put the location of the Kuroi family treasure in Jet's unconscious mind, we agreed to use code similar to the one we used during World War II. But we knew that a code alone was not enough to protect the information. So we decided to set up barriers in Jet and Soji's minds. There were two passwords. One was the memory of the sound of the wind, and the other..."

"Was the date of December fifteenth, 1996!" Hiro exclaimed.

"Right." J-Bird nodded. "More precisely, the sound of the wind was the key to accessing those particular memory fields in both Soji and Jet's subconscious minds. The date was the key to opening Soji's unconscious mind."

"But December fifteenth, 1996, was not the actual date that Soji met Satoko and was hypnotized. That was the twenty-sixth of March, 1996. If we'd used the actual date, someone could have guessed it," Neil said.

"Indeed," Soji said. "Harter tried to hypnotize me, but he couldn't. Somehow he knew I'd been in America at the end of March 1996, and he tried to unearth my memories from that time. But my unconscious mind thought I'd been in America in December, so I didn't respond."

"Uh huh. So it was a good plan." Neil looked at J-Bird and smiled.

"We were afraid something like that would happen," J-Bird replied, "but Satoko was thorough." Jet saw the love, and the sadness in his eyes.

Neil continued. "The words that the date triggered in Soji's mind were Navajo for *What happened? Where are you from?* Those were the keys to triggering Jet's memory field, where the information about the hiding place was stored."

"What did Jet's words mean?" Hiro asked.

"She said, *Doo labo hozhoo lagi nishwood sixt naa aaoo saza*, which means, *I came from a more pleasant place, my cousin, my friend*. Those words were the final key to unlocking her memory."

"Wow!" Hiro marvelled at the ingenuity of the plan.

Neil nodded. "Though I was the one who gave Jet these words, I don't remember doing it because Satoko hypnotized me, too. Then she said the words to me in English. I translated them to Jet and Soji but remembered nothing."

"And," J-Bird said, "I only knew the first two keys: the wind and the date."

"Yes," Neil added. "Satoko was extremely careful. She broke up the information and protected the secret as many ways as she could."

The four sat in silence, listening to the sound of Aska's contented breathing at their feet.

Tension filled the air.

"Are we ready to break the code?" Hiro said, breaking the silence. He could barely contain his excitement.

"Can you, Neil?" Jet asked.

Neil looked down at the sheet of paper on which he'd written the Navajo words.

He took a breath and closed his eyes. "Well…" he said, scratching his chin. "The meaning of the first sentence is: *The center of the air has vibrant eyes.* The rest of what Jet said can be translated as:

> *Angel takes the envelope for the red unit of islands,*
> *The kettle encounters the yucca and the bear acts like a cat.*
> *The owl flies and the snake takes an apple as the toy of uncle Ed.*
> *The oasis provides the elephant with nourishment,*
> *Girls request only the unit of north dogs."*

"What? I can't understand a thing!" Hiro said. "It's like nonsense!"

"Of course you can't understand it. It's a code." Neil laughed. "It's exactly the same method we used during the Pacific War."

"How do you decode it?" Jet asked.

Neil smiled broadly. "First drop every preposition and article. Then take the first letter from the remaining words and make a word from each sentence. Then put the words together to make a sentence. Got it?"

Hiro shrugged. "Sort of."

"Okay, look. For example, let's take the first sentence," he said, writing it down.

The center of the air has vibrant eyes.

"If we apply the formula it would be like this. See?"

The Center of the Air has Vibrant Eyes.

"What do you see?" Neil asked.

Hiro spelled it out. "C-A-V-E...Cave!" he exclaimed.

"Exactly. Now let's keep going," Neil said.

He watched Neil write the words without the prepositions and articles. Then Neil wrote the first letter of each word down on the bottom of the paper.

"See?" He passed the paper to Hiro.

"C,A,V,E. A,T,E,R,U,I. K,E,Y. B,A,C,K. O,F. S,T,A,T,U,E. O,P,E,N. G,R,O,U,N,D." Hiro read slowly.

"I got it! Jet, I totally got it!" He shouted, jumping up and down. "Jet! Remember the mountains in Aomori? Aterui's cave, where we hid with Ojiisan?"

Jet nodded, remembering that dreadful day.

"Aterui?" Neil asked.

Hiro turned to Neil and J-Bird. "Our lands were invaded by the Emperor's army. The Emishi were outnumbered in men and weapons, but our ancestors fought until the bitter end."

"Sounds all too familiar," Neil said, his voice sad but somehow without bitterness.

Hiro swallowed, looking at Neil's weatherbeaten face.

"Our leader was a brave man named Aterui. He realized the only thing more war would bring was more death. So he went to Kyoto with a general of the Emperor's Army to negotiate..." Hiro looked down.

Jet recalled how Aterui had surrendered, knowing it would lead to his own death and the eternal defeat of his tribe.

"But he was betrayed and executed," Hiro said quietly.

"I'm sorry," Neil said. "The Navajo had heroes like that too," Neil told him, his voice full of regret. "It's a universal story."

Hiro sighed. "After Aterui died, many Emishi were captured and sent west as slaves. The ones who stayed behind were starving, and sold their kids to the ninja clans to survive. It sounds cruel, but that was the only way for the kids to survive, too. Members of the Kuroi family were sold. They became *genin*.

"Our ancestors," he added.

With mixed feelings in her heart, Jet listened to her young cousin talk about his history. *Their* history. She looked out at the snow-covered mountains, straining her ears to catch the sound of snowmelt.

J-Bird's eyes followed hers. "Are you okay?" he asked.

"Yes," Jet murmured, but her mind was racing. "What would have happened if Soji or I had died?" she asked.

J-Bird swallowed. "Then the treasure would have been lost. If we couldn't defeat our enemies, Masakichi and Satoko wanted the treasure to stay hidden. In a way, knowing where the treasure was actually protected all of us. They couldn't kill us as long as we had information they needed."

J-Bird began to cough, and she looked at him with concern.

"It's just a little cold," he said softly. "I'll be fine." He held out his hand to her.

"I hope so," she said, taking it and holding it tightly, feeling its warmth. Jet looked up, a tear in her eye.

J-Bird closed his eyes for a brief moment, as if remembering something, then looked up.

"I promise to take care of myself if you promise to do the same," Jet said. She hoped J-Bird wasn't thinking of joining Satoko in the Great Beyond. She knew how much he missed her.

"It's what Satoko would have wanted," Jet heard herself say.

J-Bird smiled. "Now you're sounding like me."

"What's so wrong with that? If you're not careful, I'll start acting like you too. Now that'd be something to worry about!"

"Don't worry. I'm as strong as an old coyote, and I ain't going anywhere soon. You can count on that," J-Bird laughed.

"Now what?" she asked.

J-Bird swallowed. "Back to Japan. Back to the cave. Time to put this mystery to rest, once and for all."

JAPAN

日本

CHAPTER 48

祠 *Hokora*
The Cave

Hiro surveyed the distant mountaintops. As in New Mexico, snow had fallen here. The first snow came at the end of autumn, when the leaves were still red. It melted after two or three days, and only then did the red disappear. Nature was like a magician who covered a cup with a white cloth, then lifted it to reveal that the cup had disappeared.

Hiro knew the rhythm of the mountain, understood the language of snow. The next snow always fell two weeks later, but it didn't melt. It froze on the ground and covered the mountain. That snow was called *neyuki*, and it made him happy.

Hiro, Jet, and Soji walked to the family graveyard behind Kanabe. It was a stone burial mound that rose from the middle of a flat space covered in white snow. The mountain range was totally white, contrasting beautifully with the blue sky. The colors were so clear and the mountains were enveloped in such silence that Hiro wondered if the events of the past two months had really happened at all. Everything felt pure and clean.

Hiro and Jet lit incense and put flowers on the snow. There were no gunshots in the distance, no cries of anguish. Aside from their soft chanting, the only sounds on the mountain were the songs of nature—branches rustling in the wind, birdcalls in the distance. They could finally honor Ojiisan in the silence he'd loved.

Afterward, as they began their climb to the cave, Soji spoke of how he'd move back to the village and rebuild the temple there. Word had spread about his bravery, and many new acolytes wanted to study and practice with him.

"Can we really rebuild here?" Hiro asked.

"Of course," Soji replied. "People outside the village don't want to get involved so soon after a controversy, so they'll let us do what we want. I'm going to get all the supplies locally, putting money back into the area. Before we know it, the village will be back to normal, like it hasn't been in generations."

"Do you think so?" Jet asked, hopeful. Soji seemed so certain.

"You'll see," he reassured her. "The people in the clan are in hiding. But they're still alive. Once they see that we're back, they will come out of hiding. I promise."

"You can re-open the temple. Give people a sanctuary," Jet suggested.

"Right! Then we'll build a school."

"That would be great," Hiro said. "It's been years since I've had other kids to play with in Kanabe!"

Jet smiled. The Kuroi clan members were still outsiders in Japan, and this village was the only place they felt safe. It was their homeland. They had a right to reclaim it and thrive. She would do her part, too.

"When we rebuild the Kuroi house, can we put in a moon-viewing room?" Jet asked, recalling the one Satoko had loved.

Soji turned to her with surprise. "Of course we can! Would you like a traditional *tsuki-mi-mado*, or something contemporary?"

"Both," she said, smiling broadly. "Let's design it together."

"That would work out nicely," her uncle replied.

As the three of them climbed through the knee-deep snow, it collapsed like layers of white cake, falling in around them. It covered the mountains so completely that if Aska and Hiro hadn't been guiding them, they would have been lost.

"It's *neyuki!*" Hiro suddenly shouted. Jet looked at him curiously.

"*Ne* means root. *Yuki* means snow," Soji told her. "*Neyuki* covers the roots on the ground and stays there until spring."

Hiro stomped in the deep white paradise. New snow from last night's snowfall shone in all directions, reflecting the sun in the cold clear air.

"Come on. Let's go!" he shouted, running ahead with Aska. For the first time in weeks, he radiated happiness. Aska raced after him, limbs and snow flying.

They passed one peak, then arrived at the suspension bridge over the river. On the other side, the trail ascended sharply. Aska ran up, but the heavy snow made each step difficult for the others. The sun was quickly setting as they trudged toward Aterui's cave.

"That's it!" Hiro said, pointing to a dip in the land up ahead. The bottom half of the cave entrance was covered with snow.

Jet stopped at the entrance as her old fear surfaced. Dark, cold, small spaces. The fear had a name—claustrophobia. Jet breathed deeply as she tried to stop her body from shaking. Hiro went in. He glanced back at her. *Remember what I told you?* he asked her silently. *Ojiisan taught me how to call fear another name. You can do it, cousin.*

Jet smiled in response. What was another name Jet could give it? Satoko had once said that love was the opposite of fear. Could that be it?

Could she feel love for this cave, for the hero it honored, for Aterui? For the sacrifice he made for his tribe, for his history? For *her* history?

Jet breathed in the cold air. It was because of Aterui and all the others that she stood here now. How could she not go in?

A voice came through the wind. It sounded to Jet like Satoko in the height of her strength.

If we're lucky enough to discover who we really are, and if we have the courage to claim our power and embrace our fate, we can harness any emotion. We can control the world rather than have it control us. We can live with gratitude.

Gratitude! That was the word she would use.

Jet repeated the word to herself and took a step forward.

I am grateful for the bravery of my mother and my grandfather, she thought. Trembling, she took another step. *I'm grateful for my ancestors' sacrifices.* Filled with resolve, she took another. *I'm grateful to Ojiisan for accepting me.* Another. *I'm grateful to Hiro for forgiving me.* Finally she was in the dark cave.

Yes!

Not *fear*, but *gratitude.* It felt good to re-name fear, to take away its power.

Kansha, Hiro said silently. *Japanese for "gratitude."*

Jet smiled. Hiro shone his flashlight into the darkness. The beam fell on an altar carved out of the cave's stone wall. As he moved the light, a slender stone statue of a man appeared. Behind it was a mirror, round like the sun. The last time Jet had been here she'd noticed very little of this. She'd been too worried for Ojiisan to think of anything else. It had been dark. She'd been so scared.

Hiro knelt in front of the altar. He took two candles from his backpack and lit them. Then he took out an orange that he placed as an offering. The statue was so old that only a slight bump of a nose remained on its face. Hundreds of years had worn the eyes and mouth away. A musty, damp smell permeated the ancient cave.

"Jet," Soji said as he sat cross-legged on the earth, "this is the local monument to Aterui. His real cave is at Hiraizumi, in the golden hall. Basho's *The Narrow Road to the Deep North* talks about it. It's also called the Den of Akuro-ou. It means 'home of the rebel king, Aterui.'"

Hiro cleared his throat, placed his hands in prayer at his chest.

"Great Aterui, we've finally returned," Hiro said solemnly. "Ojiisan doesn't live in this world anymore, but please protect the Kuroi family as you've always done. Ojiisan lived a long life. He couldn't have lived so long without your blessing." Hiro folded his hands at his heart and prayed. Aska sat beside him. Jet prayed, too.

Soji waited a few minutes. "We need to try to move the statue," he said. "The code mentioned 'the back of the statue,' right?"

"Right!" Jet nodded excitedly.

She and Soji carefully slid it from the altar to the ground. Hiro shone his flashlight on the half circle where it had been. There was nothing. Disappointment flooded Jet's chest.

"Wait." Soji scratched his head. "Let me feel around the altar." He ran his fingers along every spot on the wall, roof, and ground.

"Do you feel anything?" Hiro asked.

Soji shook his head, then signaled for everyone to be quiet. He put his ear on the earth where the statue had been, hitting the dirt with his palm.

"Here!" he said triumphantly. He took a Swiss army knife from his pocket and cut into the earth. "Hiro, can you shine the light on this spot?" Hiro directed the beam toward the soft rock. Soji cut deeper into it, carving out a small square, then prying it up. A white clay box gradually appeared.

Jet gasped. Soji steadied his hand as he opened it with the edge of the knife. When the lid flipped, something sparkled.

"A key! It looks so new!" Jet exclaimed, surprised.

"It is." Soji smiled. "Satoko found this hiding place just seventeen years ago, remember? Even in this little village, they must have had shiny new keys then, right?"

Jet smiled.

"What is it to?" Jet looked around the cave. "The code said the hidden key would open the ground. That means the keyhole should be somewhere in this cave!"

"That's right," Soji said. There was almost thirty feet from the altar to the entrance. They'd have to dig up the entire cave, which would take forever, and they ran the risk of causing a collapse if they unsettled too much earth.

Mom must have left some clue, Jet thought. She stood at the center of the cave, analyzing the code she'd memorized. The candlelight illuminated the ground. She stepped back to study the floor.

"Wait! Jet, what's that?" Hiro shouted, pointing at her.

"What?" She turned around, frightened. She couldn't see anything. Was it a spider? A snake? The old fear rushed back.

"Look at your body." He pointed to her jacket.

She looked down, trembling. Just above her stomach was a faint white orb. She reached to touch it, but it disappeared.

"Where did it go?" she asked, stepping back into place.

"Don't move," Soji said. "Now take your hand away from your jacket."

Jet did. As soon as she moved her hand, the orb reappeared. She and Hiro gasped.

"I got it!" Soji said. "Look!" He took a cloth from his backpack and moved to the altar, where he began to polish the round mirror.

Understanding dawned on Jet. "Is it a reflection?" she asked.

"I think so, but it's also more than that. Wait! I have an idea."

Soji took the candles from the altar and looked excitedly at Hiro.

"Hiro, after I blow them out, shine your flashlight diagonally on the mirror, okay?" he asked.

"Diagonally?" Hiro repeated.

"Yes. Please move away from the altar." Soji blew out the candles. The cave went pitch black.

Goosebumps rose on Jet's arms.

"Now shine your light," Soji said.

The flashlight's beam caused them all to gasp, again. On the ground, fifteen feet from the altar, shone an image of Kannon, the Goddess of Compassion: a beautiful woman sitting serenely on a lotus flower, the orb of the sun behind her.

Jet's body tingled as she studied the figure projected onto the ground. "Look, she's holding a baby in her right arm. And there's a cross in the middle of her chest!"

"You're right. It's Mother Mary Kannon." Soji crouched next to the image and drew a circle into the earth where the cross appeared.

"Mother Mary Kannon?" Jet repeated the strange words.

"Yes, as in Mother Mary, mother of Jesus. And Kannon, Goddess of Compassion, sometimes called Quan Yin."

Jet was confused. "I don't understand. How can it be both the Virgin Mary and the Asian Goddess of Mercy?"

"I wondered the same thing at first." Soji said. "But remember, the Spanish brought Christianity to Japan in the sixteenth century.

A hundred years later, there were almost a million Christians in Japan. Christianity was incredibly popular. The Tokugawa Shogun was afraid it would undermine the *bakufu's* power, and they feared Japan would fall under the control of Spain."

"So the Shogun closed the country and prohibited Christianity!" Hiro added.

"That's right. Many Christians were forced to convert or to become apostates who had to trample over statues of Jesus and Mary to prove they'd rejected their faith."

"But some tried to hide their faith. They were the *kakure kirishitan*, the hidden Christians!" Hiro explained.

"Yes. And they created ways to hide their religion. One was to blend the image of Kannon with Mother Mary, like this," Soji added.

"*Naruhodo*," Jet said, Japanese slipping out suddenly. "I see."

"This is a *makyo*, a magic mirror," Soji exclaimed.

She went to the altar and touched the mirror.

"It's quite old," Soji said. "Look closely and you'll see thin lines carved on the surface to project the figure of Mother Mary Kannon when light is shone on it."

"But look! She can appear only at a certain distance," Hiro said.

"She's beautiful!" Jet beamed. It made sense that the Virgin Mary and Kannon, or Quan Yin, were joined in one image. Everywhere they embodied wholeness and compassion toward all who suffered.

She touched the radiant, peaceful image. A serene feeling enveloped her heart. She let it wash over her. Then she started, suddenly remembering the *itako's* words back on Osore-zan. Was Mother Mary Kannon one of the women who would help her? Jet believed so. She kept her gaze on the radiant image. She'd seen enough fighting and bloodshed. What she wanted to know was how to heal, to give life, not take it away. That was *real* power.

Suddenly, she shivered with understanding. Was that what her mother had meant about the "privilege" of being a woman? Jet thought back to her first moon day, so many years ago. Satoko, too, had seen pain and destruction.

Deep in the cave, Jet was no longer scared. She held out her palms, receiving the light from Mother Mary Kannon, sending out her own light from her heart. In their own ways, Mother Mary and Kannon had been warriors of peace. Could Jet stand in their light and quell the shadows? Her mother had said you couldn't have the light without the dark. Now Jet understood.

Kunoichi power was to combat those in the shadows, those who wished to snuff out another's light. But the real power of *kunoichi* was to give light and life, to help others with compassion, and to heal. Though the locket was not there, she knew she didn't need it anymore. It was as if the image had burned itself onto her chest and sealed itself there invisibly. Her secret tattoo.

The *itako* had seen it in her. After all, she'd prophesized that Jet would save the mountain. She would help many. She let the *itako's* words flood her consciousness, intoning them inside her mind as if to program them into her brain. They would be her GPS. They would guide her.

Jet thought of what she knew of Christianity. The Ten Commandments. *Do Unto Others. Love Thy Neighbor as Thyself.* This way of life was different from the ninja code, she thought. Or was it?

Keep secret things secret. Use whatever you have to survive. Weren't they intertwined, like light and dark? You couldn't be helped without helping others.

"Were our ancestors Christian?" she asked.

"I don't think so," Soji said, "but the family might have helped protect *kakure kirishitan* who were hiding. They might have left the mirror as a token of thanks." He lit the candles on the altar so Hiro could turn off his flashlight.

When he did so, Mother Mary Kannon disappeared.

Soji went back to where he'd traced the circle. Crouching, he started to cut at the earth with the knife. When he'd dug about four inches, a round clay lid appeared. He cut around it carefully, then stuck the knife into the side of the cover. It popped out.

A keyhole appeared. Hiro gasped, and Jet's mouth fell open.

"Go ahead, unlock it." Soji handed the key to Hiro.

"Really?" Hiro's hands trembled as he put the key into the hole and turned it. Something creaked in the earth, like gears shifting. This was followed by the sound of air pressure being released.

The cave was filled with tension as one corner of the square around the keyhole rose slightly.

"Go ahead, pull it up," Soji prompted.

"Are you sure it's okay?" Hiro looked back with concern.

"Don't worry. This isn't a Hollywood movie!" Soji laughed. "And even if there are snakes in the box, it's hibernation season."

"You're right." Hiro smiled as Soji reached under the raised corner and pulled it up, revealing a metal box.

"Open it," he urged.

Unable to stop his hand from shaking, Hiro lifted the lid. Jet held her breath.

Inside the box was another one, made of ancient wood. Soji took white gloves from his backpack. He lifted the wooden box out, then opened the cover. Inside, folded into a square, was a cloth that was brown with age. He took it out and spread it over the box, touching it with only his thumb and index finger.

"Look!" he said. The sides were frayed, making it appear to be part of a bigger cloth.

Written on it in black ink were characters completely different from Japanese. They looked more like ancient Egyptian hieroglyphs.

"Can you understand the words?" Hiro asked Soji excitedly.

Soji nodded. "Fortunately, my field is archaeology. I specialize in dead languages."

"What do they say? Is it about the treasure?" Hiro was so excited he could barely contain himself.

Soji's brow furrowed. He sighed deeply, concentrating as he read. Then he folded the cloth back up and put it carefully into the box. Holding the box to his chest, he motioned for Jet and Hiro to follow him out of the cave.

CHAPTER 49

黄金伝説 *Ogon Densetsu*
The Gold Legend

Jet looked down on the street from the top floor of the Aomori museum. Snow was still falling. Seeing its white expanse, she felt ready for spring. She recalled those March mornings years ago when Satoko put her hand in the river of melted mountain snow and said, "Spring has finally arrived."

Satoko's favorite time of year was when winter gave way to spring. Jet now understood her mother's feeling. She shivered in the cold, longing for her mother's warm embrace. Then her thoughs ran to Takumi. She hoped he'd somehow survived. "Hope is the only thing stronger than fear," Satoko had told her. She'd never believed her. Until now.

She was looking forward to when she could shake off the weight of the heavy snow. The winter had been hard. Spring would seem like a new life.

"Jet? Are you okay?" Soji asked, putting his hand to her forehead.

"I'm fine. Just a bit tired," she stammered, bringing herself back to the present.

Soji had wrapped up the cloth carefully. Then he'd taken Jet and Hiro to the museum to meet Professor Suzuki, his former colleague. Dr. Suzuki greeted them warmly at his office door. He was younger than Jet expected. He wore a tweed suit and round wire-rimmed glasses, but looked solid and handsome, like a soccer coach or mountain climber rather than archeologist.

Jet noticed he held his gaze on her for slightly longer than was necessary as he shook her hand, but she really didn't mind.

"That's to be expected. So you're not a superhero, after all!" Dr. Suzuki said as he sat and spread out a ream of papers on the desk.

Hiro laughed.

With excitement in his eyes, Dr. Suzuki looked up at Jet and Hiro.

"Remember the strange characters written on the cloth?" he asked, sitting down.

"Yes," Hiro said.

"They were *shinobi moji!*" Dr. Suzuki raised his eyebrows and grinned. "We believe that those characters originated with the *sanka* nomads, who created them as a code to protect their secrets."

"It's highly possible," Soji said, "that our ancestors came into contact with some hidden Christians. Perhaps they were given this cloth, which was guarded and protected by many, many underground believers. The *sanka* were smart. Since the cloth was guarded, they decided it was a safe place to record where the treasure was hidden."

"So there really is a treasure?" Hiro asked hopefully.

Soji smiled. "Did you notice I wore gloves when I opened the box?"

"Yes!" Hiro and Jet said in unison.

"Well, that cloth could have been two thousand years old, so exposure to the air could have caused it to disintegrate. As soon as I touched it, however, I realized it couldn't be more than three hundred years old."

Suzuki nodded. "Dr. Kuroi is right. At that time, praying to the cross was prohibited, so people had to create a safe object to pray to. They chose the cloth, believing it had once covered the body of Christ."

Soji continued, "Everyone understood it was just a substitute for the cross. But as time passed, people came to believe it was really a sacred object in and of itself. And at that time, the Kuroi family possessed it."

"You mean the so-called Kuroi family treasure is a fake?" Jet said, dejected. "So we've come all this way and so many people have died for nothing?"

"No, I didn't say that. Let's not jump to conclusions!" Soji replied. "It depends on what you mean by *fake*. There are many kinds of treasures in this world."

Suzuki looked at Jet kindly. "The *shinobi moji* sentence translates as 'Eternal sleep exists in the mountain that holds the blue lake. Let no one disturb it.'"

Hiro repeated the words, trying to coax out their meaning.

"Is that another code?" Jet asked. She turned the words over in her mind, twisting the precious *kanzashi* that held her hair in a bun.

"Eternal sleep could mean hidden treasure. And the mountain that holds the blue lake is—" Soji ruminated.

"Osore-zan!" Hiro shouted.

If Jet closed her eyes and concentrated, she could see the azure lake that spread forever. She could recall Ojiisan saying, *The people here believe that everyone will go to this mountain after death.*

"Is that it?" Hiro nearly shouted. "Is the treasure hidden on Osore-zan?"

"I think you've got it!" Soji said, handing his nephew an old newspaper article Suzuki had discovered. Hiro glanced down at it and read aloud:

Metal Miners' Association Finds Gold in Shimokita-Yagen
The metal miners' industry association of Aomori announced today that gold deposits were found in the Yagen area north of Osore-zan, one of the most sacred places in Japan.

"Yagen is close to Osore-zan, but it's not Osore-zan. I don't understand," Hiro said.

"Keep on reading," Suzuki urged.

The discovery of gold deposits in Yagen was prompted by the detection of an extremely high level of gold ore in Osore-zan.

At six thousand grams per one ton of ore, the unusually high content alerted the local miner's association to the possibility of gold.

"Wait a sec! Did our ancestors know there was gold on Osore-zan?" Hiro asked, face flushed with anticipation.

Soji's eyes lit up. "I believe that they did. And do you understand how high the gold content of Osore-zan's ore is? The average gold content is ten grams per ton of ore."

"So the mine in Osore-zan contains six hundred times as much gold as the average gold mine!" Hiro exclaimed.

"Exactly. One million tons of gold have been mined worldwide since the beginning of history. The gold reserves in Osore-zan may be equal to half of that. Or even higher!" Soji said.

Hiro almost jumped out of his seat. Jet wanted to jump up, too, but she was more cautious. "What if that's also fake? What if it's just a rumor some group started to protect its mythology?" she asked.

Soji laughed. "Listen. If that gold is mined and invested in the market, the market value will decrease, maybe by half! The value of gold as a precious metal will have to be totally re-estimated." Soji said, looking intently at both of them.

"So?" Hiro asked, trying to figure out the true significance of this new information.

"So our ancestors might have known about a huge gold mine in Osore-zan. Columbus's discovery of America caused the Age of Great Voyages, right? Well, what triggered the discovery of America?" Soji prompted.

Hiro thought about it hard, trying to recall his history lessons. "*The Book of Marco Polo*, a thirteenth-century report on East Asia!" he exclaimed triumphantly.

"Exactly," Soji said. "The European conquistadors were inspired by the description of the Golden Country Jipang, so they traveled West to find their fortunes."

He paused for effect. "But guess what?"

"I know! They found America instead of Japan!" Hiro replied.

"Right again," Soji said. "They never found what they were looking for."

"I think that's what aunt Satoko was trying to tell us," Hiro shouted.

"I think so too," Soji agreed.

"Instead, the conquistadors took Aztec and Inca gold and brought it back to Europe. The European economy soared, which led to more exploration."

"So the Native Americans became the victims instead," Jet said softly.

"Simply stated, yes." Soji nodded somberly.

"But the gold is still here?" Jet asked, her voice shaking.

"Yes, I believe so," Soji said, his face radiant.

Jet glanced over at Hiro eagerly.

"Well then, what are we waiting for?" she asked.

CHAPTER 50

ソロモンの秘宝

Solomon no Hiho

King Solomon's Treasure

"Wait just a minute," Hiro said. "I don't want to ruin the mood, but something's not right."

"What is it?" Soji asked.

"Ojiisan told me that the discovery of gold in Northern Japan led to the invasion by the Imperial Army in the eighth century, but there's one thing I just don't understand. Wouldn't they have mined it? Japan has limited resources. Everyone knows that."

"Good point," Soji replied. "These days, it's true that our underground resources are limited, especially petroleum. But there was a lot of iron or copper before. In fact, foundry ruins dating back to the third century have been discovered here. It used to be a prosperous area."

"What about gold?" Jet asked.

Soji sighed. "The first gold was found in Miyagi prefecture in Northern Japan in the eighth century. That's why the Kyoto Imperial government changed its colonization policy from gradual settlement to aggressive invasion. That's why they invaded our land."

"So what did they do with it all?" Hiro asked.

Soji considered the question. "Well, we do know that gold mined in Northern Japan was used to build almost all the beautiful Kyoto and Nara temples and shrines in the ninth to sixteenth centuries."

Jet gasped. She recalled her mother telling her about the Temple of the Golden Pavilion in Kyoto, and all the golden Buddhist statues in temples across Japan. Jet had seen pictures of them, along with gilded ceilings, ornate scrolls, golden palanquins. She'd never really questioned where all that gold had come from. Could it be as Dr. Suzuki and Uncle Soji said?

"And in the twelfth century, a lord in Northern Japan paid approximately four thousand kilograms of gold dust to China for a set of the complete Buddhist Sutras," Dr. Suzuki added.

"Four thousand kilograms? For some sutras? *Oshaka-sama!*" Hiro exclaimed.

"That's a lot of gold," Suzuki replied. "But by the fifteenth century, when the gold boom declined, there were fifteen hundred gold mines in one Northern Japanese town alone."

"It was just like the California gold rush!" Jet exclaimed.

"Yes. Many Japanese rushed from the West to the North." Soji paused and pulled a piece of paper from a stack on the desk. "Let's see… This document says that the proper name for Osore-zan is Osore-zan Entsu Temple. Ennin, a Tendai priest, established it at the beginning of the ninth century…"

Suzuki jumped in. "Way back in 802, Aterui surrendered to the Shogun Sakanoueno Tamuramaro, the emperor's general, after a thirteen-year war. The resistance was all but crushed, and the government looted everything… Many Emishi were sent to Eastern and Western Japan as slaves."

"And Western gold-diggers took over the North, often violently," Soji said. "The Emishi were afraid that Osore-zan—where they believed their ancestors spent the afterlife—would be dug up for gold. The only way for the Emishi to defend their sacred mountain was to use the power of their enemies."

"In what way? What do you mean?" Hiro asked, sitting on the edge of his seat.

"They used the power of *Tendai* Buddhism, which had a great influence over the Kyoto leaders. They taught the *Tendai* priests about their sacred white mountain."

"I still don't understand how they used the power of Buddhism to protect them," Hiro said, puzzled.

Soji folded his hands on the table and took a breath. "Religion had a huge influence on political power. Even the emperor couldn't touch sacred land. So our ancestors took advantage of the emperor's weakness for Buddhism."

Then he smiled in a satisfied way. Hiro's face flushed. "In other words, if people believed the mountain was sacred, they'd leave it alone. Is that it?" he exclaimed. "Yes, exactly. And they did," Soji said. "Over time, when rumors surfaced about a treasure, people looked elsewhere like Shikoku where some thought King Solomon's gold was buried. There've always been strange rumors like that one flying around."

"Like the one about Jesus' grave in Aomori?" Jet asked.

"Yes. And that isn't true either." Soji laughed slightly. "But that's okay, because the rumors distracted people from the real treasure. The Soto Zen temple Entsu-ji owns the mountain. A few years ago the government asked permission to do trial drilling. The temple said no, because for them, the treasure is the mountain itself—and their history."

"So did people like Harter believe that the Kuroi family treasure was really the treasure of King Solomon?" Hiro asked.

Jet turned to the window, making a circle in the steam with her hand. The snow was falling harder now.

"Yes. He wanted to believe that because he valued material wealth over spiritual wealth, even over history itself," Jet explained.

"Sadly, yes," Suzuki agreed.

"Why didn't we just tell Harter the truth?" Jet asked. "He would have left us alone."

Soji shook his head. "Not by a longshot. Imagine if someone that determined realized how much gold was here. He would have killed everyone in his way."

"That's right," Suzuki agreed. "Mountains can be sold. Entire mountains have been crushed for coal. Our ancestors have been able to protect the mountain for twelve hundred years. We had to make sure that it stayed protected. If a tribe doesn't care about its history and land, then who will?"

Soji nodded. "You see, if we could save this one mountain, then people all over the world would know that their sacred mountains are worth saving, too. Don't you think?"

"I do," Jet said listening intently. She felt empowered by her uncle's words.

"We can't forget the myths and magic of our people," Soji said. "If we forget the legends of our tribes, we will forget how the universe was born—not from science and technology—but from the integration of many worlds and lands. We must preserve our legends and their birthplace."

Jet understood why her mother had told her the legend of Hinomoto, over and over again, of the brave girl and the powerful Empire her people had fought to overcome. She would never forget.

But still...

"Couldn't anyone put the pieces together the way we did? Couldn't they read that old newspaper article and figure it out?" she asked, confused.

"Sure, if they had the resources we had, the archives, and the code. But they didn't. No one had that—except us..."

"So the treasure—I mean the mountain and its gold—are safe now?" Jet asked, worried.

"Yes. Now the secret that was kept amongst the women of our tribe is to be shared with the men. But it can't go beyond that, ever. There's only one copy of this old newspaper article, which was never digitalized," he said, "and soon there will be none."

Soji held the article up in the air, then lit the edge with a wooden match and smiled as it went up in flames.

Jet gasped. "Uncle Soji! What are you doing?"

But it was too late. Speechless, she watched the flames engulf the treasure map the way she'd watched the map of her life burn back in Albequrque with her mother's burial. Everything felt connected and sacred.

Suzuki spoke again. "What's more, we've been lobbying for a long time that the mountain become governmentally protected land, just like a National Park in America. When Osore-zan officially belongs to the national park service, mining will be expressly prohibited."

Soji watched as the old newspaper burned to a pile of ash in the ashtray on Suzuki's desk.

"To tell you the truth, we feared the government as much, if not more, than people like Harter. And now not even *they* will be able to touch the treasure," Soji said.

The evidence was now completely gone, and no one would be able to excavate the land ever again, as long as it remained a national park, so the treasure was safe.

The smell of smoke in her nostrils, Jet listened to the snow falling outside. She finally understood her mother's words about protecting the magic mountain, and the *itako*'s prophecy: *You will save the mountain and its gods from destruction. You will be a warrior for peace.*

After all Jet had been through, she didn't care if there was gold or silver or diamonds in the mountain. She felt a deep pleasure knowing that the land her people had revered, the place they held as a bridge between the land of the living and the afterworld, was finally safe.

Now her real life would begin.

Epilogue

雪 *Yuki*
Snow

Carried on the cold north wind, bright yellow powder fell from the small flowers of the hiba tree, settling on the white snow as a sign of spring's imminent arrival.

The hiba blossomed in a profusion of both male and female flowers. The pollen from the male flowers blew between the trees and covered the woods like the folded layers of a yellow kimono. It found a soft pillow to land on in the female flowers.

Aska bounded through the pale yellow snow as Hiro skied down the mountain.

Jet watched the dance of the yellow flowers. The pollen spiraled in the wind and surged upwards. The female flowers would accept the male's desire proudly. That was the beauty of nature. She thought of Takumi, wondering where he was now and if he was all right.

She would go visit the *itako* again and ask for guidance. She had a feeling the old woman would know.

Hiro pointed ahead, to where Lake Usori's frozen surface shimmered in a faint blue mist. The peaks of Osore-zan spread out behind the flat surface. Its undulating curves reached into the sky. He wanted to meet Ojiisan and his mother again, and Jet hoped to see the *itako* and speak with her mother's spirit, but the temple prohibited access to the mountain until April.

Meanwhile, they had the arms of the mountain to hold them, so they skied from the Western ridge to the other side of the lake, to the place where the golden hiba flowers blossomed in the winter.

There Jet felt that the spirits could hear them and protect them, and that they could travel to faraway lands and come back again.

"Let's go home," she said.

As they returned to Kanabe, Jet realized that as much as she loved America, she loved Japan, too. She loved it for its history, its ageless sense of honor, and its simplicity. She also loved its embrace of ambiguity, the reverence of imperfection and impermanence, which was present everywhere in nature, and which she now understood as wisdom.

She'd loved her mother's determination, her grandfather's strength. Now she loved her cousin's stubborn inquisitiveness, his dog's fierce loyalty, her uncle's warm wisdom and inner fire. And she loved her mother for sharing all of that with her, despite the hardships, despite the struggles. Or maybe even because of them. Hadn't they made her stronger?

A sob welled up in Jet's throat. She knew she'd completed her mission and that the mountain and the Black family treasure would be safe. Jet was filled with a new appreciation for her mother and all she'd given her family.

And now it was Jet's turn. Soji was her family, and Hiro, too. She would take care of them, and they'd take care of her. They'd stay in the village and help it grow. It was their home. They could put down roots. They could blossom here. Jet finally understood. *This* was the present she'd have to give up to allow the future to emerge. She had to risk losing the village, the tribe, her family, in order to gain it back.

The village had been saved from the fire, and soon, Jet and Hiro would be living there. The thought filled Jet with eager anticipation. Kanabe would be her home, the home she'd always longed for, always dreamed of, always known was out there somewhere waiting for her to discover.

As Jet approached the door, she saw a small package by the stoop.

She leaned down to pick it up. As she unwrapped it, her fingers trembled. The locket spilled out.

Had Takumi found it? Was he here? She hadn't sensed his presence, but he was, after all, expert at hiding.

Breathlessly, she opened the locket. Her grandmother and mother's pictures were still there.

She put the locket around her neck and fastened the clasp, then tucked it beneath her clothing. A strong determination lit her from the inside. She would carry these women with her, as they had carried her. She wouldn't forget. But it would be her secret, as it was theirs. *Keep secret things secret.*

Her promise had been fulfilled.

And yet, Takumi knew… how many people had he told?

Her pulse raced. She spun around, surveying the grounds for any sign of the dark leader. She didn't sense his presence, but that didn't mean anything. She knew how adept he was at slipping in and out of places. Could Takumi transport himself to different planes of reality—emanating into the dream-world and the waking world alike? She wouldn't put it past him.

Who was the real Takumi and who was the *henge* disguise? The fierce warrior or the lonely traveler seeking companionship along the way? Or both?

She knew she could easily ask the same question of herself.

"Hey, look behind us!" Hiro called out. "Look!"

She turned. Two bright rays emerged from a deep rift in the clouds, shining down like descending spirits on Osore-zan's peaks. In that moment, everything came together—her childhood, the fairytales she had read of a Japan that had once seemed distant and unreal, the America that shaped her. All the days past and all the days to come, and finally, her mother's spirit. It was true that Osore-zan was a sacred mountain for spirits from the afterworld, but Jet felt it was sacred for the spirits of the living, too. She knew it would be a mountain of healing and unity.

The light faded into the clouds, and they stood in the deep silence of the valley.

Then she heard it.

The sound of the wind.

She knew it would be with her forever, inside her. And if she listened closely, she could even hear her name in it.

Jet sighed, letting herself drop deep into the sound.

It was the sound of peace, one she hoped would last a very long time.

Glossary

Ainu—Indigenous ethnic group of Northern Japan, originating in 1200 CE. These hunter-gatherers ate fish and plants and followed a nature-based religion. Contact between the Wa (mainland Japanese) and the Ainu began in the thirteenth century but was limited, allowing ancient Ainu culture to survive intact until the nineteenth century.

Aterui—(died 21, AD 802 in Enryaku) was the most prominent chief of the Isawa tribe of the Emishi, the indigenous people of Northern Japan. Aterui led the fight against the Imperial army in the Thirty-Eight Year War, which began in AD 774 when the mainland Emperor invaded Emishi territory, taking the land from its inhabitants. The Emishi retreated to the North, but the Imperial army continued to advance. Though outnumbered and overpowered, Aterui led the Emishi in a fierce 10-year battle against Imperial conquest. Finally, in 802 after suffering irrevocable losses, the Emishi leaders Aterui and More surrendered with more than 500 warriors. They travelled to Kyoto with an Imperial Army general to negotiate, but were brutally cut down. Their betrayal marked a turning point in Emishi history, leading to fierce uprisings over the ensuing generations. Prior to this incident, mainland Japanese had captured warriors but spared their lives, or deported captured women and children to Western Japan to force their warrior husbands and fathers to join them.

Chunin–Middle-ranking ninja. Within each ninja school (*ryu*) there were three different ranks. The *chunin* were trainers and field marshals. They stayed in contact with the head of the *ryu*, but also controlled the ninja beneath them (*genin*) who carried out the orders of the highest ranking (*jonin*) ninja.

Emishi–The Indigenous people of northeastern Honshu, Japan, currently Tohoku, considered "hirsute barbarians" by the mainland (Yamato) Japanese. Some Emishi tribes were believed to be descendants of Jōmon culture and related to the Ainu. The Emishi opposed and resisted the rule of the Japanese emperors during the late Nara and early Heian eras (7th–10th centuries AD).

En–Destiny. Fate.

Ennin–Tendai priest who established the sacred mountain Osorezan in the beginning of the ninth century.

Genin–Lowest-ranking ninja of the three ninja ranks. The *genin* were given the most dangerous duties, which they took partly in order to prove their loyalty to the *jonin*, and partly to survive. Some *genin* used Emishi as slaves, and over time, the classes and races intermingled.

Genesis–The first book of the Hebrew Bible, dating from the 5th century BCE and perhaps older, containing the best-known stories in the Bible, such as the Creation of the World, Adam and Eve, Cain and Able, Noah's Ark, and the Tower of Babel.

Gilgamesh Epic–Poem from ancient Mesopotamia (current-day Iraq), among the earliest known literary works in the world. Gilgamesh befriends the half-wild Enkidu. The two embark on dangerous quests together, until both ultimately become human. When Enkidu dies, Gilgamesh's sadness leads him to search for immortality.

Henge–The ninja art of disguise.

Hinomoto–Original name for Japan. 日 (*Nichi*) means "sun" and 本 (*Hon*) means "origin." Literal translation: "The place where the sun rises," or "land of the rising sun."

Ise shrine–Ancient shrine in Nara, directly connected to the Imperial family. Reportedly the birth place of sun goddess Ameterasu, who gave birth to the unbroken imperial line from which the modern-day Emperor is descended.

Islamic Fundamentalism–Religious ideology advocating a return to the "fundamentals" of Islam as described in *The Koran* and *The Sayings of Muhammad*, and a rejection of Western values.

Itako–Blind female shamans in northern Japan who undergo intense training and austere rituals to become mediums who channel spirits in deep trance-like states.

Kannon–Japanese name for Quan Yin or Kwan Yin, the Goddess of Mercy, or "she who hears a thousand cries."

Kanzashi–hair ornaments first used in Japan during the Jōmon period, when such thin rods were believed to have mystical powers, so women wore them in their hair to ward off evil spirits. Modern kanzashi were fashioned from gold, silver, metal, tortoiseshell, and bakelight. *Kunoichi* used kanzashi and other ornaments for self-defense, and as weapons. Jet inherits a diamond-incrusted silver *tama* (ball-style) pronged *kanzashi* from her mother. The *tama* style usually has a simple colored bead on the end.

Karma–Cycle of birth, death, and rebirth, wherein our actions in this lifetime determine our fate in the next incarnation.

Ki–Life-force energy. (Chinese: *chi*).

King Solomon–Son of David, founder of the first temple of Israel. Born c. 1011 in Jerusalem, reigned from 971-931 BCE, died c. 932 in Jerusalem. During Solomon's long reign of 40 years, the Israelite monarchy gained its highest splendor and the king accumulated great wisdom, wealth, and power. In a single year, Solomon collected tributes amounting to 666 talents of gold, or 39,960 pounds (1 *Kings* 10:14).

Kojiki–"Record of Ancient Matters." Japan's oldest book, dating from the early 8th century. Composed by O no Yasumaro by Imperial request, this collection of myths depicts the origin of the islands of Japan and the Japanese Gods (*kami*).

Kuchiyose–A ritual performed by blind female shamans (*itako*), who summon the spirits of the dead and deliver messages in the voices of the deceased to their relatives.

Kunoichi–Female Ninja. The term is thought to derive from the names of characters that resemble the three strokes in the ideogram for woman: (女 onna), written as ku (く) - no (ノ) - ichi (一). Has also been read as the Japanese number ku (九) "nine" and the particle no (の) for "and" and ichi (一) for "one," literally translated as "nine and one," meaning the number of orifices on a female body. Unlike their male counterparts, *kunoichi* specialized in *henge* disguise, assassination through poison, and spying rather than in combat, which they reserved to defend themselves against capture. They would often disguise themselves as geisha, prostitutes, entertainers, fortune tellers, and servants to get close to the enemy. They also used the art of seduction.

Jonin–Highest-ranking ninja. The *jonin* were the managers of each ninja *ryu*, which they ran according to each family's philosophy and specialty.

Lake Usorisan–Emerald blue lake on the volcanic Mt. Osore. Believed to be the Sanzu River, the Japanese equivalent to the mythical River Styx, the bridge between earth and the great beyond.

Long Walk–In 1830, American President Andrew Jackson approved the Indian Removal Act, a law providing for the resettlement of Native Americans to lands West of the Mississippi River. Almost 60,000 Native Americans were forced to migrate. In 1863, after many months of imprisonment, about 8,000 Navajo men, women, and children were forced by the U.S. Army to leave their homeland in New Mexico and make a grueling 300-mile march to a desolate strip of land known as Bosque Redondo. This is remembered as "the Long Walk."

Matsumura Clan–A powerful dynasty based on a real clan which originated from a seventh century Japanese aristocrat–politician whose four sons inherited power from their father, establishing their own powerful families, and whose two daughters married two generations of emperors to gain power within the government. The Matsumura clan maintained power in the Imperial household for more than thirteen years, except from the fourteenth to the mid-nineteenth century, when Oda Nobunaga and Toyotomi Hideyoshi and the Tokugama Shoguns took over total control of Japan. In modern times, a descendent of the clan was prime minister before the Pacific war.

Mikado–The ancient emperor of Japan.

Namu Amida Butsu–"I pray to lord buddha for salvation"—a Buddhist prayer intoned to reach enlightenment, especially when dying.

Natsukashii–Nostalgia. A sense of *deja vu*, or longing for something in the past.

Navajo Code Talkers–Native Americans from the Navajo Nation who served in the U.S. Marine Corps during WWII, the Korean War, and the Vietnam War. Code talkers transmitted secret tactical messages over military telephone or radio using codes based on their native languages, enhancing the communications security of vital front-line operations. As Navajo was spoken only on the Navajo lands of the American Southwest, its syntax, tonal qualities, and dialects made it unintelligible to anyone without extensive exposure and training. Navajo was unwritten and has very complex grammar, so it made a perfect base language for military code. During World War II, fewer than 30 non-Navajos, none of them Japanese, could understand it.

Ninja–Hidden tribe of warriors who first surfaced in sixteenth-century Japan, a time of civil war. "Nin" means to hide, both physically and mentally, "ja" means person. The samurai lords needed ninja spies to help infiltrate rival strongholds. Their relationship was based on a per-job contract. The only way out of the contract was to fulfill it or die trying. A ninja could work for a rival lord once he was a free agent. *Nin* is composed of blade (*yaiba*) 刃 and heart 心 —the ninja had to steel himself against emotion, to "put the blade over the heart" (忍者). The original meaning of that character was "cruel," but the meaning evolved to "the heart that can endure cruelty."

Ninja dog–Since ancient times, dogs have been used in warfare by the Egyptians, Greeks, Persians, Romans, Britons, and Native Americans. There was also a tradition among the ninja classes of using dogs as warriors. In modern times, dogs have been used by Americans, Germans, Russians, French, and others in warfare. Canines were trained in combat as well as employed as scouts, sentries, and trackers. In recent years, canines have been used as police dogs and for drug and explosive detection.

Nodo-botoke–Adam's apple. Literally, "buddha in the throat." After death, Japanese burn bodies and family members pick out the bones with long chopsticks. This bone is considered sacred.

Onigiri–Rice balls made with various fillings such as salmon and pickled plum, wrapped in *nori* seaweed.

Osore-zan (恐山)–A mountain in the center of the remote Shimokita Peninsula of Aomori. One of the three largest sacred Buddhist mountains in Japan (the others are Koya-san in Nara and Hiei-san in Fukui). Osore-zan is the oldest, considered a sacred center by indigenous tribes such as the Ainu and Emishi even before Buddhism came to Japan in the fifth century. Animistic beliefs held that natural places themselves were god; ancient tribes revered mountain spirits. According to myth, Mount Osore ("Mount Fear") marks the entrance to Hell, with a small brook running to the neighboring Lake Usorisan. The "Bodai Temple" on the mountain holds the twice-yearly Itako Taisai festival.

Ōu Mountains–Mountains in Tohoku, northern Honshu. The range is the longest in Japan and stretches 311 miles (500 km) south from the Natsudomari Peninsula of Aomori to the Nasu volcanoes at the northern boundary of the Kanto region.

Rinzai Roku–*The Sayings of Zen Master Rinzai.* Zen was brought from China to Japan by Línjì Yìxuán (Japanese name: Rinzai Gigen, who died in 866). The Rinzai School of Zen stems from the Linji lineage and is known for its blunt style.

Ryu–Ninja school or family. There were many schools of ninja, each descendants of a family that mastered a special technique such as spying, surveillance, counter-espionage, or assassination. The Iga and the Koga were the biggest *ryu*, or schools.

Samurai–The shogun's soldiers, who came from the upper classes.

Sanka–Nomads whose ancestors were said to be the ancient Izumo people. In ancient Japan, the Sanka traveled around Japan selling bamboo crafts to survive. They built a kind of network, picking up information and carrying it from town to town. This street knowledge was of great value to the aristocrats and samurai lords, who were out of touch with common life. The nomads decided to sell that information, thus giving birth to the ninja spy.

Shinado–Meaning "wind" in ancient Japanese. The Kuroi family were entertainers—dancers, acrobats, and singers. The specialty of their *ryu* was to move like the wind.

Shinobi–Shinobi (忍) means "to steal away" and "to forbear." This ancient Japanese word for "ninja" connotes both stealth and invisibility. Mono (者) means "person." *Shinobu* means "to hide."

Shinobi kotoba–The ninja language.

Sozu–Scarecrow. The ninja art of stopping one's breath or pretending to be dead.

Taijutsu–Physical training/conditioning.

Tendai Buddhism–Tendai (Chinese: *Tiantai*) Buddhist teachings were first brought to Japan by the Chinese monk Jianzhen (Japanese: Ganjin) in the middle of the eighth century and flourished under the patronage of the Japanese imperial family and nobility, particularly the Matsumura clan. In 794, the Imperial capital was moved to Kyoto, where Tendai Buddhism became the dominant form of mainstream Buddhism in Japan and gave rise to later developments in Japanese Buddhism. Nichiren, Honen, Shinran, and Dogen—all famous thinkers in non-Tendai schools of Japanese Buddhism—were all initially trained as Tendai monks.

Tetsubishi–spiked metal caltrops commonly used for evasion and escape, constructed in such a way that when thrown, a tip always sticks up. Ninja scattered them on the ground when fleeing to halt or slow enemy pursuit. Their tips could also be poisoned to make them more deadly.

Tsubute–Flat, round metal "ninja skipping stones" used for throwing as weapons or as distractions.

Wa–Mainland (Yamato) Japanese, as opposed to indigenous tribes like the Ainu and Emishi.

Zen–A school of Mahayana Buddhism. "Zen" is translated from the Chinese word *Chán*, a word itself derived from the Sanskrit *dhyana*, which means "meditation." The aim of Zen practice is to discover this Buddha-nature within each person, through meditation and mindful awareness of daily experiences. Zen originated in China at the Shaolin Temple, and was spread by the Indian prince turned monk named Bodhidharma. Zen Buddhism was first documented in China in the 7th century AD. It came to Japan in the 11th century. There are two main schools—Rinzai and Soto.

Zendo–Temple hall for sitting in Zen meditation.

Yakuza–Japanese organized crime syndicate. The term "yakuza" comes from a Japanese card game called Oicho-Kabu. The worst hand in the game is a set of eight, nine, and three. In traditional Japanese forms of counting, these numbers are called *ya*, *ku*, and *sa* or *za*. The yakuza took this name because the Ya-Ku-Za hand requires the most skill (at judging opponents, etc) and, obviously, the best luck in order to win. The name was also used because it signified bad fortune, presumably for anyone who went up against the group.

Acknowledgments

The authors would like to thank the following people for editorial, creative, moral, and financial support during the writing of this book:

Gina Berriault, Peter Goodman, the Navajo Code Talkers Association, Richard Ruben, Abigail Davidson, Anne Brooker, Em & Phil Bettinger, Cathy Layne, Jeanie Okimoto, Kathleen Doherty, Ted Lafferty, Kimberley Theresa Lafferty, Deni Béchard, Suzanne Kamata, Art Kusnetz, Yelena Zarick, Colleen Sakurai, Eric Brinkman, Zorie Barber, Chris Mauch, NaNoWriMo, Nina and Quinn Zolotow, SCBWI Tokyo, John Gribble, The Japan Writer's Conference, and the Mendelsohn, Oketani, and Lowitz families. The great team at Tuttle Publishing—Eric Oey, William Notte, Rowan Muelling-Auer, June Chong, Anthoney Chua, and Su Yin Ngo—were sharper than any *shuriken* and a blessing to have on our side.

We are especially grateful to The Barbara Deming Memorial Foundation, Copperfields Books of Northern California and *The Dickens* Literary Award for early support, and to the editors of the following publications in which portions of this novel first appeared: Matthew Zuckerman of *Wingspan*, August Highland of muse apprentice guild, Elizabeth McKenzie of *My Postwar Life,* and Holly Thompson of *Tomo: Friendship Through Fiction—An Anthology of Japan Teen Stories.*

We are indebted to the Japanese folklorist Ken'ichi Tanigawa for his studies of Japanese history. Finally, thanks to Amanda Giacomini and MC Yogi for giving Jet her name.